Beautiful Tempest

ALSO BY JOHANNA LINDSEY

Make Me Love You

Wildfire in His Arms

Stormy Persuasion

One Heart to Win

Let Love Find You

When Passion Rules

That Perfect Someone

A Rogue of My Own

No Choice But Seduction

The Devil Who Tamed Her

Captive of My Desires

Marriage Most Scandalous

A Loving Scoundrel

A Man to Call My Own

JOHANNA LINDSEY

Beautiful Tempest

G

Gallery Books

New York   London   Toronto   Sydney   New Delhi

G

Gallery Books
An Imprint of Simon & Schuster, Inc.
1230 Avenue of the Americas
New York, NY 10020

This book is a work of fiction. Any references to historical events, real people, or real places are used fictitiously. Other names, characters, places, and events are products of the author's imagination, and any resemblance to actual events or places or persons, living or dead, is entirely coincidental.

This Gallery Books export edition July 2017

GALLERY BOOKS and colophon are registered trademarks of Simon & Schuster, Inc.

For information about special discounts for bulk purchases, please contact Simon & Schuster Special Sales at 1-866-506-1949 or business@simonandschuster.com

The Simon & Schuster Speakers Bureau can bring authors to your live event. For more information or to book an event contact the Simon & Schuster Speakers Bureau at 1-866-248-3049 or visit our website at www.simonspeakers.com.

Manufactured in the United States of America

10 9 8 7 6 5 4 3 2 1

ISBN 978-1-5011-7521-3
ISBN 978-1-5011-6220-6 (ebook)

Beautiful Tempest

Chapter One

In the large town house on Berkeley Square, Georgina Malory entered the dining room to join her husband for lunch. The twins, Gilbert and Adam, had just left the room, their empty plates still on the table, and raced past her on the stairs. At fourteen, the boys still hadn't outgrown running to wherever they were going. She'd given up scolding them for it.

But now her mind was on her husband and his impending voyage, which she hoped wouldn't commence before the end of the Season. So with one brown brow raised, a habit she'd picked up from him, and in a tone nearly as dry as his usually was, she said, "Another ship? Really, James, wasn't one extra ship enough?"

James Malory looked abashed for the briefest moment when he asked, "How the deuce did you find out about that?"

"Your newest captain came by this morning with the message that he would be away for a few days to visit his family. He needs to inform them he has one more voyage to captain before retiring as they had been expecting him to do."

James crossed his arms over his wide chest, but he was grinning now. "I can be persuasive as you well know. He was selling his ship. I wanted him and his crew with it."

"But you already bought a second ship."

"Contingencies, m'dear. In case I need to leave without your brothers."

Georgina tsked at her husband as she sat down next to him. "You mean you hope for any excuse to do just that."

"Nonsense. As long as I don't have to endure their company for the voyage, I'm quite willing to accept their aid in this endeavor, even if they're offering it only because their darling niece was used as bait and they want revenge for that."

"Now you do them a disservice. With the Kidnapping foiled and the culprit's demanding you in particular as the ransom, d'you really think they would just shrug this off as being over and done with and not give it another thought? When it could happen again? When I would be devastated if it happens again? Yes, yes, I was listening when you insisted we can't just let this go. I even understand why you won't let me accompany you this time." But then she laughed. "But seven ships, James?"

"It might be eight. Nathan Tremayne has also volunteered his."

She gasped. "Don't you dare drag him away from his honeymoon. Well, that's putting the cart before the horse, so don't you dare depart England before we see Nathan and Judy married."

"Bite your tongue, George. Watch Tony give away the bride when he doesn't want to? I bloody well wouldn't miss that."

"Your brother agreed—"

"Under duress," James cut in. "But you know how Ros can be, not to mention Judy when she puts her foot down. He was quite outnumbered in the matter of his daughter marrying Tremayne."

"You don't object to a smuggler in the family?"

James chuckled. "Ex-smuggler, but I confess it was lonely being the only black sheep."

She grinned. "I think I can safely say you still reign supreme in that regard—and you loved every minute of your notoriety, don't deny it."

He didn't. The ten years he'd spent as Captain Hawke, gentleman pirate, had been among the best times of his life. "In either case, Nathan's offer was appreciated, but I already intended to decline and my third ship is a ready excuse to do so. Don't want to ruffle Nathan's feathers when he can be so touchy about his welcome to our family."

"I suppose your three ships are already crewed and ready to sail at a moment's notice? Well, after this third captain returns."

"Of course. As are Warren and Boyd's ships, and yours.

"Drew will be joining us, too, either here if he brings us the information he's gathered, or in the Caribbean if he sends us a missive. In the latter case, he'll let us know where to meet up with him. We merely await his presence or a missive from him. But he's had enough time to find out who our culprit is. If we don't hear from him within the month, I will depart to personally assist in the search for answers."

Georgina had never doubted that James would return to the Caribbean for retribution. You don't provoke a Malory in the extreme manner in which James had been provoked by kidnapping his daughter and demanding *he* be the ransom without bearing the consequences.

Georgina's five brothers had also been furious about Jack's abduction, and their feelings of guilt had only exacerbated their fury. But then they blamed themselves for Jack's ordeal because they'd insisted she be allowed an American come-out before her first Season in London. They were still hoping she'd marry an American instead of an Englishman. If not for that, Jack wouldn't have been in Bridgeport, Connecticut, where she was stolen right out of the Andersons' garden. And Jack's abductors had sunk every ship in the harbor that night so the Malorys and the Andersons couldn't give immediate chase. But Nathan Tremayne's timely arrival with a ship of his own foiled that part of the culprit's plan. Nathan, James, and Judy, along with Thomas, Warren, and Drew Anderson, had been able to follow the kidnappers' ship to the Caribbean. And fortunately, Jacqueline had managed to escape on her own unharmed and had been waiting for them in St. Kitts. She'd been unable to solve the mystery, though, of who wanted James dead.

"Regarding your departure," Georgina said, "shall we settle on one month then? That will be almost the end of the Season, or were you planning on explaining to Jack why you won't be here for the end of it?"

"Our darling girl barely notices I've been in attendance at those balls and soirées," James reminded her.

That was a very real complaint. He didn't even try to adjust his tone to disguise it. Georgina tried not to laugh but couldn't help it, which got her one of James's more intimidating stares, which he knew very well had no effect on her. He certainly had planned to frighten away all of Jack's suitors. It had taken a long round of cajoling from both his wife and daughter before James had agreed to remain inconspicuous at the parties Jacqueline was invited to. And while it was definitely hard for a man his size to be inconspicuous, he did try to keep to the sidelines, occasionally even standing outside by the terrace doors if the events weren't large enough to have sidelines. As it turned out, Jack so bedazzled her beaus that the young lords didn't notice him, which James found quite annoying.

Then again, James would never have agreed to try to be inconspicuous if Jack hadn't assured him she refused to fall in love during her first Season and certainly wouldn't be marrying anyone for at least a year. Georgina recalled that Jack's cousin Judy had shared those intentions, but they all knew how that had turned out, with Judy's wedding occurring this week. But Georgina wasn't about to remind her husband that well-laid plans, particularly those involving the heart, could go awry.

To ease her husband's annoyance at his lack of success in sending every one of Jack's beaus running for the hills, Georgina remarked, "She doesn't favor any of them, you know."

That got a brilliant smile out of James, which earned him a glare and the complaint "Why are you so happy about that? The purpose of this Season is for her to meet and fall in love with a fine young man and get married. Instead, she wants to be like you. She'd be a rake if she could. She'd be a pirate if she could. She's taken every one of the unladylike things you've taught her quite to heart. I should have drawn the line at swords and pistols. But fisticuffs? You wisely didn't mention that, and I wouldn't even have known if she didn't offer to give me a demonstration."

"Where exactly is the harm? She's a Malory and my daughter. I want her to be able to protect herself with whatever is available to her, if I'm not there to do the protecting. And from what little Jack has told us about the time she spent on her abductor's ship, she did put her pugilist skills to good use in venting her anger on the ship's captain and keeping him from taking unfair advantage of her. You can't imagine how much I'm looking forward to getting my hands on that man m'self."

"Still, you should have refused. It was so utterly inappropriate to teach Jack those skills. They didn't help her defend herself when someone was intent on abducting her. Instead they made her think she could fight those men herself after the fact, when she was already captured—which could have gotten her more hurt than she was."

When Georgina saw the thunderous expression appear on James's face, she knew it wasn't directed at her, but due to the impotent rage he'd felt at having been as helpless as Jacqueline had been to hurt the men responsible, so Georgina quickly changed the subject. "Well, she's breaking countless hearts, you know—just as you did. And enjoying every minute of it. You weren't really that callous, were you?"

But he didn't like hearing that, either, and sat forward. "I know for a fact she's not the least bit callous. She's honest to a fault. She's not leading them on, George. She's not giving false hope. She's just having fun. Isn't that a good part of what this bloody Season is about?"

Georgina rolled her eyes. "You know very well it's a marriage mart. For her to attend all the balls and soirées is misleading when she doesn't want to marry yet."

"Shall we cancel the rest of the Season? Problem solved."

"By all means. You can tell her."

He chuckled. She snorted. They both knew there would be no canceling when Jack had so been looking forward to this Season—if not to landing a husband during it.

"Well, I know that you're as relieved as I am at how quickly she's put that ordeal behind her," Georgina said.

"But has she really? When her anger returns every time it is mentioned? So does mine, if you haven't noticed."

"Then I should have put it this way—at least she hasn't spent the last month since we got home crying in her bedroom and refusing to step foot out of it, Season or no Season."

That got a laugh from him. "Our darling girl? Cry?"

"Any other girl her age—"

Georgina didn't finish as Jacqueline suddenly stepped into the room, saying, "Help me decide."

Georgina raised a brow at her daughter, hoping she hadn't heard what she and James had just been discussing. Jack's neutral expression suggested she hadn't.

Jacqueline was still wearing a robe and nightgown even though it was already past noon, but then she had no reason to prepare to receive her many callers when they continued to be turned away at the door. It was a bold move on her part, but it didn't discourage any of them. Nonetheless, she had decided early on to simply enjoy the entertainments, not to be the entertainment herself. But she was breaking so many hearts. Her parents, her whole family, knew she would. She was too pretty, their Jack. Georgina was beautiful, but Jack didn't take after her mother at all. She was taller at five feet six inches, and while she was blond and green-eyed like her father, her features were uniquely her own. High cheekbones, stubborn chin *and* disposition, a pert nose, and lips much too lush, and at the moment long golden curls loose about her back and narrow shoulders.

As for Jacqueline's request, she held a mask in each hand, one a full porcelain mask that would cover her entire face, the other an exotic white domino edged with feathers that was long enough to conceal her face nearly to her mouth.

"Another ball?" Georgina said. "When did the invitation for a masquerade arrive?"

Jack shrugged as she came forward, dropped the heavier mask on the table, and swiped a sausage from her mother's plate. "Yesterday would be my guess since we were quite busy elsewhere all day. And don't worry, this ball isn't until next week, after the wedding."

Watching Jacqueline devour the sausage, Georgina said, "You haven't eaten yet?"

"Who has time to eat?"

"We do," James said pointedly.

Jack grinned and sat down next to her mother, yelling behind her, "I'll have what my mother is having if there's any left!"

Georgina remarked, "I requested breakfast. You wouldn't rather have the sole that was prepared for lunch today?"

"I'm heartily sick of fish. That's all Bastard offered on—" Jacqueline's lips snapped shut and her cheeks flushed with furious color.

Georgina and James exchanged a concerned glance, seeing again what they'd just been discussing. Jack's brief stay with the kidnappers continued to remain far too touchy a subject, and Bastard was the name she'd given the captain of the ship that had whisked her away from Bridgeport.

She'd never learned his real name, hadn't been given even a fake one, and hadn't found out whom he worked for. All she knew about him was that he was Catherine Meyer's lover, if that was even the real name of the woman who had lied her way onto *The Maiden George* to cross the Atlantic with them, pretending to be Andrássy Benedek's stepsister. Nor was it true that Andrássy was distantly related to the Malorys as he'd claimed. The two scoundrels had told elaborate lies so they could rob the Malory women of all their jewels on that voyage and then kidnap Jack to boot once they arrived in Connecticut.

Every time Jacqueline was reminded of that unpleasant experience, she got angry all over again. Her parents had witnessed many of these sparks of rage and understood them. She'd been helpless, she'd been bested, and not one of the skills James had taken pains to teach her had come in handy during the Kidnapping. But at least the sparks of anger were brief.

Jack was already grinning when she changed the subject. "I'm running out of ball gowns. Shall we order a few more?"

"I suppose we must," Georgina agreed. "I really wish these hostesses wouldn't try so hard to outdo each other. There should be a law to restrict them to giving just one ball each per Season."

"I like to dance, so I'm not complaining. Which mask?"

"The domino, of course. Full masks are far too hot and uncomfortable. You'd be removing it before we even arrive. Your father, on the other hand, should definitely wear one—then he won't have to hide in the garden for this ball and I might even get to dance!"

James snorted. "Not bloody likely, George. But I'll drag Tony along if you feel like dancing. He'll need distracting for the duration of Judy's honeymoon."

Georgina laughed. Both of these Malory brothers hated balls, and everyone in the family knew it. If Tony did need distracting, he'd choose any means other than a grand social event.

Henry, who was serving as butler today, a duty he shared with his good friend Artie, hurried into the room with a look of urgency and handed James a missive—which he didn't open. Georgina raised a brow, waiting. Jacqueline raised a brow, waiting. But James just put the letter in his pocket and smiled.

That particular smile, filled with relish, suggested the letter was from Drew. James finally had what he'd been waiting for, which meant he'd be leaving for the Caribbean soon.

Both women drew that conclusion. Georgina sighed, but Jack crossed her arms over her chest, her expression and stance as stubborn as they could get, and told her father, "I'm going with you."

"The devil you are."

"I want revenge just as much if not more'n you do!"

"I'll bring you home a full accounting, every bloody detail!"

Georgina smacked the table sharply with her hand to stop the head-butting before it got any louder. "Jack, use your head instead of your emotions. Your presence on such a trip will divide your father's attention. Instead of dealing with the matter at hand, he'll be worried about you if you're anywhere near those waters."

"I could wait at Gabby and Drew's—"

Georgina cut in, "Their island is too close to St. Kitts, where whoever wrote the ransom note wanted your father to go to secure your release. And what's the point of waiting it out there rather than here? You'd still be in the area where those villains operate, and you could get captured again while your father is pursuing the fight elsewhere. Then James would be helpless again to vanquish whoever is determined to harm him. Is that the outcome you want, to let them win?"

Jacqueline opened her mouth to protest, but, looking angry, said, "I get it," then she stomped out of the room yelling, "But I don't like it!"

Georgina sighed. "I can't say I'm surprised. I had a feeling she'd make that demand."

"I would have been surprised if she didn't," James agreed.

Georgina held out her hand for the letter even as she said, "Make damn sure you search your ship from top to bottom for a stowaway before you sail. She might have said she understands why she shouldn't go with you, but that doesn't mean her anger won't get in the way of her common sense."

"I can sail before she notices."

"Better you see her standing firmly on the dock with me as you leave. Now let's see if this letter contains the information you were expecting." She read it first, then handed it to her husband. "I don't think it does."

Chapter Two

QUITE A FEW PEOPLE in the church were frowning and whispering about the five men moving furtively down the aisles on both sides of the left set of pews. They appeared to be conducting some sort of important mission that required stealth, speed, and split-second timing. Even Georgina, sitting next to Jacqueline, whispered, "What the devil are they doing?"

Jack had wondered why her father wasn't sitting with her and her mother, but had assumed he was keeping his brother company while Tony waited to walk his daughter down the aisle. But that was done and Judy was standing at the altar next to Nathan taking her vows. So it wasn't at all clear why the five men were behaving so furtively.

James did not join his wife and daughter, but casually sat down in the first pew next to his brother, the father of the bride, instead. Jason, their oldest brother, sat down next to Roslynn, who was seated on Anthony's other side. And their second-oldest brother, Edward, as well as Nicholas Eden and Jeremy, moved into the pew behind them, squeezing in next to their wives, Charlotte, Reggie, and Danny. The men were so quiet and unobtrusive about it that Tony, who appeared to be listening closely to every word being said at the altar, didn't notice them or feel James put his arm on the back of the pew, not quite touching Tony, but obviously ready to if necessary.

The wedding guests' frowns turned into smiles and grins, and instead of whispers a few discreet chuckles were heard. It was clear now that the five men had positioned themselves to restrain Anthony if he made any objection to the marriage when the clergyman raised the question. They obviously thought he still might!

Jacqueline admired their heroic deed, though it wasn't necessary. Moments later, without any interruptions, Judith and Nathan Tremayne were pronounced man and wife, and Nathan was kissing his bride. Jack smiled despite the tears on her cheeks. She had started crying the moment Judy had entered the church because she was so happy for her best friend. They were cousins but had been closer than sisters their entire lives.

And it had been such a beautiful wedding ceremony with the children in the family, including Nathan's nieces Clarissa and Abbie, scattering rose petals down the aisle, and Jacqueline's twin nieces carrying the long train on Judith's exquisite gown. Judy was breathtaking in that silk and lace gown with its bodice glittering not with sequins but actual diamonds, one of Roslynn's many extravagances. And Jack knew her cousin was quite in love. Judy was supposed to wait a year for love to show up, the way Jack was waiting, but getting stuck on a ship with that smuggler she'd lost her heart to had made it impossible for her to avoid him.

The plan was to adjourn immediately back to Haverston for the wedding party since it would get uncomfortably tight in the church if everyone tried to wish the happy couple well there. Sometimes the size of a family had to be taken into account, and there were so many Malorys now that it was a wonder they'd all fit into the church. In fact, it had been quite a few years since the entire family had gathered at Haverston. Jason, the eldest of the family and third Marquis of Haverston, used to insist they all come for Christmas, but that was before there were so many Malorys that he no longer had room for them all despite the huge size of the ancestral mansion.

Judy's mother, Roslynn, had solved that problem last year when her immediate family had arrived late for the annual gathering and ended up staying in the hotel in Havers Town. So she'd found a young solicitor who didn't know her family and had him handle the details of buying the property next to Haverston, which she completely refurbished and added many more bedrooms to, then secretly deeded it over to Jason with the stipulation that he not tell his brother Anthony about it. It was her bane that Tony only allowed her to spend her enormous fortune on frivolous things. She knew he wouldn't consider a big house frivolous and would have been quite put out about it if he'd found out.

Everyone who had arrived for the wedding yesterday had rooms at Haverston. Those who had arrived this morning had been directed next door. The children shared rooms, the nursery had a few babies in it, including Jacqueline's new nephew, who was not quite a year old yet. But Jack had already been made an aunt when her oldest brother Jeremy's wife, Danny, had had twin girls seven years ago, the third set of twins in the family!

As Jack left the church with her parents, Amy caught up to whisper in her ear, "I can guess who will be next to the altar."

Jack started to bristle until Amy actually pointed at their cousin Jaime, Judy's sixteen-year-old sister, who they both knew flirted with every young man who wasn't family.

Jacqueline chuckled. "She'll never make up her mind about who to marry. I can't keep up with how many times Jaime thought she was in love."

Just ahead of them, Katey was trying to cheer up her father, Anthony, and her husband, Boyd, tried to console him by pointing out, "At least Judy didn't marry a Yank!"—which only got him a dark look from his father-in-law.

"Jack, wait up!" Brandon Malory called as he ran up behind her and steered her toward his coach. "Ride back to the house with me? I'd like a chance to talk."

Jacqueline didn't object. She hadn't seen her cousin Brandon since she and Judy had visited his ducal estate just prior to departing for their American debut. The last night of their stay in Hampshire, Judy went ghost hunting one last time—and was successful. She'd not only caught a ghost, who turned out to be Nathan Tremayne, hiding his smuggled goods in the ruined old manor house his grandmother had left him, but a husband!

Brandon's sister, Cheryl, caught up with them and exclaimed to Jack, "I can't believe Judy married her ghost!"

Cheryl started to get into the ducal coach to ride with them, but Brandon told her, "It's bad luck for girls to ride with their brothers after a wedding; it raises their chances of becoming old maids."

She looked aghast and ran off to find her mother. Jacqueline chuckled. "Did she just believe that nonsense?"

Brandon grinned as he helped Jacqueline into the coach. "She's still gullible at her age."

"She's only two years younger than you!"

"Every year makes a difference. I shudder to think what she'll be like next year when she's Jaime's age." But as soon as they were seated, he said, "Everyone keeps telling me, 'Don't ask,' it will make you lose your temper. But you won't with me, will you?"

She didn't need to ask what he was referring to. The family had been tiptoeing around the subject of her kidnapping because she got angry every single time her ordeal was mentioned. She rarely stopped thinking about it—and him. Only the Seasonal parties had been a distraction. But she didn't feel angry now. Maybe the memories were finally going to stop plaguing her.

"I'm fine," she assured her cousin.

"Tell me about the pirates."

"There's not much to tell when I never saw any of them other than the captain and his paramour, Catherine. You have heard about her, right? The damned liar who plotted her way aboard *The Maiden George*?"

"Yes, and her supposed brother they tried to convince the family was a relative of ours."

"They were good liars. Most of the family believed them. Only my father and I had doubts about them prior to our learning the truth. But while Andrew—that was Andrássy's real name—helped with the theft of our jewelry aboard ship, he had no part in the kidnapping, even tried to stop it, only to get dragged along with them for that effort. And he helped me escape, so I've forgiven him for being in Catherine's thrall. He was her lover, too—she does spread herself around."

Brandon blushed at her bluntness. "And the captain?"

The captain. Bastard. Too handsome with his long black

hair and dark turquoise eyes. That handsomeness had distracted her a number of times she'd been on a tirade, which had made her even more furious.

Her tone was contemptuous when she answered, "He was handsome, but an idiot."

"Because he kidnapped you, of course he was, but—"

"No, because he tried to do it at sea!"

"With both ships moving?" Brandon said in surprise. "Is that possible?"

"Well, it didn't work, so I don't know. Nathan found the man they had planted on our ship to hie off with me. We thought he was a stowaway. No one realized that was their first attempt to kidnap me."

"Bastard was talkative, eh, to tell you all that?"

"Not really." Then she grinned. "I was frustrating him to the point of anger because I refused to eat the first four days they had me on their ship. He inadvertently said it would have been much easier if his friend had gotten me off our ship before he was discovered and had to abandon that plan."

"So they tried again in Bridgeport and succeeded—partially." Brandon looked angry.

"They were working for Catherine's father, and apparently he's not known for his patience. As soon as I became their hostage, he expected my father to be hand-delivered to him. But Bastard failed." She ended with a smirk. Maybe Bastard was already dead for returning to his boss empty-handed. For a moment she relished the thought.

"Well, you're a brave woman, Jacqueline Malory. I'm glad you're all right. Still, I'd like to get my hands on those pirates!"

"Don't worry, Brand. My father will take care of them. You should come to London for the rest of the Season. You certainly look like you're old enough to be there." He did, too. Already as tall as his father, Derek, strapping of build, he looked several years older than seventeen.

"Wish I could. But the title causes too much of a stir."

She grinned. "So don't mention it. It's not like the *ton* knows you by sight yet. And there are so many Malorys, who can keep track of all of us? Sneak in, have some fun, sneak back home."

"I can't be like our fathers, so don't even suggest that, Jack. Dukes can't be rakes."

"Who says they can't?"

At the party, James and his four conspirators got ribbed quite a bit for thinking Anthony might ruin his daughter's special day. A pact was made not to let Judy find out about it, though Tony was quite annoyed when he heard.

Anthony even cornered James to promise, "We'll be meeting at Knighton's as soon as we get back to London, and it's going to be a particularly grueling round in the ring."

James, feeling a tad guilty by then for doubting his brother's professed acquiescence to his daughter's marriage, still said drily, "Does this mean I'm going to have to let you win?"

Nicholas Eden heard that and started laughing, which provoked glares from both brothers and had Regina, Nick's wife, rushing in to whisk her husband out of harm's way. Usually, the brothers' long-standing dislike of the man who had married their favorite niece was merely expressed in disdainful remarks, but with Anthony currently annoyed, Regina wasn't taking any chances.

And Jack was told one time too many at the party that her "special day" would be next. Not bloody likely, but she smiled anyway, determined not to do or say anything that might ruin the happy occasion. But the moment she caught sight of Judith slipping away from the party to run upstairs to change into traveling clothes for her wedding trip, Jacqueline followed, wanting a last few private moments with her best friend.

Judith, turning to see who closed the door behind her, asked, "Are you here to call me a traitor again?"

It wasn't an unfounded question, though Jack had stopped calling Judy a traitor a while back, and she had only said it in jest a few times anyway. They had sworn to each other that they would have fun together this Season without its ending in matrimony. But so many of their family members had assured them both that love happens when it happens, insisting Jack's intention to hold it off was quite unreasonable. But Jack was stubborn, whereas Judy wasn't. Besides, there was also the simple fact that Jack's interest wasn't getting piqued this Season, not enough for it to matter. Nor would she be stuck on a ship with a handsome young man as Judy had been. Actually, Jack had been stuck on a different ship with a handsome young man, but all she'd wanted to do with Bastard was kill him, so that didn't count.

So she smiled at her dearest friend. "No, I'm here to tell you how incredibly happy I am for you."

"Oh, Jack!"

They both started crying and hugging each other at once, which had Jacqueline saying gruffly after a moment, "Stop it, really. You don't want red eyes when you'll soon be using them to ogle your husband."

Judith stepped back with a grin. "Do I really do that?"

"Course you do. Everyone has noticed—even your father."

Judy laughed. "Maybe that's why he gave in so graciously and allowed the wedding to take place."

"Was it gracious? Thought it was kicking and growling."

"There were only a few threats in the end; yes, that was definitely gracious behavior for him."

"I'll trust your word on it, since I didn't get to see it."

Jack wasn't going to get to see much more of her cousin either after today. Judy was going to be living in Hampshire with her husband in the house he'd inherited from his grandmother, and Jack would be living miles away in London. She could visit, but she couldn't visit year-round!

"I'm going to miss you so much!" Jack suddenly burst out.

"We're not going to be on different sides of the world, Jack."

"I know." It was just going to feel like it!

"What you need is a distraction."

"I have one. My father will be sailing to the Caribbean on *The Maiden George* after we return to London, and I haven't been thinking about much else."

"I heard, but I meant a romantic distraction. Not one of your beaus has caught your fancy yet?"

"No, but I do like them all. I just don't love any of them."

"Maybe because you haven't tried to."

Jacqueline laughed as she started helping Judith out of her gown. "I didn't know I was supposed to work at it!"

"You know what I mean. If you'd just put that nasty kidnapping behind you, the anger will go away, then your heart might open to new possibilities."

With Judith's back to her, Jack rolled her eyes. She understood that Judith was happy and wanted everyone to be as happy as she was. It even made Judith forget that Jack would be happiest if she *didn't* find love this year.

But rather than remind her of that, Jacqueline said, "I'm still worried about my father, now that he's sailing this week to take care of Bastard and his boss." In fact, she was sure a Malory family meeting to plan the attack would be taking place soon, maybe even there in Haverston tonight, since both Warren and Boyd were here for the wedding. But, of course, she wouldn't be included!

"So he knows who is responsible now?"

"I don't know!" Jack complained angrily. "They won't tell me anything!"

Judith turned around, frowning. "But you were sure Uncle James would know exactly who the culprit was as soon as you gave him—oh, Jack, tell me you're not still keeping it a secret! You have to tell him about the original, more goading ransom note you found on the pirate ship."

"Since he's sailing to the Caribbean anyway, there was no point in keeping it from him. I gave him the copy I made of the note the same day he got Drew's letter."

When she'd discovered that note in Bastard's cabin, she'd thought that he hadn't left a ransom note in Bridgeport and her family would have no clue where to look for her. She'd been livid about that. She'd tried to kill Bastard that day—well, and many other times—and with her usual lack of success. The bloody sod had been far too strong for any of her attacks to do anything other than make him laugh. But he'd actually assured her that he'd penned a more polite version of his boss's note that would be delivered to her father. As if that would matter in the scheme of things.

"I even explained to my father that I didn't mention the original note to him sooner because I was sure he'd be walking into a trap if he sailed back to the Caribbean right away. He read it and just smiled without saying another word! It made me so angry!"

Judith tsked as she stepped out of her gown and turned back around. "Jack, enough time has passed that there won't be any trap. So let your father do what he does best, while you enjoy the rest of your Season."

Jacqueline sighed. "I know. I'll try to."

Judy rolled her eyes. "You don't try, you do or die. Isn't that your motto?"

Jacqueline laughed. "Something like that. Very well, I will get back to having fun in London."

"Promise?"

"For you, yes."

Nathan chose that moment to step into the room, making Jacqueline realize why Judy's maid hadn't been waiting for her there to help her change into her traveling clothes. Because her new husband must have wanted to assist. And he took one look at his bride wearing only her chemise and petticoats and crossed the room to gather her close for a passionate kiss.

Jack was quite sure he hadn't even noticed her in the room! She smiled as she slipped out and quietly closed the door behind her.

Chapter Three

JACQUELINE MUCH PREFERRED EAVESDROPPING at doors—except at Haverston. The doors in that old mansion were much too thick, some even reinforced with metal, so it would be hard to hear through them unless there was shouting on the other side, which there wasn't. She did check first, but only for a second. And since members of her family could traverse the halls at any moment, she couldn't have stood there in plain sight with her ear to the study door anyway.

She hurried outside instead, leaving unnoticed through the back door of the house, and ran around to the study windows. She expected them to be open on that warm summer night and they were. She even peeked inside to confirm who was in there with her father—her uncles Warren and Boyd.

Anthony arrived just as she ducked below the window ledge. He wasn't sailing with James, so what input he might have Jack couldn't guess. Or he might just be there to provide moral support. No matter how angry Tony might be with James, he would still stand firmly with his brother against the

Yanks, as her father and Tony called the Anderson side of her family. But there wasn't going to be any sort of confrontation with Boyd and Warren tonight, verbal or otherwise, not when James had accepted their help on this mission.

Jacqueline was waiting so tensely to hear something from inside the room that she was startled when her brother Jeremy squatted down beside her, whispering, "I should have known I'd find you here first."

She just put her finger to her lips as she scowled at him for finding her hiding spot. But he still asked, "What'd I miss?"

"Nothing yet," she hissed, though she glanced quickly beyond her brother to make sure Percival Alden hadn't tagged along with him. Percy was a long-standing friend of the family who could be depended on to do one thing—blunder. And in this case, that would be alerting her father to their eavesdropping outside the window.

"You heard from Drew?" Warren said inside the study.

"It's not encouraging," James answered. "Read it for yourself."

Warren must have picked up Drew's letter because he quickly pointed out, "Says here it's not the pirate you and Drew suspected, that Pierre Lacross is still in prison on Anguilla."

"Read the next part," James prompted.

Boyd proved he was standing next to his brother and reading the letter at the same time when he said, "So the warden of that prison seemed a little nervous to Drew at the mention of Lacross? That's actually understandable for a man living behind stone walls with hundreds of convicted criminals, don't you think?"

"I do," James agreed. "It's the part about the warden refusing to allow your brother to see Lacross for himself. Drew is the only one of you who would recognize Pierre Lacross if he saw him because he was with me when I captured Lacross."

"The warden could have denied Drew's request for any number of reasons," Warren put in. "Knowing Drew, he's just annoyed that he couldn't talk his way around that warden."

Boyd added, "And that could mainly be because it's a British prison and Drew's American origins become obvious the moment he opens his mouth."

Anthony chuckled. "Now that's the more likely reason when Englishmen tend not to be cooperative with you Yanks even on a good day."

"We're not antagonizing them, Tony," James warned his brother. "Keep your annoyance with me on me, not on them."

"Then what am I even doing here?"

"I thought you might want to be included, in case you change your mind and decide to sail with me."

"Not bloody likely, old boy. I'm staying close to home in case Judy changes her mind about that bounder Tremayne and returns home, needing a father's shoulder to cry on. You can tell me all the gory details when you get back to England."

"Then you might as well return to the party," James suggested.

"Didn't say I wasn't interested," Anthony grumbled.

Warren said, "Well, even if we still don't know who we're looking for, I'm game to leave now. I've been landlocked far too long. And we can investigate more once we get to the West Indies."

James said, "If Drew and I didn't both suspect Lacross is responsible for Jack's abduction, I wouldn't have given him this much time to try to confirm it. Drew checked Pierre's old fortress island. It was deserted, but there were signs of recent occupation. And he wasted weeks trying to find out who had been there recently and where they went, which is why we didn't hear from him before now."

"But if Lacross is still in prison, what did Drew even hope to find there?" Boyd asked.

"Not all of that pirate's men were captured the night we defeated him. But in any case, I should have been on my way back there long before now, considering that when I retired from the sea, I left more'n one enemy behind in the Caribbean. Drew wouldn't know them if he met them. I need to talk to them myself to determine if any of them hatched this plot. Drew doesn't know who to question to get answers that might be helpful, whereas I—"

"Get answers by any means," Warren said, then added abashed, "That was a compliment, James, not a slur."

Anthony chuckled. "You're taking all the fun out of this, Yank." But then he said to his brother, "No need to fry me, old boy. You might have upped your truce with them a notch for the duration of this mission, but I haven't."

James ignored that remark, saying, "I would have left sooner if my darling Jack hadn't kept this from me. She found it on the ship that sailed off with her from Bridgeport. Her abductor, the ship's captain, insisted on sending us a more polite version of the original ransom note."

"A polite kidnapper?" Boyd said in surprise.

Warren snorted. "What kind of pirate writes a polite note?"

Anthony read it aloud: " 'Your life for hers. Sound familiar? You know the place. Do hurry, *mon ami*.' "

James explained, "Jack made a copy of this more goading note penned by her abductor's boss before she forgot the exact words."

"Yet she kept it a secret from you all this time?" Anthony asked. "Why?"

"She was afraid I would be walking into a trap if I returned to the Caribbean too soon, that they would be expecting me. The writer, who she knows is Catherine Meyer's father, obviously thought I would know exactly who he was by those otherwise cryptic words."

"Do you?"

"Yes, except he's still in prison."

Warren said, "Lacross again?"

"Now wait," Boyd put in. "You can't assume the man is French just because of that *mon ami*. I'm not all that familiar with the French language, but doesn't that particular phrase mean 'my friend'?"

"Sarcasm at its best," James replied. "That note implies he wanted me to know exactly who was orchestrating my demise without providing proof that could be used in a court of law. And that, more'n anything else, sounds like Lacross. I also wouldn't be surprised if Lacross has a daughter who's a jewel thief and as clever as a fox, that shrew Catherine Meyer, who our fake distant relative Andrássy brought aboard *The Maiden George*."

"Does she resemble Lacross?" Warren asked.

"Not closely enough for me to conclude that she's his daughter," James admitted. "But she could be doing Lacross's dirty work. Either the warden in Anguilla lied to Drew, or Lacross is pulling strings from inside that prison. The point of this entire plan could have been to hand-deliver me to that prison and right into his cell."

"Not possible," Boyd disagreed. "I thought you nobles never got locked up for anything."

"That's usually the case," James said. "But Captain Hawke would be."

"Captain Hawke died in England. I could have sworn you made sure of it."

"I did," James said. "But news of Hawke's demise might not have reached all the islands in the Caribbean, where warrants for Hawke's capture could still be active. And I've been back there and someone who knew me as Captain Hawke might have spotted me. More to the point, Lacross saw me when I helped Drew rescue Gabby and Lacross was captured, so he knows I'm not dead. What I can't figure out is how Lacross or whoever is behind this plot figured out that Hawke is James Malory. I went to great lengths to keep Hawke's true identity a secret."

Warren groaned. "Are we going to have to attack a British prison?"

"No—well, I hope not," James replied. "I do need to have a talk with that warden, though. However, I can also think of two other men who might have said something similar to what's in that original note. So many questions remain. Nothing is conclusive other than I'm sailing the morning after that damned masquerade ball I got browbeaten into attending."

Boyd chuckled, guessing, "Georgie at her finest, eh?"

"On the contrary. I just bloody well hate balls. My George, however, can be enjoyably persuasive."

"Oh, God, he didn't just imply—?" Warren started to complain.

Anthony cut in with a snicker. "Course he did, Yank."

Outside, Jeremy helped Jacqueline to her feet to escort her back inside the house, complaining, "I should have been in that room, but he's refused to let me participate."

"You think I didn't try? He's adamant that neither of us can go."

Jeremy snorted. "I understand why you're being excluded, but I lived in the islands and know the Caribbean like the back of my hand. I would be a real asset and he knows it."

"Let's try not to insult me, Brother," Jack said drily. "You or I would make a perfect hostage that could stay his hand in a battle with his nemesis. So we need to bow out even if we don't like it."

"You do, but I still have time to change his mind. When is that ball that he referred to?"

Jacqueline rolled her eyes. Jeremy wasn't going to win that argument with their father any more than she had. But still smarting over her own exclusion, she wasn't about to stay there and try to convince him. She had to find Gabby and get her to tell her everything she knew about the pirate Pierre Lacross.

Chapter Four

Y OU DON'T SEEM AT all upset that Father will be sailing in the morning without either of us," Jacqueline said to her mother as she looked at herself in the full-length mirror in her bedroom.

"I do hide it well, don't I? Though I have every confidence that he will return from the Caribbean triumphant so we can put this nasty business behind us, that doesn't mean I'm not going to worry every moment that he's gone."

"And miss him."

"Of course I will, terribly. And I know you will, too. And, no, you're not going to mention again that you'd rather be sailing off with him in the morning instead of staying behind with me."

Jacqueline grinned. "I wasn't going to. I know bloody well when I'm outnumbered in the argument, even though I'm more deserving of an opportunity to exact revenge than—"

"Jack," Georgina cut in warningly.

"That just slipped out, really, it did."

Georgina tsked. "At least the rest of the Season will be a distraction for you and me."

Jack hoped that would be the case. She just wished she could be distracted sooner, say tonight, from her father's departure. At least with her wearing a black wig and a domino no one was going to be able to tell that she was also experiencing emotions—of the vexing sort. Not when on the surface she looked vivacious. And truly, she couldn't deny she was quite excited about the evening's festivities. For once she wouldn't know whom she was dancing with. She loved harmless little mysteries of that sort.

They were both already dressed for the ball tonight. Georgina had surprised Jacqueline with a new emerald necklace to match her pale green ball gown, which she fastened behind Jack's neck.

"Now, come along. Your father is no doubt anxious to get this over with! He's waiting downstairs with Brandon."

"Brandon? When he said he wouldn't come!"

"He told us you insisted, and we all know that meant you browbeat the dear boy mercilessly."

Jack grinned. "Well, only a little. But a masquerade is the perfect opportunity for him to sneak in for a little fun without being announced as the Duke of Wrighton at the door. I had to try to convince him after he said he's not planning on joining any Season. He doesn't know what he'll be missing, but after tonight he will, so maybe he'll change his mind."

"I wouldn't count on that. Brandon takes his consequence quite seriously, more's the pity, but then you know how I feel about titles. You need to recall that he's the first duke in this family, and his parents have raised him as such. And you aren't to interfere, Jack, not even a little. I wouldn't be a bit surprised if his future wife is picked for him. She will need to have impeccable credentials."

Jacqueline snorted. "Doom and gloom. You're forgetting he's also a Malory."

Georgina raised a brow. "And Malorys tend to get what they want?"

"Exactly."

"I CAN'T BELIEVE HE'S actually dancing."

As Jacqueline danced with Brandon, she followed his gaze and laughed when her parents twirled past them on the dance floor. "I can. Mother entered with you and me, but my father was a few couples behind us in the line, so no one will guess it's him even if they were able to guess it's me. This black wig I'm wearing and the domino were supposed to keep my identity a secret."

"They didn't."

"I know that," she complained. "I am quite annoyed that Bernard Morton's rushing over to me for the first dance alerted the others that he'd found me out. How the bloody hell he did, he wouldn't admit. If he bribed my maid to find out the color of my gown tonight, I'm going to fire her as soon as I get home."

"No, you won't, when he could have likely bribed your seamstress or posted a man near your house to race the particulars to him. But it hardly matters, Cousin. Certainly not worth firing a loyal—"

"Disloyal."

"—servant."

"I suppose, though it has quite ruined the masquerade for me, when the delightful point of it was not to be recognized. It's just any old ball, now."

He chuckled. "I thought you loved balls?"

"I do, that's why I'm only grumbling, not snarling."

"Good point," he said drily.

She grinned up at him. She was glad he'd come to the ball. With his mask, no one was going to guess that he was only seventeen or find out that the Duke of Wrighton was in attendance.

"As for my father," she said, "while he most certainly does hate to dance, he loves pleasing my mother more, and she enjoys dancing. What about you? Well, you must. You've had six partners in a row before I could get you on the floor m'self, and I had to almost run to grab you before you were asking someone else!"

"I do indeed like it, but it's not so much the dancing as the—touching."

She chuckled. "A light touch on the waist excites you, does it?"

She knew she'd just made him blush under his half mask, which covered his cheeks but not his mouth. Sometimes she spoke without thinking first—well, most times she did that— but she hadn't meant to embarrass her cousin, who had probably never had a chance to interact with a young woman his age other than relatives because his parents kept him so cloistered. A seventeen-year-old might well be quite touchy, too, about his relations with the opposite sex, and she should have known better than to tease about his sexual prowess or his lack thereof.

So she jumped back in with "Don't answer! I put my foot in my mouth quite often, as you well know. Instead, tell me what you think of your first foray into the world of debutantes? Is it what you expected? Or perhaps it's difficult to form an opinion when everyone is hiding their faces?"

"Personalities aren't hidden, nor are their delightful—gowns."

Jack burst out laughing. What an amusing way to refer to shapely feminine bodies! She knew he wasn't embarrassed anymore because he'd said it in an exaggeratedly prudish tone.

"Has anyone piqued your interest yet?"

"Indeed. I'm already in love, with her, and her, oh, and her, too."

He'd just pointed to three different debutantes, one dancing, the other two giggling as they gazed in his direction. Jack rolled her eyes. She might even have thought he was teasing if it were anyone other than Brandon.

So all she said was "You sound like our cousin Jaime. She fancies herself in love with a different man every few months. Please tell me you know the difference between infatuation and love, the abiding sort, the knock-you-on-your-arse sort."

"D'you? Or are you so determined not to find it this year that it could smack you on the head and you'd ignore it?"

"Well, since that wasn't a serious question, I can say I know bloody well that attraction ain't it, because I was utterly attracted to Bastard while I hated every bone in his damned body."

"Then rest assured that I also know the difference, Jack, so I'll let you have your leg back now."

She laughed. "You're usually so serious. When did you start pulling legs?"

"Since I discovered how gullible my sister is. She's still carrying on about Judy's marrying a ghost!"

Chapter Five

When the dance ended, Brandon quickly returned Jacqueline to her parents before he hurried off to find another partner. Jacqueline didn't mind since she'd intended to join them herself. Her father, for the first time standing with his wife instead of on the sidelines, made an exceptional shield, and Jack wanted that shield for a moment, so she inserted herself between them.

Since her decision to join her parents so deviated from her request that her father not frighten off her beaus before she got to know them, James immediately asked, "Who has annoyed you?"

"They appear to know exactly who I am tonight," Jack complained, then grinned. "And now they know exactly who you are, despite your mask, because they saw me enter with Mother, and now you're standing with her when you haven't done that at any of the other parties we attended. They always ask if you're present, you know. And I always lie and assure them that you aren't. Shall we see how brave they are now?"

"If you want a respite, m'dear, we can adjourn to the terrace," Georgina suggested.

"No, I really do want to see how brave they are."

James said nothing to that. Georgina just tsked. That her father's notoriety was still as powerful as ever had never been in question. Because he refused to socialize with anyone outside the family, the *ton* still didn't know him and rumors about him still abounded. That he and his brother Anthony still occasionally visited Knighton's Hall for brutal exercise in the boxing ring didn't help put to rest those rumors of how deadly James could be. Young rakehells relished those matches, which gave them something unpredictable to wager on, but less daring young lords didn't want to get anywhere near James Malory, even if they were in love with his daughter.

The music started again, but the level of chatter got louder for a different reason. Word of James's possible presence was spreading through the ballroom and causing quite a stir. And Jacqueline knew it was her fault for joining them while he was still with her mother, drawing every eye to him, just because she was annoyed with her suitors for knowing who she was and telling her who they were. Utterly childish bit of pique that she now regretted.

"Bloody hell," James hissed. "Is that our hostess bearing down on us?"

"Yes, that's Lady Spencer indeed," Georgina replied. "We attended her first ball of the Season soon after we returned from Bridgeport. You avoided being announced at it, if you recall, so you didn't get to meet her."

"If she's going to ask me to leave, I may have to pummel her husband," James promised.

"She's a widow," Georgina said with a grin.

"I'll ferret out a male relative."

"No, you won't, and she wouldn't dare," Georgina said staunchly. "Your name was on the invitation. Even if none of these hostesses actually expect you to make an appearance, it would be a coup for them if you did."

Lady Spencer confirmed that when she gushed, "Lord Malory! I am so delighted to make your acquaintance. I never dreamed you would accept my invitation, but now you have single-handedly assured my success!"

Jacqueline knew her father hated being cornered like this and would probably just let Georgina deal with the lady and her effusive greeting. But he surprised Jack when he gave their hostess a courtly bow and said, "The pleasure is mine, Lady Spencer, but you do yourself a disservice. Your balls are so legendary, I couldn't resist the temptation when my wife suggested I see for myself."

After what Jack had overheard at Haverston while she and Jeremy had eavesdropped, she wondered if her mother was blushing under her domino. The real temptation was what Georgina had dangled in front of James to get him here. But their hostess wouldn't know that and seemed utterly thrilled by his words. Jack's father certainly hadn't lost his touch with the ladies.

But he didn't fail to notice that one of Jack's beaus had found enough courage to approach her while James spoke with Lady Spencer. Jack noticed as well and was pleased that not all of her beaus were afraid of her father.

The tall, blond-haired fellow, whom she couldn't immediately identify because he was wearing a full face mask, gave her a half bow and extended a hand. "Would you do me the honor?"

Gallantly said, and he cut an impeccable figure in his black tailed coat that fit his muscular physique extremely well. Jacqueline placed her fingers lightly over his and allowed him to lead her onto the dance floor. She felt a distinct measure of excitement, but only because she hadn't placed him yet and was determined to.

It was the first thing Jacqueline asked. "Which one are you?"

"I'm supposed to tell?" He had a deep voice, but it was muffled by his mask.

"My other beaus have revealed themselves. Quite takes the fun out of a masque ball when you no longer need to figure out who you're dancing with."

"Then I won't tell."

"Really?"

"I promise."

So, she'd have to rely on deductive reasoning! Now this was the fun she'd expected to have tonight. "I already know who Bernard, Jasper, John, Addison, and Ellis are, but that still leaves Lewis, Rupert, Peter, Giles, Hugh, Thaddeus, and Chester."

He laughed under his mask. "D'you really have that many suitors?"

"It does sound a bit much, doesn't it?" She laughed softly, but then she realized he would already have known that if he were one of them. "Are you pretending you don't know who I am?"

"Who are you?"

She was taken aback. "If you really don't know, why did you ask me to dance?"

"How could I not, when you're the most beautiful woman here?"

She laughed again because he couldn't say that when her face was mostly covered by the domino, not without knowing exactly who she was. So he was teasing and she was actually delighted by it. It was quite refreshing, from one of her beaus. But she still hadn't guessed who he was.

She got back to the matter of figuring that out. "I'm sure a few of my suitors aren't really serious in their pursuit. I know Giles isn't, since he fancies himself a bit of a rake. However, three of those who haven't revealed themselves to me yet tonight aren't as tall as you, and Peter isn't as strapping." She paused for a quick admiring glance down his length. "So that just leaves Lords Hugh, Rupert, and Thaddeus."

"Maybe I should give up before I start?"

"Start what?"

"Winning your heart."

She chuckled. "Afraid of a little competition, are you?"

"You call twelve men a little?"

"To be honest, they weren't all mine to begin with," she admitted candidly. "I inherited some of my cousin's suitors when her wedding was announced recently. And you can certainly give up if you like, but there won't be any heart winning in either case."

"Then, like your cousin, you've already decided whom to marry?"

"Gads, no. What I've decided is not to marry this year a'tall, maybe not the next, either. I'm quite on the up-and-up about that and have made sure to tell them all. They just think I'm pulling their collective legs, when I'm not."

"Why?"

"Why follow the pack?" She laughed. "That's definitely not for me. And what's the hurry anyway? Because it's expected of a young lady to marry during her first Season?" She gave a soft snort. "So you've been warned, as have the others. But then you already knew that, if you're one of them."

"I'm not."

A shimmer of excitement ran through her when she heard that. So he hadn't been teasing after all? He was someone new who'd come late to the Season? But, no, latecomers stirred up the gossip mills for a few days, so she would have heard by now if a new lord were in town.

He might be one of the young men she'd met at the start of the Season who were interested only in marriage and expected to be engaged before the end of it. Once they heard her candid declaration that she wouldn't be marrying this year, they'd wished her well and ignored her after that. But one might have changed his mind and was now determined to change hers—by gaining her interest before she knew who he was.

The only other young lords in town wouldn't ordinarily come to an event like this since they weren't interested in getting married yet. Most rakes were determined to spend some years gadding about before they got down to the business of producing an heir. And the second and third sons of a titled parent felt less pressure to marry than the family's heir. But due to the masquerade theme of this particular ball, they could more easily sneak in without an invitation. And the thought made her realize, so could anyone else.

"You're too quiet. Already bored with me?"

Having her thoughts interrupted brought the complaint "It's bloody annoying when variables sneak up on you."

"Is that what I am? A variable?"

"Didn't you say you wanted to be?"

"I wouldn't put winning your heart in that context, but if you're whittling down your extensive list of suitors so you can add me to it—"

"I don't whittle it down," she cut in. "I just keep count. But I like to do a little research, so if you aren't one of the fellows who frequent these parties, are you a rake, a second son, or a workingman?"

"That would be revealing too much."

Jacqueline grinned. "Sticking to an aura of mystery, eh?"

She imagined he was smiling when he replied, "It does seem to amuse you, so, yes, I believe I will."

"Well, at least you're not a beggar, dressed as you are," she said with confidence.

"I could have stolen these clothes."

Her brows shot up. "A criminal?"

"Overlooked that variable, did you?"

"Indeed I did, and that won't do a'tall."

"You could reform me."

"I could say good-bye."

"Even if I'm otherwise quite dashing, charming, and just what you need to keep things interesting?"

She started to turn away, quite disappointed that he was the one thing her father could never be brought around to accept, even if she could. But he kept her there by tugging her closer to him for the briefest moment, brushing her chest against his. It was quite surprising, that touch, and titillating, making her nipples tingle. But that he would dare detain her was the bigger surprise.

"I was jesting," he was quick to say. "I've only ever broken the law one time that I can recall, and it was a minor offense where no one got hurt, certainly nothing to warrant me being called a criminal."

If he would admit that much, then it must be true, but she still wanted to know, "Then what was it?"

"I don't make confessions to strangers. D'you?"

"Only about marriage. Don't want to give them hope when there isn't any."

"If I'm only destined to be a friend—for a year or two—perhaps you will meet me after the ball so we can start getting better acquainted?"

Instead of being affronted by such a breach of etiquette, Jacqueline chuckled. She was pleased that one of her guesses appeared to be on the mark. "So you're a rake of the more daring sort? Much as I'd like to be one m'self, I'm not going to tempt my father into killing you. So, no, I shan't meet you so late at night."

"A stroll on the terrace then, where I won't have twelve pairs of eyes frying me?"

She chuckled. "What you would get is my father tossing you over the railing out there, or did you think his eyes aren't also watching you like a hawk? But you might find me riding in Hyde Park tomorrow afternoon, should you care to join me—without your mask."

"Then until tomorrow."

Chapter Six

T HE NEXT DAY, JACQUELINE didn't doubt her mystery man had deliberately left the ball prior to the unmasking. She'd kept track of him in the crowd for a while, noting that he didn't ask anyone else to dance after he returned her to her parents. They'd been surprised when James had asked him his name and the fellow replied, "Your daughter is amused by mysteries so I'd prefer not to tell you right now." He'd bowed to the ladies and walked off, and since James had taken off his own mask by then, Georgina and Jack had laughed at his thunderous expression.

She couldn't get out of her mind the man's risqué suggestion that they meet after the ball. Daring stuff, his willingness to risk her father's finding out that they'd gone off together. Which made her think again that her mystery man didn't really know her or her family, and, more to the point, the many rumors of the more lethally unsavory sort that still abounded about her father.

But then one of her other beaus finally got up the nerve to draw her away from her parental shield, and once he did, the others formed a solid barricade on the edge of the dance floor to request their dances before she could return to her father's side. She found that so amusing she forgot about the daring stranger for a while. Until the unmasking and finding out that he wasn't there for it.

She was still intrigued and incredibly excited about her rendezvous in Hyde Park today. She was also glad to have the ride on her agenda to distract her from her father's having left for the Caribbean early that morning. A fait accompli, so she shouldn't still be miffed that he hadn't let her go along, but she was. After all, she was the one who'd been directly victimized by those damned pirates, so she should have a chance to get her own sweet revenge against Bastard, while her father took care of the culprit who'd pulled Bastard's strings. But so much for her wishes . . .

She was already dressed for her rendezvous in a deep blue riding habit, the only darker-colored outfit she was allowed to wear. Carrying the feathered hat and jacket into the dining room, she wondered if she could manage to eat anything before she left the house. She scoffed at the notion of being nervous about meeting the stranger again. She might be heaping more importance on this ride than she ought to. The stranger might have a physique to admire, but he might also have the visage of a toad.

That thought made her laugh aloud, which was when Amy Anderson appeared in the doorway, still removing her gloves. Amy had brought her twins, Glorianna and Stuart, with her, but then she would never have heard the end of the complaints if she hadn't. They were the same age as Jacqueline's twin brothers, and those four loved getting into trouble together when Amy and Warren were in London. Stuart and Glory were already rushing past their mother to the stairs.

"Eating alone?" Amy said as she took the chair next to Jacqueline.

Amy was Jacqueline's cousin and had become her aunt as well when she'd married Jack's uncle, Warren Anderson. Amy sailed with her husband, even raised her children at sea, bringing along first their nannies, then their tutors. But Warren's ship had departed that morning, along with Boyd's and Georgina's, all sailing with James back to the Caribbean, and none of them were taking any women along.

"You missed my mother. She's off having lunch with Aunt Roslynn."

"I did think she might need cheering up, which is why I stopped by, but I'm sure Ros will see to that."

"And you don't need cheering when you get left behind?"

"It's actually the first time Warren has sailed without me since we married. When I was expecting, he stayed home with me for the duration."

"So you're as miffed as I am not to be included?" Jack asked.

"No, but if you are, then maybe you need cheering up more'n your mother."

"So everyone keeps telling me," Jack mumbled.

"Then let's start with you telling me who he is?" Amy said with a grin. "I'm dying to know."

"Don't be so cryptic, Cousin." Jack rolled her eyes. "I'm not a mind reader."

"You've met your true love."

Jack's eyes flared. "Bite your tongue, I did no such thing. Take it back, Amy, right this minute."

Amy frowned before admonishing, "Well, don't get upset about it. I know you didn't want to meet him during your first Season and maybe you didn't actually meet him. Maybe you only encountered him in passing so he didn't make an impression on you. You didn't even see him? Maybe he only saw you and hasn't started the pursuit yet?"

"That's enough maybes, thank you very much. If you've just cursed me by saying I've found the man of my dreams, I'll never forgive you."

Amy tsked. "I didn't. There's been no wager, I assure you, and I've learned my lessons about not pushing things along by betting that they will happen. I just had one of my feelings, and you know they aren't always spot on the mark. It might not even have been about you. The family assumes you'll be next to the altar, so I was only guessing. It could be Jaime."

Jacqueline didn't believe a word of that, but as long as her cousin didn't make one of her infamous wagers that she *never* lost, then Jack wasn't going to worry about it. Especially since Amy's premonitions weren't always time-sensitive. If Amy was predicting that Jack would find true love, it could happen next year or the one after, which would be on Jack's timetable and suit her just fine.

But Amy could be a font of information of the mysterious sort, too, which prompted Jacqueline to suddenly ask, "Have you had any feelings about my father or your husband and what's going to happen when they reach the Caribbean?"

"Nothing like that powerful feeling that something bad was going to happen when you all set sail for Bridgeport, Jack, which is why I'm not worried about their trip."

Well, that wasn't satisfying. It could mean they wouldn't come to harm, but it could also mean they weren't going to succeed in finding the culprits. If she had just told her father immediately about that damned original note from Bastard's boss while they'd all still been in the Caribbean . . . No, her father would have walked straight into a trap and would still have left her behind somewhere. But she should have told him as soon as they got back to London; then he would have been gone for a full month by now instead of a few hours, and she would only have to wait one more month to find out what had happened or was going to happen, rather than two or more. She growled to herself because there was no winning for her in any of those scenarios.

But thinking of the secret she'd kept longer than she should have, she suddenly asked her cousin, "Can you keep a secret?"

Amy chuckled. "I'm not sure!"

Which changed Jack's mind about mentioning the note and asking if Amy had any feelings about what might have happened if Jack had handed it over sooner. So she said instead, "I met someone at the masked ball last night that I can't place."

"You have such a legion of beaus, surely he—"

"No, he was quick to say he wasn't one of them."

"And the secret is?"

"I was interested," Jack admitted, abashed.

"But that's wonderful news! And shame on you for trying to convince me my feeling wasn't about you."

Jack tsked. "But this isn't wonderful a'tall when he could be anyone, even someone quite inappropriate. Besides, I was merely intrigued."

"Clever fellow. Perhaps that was his strategy. He wanted to pique your curiosity so he would stand out from the pack, and he succeeded. It is going to take someone quite out of the ordinary to win you, m'dear, and that's not just my opinion. All of our aunts have said the same thing, including your mother. But I'm not sure I like that reference to 'inappropriate.' You've really no idea who he might be?"

"No, and he didn't stay for the unmasking at midnight, so I don't even know what his face looks like. It's annoying that I could pass him on the street and not know it."

She did worry that she might not recognize him in the park today. Or that he'd found out exactly who her father was last night after their dance—how could he not when James's confirmed presence had put the gossip mill in full swing? But that might have been why the stranger had left early. He could be a coward after all and not want to tempt fate by getting anywhere near James Malory again—or his daughter.

Finished eating, Jacqueline stood up to put her jacket on, then her jaunty hat with the single powder-blue feather. Noting the riding habit, Amy raised a black brow and asked, "D'you need an escort? I'd be happy to join you."

Jack laughed. "You don't know about the four bruisers my father hired? I can't leave the house without them. And Artie wouldn't have had my horse brought around without sending for them first. I'll see you later, Aunt Minx. And stop having your feelings about me!"

"I've agreed my feeling might not have been about you, but it was still a good feeling!" Amy yelled after her as Jack rushed out of the room.

Her escorts were indeed waiting for her, one of them dismounting to help her onto her sorrel mare. She imagined she was still early for her meeting with her mystery man, so she rode slowly on the way to the park. She couldn't really call it a rendezvous with the man with her bodyguards tagging along. But the two of them could ride side by side while they got better acquainted. And she'd find out who he really was!

Chapter Seven

JACQUELINE FOUND THE SINGLE red rose with the small sealed envelope attached lying on the side table with a new stack of party invitations next to it. She picked up everything and took it to her bedroom, tossing it onto her vanity before she flounced on her bed with a forlorn sigh. She wasn't angry, though she was definitely vexed and keenly disappointed, and the combination wasn't pleasant. Anger was preferable and easily dealt with. She could yell and scowl, then put it aside, but this crushing combination of feelings would linger until some other emotion took its place.

She finally sat up with another sigh to remove her hat and shrug out of her riding jacket. And stared at the single red rose across the room. If it was from *him*, she'd shred every petal, but she didn't think it was. Her many beaus were in the habit of sending her flowers. They filled every room of the house, and before those withered and died, they were replaced with new flowers that were even more extravagant. But none had ever sent her just one rose.

She didn't exactly rush back to the vanity, but she was a little breathless when she opened the envelope and held the note in her hand: *A thousand apologies. I was unavoidably detained.* And signed, *Yours truly.* He even underlined the *truly.* But she wasn't the least bit mollified after she'd stayed in the park for hours, traversing the riding path back and forth a dozen times. He could have sent someone else to tell her they wouldn't be riding today.

Then her maid arrived to prepare her for the soirée she was to attend tonight, another reminder that the hour had grown late because she'd wasted far too much time in the park. But she was excited again by the time she was dressed in a new evening gown of the palest aqua and hurried downstairs. Only a little of that excitement was due to her expectation of seeing the stranger tonight. Most of it was because her brother Jeremy would be escorting her, with his wife, Danny, to give Georgina a respite from the round of parties. And aside from Judy's wedding, Jack had seen far too little of her older brother since spring when she and Judy had sailed to her American debut.

She grinned at her brother's wife, who had snow-white hair and looked stunningly beautiful as usual. Danny had never let her hair grow out, despite not needing to disguise herself as a boy anymore. Having been separated from her parents when she was a child, she'd grown up in one of the worst sections of London with a pack of orphaned thieves, and the short-cropped hair had been to pass herself off as a boy to avoid trouble of the salacious sort. Jeremy would never have met her if he hadn't needed to hire a thief to help his friend Percival Alden with a personal matter. It had been amusing when Danny had met Nathan Tremayne for the first time and he'd asked if they were related by blood, since his hair was as light a shade of blond as hers.

"Tell me who I need to scowl at and who gets a friendly pat on the back tonight," Jeremy said as he put her arm through his to lead her outside to his coach.

"You don't need to scowl at anyone. They're all nice enough chaps. Besides, you really can't pull it off the way our father does. You're too handsome, Brother. It quite keeps you from being intimidating. Why don't you tell me instead why you didn't show up this morning to bid our father good-bye?"

"I was too angry," Jeremy mumbled, then added in a growl, "I hope he thought I stowed away on *The Maiden George* and he wasted time searching for me before he sailed."

Jack burst out laughing. "No, you don't." Jeremy helped Jack into the coach and, once inside, sat near to his wife, across from Jack.

"I don't doubt he did," Danny put in. "I've never seen him this angry."

Jacqueline raised a brow. "Well, I can't say I'm surprised when I feel the same way."

Jeremy suddenly unrolled a map, put it on Jack's lap, and pointed at an island. "That's where Father's fleet is going. And this is where he captured Pierre Lacross all those years ago."

She stared at the spot Jeremy was pointing to. "But there's nothing there."

"Because that island is unnamed and too small to appear on this map. There are many tiny islands in the Caribbean where criminals of one sort or another can hide. Like I told you before, I know those islands well."

Danny leaned back with a sigh. "He's obsessed with this mission, if that's not clear to you yet, Jack. I'm having a hard time talking him out of catching the next ship that's heading that way."

Jacqueline debated for a moment whether to say she'd go with him, then said instead, "For what purpose, Jeremy? To catch up with Father so he can lock you in a cabin for the duration of the voyage—and be furious that you didn't obey him and stay out of it?"

"See?" Danny said, gloating only a little. "I said nearly the same thing, didn't I, Jer?"

"You two do know that I'm not still the teenager he found in that tavern all those years ago, don't you?"

Danny suddenly chuckled. "I do wish I could have seen James's face that day when you told him you were his son, yet you stood there the spitting image of his brother Anthony when Tony was that age."

Jeremy still looked uncannily like their uncle Anthony, but then Anthony and Jeremy shared the black hair and cobalt eyes of their Gypsy ancestors, while James didn't. Tony's wife had actually accused Tony of lying about Jeremy's parentage. Even James found that to be amusing—mostly.

"So he didn't believe me at first, at least, not until I told him who my mother was," Jeremy said. "All beside the point, which is he still treats me like that child."

"It couldn't have been pleasant, growing up in taverns," Jacqueline remarked. "At least, until he found you."

"It wasn't that bad, though I would have much preferred taking to the seas with him. And I got to for a while, until that sea battle with Nick. Father bought that plantation in Jamaica so he could have a place to park me after I nearly got injured in that battle. But at least he took me with him when he went back to England to get even with Nick, and you know what a surprise that turned out to be, with Nick having married our cousin Regina. Then Father left me with Uncle Tony while he went back to the Caribbean to dispose of that plantation. Of course, you never would have been born, Jack, if things hadn't played out that way."

"I still find it amazing that your father was actually a pirate," Danny said.

"Gentleman pirate," Jeremy and Jack said at the same time, then laughed because they'd both corrected Danny.

But Jeremy continued, "It was just a game to him, bedeviling any ship that appeared to offer a challenge so he could test his skills. And I had it straight from his first mate, Connie, that the only reason he went to sea was because he'd gotten so jaded being one of London's most notorious rakes that nothing stirred his emotions anymore, not even duels."

"So it took a full decade for him to start feeling again?" Danny asked.

"No, he was gone that long because his brothers ended up disowning him. But his time on the high seas was his salvation, too. He enjoyed it and might never have returned to the fold if he hadn't found me."

"Your father's decision to return to England is directly responsible for quite a few marriages," Danny remarked. "His, mine, Amy's. Even three of Jack's uncles wouldn't have met their wives if your father hadn't brought their sister to England. Think of all that happiness he created for himself and the rest of us by making peace with his brothers—for you. We should start calling him Cupid."

"Bite your tongue," Jack choked out.

"Hell's bells, Danny, you don't want to insult m'father," Jeremy said with a groan.

"I was joking." Then with a wink at Jacqueline, Danny added, "But kindly remember how a few minutes ago you were ready to make him angry at you for hying after him. I believe I've made my point?"

Jeremy said no more about it, but that didn't mean he wasn't silently stewing. But they'd arrived at the home of Gladys Marshall, who was hosting tonight's soirée, where there was to be music and a buffet. And Jack's curious stranger wasn't there. If he was, he didn't make himself known, and after glancing around the room for a few minutes, she was pretty sure she knew every man there.

She came up with dozens of excuses why he appeared to be giving up the pursuit. He couldn't get an invitation because he wasn't even gentry. He was so hideously ugly that he was ashamed to show her his face. He was a coward after all who didn't want to bother with someone who had such a dangerous father. He didn't want to settle for just friendship, which she had assured him was all she was offering this year. All of her other beaus knew that, too, and only a few had given up early on. The rest were confident they could change her mind given enough time.

There was still no gossip about her mystery man either, though a few debutantes mentioned to her that they'd noticed him at the masked ball and wondered who he was. But even they were more interested in asking her about her father, since he was still the prime tidbit for the week.

Giles was the first of her beaus to approach her. He was one of the more handsome young lords pursuing her, and she liked his wit and humor. She even hoped he'd still be unattached next year when she would get around to choosing a husband. It was likely he would be since he was a professed rake.

"Are you ready to marry me yet?" he whispered beside her so Jeremy wouldn't hear.

"You can't maintain your rakish reputation if you keep asking me that," she scolded with a smile.

"I've sworn I'll give up everything for you, Jack." But then he glanced around, no doubt to make sure James wasn't there, before adding, "I couldn't help but notice how intimidated my competition was last night by your father. I'm not, you know. In fact, I was thinking about inviting him for a round or two at Knighton's Hall to get to know him better. I've heard he enjoys exercising there occasionally."

Jack laughed. "If you want to call it that. But you'll have to wait until he returns to London. He's away for a few months."

Giles looked thrilled and swept her onto the small dance floor. Jack chuckled to herself. She'd have to warn Giles that he ought to watch one of her father's matches before he took the plunge—if he was actually serious about such a silly notion.

THE NEXT DAY, JACK rode in the park again just in case her mystery man showed up, but she didn't stay long this time. With a shrug, she decided she'd wasted enough time and thoughts on a man she didn't know and would likely never know. It was time to forget about the curious stranger and get on with enjoying the Season.

Returning home, she found another single red rose on the side table in the front hall. Jacqueline laughed and ran upstairs with it, placing it carefully on her bed while she quickly changed out of her riding habit and into a comfortable skirt and blouse for the rest of the afternoon, until she had to dress for tonight's party, which was still hours away.

She opened the new note and read:

Circumstances have conspired to thwart me. I must leave England on a family matter and don't know when I can return, or if I should. Only you can draw me back to London, Jacqueline Malory. I merely require a little bit of hope that you might want me to return and you can give me that if you will come to bid me farewell. My ship sails at dusk with the tide and is anchored in the Thames near the London Docks at Wapping. I will await you at the Wapping dock stairs until the last minute.

Once again, he signed off with *Yours truly.* And once again he underlined *truly.* Jacqueline smiled to herself. Of course she was going to go and . . . She paused. The docks? At dusk?

She read the note again, then again. Why the devil would he suggest such an unsavory location? And his handwriting seemed vaguely familiar in this longer note. She compared it with his first note and still felt she'd seen it somewhere else, she just couldn't remember—and then she did.

Her smile was back. She was definitely going to meet him at the docks; she just wasn't sure how yet.

Chapter Eight

Our plan is in motion, so there's no turning back now," Jeremy remarked. "Nervous?"

"Not even a little." Jacqueline sat beside him in the chaise, offering a grin to prove it.

"I hope you're right about this, Jack."

"So do I. But in either case, we're prepared."

"But if it is the blackguard who abducted you and we capture him, just imagine what the elders will say. They'll see I'm as capable of handling a dangerous mission as my father. Much obliged for the opportunity to prove it, minx."

She grinned. "My pleasure."

It was still a long ride to the docks at Wapping. But any of London's docks or riverfronts could be dangerous even in the bright light of day, let alone near dusk, so she and her brother were well armed for their mission. And well protected. She glanced behind her to make sure all four of her big, muscular guards were keeping up with them on their mounts. They were.

And she hadn't lied to Jeremy. How could she be nervous

when she was exhilarated? No matter the outcome, she'd have answers tonight.

Jeremy was driving his two-wheeled, single-horse chaise, which only had a wide perch that was designed for one but could accommodate two. He used this vehicle to get around London by himself, when he was out and about without his wife and children, since he wasn't fond of riding a horse. He'd brought it tonight so they could both sit on the wide perch, which would allow them to see far ahead of them when they neared the Wapping dock stairs.

A while later, Jeremy remarked, "You know, if this is actually a suitor of yours, he had time to call on you for any farewelling in a nice, safe parlor. Didn't that occur to you?"

"My beaus get turned away at the door, so he couldn't. He might have tried, then left the note instead."

"No callers a'tall? Hell's bells, Jack, I thought you were going to have a normal Season. This doesn't sound the least bit normal."

"I am, and I was, but—"

"Never mind, there's nothing normal about the number of your suitors, either. You're going to force Artie and Henry to retire, you know, if they've been having to slam the door shut so often."

"Nonsense, those two old salts love slamming doors. They complained when they had to let my suitors in!"

Jeremy tsked. "I would have thought you, of all women, would have had no trouble a'tall dismissing the men you aren't interested in marrying. You're certainly not known for being subtle, Jack."

"Nor was I. I warned them I'm not considering marriage proposals this year. They're just being stubborn. So it's not my fault if they figure out too late that when I say something, I bloody well mean it."

"Did I strike a nerve? Or are you nervous?"

"Neither, but maybe you can tell me why a man thinks he can change a woman's mind about him simply by persevering?"

"You're joking, right? A no never discouraged me, it merely made me more charming."

"So it's just the chase that keeps men interested? Or more likely the competition in this case?"

"Probably both, but foremost, it's simply you, minx. You're the prime catch of the Season. It would also be the coup of the century for a young buck to marry James Malory's daughter without getting trounced first."

She laughed. "There is that, I suppose."

"But what if you've got it all wrong," Jeremy persisted, "and we only have to contend with an obnoxiously determined suitor. D'you actually favor this fellow above the others?"

She grinned. "I told you. He piqued my interest because he posed a mystery, professing to want to win my heart but refusing to give me his name. I'd like to solve that mystery before he leaves England."

"Hell's bells, Jack!" Jeremy stared at her for a moment before he shook his head. "You're being played. Sounds like something I might have done if I was determined when I was still chasing skirts. He's worked his way to the top of that ridiculously high stack of yours, hasn't he? So his ploy worked. And I'm going to bloody well pummel him m'self if he's lured you to the docks just to get you alone, away from his competition. He probably wants to steal a kiss before—have they been stealing kisses?"

Suddenly Jeremy looked quite angry. Jacqueline chuckled.

"Course they have—well, course they've tried—but I'm not interested in kissing yet. Even had to sock Lord Giles to get that point across a few weeks ago. Blackened his eye and didn't feel the least sorry for it, though I did accept his apology the next day. But when I'm ready for kissing, I'll likely be the one stealing them, so you needn't worry about that."

"That's supposed to put my mind at ease?" Jeremy snorted with a roll of his eyes, but said no more about it.

Chapter Nine

THE DOCKS BUILT AT Wapping were well protected with high walls surrounding them. Ships had to pass through basins to get from the Thames River to the dock's fancy warehouses, which housed only luxury goods. But to find the old stairs that accessed the river at high tide, Jeremy and Jack's guards had to follow the winding road outside the large enclosed docks to get to Wapping Street, which ran along the riverbank. The street was high enough above the tidewater mark to offer extensive views of the ships on the water, some already sailing toward the Channel. Even this far from the dock entrance a few vehicles were going in both directions.

"Are you still hoping this is legit, Jack?" Jeremy asked.

"Oh, no, I'm hoping it's not."

To come face-to-face with Bastard again, to finally have her revenge, that was going to be a sweet dream come true. She would never have guessed that he was behind this new plot if she hadn't finally recognized his handwriting in that longer note he sent today. At her insistence, her father had showed her the ransom note that the Andersons retrieved from the post office the night she was abducted in Bridgeport. She didn't have that ransom note so she couldn't compare it to the one that had been delivered today, but she was almost positive the writing was the same. And "almost" was enough to convince her to come prepared to this meeting and turn the tables on Bastard—if it was him.

She was still fuming over his success at tricking her by wearing that blond wig and a mask that covered his face and muffled his voice. And he'd obviously studied his betters because his gentlemanly manners had deceived her.

If it was him, Jack would prefer to just shoot him, but Jeremy had convinced her that Bastard might have valuable information about his boss and where he was located, information that could help their father. They could send it to him and Drew posthaste in the Caribbean. So Jeremy had persuaded her that the best course of action would be interrogation first— brutal she hoped—then a quick ride to prison, where Bastard would await trial and the gallows.

But if it wasn't him—damnit, she really did hope her mystery man wasn't a legitimate suitor despite how much he'd intrigued her. She'd rather have revenge tonight.

They passed a set of stairs where two women and a child had just been rowed ashore from a passenger ship and were waiting for their baggage and probably hoping to hail a passing hackney carriage as well. But with the enclosed docks, it was not an ideal place to come ashore. Most passenger ships that were going to unload prior to getting cleared for a berth did so near wharves where vehicles for hire were more easily obtained. But the river was extremely congested, and captains couldn't always anchor in ideal spots.

The next set of stairs was quite a distance farther up the street, but as they approached, they could see a man standing at the top of them. If there was a plaque on the wall next to the stairs naming them, they couldn't yet see it. The vehicle behind them was following closely and had only just cut in front of Jack's mounted guards and would probably have passed Jeremy's chaise if a coach up ahead weren't blocking the other side of the road, making it too dangerous to attempt. But Jeremy waved at it to pass them when he began to slow his chaise.

"At least Percy came through," he said with a grin, seeing the coach that had stopped a little ways beyond where the lone man was standing, his back turned toward them.

"You had doubts?"

"Well, we put this scheme together at the last minute. And Percy has been known to muck things up."

"Known? It used to be guaranteed!" Jack said. "But that hasn't happened in years, correct? Or you wouldn't have enlisted his help."

"Indeed, Percy can be depended on these days to follow instructions to the letter. He even writes them down!"

Percy had been sent to Knighton's Hall to hire every brawny fighter he could find and to go elsewhere if there weren't enough there, until he couldn't fit any more in his large coach. The lone fellow stood gazing in the opposite direction, not even glancing back their way. He appeared to be watching Percy and his driver, who were bent over, pretending to inspect one of the coach's wheels.

"The moment of truth has arrived," Jeremy said.

"He's tall enough to be the mysterious chap," Jacqueline told her brother. "And has the same color hair, though I didn't think it was that long." The blond queue fell halfway down the man's back. "But Bastard has black hair, so if that was him at the ball, he was wearing a wig then and is now."

"So you think it's Bastard?"

"I'm not absolutely sure, but I'll know as soon as he turns around. I'll never forget that face."

Jeremy jumped out of the chaise, looking up at her to say, "Wait—"

She jumped down beside him before he could finish, eliciting a distinct sound of annoyance from her brother. But they approached the man together. And the man must have finally heard them because he turned. He was wearing the damned mask from the ball? A suitor wouldn't at this point—would he? But Bastard certainly would, because he knew she wouldn't go near him if she saw that he was the man who had abducted her in Bridgeport.

She was incredulous that he would still pretend to be her mystery man. Jeremy put his arm out to stop her from getting any closer.

"That's not going to do, mate," Jeremy said in one of his more unfriendly tones. "Take off the mask or my sister gets back in the carriage."

"I will," her mystery man said.

But he made no move to do that—and that's when men charged out of the coach behind them, which hadn't gone around them after all, and more men were hopping over the low wall by the riverbank beside them. Percy and his men, some twenty feet away, were running forward to help, but they weren't close enough yet. And despite the extra thugs who had jumped over the wall to surround Jeremy, someone still tried to disable her brother with a board to his head. At the horrible-sounding crack Jack turned with a gasp to see her brother stagger, but he had a hard head. He shot that fellow, then dropped another with the butt of his spent pistol and took his fists to a third. And where the devil was her escort?

Also surrounded. She saw it now beyond that other coach. Her guards had been rushed upon, too. She wasn't even sure those four bruisers, as big as they were, could win against dozens of men trying to get at them.

It was a bloody army of riffraff, back there, here, and she felt a moment of terror when she saw that some of them looked like pirates. Those near her had split up, half of them surrounding Jeremy, and the other half turning to deal with Percy's men. But Jeremy was holding his own. He was extremely tall like Anthony and just as muscular. And while he wasn't as good with his fists as their father was, he was still an exceptional fighter, brutal when needed, and had already dropped four more of the attackers to the ground. But when one fell, another took his place. There were simply too many of them! He got tripped, and the moment he was down, fists and boots descended.

Jacqueline went a little crazy seeing that and leapt at the men blocking her view of Jeremy, afraid they were going to kill him. "I don't think so" was said as she was yanked out of the fray and then cheekily, "I knew you couldn't resist me, Jack."

She sucked in her breath, recognizing that voice clearly now and started to reach for her pistol. But Percy had reached her by then, yelling, "Jack, let's go!" He grabbed her arm, which yanked her hand out of her pocket! Damnit, bad timing as usual for him, yet he let go after nearly dragging her down with him when one punch knocked him out. And the puncher was the Mask. Bastard!

Fear and fury overwhelmed her, that she'd underestimated him. They were supposed to capture him, not be captured! And she felt horrible that she'd put Jeremy and Percy in danger, for nothing! And even worse, she'd given her father's enemies exactly what they wanted—something to use to manipulate him.

In a rage, she turned with her right fist swinging, only to get instantly flipped about, but he'd already removed the mask, revealing that handsome hated face. "Tactics I remember well," he said, actually sounding nostalgic! Then to his men: "Bring the gents if they still live."

He'd already put a hand over her mouth so she couldn't scream at him. His arm went around her waist now to clasp a steely grip on her other arm near the elbow. She was lifted off her feet and only saw in the briefest moment that the eight burly men surrounding her brother had stepped back—because Jeremy was no longer moving.

Horrified that Jeremy might be dead, she clamped her teeth on the palm across her mouth, then tasted blood, she had no idea whose, then the hand pressed tighter against her mouth.

But she was halfway down the stone steps by then, he was hurrying so fast with his prize.

Carrying her like that, he might as well have tied a strong rope tightly around her arms and torso. She couldn't maneuver either of her hands to reach her pocket and the weapon in it. But her feet weren't restrained and were dangling near his shins, so she lifted her legs to slam her boot heels back against Bastard's knees to cripple him, bracing herself for a fall down the remaining stairs if she was successful. It would have worked if he were shorter, but all she got was a hiss out of him when her heels slammed against his lower thighs. Well, the arm about her middle tightened, too, which cost her some breath.

That wouldn't have stopped her from kicking him again, but there was no time left to try it. She'd seen the two waiting longboats at the bottom of the stone steps where the water was lapping at high tide. The two boats were big enough to accommodate ten rowers each, but that didn't account for all the men who had been on that street, more men than a ship would need for a crew. Were they not all sailors?

Two men had even been left with the boats, one in each of them. And Jack was utterly jarred when Bastard leapt into one of them.

She was set down hard on the back bench to face the ships anchored directly ahead of them out in the Thames. With absolute efficiency one of the other rowers put a gag over her mouth so the hand, bloody she hoped, could be removed. She was reaching for her pocket again but the two men behind her were quicker. Even as the gag was tied, her arms were dragged behind her back and her hands tied there just as quickly.

Another loud thud came from behind her, which she guessed was Jeremy being tossed into the boat as well. They wouldn't bring him along if he was dead, would they? Small hope, but hope nonetheless. Then the boat swayed alarmingly as the others got into it and took up the oars.

Not much had been said during the entire kidnapping other than shouted curses, groans, and what Bastard had said there at the end. The thugs remained silent as the longer rowboat was maneuvered about and swiftly rowed away from shore. She faced the riverbank now and saw other men being carried or helped down the stairs to that other longboat. She couldn't see Percy's coach, but she could just make out the top of Jeremy's chaise beyond the low wall at the top of the stairs, and the bigger coach behind it. Had it followed them all the way from Berkeley Square?

Were the coaches going to be abandoned there? Someone

would find the vehicles, but they wouldn't know whom they belonged to unless some of Jeremy's men escaped—if any of them were still alive. But then she saw the coach behind the chaise turn about and head back the way they'd come, and Percy's was close behind it. So the coaches were going to be disposed of? Oh, God, the bodies, too? And the continued silence was telling. Only the one order had been given, making her realize how well planned this abduction must have been.

And then a sack was placed over her head—again. Why? She knew who had her this time, so what was the point of blindfolding her? Unless it was to cover her face? He'd done that before, kept her completely isolated from his men. Did he not want the pirates to get a good look at her?

A damned small sack had been tugged down over her head and now pressed tightly against her nose. Small compensation that it blocked most of the stink of the river, a smell she was actually familiar with, as many times as her family had come down to the docks to bid one of her five Anderson uncles goodbye before he sailed.

She knew their destination had been reached when the boat rocked against one of the ships. She was picked up, twisted about, and hefted over a shoulder for the climb up the ladder. If that sack hadn't been so tight, it might have fallen off with her head halfway down the man's back.

The deck was crossed, a door was opened, and she heard more than one set of footsteps entering the room behind her. She was startled when someone said, "I think he broke my bloody jaw."

A chuckle. "If it's broke, you wouldn't be saying it's broke, now would you, mate?"

Neither voice belonged to Bastard, but a grunt was the

response. Then Jack was dropped on something soft low to the floor. Whoever had carried her aboard had at least bent over to do it, so the landing didn't quite knock the breath from her. Bastard? She didn't know if he had carried her or was even in the room.

But she wasn't untied. Her boots were pulled off instead, though she got in a good kick to someone's chest before the last boot was confiscated. Her dagger clattered on the floor when it fell out of one. One of the men snickered. But they hadn't yet found the pistol in her pocket, and she turned over to lie on it, not very comfortable, but she wasn't about to make it easy for them to find it.

But they weren't looking for more weapons; they were binding her feet together. Once that was done, she heard a marching away and the door was closed. But one of them might still be in there, unmoving. Bastard. And she wouldn't know if he was there unless he moved or said something because they hadn't removed the sack from her head!

Chapter Ten

SHE WAS LEFT ALONE too long, giving her too much time to think. It was such an elaborate plan, charming her at a ball, the notes, the roses. If he had picked anywhere else in London for this final rendezvous, it would never have occurred to her that it was Bastard pulling these strings. She still found it hard to believe he'd actually been her mystery man, and maybe he wasn't. He had arranged it, certainly, had even used the disguise tonight until she got close enough for him to spring his trap. But it took finesse to pull off the role of a gentleman, so it was far more likely that he'd hired an actor to charm and intrigue her at the ball. The man had been English. His diction had been cultured. He'd been everything Bastard wasn't!

Frustrated by their utter failure, still worried about Jeremy's condition, still lying uncomfortably on her pistol to keep it hidden beneath her, she closed her eyes to wait out this ordeal. Before much longer, she heard the door open and close, then a single set of footsteps moving toward her and stopping near her back.

"Your brother isn't dead—if you were wondering."

If? If! Bastard again. Like his handsome face, he had a voice she'd never forget either, deep, husky, sometimes amusing, and so aggravating because she hated him so much.

The bindings on her wrists pulled against her skin as he cut through them. She sat up immediately and tugged the sack off her head. Her coiffure was undone, so half of her hair came tumbling down her back. His back was all she saw of him as he walked away from her toward a desk across the room, his long raven-black hair floating about his wide shoulders.

He sat down behind his desk, giving her the full brunt of that unforgettable face she hated, the alert turquoise eyes, the high cheekbones, the wide jaw, the full lips that smiled a lot and were smiling now. She remembered that, how often he'd smiled for no bloody reason and how much it had infuriated her—at least until her refusal to eat had finally gotten *him* angry.

And the black stubble on his cheeks and upper lip, she remembered that, too. He didn't like to shave and definitely didn't do so daily. But he was dressed like a gentleman, in a finely tailored brown coat that he shrugged out of now, black pants, glossy boots, white shirt replete with cravat that he also got rid of. Dressed to deceive tonight, so she might still believe he was the Mask right down to the last moment.

The nefarious Bastard whom she hadn't succeeded in capturing as she'd so hoped.

She pulled the gag off her mouth to demand, "Who is that liar you hired to lure me here? I want to know who to gullet—after you."

He dipped his head and spread his hands a little to indicate something on his desk. She had to stand up to see it, which wasn't easily done while sitting on a low cot with bound feet. She managed it with a hard push from both hands.

The porcelain mask was lying on his desk. "Nice try, but no bloody way. You at a ball in formal wear? Even if you could steal the togs for a fancy event like that, you don't know the first thing about being a charming gentleman of refinement. The mask proves nothing. He could have given it back to you."

"You wound me."

"I wish I could!"

"You were apparently bored and easily intrigued," he replied offhandedly, but with that damned smile she hated. "And it worked, didn't it, to lure you right into my hands again?"

She still refused to believe it, but if she did, she certainly wouldn't admit it to him. The man who hadn't just intrigued her but had also excited her couldn't be the man she hated above all others. But she could end him right then and there because the fool hadn't been smart enough to search her for other weapons, leaving her with two.

She pulled her pistol out of her pocket and aimed it at him, but he dropped below his desk the second he saw it and stayed hidden behind it. She didn't dare try to hop over there with her feet still bound. She'd fall on her face and he'd have her pistol in hand in an instant.

Then she heard him say with infuriating calm, "You can't shoot me, Jack. They'll kill your brother if you do."

She blanched. She'd had no one to protect the last time he'd abducted her and had tried to kill him every chance she got. Failing each time. The man was too big, too swift, too calculating, guessing her moves before she made them. Her single shot would be heard and draw his whole crew in here.

Furious, she snarled, "Come over here so I can bash your head in instead!"

He didn't, but he laughed at the suggestion. "You're going to slide your weapon across the floor instead."

"Not bloody likely. Show yourself, coward. They won't kill James Malory's son—not if you still want our father as a willing sacrifice."

"We only need one hostage. I appreciate your giving us three."

He sounded far too confident, as if he weren't still cautiously hiding behind that desk. Maybe she could hop his way without falling, at least get to the desk so she could crawl on top of it and . . . He stood up, presenting her with a big target she couldn't miss. If she were in a rage, she would have thoughtlessly pulled the trigger. But then she'd be without a decent weapon to use in dealing with his crew after she killed him, and they'd all come charging into the room when they heard the shot. The dagger strapped to her thigh wouldn't be much help against the lot of them. Then again, Bastard could be her weapon and her shield to get herself, Jeremy, and Percy off that ship. His crew would do nothing if they saw she had a pistol pressed to his back.

He must have noticed the calculating look on her face because he said, "You care so little for your brother?"

Having Jeremy here was obviously going to be a distinct disadvantage—for her. Bastard would hold Jeremy's welfare over her head every time she did something he didn't like. He wouldn't need ropes to keep her hands tied. She had to get them off this ship now, while England was still a short swim away.

"On the contrary, I love my brothers, but they're not here.

I lied to protect the fellow who was with me, since if your crew thinks he's a Malory, he'll be safe from harm."

"Then who is he?"

"No one of import, just a penniless lord who resembles my older brother. Which is why I occasionally hire him to pretend to be Jeremy, and that was necessary tonight since you wanted to meet in such an unsavory part of town."

"And the other gent?"

She shrugged. "Those two chum about together, so he was invited along. Besides, d'you really think anyone in my family would have allowed me to meet anyone in this part of town? My older brother would have locked me in my bedroom if I had even dared to mention it to him."

Bastard sighed. "Too bad."

"Too bad?"

"That I don't believe you. But your claim about your family's not allowing you to go to the docks does beg the question, why did you come?"

"Because I suspected it might be you and wanted to make sure you hang!"

He was smiling again. "No, you didn't. You were caught up in the romance of having a secret admirer. It warms my heart to know how eager you were to see me again, that you, the most sought-after debutante in London, came to the docks for our rendezvous."

"I was eager to see *him*, the puppet you hired, not you. You I want to see dangling from a rope, or lying in a pool of blood, which is still an option." She waggled the hand that was holding the pistol. "So you're going to slide one of your daggers over here, and I know you have at least one on you, so I can cut my feet loose." She wasn't about to let him know she still had one of her own. "Then you're going to walk me out of here and off your ship."

"Am I?"

She gritted her teeth. "*Now*, Bastard, the dagger."

He leaned down to extract one from his boot and placed it on the desk in front of him, within his reach, but nowhere near hers. She sighed. "Can you even imagine how much willpower it's taking for me not to pull this trigger? Did I ever give you the idea that I might not enjoy killing you?"

"No, you made that abundantly clear. But did I ever give you the idea that I wanted to harm you in return?"

The absurdity of his question boggled her mind, making her snarl, "The very nature of your mission was the worst harm I could imagine!"

"Are we really going to do this again? Rehash the same arguments? Yes, you love your father so much you'll kill anyone who wants to harm him. Yes, I had no choice in the matter. But that was then, when I had a shrew on my back pulling the strings."

He was talking about Catherine Meyer, and the very mention of her made Jack growl, "Is she here again?"

"No, thank God, her father didn't let her come along this time. If he did, I don't doubt I would have just tossed her over the side as we got under way. It would have been too much of a temptation to resist."

He was grinning as he said it. Jack wasn't. Much as she would have liked to do the same thing to that lying jewel thief, Catherine had been his mistress, too, which Catherine had crowed about during Jack's previous kidnapping. And Catherine was his boss's daughter, no matter what name she went by, no matter if his boss was Lacross or some other nasty villain, so Bastard wouldn't dare harm her.

Jack didn't believe he would have thrown Catherine overboard. Actually, Jack wouldn't believe anything he said.

But she was running out of time! She didn't need to be told they were under way, she could feel the ship moving. And she didn't doubt everything he'd been saying was meant to distract her until it was too late to extricate herself from this second kidnapping. And he was too late anyway! Her father had already sailed, wouldn't even know that Bastard had her again.

She'd been insane to think she could capture this wily bastard herself. But she smiled to herself that he'd failed his mission. By the time he got her to the Caribbean, his boss would already be dead and her father would be on his way back to England. Whatever ransom note Bastard left this time would—terrify her mother. Damnit!

"Are you cannoned up, or fast?"

He raised a black brow at her. "If I wasn't in command of a ship, that would make no sense to me, and why do you want to know?"

"Could you just answer a question for once without asking another?"

"I won't be participating in any sea battles, if that has you concerned. This ship used to be a trading vessel. It's never been fitted with cannons." But then he chuckled. "Other than fake ones that Mort assembled for us."

Her shoulders drooped. He could easily overtake her father's fleet, which was fully cannoned for the battle they expected. That would allow Bastard to get her to his boss first. So she couldn't admit to him that his ransom note wouldn't reach his target this time or he would make sure his ship got in the lead. It probably would anyway, even if he didn't know he was going to be in a race. And she would be in the hands of

Bastard's boss before her father found the pirate to dispose of him. And that would mean her father would be walking into a trap again. . . .

She pushed that thought away and said, "I think I need to shoot you anyway and take my chances with your crew."

Chapter Eleven

THE SHARP RAP ON the door startled Jacqueline, but she didn't turn her pistol in that direction, keeping it steady on Bastard, and said softly, "Whoever that is, tell them to go away."

"Enter," he called out. He didn't even take a moment to consider doing that!

He'd never done that before, either. Anytime his crew needed him on that previous voyage, they'd knocked and he'd left the cabin to talk to them instead of allowing them access. Always locking the door behind him, too. She'd assumed he'd been protecting his crew, making sure she wouldn't be able to recognize any faces other than his. She wondered why he was behaving differently on this second kidnapping.

A frightening thought struck her. She wasn't going to survive this time.

The crewman who stepped inside the captain's cabin was nearly as tall as Bastard. He wore his blond hair queued back and had a pleasant visage—well, he was actually handsome.

And he didn't exactly look like a sailor in that billowing lawn shirt open at the neck, tight britches, tall boots, a fancy gold chain around his neck. It was uncannily similar to how her father dressed aboard ship! The only thing missing was the single gold earring James often sported at sea and even occasionally in London. And then it hit her. The man was blond and the right height, and just as strapping as her mystery man.

"You're the masked man I danced with at the ball!" she accused.

The blond man had the audacity to grin at her before saying, "No, ma'am, I'm not. Wouldn't be caught dead in one of those torture chambers." But then he glanced at his captain. "Do you need help?"

"No, she's only got a single bullet. She's not going to waste it." Bastard tossed a key to the crewman, though it didn't quite reach him and slid across the floor to stop near his feet. "But you can lock the door on your way out."

Jacqueline's eyes flared. Get locked in the room with Bastard? He'd take cover again, forcing her to get closer to him, and she knew exactly how that would play out. So she pointed her pistol at the blond.

"I'll waste this bullet if you reach for that key, I promise you I will. Kick it over toward me."

The man didn't do that; instead he looked at his captain to tell him how to proceed.

Bastard sighed. "Let it go. She's angry enough to do something rash. Your business was . . . ?"

"You wanted to know when her brother woke up."

Bastard smiled at Jacqueline as he replied, "She wants me to think they aren't related."

"Get rid of him then?"

"No, we're well stocked. At least we don't need to fish for our dinner this time, so another few mouths to feed doesn't matter. Both those gents might still come in useful."

"He won't be a bargaining chip," Jacqueline warned. "You might as well let him go while you still can."

Bastard raised a brow at her. "You don't think we'd kill him before tossing him off the ship when you have frequently called us a murdering lot? We can't let him go alive. Dead men tell no tales, you know. So which is it: Do you care about this fellow or do you not?"

She wasn't going to answer that and said instead, "I recall hearing you assure me you weren't a murderer. Of course, I didn't believe you at the time and never will, so it's moot. But the fate of my hirelings isn't going to be decided by either of you." She waved the pistol at the crewman again. "Close the door, then walk over to Bastard so he can tie you up. You're not letting his crew know that I have the upper hand."

The blond man laughed at the absurd order.

Bastard said laconically, "I think she's serious."

Amusement gone, the crewman, or whoever he was, said, "The devil I will. Take your best shot, Jack Malory, if you're going to. Otherwise, I'm getting back to work."

She was angry enough to shoot the man, and she wanted to! But she couldn't waste her only chance of getting off that ship by using the captain as her shield. So she watched the door close behind the man before glancing at Bastard again.

"He's not a sailor," she said, pointing out the obvious in a contemptuous tone.

"Neither was I, but my friend and I have adapted fairly well."

"Your friend? You consider your crew to be friends? Yes, of

course you do," she sneered. "Pirates are all for one and one for all."

He chuckled. "I wouldn't know. I did tell you before that we weren't pirates, didn't I?"

"If you did, I wasn't listening."

"You listened, you just chose not to believe anything I said. But Catherine isn't here now watching my every move, so perhaps we—"

Jacqueline cut in sharply, "I don't believe she pulled your strings, and I certainly don't believe you would have tossed her overboard if she were here, though I would have liked to see what would happen to you if you told her father you abandoned her in London."

He shrugged. "I doubt it would matter to him. He didn't strike me as a loving parent. But she seemed desperate for his love, would do anything to get it. Stealing those jewels from you and your relatives was just for him, to prove that she could be useful to him so he wouldn't send her away when she'd only just found him."

"So that part of her tale was true, that she was searching, or had searched, for her long-lost father?"

"It's probably easier to make a tale believable if some parts of it are true."

Jack made a sound of ridicule. "I'm sure you would know from experience."

"I don't recall lying to you, Jack. If I did, it was only to protect your health, which you were determined to wither away."

"I was too angry to eat back then!" she snarled. "I would have puked it all up."

"I'll agree you were angry without respite. Your starving yourself kept you from sleeping. It made you weak. Your attacks became pitiful. And I was infuriated every time I heard your belly growl, since it was never my intention to harm you—physically. Can you at least agree that starving yourself wasn't a well-thought-out plan?"

"And miss another opportunity to infuriate you?" she shot back. "I still need your dagger. Toss it over."

He crossed his arms over his chest, a clear no. She growled low in her throat and sat down on the cot behind her to test the thin rope around her ankles. It had been looped four or five times before it was tied off. She tried sliding one foot out, but it had been wrapped too tight.

With another glance at Bastard first to make sure he was still standing behind his desk, she bent forward over her knees to find the knot and work it loose with her fingers. It wasn't working, not when she could only use one hand because her pistol was in the other.

She was about to take out her dagger to cut the rope when she saw the top of his head in front of her and gasped. Good God, he was too quick. She'd only been distracted for a moment!

"Be easy, Jack. I'm just helping."

He didn't look up as he spoke, and she felt the rope fall away. Then he looked up at her smiling, even though her pistol was aimed at his face only inches away. Those eyes, such a starkly bright turquoise with that dark ring circling the outer edge of the irises, were mesmerizing, but especially so with that face.

A villain such as him shouldn't have eyes like that. Or smiles that were genuinely amused rather than sneering or mocking. Too many times she'd gotten distracted by his face and how handsome he was. Such as now. In that brief, arrested moment, he could have grabbed the pistol from her hand and she wouldn't even have noticed!

He didn't even try. "I've risked a bullet to show you that you can trust me."

She leaned back to put some distance between them and slow her heartbeat. He stood up, towering over her, and simply offered her his hand.

"Shall we?"

Thoughts, where did they go!? She stared at the hand and leaned back even more until she was touching the bulkhead behind her. Shall we what?

She meant to say that aloud. He shook his head, probably because she was ignoring his proffered hand. "I could have reached for your weapon instead of the ropes and easily taken it from you. Does that tell you nothing?"

"That you missed your chance?"

"That this voyage will be different."

He started to walk away, back toward his desk. She shot off the cot and jammed the pistol against his back. "We're going this way, out the door. Make that happen."

"And if I don't?"

She glanced up at the back of his head, so far above her. Hitting him with the pistol might do what she hoped if they were the same height, but they weren't. If she tried it now, it might not knock him out or even daze him.

Why the devil wasn't he more concerned about being shot? And why hadn't he taken her pistol when he'd had the chance?

The man wasn't taking her at all seriously!

He only sighed as he turned carefully and slowly walked to the door, giving her time to maintain her position behind him.

Still, she bumped into his arse when he bent over from the waist to pick up the key from the floor. She hissed through her teeth and was surprised he didn't laugh about it.

But he opened the door and walked up the few steps that led to the quarterdeck. It was dark, except for the light from the two lanterns on either side of his cabin door. Bastard didn't move any farther. It wasn't difficult to see why. She might not be able to see over his shoulders, but she could see on either side of him that his men stood in a tight half circle at the top of the steps, forming a solid barrier, undoubtedly put in place by the blond crewman.

She pressed her pistol harder into Bastard's back. "Tell them to back off."

"No. This is what can loosely be termed a standoff. You might as well give up graciously, Jack."

Her mind churned frantically. Among the mostly brawny men who formed that blockade, she saw only one skinny fellow to her right and a nervous-looking boy next to him. She would have given anything right then for her rapier instead of a damned one-shot pistol. With two arm's lengths of sharp metal in hand, she could have slashed an opening to get past them.

She leapt toward the boy, but socked the man next to him first before pushing the boy out of the way, clearing a path to the railing. She almost made it, was only three feet from it, about to leap into the water, when an arm went about her waist, lifting her off her feet, and the pistol was yanked out of her hand. She should never have turned her back on Bastard! She screamed in fury, but she was facing nothing but an empty deck now, his men having scattered to get out of the way of any gunshots.

She was let go inside the cabin and then pushed forward into the room, just far enough for Bastard to close the door and lock it—with him on the other side of it before she could even turn around. But she didn't pause to bemoan what had just happened. She ran straight for the long row of drapes covering the bank of windows she'd escaped from once before.

Chapter Twelve

❧

Damon Reeves gripped the rail, trying to calm his breathing. That had been too close, she'd almost made it over the side. He would have jumped in after her, of course, but the Thames definitely wasn't the clear aqua waters of the Caribbean. If she'd dived into its murky depths, he might not have found her. And if she'd drowned, her father would have been after him before the night was done, instead of a week from now per Damon's plan, which was to make sure Malory didn't follow too quickly this time.

"What were you thinking, letting her keep that weapon?" Mortimer Bower said angrily as he joined Damon.

"I don't want to fight with her for the duration of this voyage."

"You'd rather take a bullet?"

"No danger of that now." Damon showed Mort that he had the weapon.

Mortimer snorted. "You shouldn't have gambled that she would come or wasted all that blunt hiring that small army in case she did. I know those four bruisers who escort her stayed your hand in the park that day, but did you really think you'd need so many to deal with them tonight?"

"No, I actually hoped her father would be escorting her. We definitely needed those numbers for James Malory, as we learned firsthand on the last trip."

"So you would have taken him and not her?"

"No. I want his cooperation. I won't get it without leverage, so having them both would have been ideal."

"I still can't believe she even showed up, young lady like her."

"And I was sure she would. I piqued her interest just enough. And by all accounts, she's recklessly daring. Probably gets it from her father."

"Well, she came prepared, if you didn't notice," Mort grumbled. "As if she expected you to be waiting for her here. So I'll allow it was a good thing you overdid it. But if even one of her men escapes, you will have lost your advantage."

Damon laughed. "When did you become such a doom-sayer? We picked that location because it's a street with hardly any traffic in the evening and it's secluded due to the high walls of the London Docks. We were successful, Mort. Johnny signaled that by waving the lantern from shore. The street will be cleaned. Her family will waste time looking for her in London."

"Unless she left a note about where she was going."

Damon frowned. He'd have to ask her about that—or not. If she left a note, she probably wouldn't be able to resist gloating about it.

"And you weren't expecting another coach full of guards tonight," Mortimer said, continuing to point out what hadn't gone according to plan. "That flat you rented to hold the prisoners for a week is going to reek by the end of it, with all the extra bodies in it."

"Better than killing people who don't deserve killing. Which is what those damn pirates wanted to do. Hell, they wanted to storm Malory's house, you know. They would have got us all arrested, trying something that stupid in that part of town. It was hard enough getting them to agree to let me handle the details of Jack's arrival. I'm still a little surprised it worked."

"I suppose young ladies love mystery and romance."

"It was worth a try, though she's not a typical young lady. And the proof is, I think she came to capture me. She alluded to as much."

"But how would she have guessed?"

"I don't know—yet. Now stop being so negative. Nothing ever goes exactly according to plan. I'm pleased with our progress. My only regret is that we had to involve his daughter again."

"You had no choice. We already learned Malory is impossible to take down. Trying it twice on our first trip to London just got six of our crew so injured they had to be replaced and forced us to follow Malory and his family to America. At least Malory just thought we were thieves trying to rob him, so he never sent the watch after us. But your target did warn you it would be nigh impossible to capture Malory. Why else would he have told you to take one of Malory's female relatives instead and given you the ransom note for that scenario?"

His target. The irony was that they were both his targets, but originally there had been three. One was too easy and had been captured in days. The other two were so difficult that Damon had decided to pit them against each other and then deal with the remaining survivor. It had seemed a good plan, but it hadn't worked the first time around. That failure had landed him in a dungeon where he'd been quite sure he was going to rot.

The scarcity of food had brought despair. He'd eaten nothing the first four days and after that only when someone remembered to feed him. The small dungeon had been newly constructed and so secure, no guard had been needed. Damon had been alone in the single cell, but he had heard Andrew's screams coming from somewhere aboveground. He'd wondered if that was the fate that awaited him.

Catherine was responsible for his imprisonment in her father's dungeon. She had blamed her lover, Andrew, for Jacqueline Malory's escape and Damon for not preventing it. The first time Catherine brought him some food and water, he'd asked her if Andrew was still alive, but she hadn't answered his questions, so he figured Andrew was dead.

The solitude had given him time to reflect on all the things he could have done differently. He'd been assailed by regrets that he hadn't succeeded in helping the one person most dear to him. And his ship and crew had been captured. Catherine had taunted him with that, though he'd hoped it was a lie, and it was. But Catherine didn't admit that until she finally approached him with a new deal three long weeks later.

"Your men are fine," she'd told him that day. "My father wasn't interested in punishing them for your failure. He was keeping them on your ship until he decided on a new captain for it. Then I think he forgot about it. He doesn't go outside often these days and probably failed to notice that it is still anchored in the bay."

"I'm not surprised, as sickly as he looks."

"He's not sick, he's recovering," she'd said angrily. "He wasn't treated well in prison and it hasn't been that long since he's been out."

"Why didn't my men sail away?"

"And leave you? That big lummox you call a friend probably would have skinned them alive at the suggestion. Treats you like he's your mother, as protective as he is of you. Why is that?"

"I'm all he has left. He lost his family to a hurricane while he and I were away at school."

"So you adopted him?" she'd asked sneeringly.

"We were already best friends" was all he'd replied, and he hadn't meant to say that much.

Giving Catherine any information about himself would be as foolish as succumbing to her seductions, which he was heartily sick of. He'd rebuffed her from the start. She should have stopped trying long ago. But for some reason she didn't seem to believe that he disliked her.

"He did try to sneak onto the island to rescue you a half dozen times," she'd gone on to say. "I had to assure him you were chained to my bed enjoying yourself to get him to stop risking his life. But the idiot actually doubted me. So I let him know you would be released soon if he behaved, and that put a stop to his recklessness. You can thank me later."

"Was that a lie, too?"

"At the time, yes."

"And now?"

"Now you're lucky I'm on your side."

Having her on his side was a curse, not luck, and he'd told her so that day. She'd merely tsked, dangling the key to his freedom on her finger.

"You need to start being nice to me," she'd said. "You have no idea how difficult it was to talk my father into giving you another chance. I had to convince him we are going to be married."

"Go away."

"You'd rather rot in here than marry me?"

"Yes."

She'd left, taking the key with her, but was angry enough to return a moment later to snarl, "I lied. Marriage isn't a condition. But I did make a lot of promises to gain your release. So we're going to be successful this time. One way or another, we're going to deliver James Malory for my father's vengeance. You don't know what he's like when he's angry, and he's very angry."

"Then he did kill your friend?"

"Andrew? Well, not exactly. He thought he did, whipped him so bad it was hard to imagine Andrew had any blood left. But he merely had his body tossed out of the hall. I managed to secrete him onto your ship so your crew could tend him. I have no idea if he survived or not. I didn't bother to ask. But I suppose we can drop him off at St. Kitts when we stop there to stock up for the voyage—if he's still alive."

She was so blasé about it, but he hadn't been surprised. From his dealings with Catherine, he'd learned she cared about no one but herself—and that old pirate she called her father.

She took him to see her father that day. On the way, Damon told her, "You should be running in the other direction, Catherine, not trying to please a man like that."

"Whatever he's done, he's still my father. And his anger will dissipate once he gets what he wants. For your sake, I hope you can assure him we'll succeed this time."

In the large hall, Pierre was sitting alone at a table, but a half dozen other tables were filled with the cutthroats who'd eagerly joined the old pirate. Tall, maybe even muscular prior to his stay in prison, he was slow in recovering from that, was still too thin and haggard, and yet his icy-blue eyes were uniquely chilling. His black hair and beard were laced with gray and matted. He might have been handsome in his youth, but it was hard to tell now.

He stood up when Damon and Catherine reached him, remarking, "At a simple first test of your loyalty, Captain, you failed grandly. I'm sure spending a few weeks in my dungeon has made you eager to prove you can be trusted never to fail again. A prison cell in Anguilla isn't much different from the one I built here. It's not easy for a man to survive in either. Are you ready to try again?"

"I'll take on the mission, but only if I can go alone, without Catherine. She only complicates the situation."

"How dare—!" Catherine started to yell.

Pierre held up a hand. "He's right, *chérie*. You're too attractive and tempting. You'd only distract the captain when he needs to concentrate on the business at hand. Besides, I have a different jewel-stealing mission in mind for you."

Catherine had been mollified, seeming to bask in her father's complimentary remarks.

Pierre had turned to Damon. "As for you, Captain, no, you will not go alone. You will take my men to serve as your crew."

"I have a good crew, good at following orders. Your men—"

"Follow my orders and will keep an eye on you and ensure your success this time. You can keep some of your men, but you do not leave without some of mine. If all is well when you return, then you will be given our new location."

"You're moving?"

"An old habit of mine. I never stay in one place very long. Once you have the girl, follow these instructions." He handed Damon a folded small sheet of paper. "If she is not with you, you will be killed instead. Do you understand? I will not accept another failure."

"That is perfectly clear."

But then Pierre said in a darker tone, "You should have succeeded. The girl would have been let go if you had lured her father here in a timely manner so I could have my revenge. But I've been made to wait, so now I will have a better revenge. Can you imagine what that is?"

"Both of them dead?"

"Exactly."

That single word had had a profound effect on Damon. He might hate James Malory, but he certainly didn't hate the man's daughter. And he wasn't about to let her die at an old pirate's whim.

Chapter Thirteen

JACQUELINE STOOD AT THE large windows, watching the English coast in the moonlight behind the ship. She turned around with a snarl because she'd been unable to get to it. Failure, it was the bitterest pill. But she still had to do something to stop this from playing out according to Bastard's agenda. If she couldn't escape, she could slow his ship down so her father got to the Caribbean first to deal with whoever was behind the plot to kill him.

But it wasn't as if she hadn't tried to sabotage Bastard's plans on the last voyage. He slept too lightly. Every time she attempted to get the key to the cabin door, which he kept on him, he woke. But she didn't have a dagger last time. She might be able to pick the lock with it and slash through his sails, if she could do it late at night when she wouldn't be noticed. Or toss one of the lanterns at the wall and hope the helm on the other side of it would burn before the fire could be put out, but she'd have to do that while Bastard was in the room, since he never left her alone with lit lanterns or left tinder in the room so she could light one.

The man took too many precautions. Nothing sharp in the room she could use against him, nothing heavy to throw at him. She hadn't had a cot to sleep on last time, either. He'd offered his bed, which she'd rejected, so she'd been given several blankets instead. The cot was new. And the bars on the windows were new, too. He wasn't about to let her escape through them again as she'd done the last time.

The dagger on her thigh at least gave her more options this time. She could sail this ship if she could just get control of it. She could do that by killing Bastard to get his key, then sneaking out to find Jeremy and Percy and release them. If any of the crew were Englishmen, she might be able to convince them to change sides. If that didn't work, the three of them could get the ship back to England at least, as long as they didn't run into any storms. And now would be the time to do that, when England was still so close.

She went to the door and pressed her back against the wall close to the door handle. The moment Bastard opened it, she could slip out behind him before he turned to lock it.

Seconds later, the lock clicked, the door opened just enough for him to enter, and she shot out of the doorway. "At least have dinner first, Jack," he suggested.

His damn long arms pulled her back into the room. Well, that had been a little too hastily planned, so she wasn't infuriated that it didn't work. And he'd sounded amused. She supposed she would have been, too, if she were the one foiling such a sloppy escape attempt.

"I'm not hungry," she mumbled, and moved to sit on the cot while he lit the lanterns.

She noticed that he hadn't locked the door when he'd closed it, but that was his habit, too. As long as he was in the room with her, he was confident that he could keep her in it. He only locked it before he went to bed or when he left her alone in the cabin.

When he turned to face her again, he warned, "I will not allow you to starve on this trip. Every plate of food you refuse is one plate your brother and his friend won't be given."

"I told you he's not my brother, and I demand to see them."

"No."

"Why not?"

"Because you aren't leaving this room and they aren't leaving their confinement. You'll just have to trust me that they aren't being deprived—unless you deprive them by ignoring the food you're given."

"I wasn't planning on not eating—as long as you don't try to feed me fish again."

He actually laughed. "That wasn't my fault."

"Everything is your fault."

"Be that as it may, we're carrying livestock on this trip to keep the meals fresh, and even a real cook. In Bridgeport, all we were able to stock was fish because your relatives there had cleaned out the town of all supplies for their fancy parties. You can dine as you're accustomed this time around."

He waved a hand toward the dining table, with six plush, padded chairs and a candelabrum at the center. She'd noticed it; she just wasn't interested in anything bolted to the floor that she couldn't use to her advantage. Last time, he'd offered her the chair at his desk, since it had been the only seat in the room. Last time, she'd thrown all those plates at his head. Until Andrew had convinced her she'd need her strength if she hoped to escape.

Thinking of that fake Malory relative who had helped her more than she could repay, she asked, "What happened to Catherine's actor friend?"

"We returned him to England."

She'd seen that brief frown before he turned his back on her to move behind his desk and sit down. "You punished him for helping me, didn't you?" she accused.

"Not I."

She blanched. "Catherine's father did? A man who favors the cat-o'-nine-tails?"

"How the devil do you know that?"

"Because we suspect you work for Pierre Lacross! And my aunt Gabby saw firsthand what that evil man is capable of. Are you working for Lacross?"

She would have loved to hear confirmation. Even her father, suspecting it was Lacross, was going to get confirmation first by visiting the prison in Anguilla before he set out to find the pirate.

But all Bastard said was "Andrew required a doctor so I hired one for the crossing. He may eventually recover completely, but at least he was able to walk off my ship without needing assistance."

"Are you implying you rescued him?"

"That surprises you?"

"The only surprise is that you would try to convince me you have any sort of compassion."

"Very well, I'm sure you'll believe that it wasn't my intention to rescue him, although I did end up doing that."

Jack didn't believe that he'd helped Andrew, but she was convinced that Andrew had been brutally punished for helping her escape. She cringed as she imagined the sting of the whip on his back. She hoped that one day she would be able to repay him. But now she had to deal with Bastard.

"Having bloodthirsty thoughts again, are you?"

She met his amused eyes and quipped, "When you're in them, of course."

"You are entirely too easy to read, Jack."

He wasn't. This amused, cavalier manner smacked of his being smitten with her, but that was absurd. He'd been like this before, too, but last time he'd assured her repeatedly that she'd be let go after the exchange. He hadn't yet made the same assurance in the last few hours. This time he had to know that he was taking her to her death. And that amused him? Was he every bit as evil as his boss?

She shoved that thought away. She didn't want to think that. She'd never get any sleep sharing a room with him if she did, and it was going to be a long voyage if she couldn't turn the tables on him. She needed more information about him. She hadn't tried to ferret out any the last time, when she'd attacked him every chance she got. She had to be more cunning now because she had different goals this time, to slow his ship down or capture it. Killing him in the process would just be a perk.

"By the by, I offer you my bed again, and no, that wasn't an invitation to share it. The cot is for me."

She looked at the bed. It was large. It was probably comfortable, with such a thick mattress. She ought to accept, but it just seemed wrong somehow to sleep in the bed of a man she was going to kill.

She shook her head. "I've already claimed the cot. You'll stay the hell away from it."

"As you wish."

"But I'll accept your offer of the bed if you take the cot out of here and yourself with it."

He laughed. Of course he did, the bloody sod. She really was going to have to stop amusing him.

So she said, "I still want to know who you hired for that charade at the ball. An actor, or was it some destitute gentleman who didn't realize he'd be risking the wrath of my family?"

"You still don't think it was me?"

"You keep forgetting he had blond hair."

"A wig, but then you also wore one that night." Then he grinned. "Like minds . . ."

She snorted rudely. He opened one of his desk drawers, pulled out the blond wig, and twirled it on his finger, adding, "It never even occurred to me to hire someone else, but then I wouldn't trust anyone else to pique your interest. Which reminds me . . ."

He stood and came around his desk. Jack bolted to the door. As usual, he got there first and positioned himself in front of it. She plowed a fist into his stomach, but that hurt so badly she wondered if she'd just broken some knuckles. He didn't make a sound, lost no breath at all to the punch. Instead he caught both of her hands and gently locked them behind her back, leaving her entirely too close to him, their chests touching.

She looked up at him, about to scream, but that's when he kissed her. It utterly surprised her, long enough for his lips to brush over hers once, then again, so sensually soft, so . . .

She head-butted him, hoping to bloody his nose. At least she tried to, but as usual, he anticipated her moves and lifted his head out of the way, so her forehead only struck the top of his chest.

"That was for looking so bloody beautiful at that ball, so don't begrudge me one kiss. It won't happen again—unless you want it to."

Chapter Fourteen

H OW DARE YOU KISS me?" Jack snarled. "If you do that again, I'll do more than try to bloody your nose." She pulled away from him, able to do so because he'd loosened his grip on her hands.

But all he said was "If you keep hurting yourself on me, I'm going to have to restrain you again."

"It's the only way you're going to be safe. Go ahead and tie me up. It's no more'n I expect from a bloody pirate." She quickly turned her back on him because she didn't want him to see her rubbing her hand. Her knuckles were red, but no bones were broken.

He laughed. "I'm not worried about myself. Give it up, Jack. I've seen you soft and flirtatious. You liked me."

That ridiculous remark made her swing about. He was standing behind his desk.

"Not you, fool! The mystery was all I liked that night. It's what I expected from a masked ball and was disappointed that my beaus ruined that for me."

"You mentioned that."

"Yes, I did, so you should know that you merely supplied the mystery that was missing. I appreciated that. If you mistook that for 'liking' you, you're dead wrong."

"Yet you showed up at the park to meet me the next day. It's too bad you didn't come alone." Then he sounded a little more than curious, almost indignant on her behalf, when he asked, "What could your father have been thinking, letting bruisers like that escort you? A dozen footmen wouldn't have drawn as much notice as those four and would have been just as protective."

"It worked to frighten you off, didn't it?" she shot back with a smirk.

"I wasn't frightened, Jack. I do lean on the side of caution though, and I like my face the way it is. It would have been quite a fight and would have served no purpose other than to let you ride off without me."

She snorted. "You wouldn't have won. Those four are long-time sparring partners of my father's—when his brother Tony isn't around to accommodate him in the ring. And answer me. Did you have my guards killed?"

"No, but detained, yes. All of the men you brought along tonight will be released after my . . . suggestion is delivered to your father. I'm not taking chances this time. I'm letting a full week pass before your father is informed that I have you and he comes after us."

"Not if you left it to the posts again."

"I didn't," he said a little smugly. "I left a trusted man behind to see to it."

A full week? Her mother was going to be out of her mind by then!

"I hate you!"

"I'm aware of that."

"You have no idea what you've—I should have shot you while I had the chance!"

"I agree, though it might not have accomplished all that you hoped for."

"But your blood all over the room would most certainly have been a pretty sight."

"Or no blood at all depending on what you aimed at." He began to remove metal plates from inside his shirt.

She stared at him incredulously. It was laughable, that he'd taken a precaution like that. No wonder her hand hurt so much!

"This was an all-or-nothing plan, wasn't it?" she demanded. "Telling me you were sailing tonight. Would you have sailed if I didn't show up?"

"No."

"But you played your final card in that last note, implying that you wouldn't return to England if I didn't see you off. What would you have done next? Wait a few days and then say you returned to England anyway?"

"I would have thought of something."

"Playing it by ear instead of plotting far in advance? Doesn't sound very piratelike."

"And you didn't come for a romantic rendezvous. How did you guess?"

She clamped her mouth shut. He sat down and crossed his arms. "You want answers, you have to give some in return, Jack."

"What makes you think I play by the rules?"

"You don't? Then I guess you have no more questions for me."

She did. Before she turned the tables on him, she'd like to know where his boss was hanging his hat these days. Her father had suggested that if it did turn out to be Lacross, the pirate might have set this plan in motion right from his prison cell, but she couldn't believe a man that evil had ever won any type of loyalty from the few men who might have escaped capture the night his fortress got raided, at least, not enough loyalty to do the bidding of a man already behind bars. Besides, that particular pirate didn't win loyalty, he coerced it.

Which brought an incredible thought: "Is Lacross holding family of yours hostage to get you to do his bidding?"

"No."

Completely wrong about everything? Or he was lying. "If you don't work for him, then who?"

"First, please answer one of my—"

"Yes, yes," she cut in angrily. "I didn't know for sure it would be you at the docks, but I thought it was a likely possibility because your handwriting is so similar to the writing in that more polite ransom note you told me you wrote and posted in Bridgeport."

"You weren't there to see that note."

"Because of you!" she snarled, but after a moment added, "My father kept it and I beteviled him into showing it to me on the trip home."

He chuckled. "My, what sharp, beautiful eyes you have."

She scowled at him. "It could have been a minuscule chance and I still would have come prepared for a fight if it meant capturing you!"

"I'd hoped you'd bring your father."

She choked back a derisive laugh. "You should pray you never do come face-to-face with him. He has splendid plans for you, Bastard—in my opinion, that is. You will find them so painful you will beg for a quick end. But it won't be quick, and you won't walk away from it."

He shrugged. "Sounds like the same thing you predicted previously, torn limb from limb, et cetera. Nonetheless, I hoped he would escort you, which is why I hired so many men. Even the mightiest can fall to overwhelming numbers."

"Then why didn't you do that before, instead of following us to America?!"

"Because he didn't go slumming, and you can't take an army of riffraff into the upper-crust end of town without raising a hue and cry. But we did try unsuccessfully a couple times with a few of my crew."

She shook her head at him, pointing out, "He would have mentioned it."

"Does he tell you every time he's accosted by men he believes are thieves?"

No, he actually wouldn't. He'd just deal with it and go on his way as if nothing had happened.

She raised a brow. "How many died?"

He choked back a laugh this time. But a knock at the door drew him to open it, and a moment later he set the tray of food on the table. She moved over to the table to see if he'd lied about having a real cook this time. Apparently, he'd told the truth. The food on the two plates looked appetizing: fresh peas, roasted chicken with a caramelized sauce that smelled divine, rolls still steaming, even dessert.

She sat down and reached for a plate, the aromas reminding

her that she was hungry. But when he started to do the same, she said adamantly, "I won't dine with you as if I'm not your prisoner and you're not a bloody pirate." She pointed at his desk. "You eat over there if you want me to eat."

"For now," he allowed, and took one of the plates with him back to his desk. "But we will dine together, perhaps do much more than that, before this voyage ends, Jack. I may even invite your brother or rather the man who looks like your brother up here for a meal if you ask me nicely."

Bloody smiling liar, she thought. He wouldn't. He just liked to dangle carrots.

But as Jack took a bite of the roasted chicken, she thought about what Bastard had told her about his attempts to capture her father. Was that a lie, too? Or was he crazy and desperate enough to think he could take down James Malory? Her nemesis was more dangerous than she'd thought.

Chapter Fifteen

IN BERKELEY SQUARE, THE vehicles were lined up two deep at the curb outside James and Georgina Malory's town house. The elders, as James and Anthony referred to their two older brothers, were there. Anthony and Roslynn were there, since he'd been the first one whom George had sent for when Jacqueline hadn't come home for dinner. Danny was there, too, since her husband was also missing, and she knew that Percy was with him. And Amy had been fetched in case she had any out-of-the-ordinary insight into the situation.

They were gathered in the parlor. Edward was seated next to Georgina with his arm around her shoulders. She'd stopped crying for the moment. They'd already searched the house for a note Jacqueline might have left about where she'd gone and questioned all the servants. They knew only from Jacqueline's maid that she'd decided not to attend the scheduled party that night and was going for a ride with Jeremy and expected to be home in time for dinner or shortly thereafter. And Artie had confirmed she'd left the house with Jeremy. But dinner had been hours ago.

"Would she elope?" Amy asked.

"With whom, all twelve of her suitors?" Georgina replied.

"She was interested in a new one she met at the recent masked ball you took her to," Amy continued.

Georgina frowned, remembering. "James didn't like that fellow because he refused to introduce himself when the young man returned Jack to us after a dance."

Amy said, "She didn't know his name when she told me about him yesterday, but she's had time to find out."

"I'll be the first to admit Jack is impulsive, even reckless," Georgina said. "But she's not crazy. No one marries someone they've only just met, certainly not our Jack, who's touted repeatedly that it's not her goal to marry this year—much to James's delight."

"But she's obviously enlisted Jeremy's help with something," Danny put in. "And both Jeremy and Jack are angry and hurt that James wouldn't let them go with him. They talked a lot about this last night when we escorted Jack to the soirée."

They all stared at Danny, which had her add, "No, Jeremy would *not* leave the country without telling me."

Georgina sighed in agreement. "Jack might have wanted to follow her father, but she'd leave a damned note if she was going to do something that foolish. And they certainly wouldn't take Percy with them."

"Do you have any feelings about this, Amy?" Edward asked his daughter.

Amy sighed. "Nothing that will help."

"Anything at all?" Georgina persisted.

But Jason added, "Jacqueline has Jeremy with her, and Percy, and her four-man escort. She must still be in the city and is just delayed for some reason. That she didn't leave a note means she expected to be home before she was missed. She's probably going to show up here any minute."

They all stared at Jason for making that prediction, then immediately turned to Amy again. Amy rolled her eyes. "I'm not a bloody magic ball. I'm sensing nothing about this situation, which you should take to be a good sign, no harm, no danger, no disaster. I haven't had any special feelings a'tall since yesterday when I shared with Jack that she's found her man."

"Her man?"

"The one for her. And she got quite angry at the suggestion, flatly denying it. But she was also excited about the masked man. But as I said, as of yesterday, she still didn't know who he is—unless she lied to me." Amy shook her head. "No, she wouldn't do that. Maybe she found out who he is or figured out how to find him."

"So you think she's gone off to meet him and dragged Jeremy along as a chaperone?"

Amy shrugged. "As good a guess as any."

"Now that sounds like something Jack would do," Roslynn put in. "Especially if the man posed a mystery to her and she hasn't solved it yet. But I do agree with Jason. They are probably just delayed in getting home."

"We can't depend on that," Georgina said. "We need to start looking for her. I'll make a list of Jack and Judy's friends here in the city. The rest of you, figure out where an innocent rendezvous might take place in case she did run off to meet that man from the ball."

"A restaurant, since she left near dinnertime."

"It's way past dinnertime, but that's not a bad idea."

"The man's hotel if it has a restaurant. If he's new to town, he might be staying in one and could have suggested they dine there. And Jeremy is chaperoning her."

"But we don't know his name."

"Won't need to know," Danny said. "If they've gone to either a restaurant or a hotel, her four-man escort will be waiting outside and will be easy to spot. Jeremy took his chaise, that's also easy to spot."

Jason started giving orders. "We need more men for the search in case she doesn't walk in the door soon. George, send a man to every Malory household in town to collect all available footmen. I need to attend to something, but won't be long. I imagine she'll be back by the time I return."

"What the devil, Jason, where—?"

Anthony didn't finish his question because his eldest brother was already out the door. Georgina had started crying again on Edward's shoulder. Anthony sighed and dropped down on the sofa next to his wife.

"Are we sure we've searched everywhere for a note Jack might have left to explain where she went?" Edward asked Georgina gently.

"Her room, mine, the parlor. The maids are still searching the rest of the house, though Jack would have left the note in a place where I'd surely see it."

"Who was manning the door today?" Danny suddenly asked.

"That would be me," Artie said, standing just inside the parlor door.

"So you got left behind this trip?"

The two old salts who'd sailed with James during his

ten-year absence from England usually drew straws to see which one would accompany James if he sailed without the rest of his family. But Artie was shaking his head.

" 'E left us both behind with the womenfolk this trip," Artie grumbled. "We were to guard them with our lives—fat lot o' good we did, eh."

"Nonsense," Danny told the ex-pirate. "Amy has assured us there's no danger yet, and for the time being we're going to assume there won't be. But did Jack receive anything today out of the ordinary?"

"A single rose, same as the one she got yesterday. She took them to her room."

"I saw the two roses on her vanity when I looked earlier," Anthony remarked, "lying side by side."

"Were there notes with them?"

Anthony leapt up from the sofa and headed for the parlor door. "We only looked for notes that Jack might have written to George. Bloody hell, didn't even think to look for any others written to her."

Chapter Sixteen

JACQUELINE HAD NOTICED THE last time Bastard abducted her how circumspect he was about his body. She'd thought at the time that he must be badly scarred and wanted to hide it from her. Why else would a pirate not want to get undressed in front of her? Now, he was doing it again, getting into bed with his clothes on, removing only his belt and boots. The last time he'd never changed clothes in the room, either. When he'd needed fresh pants and a shirt, he'd leave the room with clean clothing. To do what, change out on the deck? That must have gotten a few snickers from his crew.

If he was scarred, she'd gloat. No doubt he deserved every wound he'd gotten. But she had a feeling now that his bedding down in a less than comfortable manner was more for her benefit than his. Did he really not want to offend her sensibilities? That smacked so much of being a gentleman that she couldn't credit it, yet she had seen how he'd behaved at Lady Spencer's ball.

He'd cut a fine figure in his black tailed coat and had

known exactly what to do and say that night. And his speech was refined, not fresh out of the gutter. He'd even managed to excite her with his air of mystery. She wondered if he could have been reared gently by English parents. Was that why he'd managed to deceive her that night? And whom was she kidding? Her own father had raised enough havoc on the seas to be labeled a pirate. So it was definitely possible that Bastard had been a gentleman prior to becoming a lying kidnapper.

It didn't change her worse-than-bad opinion of him; she just found it amusing that he'd want to spare her the sight of his nakedness. She ought to do the opposite herself, at least remove her blouse, skirt, and petticoat. She enjoyed the idea of shocking him, but only briefly. He probably wouldn't be shocked and would see it as an invitation, and she certainly didn't want to extend one. She recalled how he'd looked at her on the last voyage after she'd taken off her wilted ball gown and donned one of his white shirts for the sake of comfort. The sensual expression in his turquoise eyes had so unnerved her that she'd punched him in the jaw. Well, she'd tried, but he was quick and had caught her hand, laughing. No, she wasn't going to do anything he might interpret as an invitation. She was and would remain fully clothed, right down to her boots. She would have slept in her spencer jacket, too, if she hadn't already draped it over the back of a chair.

After he turned off the lantern, she asked, "D'you have scars?"

"Not many, why?"

A lot of moonlight was in the room, so she looked in his direction, waiting for him to sit back up to talk, but he didn't.

"No reason." She lay down on her back to ignore him.

"I can guess."

"No, you can't."

"You wonder why I don't sleep naked when that is my habit."

Damned mind reader. "Since I don't know your habits or care to know them, your guess is wrong. But why don't you move me in with your other hostages? The hold would be preferable to your cabin."

"And miss these scintillating conversations with you?"

"Is that where you put them? In the hold?"

He didn't answer, said instead, "I take it you aren't blushing?"

"I have a good imagination. I frequently imagine you walking about naked. It's amusing." After a silent moment, she wondered aloud, "Are you blushing?"

"No," he said in an amused tone. "Just surprised that we have the same imagination."

She drew in her breath and her cheeks got hot. Bloody hell. She turned over loudly to face the bulkhead, but her remaining dagger was strapped to her thigh, so she turned again.

"Sweet dreams, Jack." A definite chuckle.

"They will be, full of gore and you dangling from a hangman's noose and—"

"Spare me the details, please."

The room suddenly blackened when clouds got in the way of the moon, but she wasn't going to let the darkness lull her to sleep. She had to do something tonight before the ship sailed farther away from England. She had to find Jeremy, commandeer the ship while most of the crew were sleeping. Finish off Bastard . . .

The thought of hurting anyone disturbed her, but this man deserved it. Not only had he kidnapped her twice, he was now holding Jeremy and Percy as hostages. And he was in the employ of some nefarious pirate who was determined to kill her father. She had to do it. It was the only way she could get the key and unlock the cabin door. If she tried to pick the lock with her dagger, she knew he'd hear it and take away her last weapon, rendering her utterly helpless again. She hated that he was such a light sleeper, wouldn't even be surprised if he slept with one eye open.

The moonlight came back, but only for a second. But its absence made her worry that storm clouds had arrived. There'd been none the last time she'd looked out those barred windows, but that had been hours ago.

Rain and a thunderstorm would be the worst luck. There was no way Bastard would sleep through that. But she had no clue if he was sleeping yet and probably wouldn't get one since the man didn't snore.

When enough time had passed to ensure he was asleep and the moonlight had come back, she got her dagger from her thigh sheath before she stood up and tiptoed over to Bastard's bed. The nice weapon had a seven-inch blade, sharp and light-weight, made just for her. She positioned herself at his bedside and bent over him before she reached for the key. It was where he usually kept it, in the right-side pocket of his trousers, but she wondered why her removing it didn't wake him, light sleeper that he was. Then she saw that it had. His eyes were open and locked to hers. The only reason he remained perfectly still was because now that he was awake, he couldn't help but feel the blade she held pressed to his neck. It was now or never.

But before she delivered the coup de grâce, she couldn't resist telling him, "You shouldn't have done this again. You should have stayed far, far away from me and my family."

He said nothing, didn't even try to talk her out of killing him, but she felt his hand on the back of her neck, drawing her head slowly down to his. She pressed her blade more firmly against his throat as a warning, but he didn't stop until their mouths touched.

It was almost magical, how arrested she suddenly was. And it was no brief kiss this time. His lips moved over hers slowly but with such passion, she was drawn deeper and deeper toward an intimacy she'd never before shared with anyone. The thrill was in full bloom, making her heart pound erratically, stealing her breath. This is what she'd wanted that night at the ball when she first met him, what drove her to the park with such excitement to see him again.

First met him? No, not *him*, but the charming, mysterious . . . What she felt in that moment was overwhelming her senses, so much that she was helpless to resist temptation like that. Then she tasted his tongue against hers, and the thought intruded—shouldn't she bite it?

That was a cold dousing. She lifted her head and heard him say, "Does that tell you why this happened again?"

"Not bloody likely."

But she realized the dagger was still in her hand, still pressed to his neck. He'd missed his chance to disarm her so he could kiss her instead? Fool! But she couldn't bring herself to slash his throat now. That was a little too gruesome for her. So she moved the blade to the side of his torso and thrust it in, hearing him groan, before she broke away from him and ran to the door.

"Jack. Jack, wait—"

She didn't hear the rest if he said anything more. With the key turned and the door pushed open, she bolted out of the cabin. The deck was dark, but still someone spotted her and shouted to alert the crew. So much for finding her brother and gaining control of the ship. She hesitated only a moment to kick off her boots before she dove over the railing. She might or might not make it back to England, but either way, the pirates wouldn't be able to use her to control her father.

Good God, the water was cold, but in moments she was behind the ship as it sailed on, and she continued to swim in the opposite direction. She could do this. She was a good swimmer. And she could rest from time to time, floating on her back. Surely another ship would come along and rescue her before too long.

At least she didn't have to worry about Jeremy and Percy. She'd convinced Bastard they meant nothing to her, and he'd shared that with the crewman he'd called Mort, so surely they'd be let go as soon as they reached land. Bastard obviously hadn't died immediately, but she hoped she'd hit something vital and he would bleed out within the hour.

Would his crew sail back to England without him to try to capture her again? If they did, they would definitely beat her back there. And then it started raining. She stopped to glance back, but she couldn't see the ship, probably because the rain was coming down so hard. But she couldn't have gotten that far from it yet. She looked on each side of her, but still couldn't see it, so continued on. After a moment she stopped again with the horrible realization that in turning about, she might have lost her direction to England. If she swam right back to that bloody ship . . .

Chapter Seventeen

JACQUELINE SCREAMED WHEN SHE felt something touch her side, thinking of scary things in the sea. But she couldn't mistake the arm that was suddenly wrapped around her chest, or the voice that said, "You are the most aggravating woman."

Enraged by her failure, she turned and fought Bastard tooth and nail, tried to kick him where she'd wounded him, tried to drown him. She struggled so hard they both sank several times. She might have won that fight, too, but unfortunately he hadn't swum after her alone. Mort was with him, and when the blond got there, he took her in hand to swim both her and Bastard to the rowboat that had also been lowered for the search.

She might have heard the oars approaching if not for the rain. She might have had time to dive deep so they would have gone on searching endlessly with no luck. The dark would have been on her side. They couldn't see anything out here in the water any more than she could. But Bastard was tenacious. He had to have been getting weaker and weaker himself from his wound, but he'd continued to swim after her, determined to save her from her folly.

And it was so bloody galling that she hadn't even gotten far. Within minutes the rowboat stopped below the ship's lowered ladder. She slapped away the hand that reached for her and climbed it herself. But she didn't move any farther when she landed on the deck because she found herself surrounded by pirates. These definitely weren't ordinary sailors, being garishly dressed and armed and making scandalous remarks about her attributes, which she knew were outlined by her clinging, wet clothes. And they were laughing, especially at Bastard when he came over the side.

"If you can't handle the little vixen, we can!"

"You nearly lost our prize," another man sneered.

"She's not your prize," Bastard retorted, in a chilly tone she'd never heard him use before. "And she won't be taking any more evening swims. Get off my deck, now!"

Mort pushed the lot of them out of the way when they didn't depart quickly enough. Bastard took her arm and walked her up to the quarterdeck to reach his cabin and get her away from those leering eyes. She was too abject to be embarrassed. She still couldn't believe he'd jumped in after her with his wound. That was a stupid thing for him to do, considering his friend had also jumped in. And the wound was bleeding a lot. His wet shirt was pink with it.

The blond followed them into the room to get the key from her. He didn't ask for it, just stood in front of her with an angry expression, holding his hand out. She would have thrown it at him if she weren't so dejected. He then moved to his friend and helped to strip the wet clothes off him and get him into bed.

She'd watched without interest as she stood in a puddle

from her own clothes, taking in the wide chest, a bare flank, but not much else with that big blond standing between them. The door had been left open, but she saw at least one man had moved in front of it to stand guard, so she didn't look that way again.

Then another man entered, a short, skinny fellow of middle years dressed all in black with a long braided beard and a pink bandanna on his head. And two silver hoop earrings, which were barely visible beneath his shaggy long brown hair. She stared at him incredulously, but her eyes got really wide when he marched straight to her.

"Please say yer my patient, pretty."

Mort snapped, "The wound is over here, as if you haven't heard, you nasty old sod. It needs stitching."

The doctor, if that's what he was, still gave Jack one more suggestive look before he moved to the bed and opened the long bag he'd brought with him. He lifted a saw out of it, then a hammer, before he said, "Aha!"—and brought out a threaded needle.

Jack was still staring at what appeared to be a toolbox rather than a doctor's bag and asked incredulously, "A hammer?"

"Easier to cut bone if ye break it first," the man said as he began to ply his needle without any preparation first.

"Are you a real doctor?"

He glanced back at her with a chuckle. "Course I am. I'm just better at chopping off legs—and getting under skirts." He actually wiggled his eyebrows at her.

She turned her wide eyes on Mort. "Is this who treated Andrew?"

"No, that doctor left us in England. He only agreed to join us for the free passage home."

"Then who exactly is this?"

"Already told ye who I am, girly. Name's Dr. Death and I'm the only doc aboard, so don't be insulting me, eh."

She clamped her mouth shut, guessing he was one of the pirates. A real doctor would never have a name like that.

Mort left, still without closing the door, and then Bastard said from the bed, "I really didn't think you'd actually try to kill me."

The words rang hollowly in Jack's ears. Her last and worst failure yet, that Bastard wasn't dead—that she wasn't on her way to England. But she didn't react. She was too numb with dismal despair.

She was tired, exhausted, but she didn't sit down on her cot, didn't want to get it soaked when she guessed she'd be sleeping in it sometime tonight. And the doctor was still there, stitching the wound. Bastard hadn't waited for them to be alone before he'd made his remark.

He wasn't giving up on a reply, either, and said warningly, "Jack?"

Wearily, she reminded him, "I've lost count of how many times I said I would kill you. You've lost your mind if you think I wouldn't."

"No, I just thought there might be more between us than blood and gore."

"Ah, yes, what were your deluded words? That I 'liked' you?" She laughed scornfully.

"You give me this paltry wound instead of a real one that could have ended me? Admit it, Jack. Your heart is no longer in it—not since we danced together."

That revitalized her anger. "How many times must I say it? I thought that man was someone else, not you. If I'd known it was you, I would have shouted to the rafters that you were a murderer and needed to be apprehended. You wouldn't have gotten out of that ballroom alive."

"Perhaps. But now you do know it was me. Changes everything, doesn't it?"

He sounded so bloody smug—until the doctor asked, "You're a murderer, Captain?" Dr. Death sounded impressed.

"No."

"He is, too!" Jack insisted.

"She's just predicting I will be, Dr. Death. Hardly makes it true, now does it?"

Bastard might have addressed that to the doctor, but he'd said it for her. Not that it mattered in the least when he was using her to lead her father to his death.

But the doctor shook his head as he closed his bag and headed to the door. "I suppose the bandage will need changing over the next few days, Cap'n," he said in parting. "But that's woman's work, not mine."

"Jack will do it."

"No chance in hell."

"You will. Would you really throw your . . . hirelings to the wolves?"

She drew in her breath. Was he actually going to play that card? And he wasn't even looking at her when he made that threat. His eyes were closed. The blood loss and his exertion in the water had weakened him more than he was trying to let on. But he hadn't passed out yet.

"You know where my shirts are, put one on. I haven't locked the trunk yet."

She almost laughed. He obviously remembered that she'd confiscated one of his shirts on the last voyage just so she could get out of that uncomfortable ball gown she'd been wearing when he'd kidnapped her. She'd shredded all the rest of his shirts that day and would have ripped apart his pants, too, if they weren't so sturdily made. But he'd locked his trunk after that.

Now she just said adamantly, "No."

"It wasn't a suggestion, Jack. Considering what happened tonight"—he paused to place a hand over his bandage—"I need to see what else is in your arsenal."

"That was my last dagger."

"I'm afraid I'll need proof of that now. But it's up to you whether you strip in front of me, or if Mort takes your clothes off for you. Although considering how angry he is at you right now, I think you'd prefer to do it yourself."

She wished he were bluffing, but knew he wasn't. The doctor had closed the door behind him, but Bastard's friend would probably be back to tie her up for the night or take her to the hold so Bastard could recover in peace. That was a promising thought. . . .

She crossed over to the trunk at the foot of his bed and opened it. Most of his shirts were white, but she saw a blue one and, under it, a pink one. She would never have taken him for a dandy, but then pirates were known for gaudy attire according to Gabby.

She grabbed the pink one and moved back across the room to toss it on her cot before she faced him. This wasn't going to be difficult, certainly nothing to be embarrassed about. She might even make it uncomfortable for him, enough that he might wish he hadn't suggested this.

She turned out her pockets first before she unfastened the

soggy skirt and let it drop to her feet. The thin petticoat was still sticking wetly to her legs, so she had to push that down. She glanced at him then to see if he was actually watching her every move. He was, maybe a little too avidly. He'd even leaned up on his right elbow. The bandage had been wrapped around him, but his chest was so damned wide and long, she was still seeing too much of it. And he was naked under that blanket. . . .

So maybe she felt a little embarrassed, but not because of what she was doing. Standing there in her blouse and fancily beribboned drawers, she turned one hip toward his view, then the other. Unlike his shirt, which would reach her knees, hers barely reached her hips. She unbuckled her leather sheath next. It had fit so nicely over the leg of her drawers that it hadn't chafed her skin, but it was useless now that her last weapon was gone. She would have kicked it angrily away if her feet weren't entangled in the pile of wet clothes.

She brought her eyes back to his before she began to unfasten her blouse. Her fingers slowed. It wasn't intentional, she was just fascinated by what she saw in his eyes. She'd seen that look once before, the last time her calves had been exposed to him. She'd been too enraged then to wonder if she might utilize that he liked what he saw, too enraged to wonder if she could get close to him without swinging her fists. She still didn't think she could, so it was moot, but it was still fascinating that she could dazzle him, however briefly.

She removed the blouse and held it in her hand as she made a full circle so he could see that nothing was tucked into the back of her drawers or inside her thin chemise. "Have you embarrassed me enough?"

He raised a brow. "I expected to, but as usual you surprise me. You don't seem the least bit embarrassed. You *are* a lady, correct?"

"I'm my father's daughter," she said offhandedly. "He used to be a rake of the worst sort, you know."

"Please tell me you aspire to be the same?"

She snorted. "I used to when I was a child. I wanted to be like him in every way. But I grew up. I'm aware I can't follow in all of his footsteps."

"I'm devastated to hear it."

"No, you aren't. If I were just like my father, you'd be dead right now."

He smiled. "There is that, and later we'll discuss why you spared—"

"I still wounded you!"

"It's a paltry wound. But come here, Jack, if you want to leave that on."

She knew he was talking about her chemise, which she wasn't about to take off when he was gazing at her so sensually. She stepped out of the pile of wet clothes and bent over to pick them up and took them to the dining table, where she draped them over the chairs to dry. She started back to the cot, hoping he'd forget about any more disrobing.

"Mort will be returning. You might want to get this over with before he comes in. I repeat, come here."

Get what over with? But she swung about and marched to his bed and glared down at him. He didn't notice the glare, he was so intent on her breasts. He lifted his hand and dipped a finger under the low neckline of her chemise, running it slowly over the tops of her breasts. Her nipples tingled as they hardened, but she was still incredulous. Did he really think she'd keep a dagger between her breasts? She almost laughed. But him touching her like that . . .

There was an easy way to stop it, and she even surprised herself when instead of backing away, she pulled the neckline of her chemise right down to the edge of her nipples, telling him, "See? There's nothing there."

It sounded as if he was choking before he said, "Oh, there's definitely something there, but I accept defeat graciously. You no longer have any weapons—that can do physical damage."

What other sort . . . ? She stopped the thought. Really? He considered her attributes a weapon? That was so interesting that she was slow to raise the edge of her chemise again. And meeting his eyes . . .

She swiftly swung about again and returned to her cot to grab his shirt. She put it on before she untied her chemise and drawers and, after turning her back to him, let both undergarments fall to the floor. Then she quickly fastened the shirt down to the last button. She still heard his groan. Ha! He didn't expect that, did he? But really, she wasn't sleeping in wet underwear just for modesty's sake. She even draped those undergarments on the chairs, too. But remembering his warning that Mort would be returning soon, she quickly got under the covers.

Chapter Eighteen

DAMON ENJOYED WATCHING JACK sleep, a little too much. So much fury in such a small bundle, but not when her eyes were closed. But he knew she wouldn't like his taking advantage of her slumber, even innocently, so he pried himself away from her side before she woke.

The morning sun blinded him for a moment when he left his cabin and locked the door. He took the two guards that he'd stationed outside his quarters with him as a precaution. He wished he could trust his own crew, but he couldn't yet. These two new crewmen at least appeared to be following his orders, but nothing had yet occurred to test their loyalty. Nor would it, he vowed, until he was ready.

He headed down the stairs to the lower deck. Two of the three cabins located there were occupied, and the new cook had demanded yet another cabin for his personal culinary supplies. Damon grabbed the key from the wall and opened the first door to his left. Mortimer had been too generous. He hadn't restrained these two, was giving them the freedom of his cabin, if not the ship. Which probably wasn't a good idea, considering how big one of the men was.

Damon leaned against the doorframe, a pistol in his hand, the two guards behind him, also armed. He should have paid Jack's hirelings a visit yesterday before he'd been wounded. He wasn't exactly going to strike fear into either of them today with a bandage wrapped around his torso, not that he cared to go that route.

The younger of the two, the bigger one, was quite injured, his face bruised and swollen. Damon imagined the rest of him hadn't fared much better. It was too bad it had taken so long to knock him out. Damon should probably send the pirate's doctor in to check on both of them, if Mortimer hadn't already seen to that, not that the pirate sawbones was anything close to a real doctor. Actually, the man might make matters worse. Not for the first time, Damon wished that Dr. Caruthers, whom he had obtained for Andrew, hadn't abandoned them as soon as they'd reached London.

The larger man who had chaperoned Jacqueline was sitting on the edge of the narrow bed, half bent over, an arm protectively about his middle, and he didn't change his position when the door opened. His friend had pulled a chair over to the bedside next to him. This fellow, who looked older and was rather portly, was a little too well dressed for destitute gentry, but Damon supposed even poor ones would want to keep up appearances.

Both men were staring at Damon, not wary, not bothering to hide their antipathy for him. Damon supposed he wouldn't either if the situation were reversed. But then the younger man suddenly pushed off the bed and lunged at Damon.

"Where's Jack? If you've hurt her—!"

Damon cocked his pistol, a loud sound between them that stopped the young man's hand from reaching for his throat. "You're injured enough," Damon warned the man coldly. "Do you really want to make it worse?"

"Answer me?! You'll get off one shot but I'll still snap your neck before your guards get off theirs."

"You can try, but there's no reason for anyone here to die. Sit back down and you'll have your answer. I've already gotten mine. She tried to convince me you're not her brother, but you have the same temper. You're obviously a Malory."

"I'm not," the younger man denied sharply, but he backed up and sat down again carefully. "How is she?"

"Fine, and the least of your worries."

Damon's assurance only relaxed the man a little. His glare and antipathy remained potent. His risking his life merely to find out how Jack was faring convinced Damon that both Malorys were lying to him. This one might not be her brother since there was no remarkable family resemblance, but he did strongly resemble Anthony Malory, so he was sure they were somehow related. But for the moment Damon could play along with their denials to humor his illustrious prisoner.

"You won the toss for the bed?" he said to the younger one, who was sitting on it.

"We'll be taking turns."

"I confess I didn't plan on capturing you, so there are no spare cots aboard, but there might be extra hammocks. I'll have one brought round if there are, and some books to help you pass the time."

"We don't want any favors from you," the younger man snarled back at him.

"A little too late for that, when I asked my first mate to

give up his cabin for you. He wasn't at all pleased about it, so other accommodations can be arranged if you'd prefer, though I doubt you'll like sleeping with the livestock, which would of course require some chains, too, since we can't have you doing damage down there. You might have noticed you aren't restrained in here?"

"Appreciate it," the other man said. "'Deed I do. But I insist you return us to London."

"My friend speaks for himself. I'm staying right here as long as Jack is here."

"You both are, but restrained or unrestrained is the question. Did you miss that it was a question?"

"If you think I'm asking for bloody chains, I'm not."

"Excellent," Damon replied. "I agree that wouldn't be a pleasant way to spend the next month. All that is required to keep these accommodations is that you don't try to vacate them. If you can restrain yourselves, then you won't be restrained—no pun intended. Now then, it's time for you to tell me who you are."

"Who did Jack say I am?"

Damon laughed at the cautious reply. The man was making it hard for Damon to humor him with answers like that. But he didn't need confirmation when neither of these two would come to further harm on his ship.

"I'd still like an actual name, but Jeremy will do if you're hesitant to give one. She says you look like her older brother. Do you?"

"From a distance, I suppose I do. That name is fine, if you have to call me anything."

"And you?" Damon asked the other.

"Lord Percival—"

"Percy talks too much," Jeremy interrupted in a warning tone.

"So a couple of destitute lords, after all?"

"Eh?" Percival said quite indignantly.

"We're not all rich like the Malorys," Jeremy said quickly.

Before Damon could reply, the man elbowing his way past the guards poked his head in the cabin, then complained bitterly, "That's the toff who nearly broke me jaw. Why's 'e being treated so royally when 'e ought to be in chains down in the 'old, eh?"

Damon walked the intruder backward by not giving him any choice but to move or get knocked over. "Did I ask for your opinion?"

"No, but—"

"Tolerated but silent, that was the deal. Stay out of my way or you will find out just how unnecessary you are to the completion of this mission."

"That goes both ways—Captain," the man sneered before he scurried up the stairs.

Damon closed his eyes for a moment. It was telling by the pirate's answer that he was confident he and his cutthroat friends still held the upper hand. Damon couldn't protect Jack if he gave in to his rage and failed to rid his ship of its infestation. He turned back to the open door, but his eyes passed over the two guards. One looked indignant on his behalf, the other looked uneasy. It was still too soon to try. And considering what had just happened, the key to this room probably shouldn't be left where anyone could grab it.

"Trouble with your pirates, Captain?" Jeremy asked, nodding toward the bandage on Damon's side.

A logical assumption after what the hostages had just overheard. "No, that's Jack's handiwork. Quite the hellcat she is."

"Did you hurt her?" Jeremy tried to get up again.

"Be easy, man, I told you she's fine. And you mistake the situation. She's very precious cargo. She won't be hurt no matter how many times she tries to kill me."

"Then we'll hope she has better luck next time," Jeremy sneered.

"I'm sure you will."

"You mentioned a month," Jeremy said next. "Where are you sailing to?"

"Warmer waters."

"A whole month at sea?" Percival said, looking appalled.

"You could work your way across, if you want exercise to alleviate the boredom. Although you"—Damon paused to stare at Jeremy for a moment—"maybe not. It took quite a few men to take you down. Reminds me of Jack's father."

"You still think I'm somehow related?"

"You could be, even though you don't look like her or her father."

"There's a reason—" Percy stopped talking before Jeremy could kick his chair over.

Damon raised a black brow. "Maybe you and I should have a talk?" he suggested to Percival. "Would you like a spot of fresh air?"

"Leave him be!" Jeremy snarled. "He's not used to pirates."

"But you are?"

"I want to see Jack. I need assurances that she's all right."

"Perhaps another time. For now, you'll have to take my word for it."

"I *will* need the exercise. You can't keep me locked in here for a whole bloody month."

"Of course I can. However, I'll consider the request after you've recovered sufficiently. But you'll need to bargain for it."

"With?"

"With a promise of no trouble, and no attempt to rescue your employer, relative, or whoever she is to you. And you won't be let out together. One at a time or neither of you. By the way, I'm not a pirate."

Jeremy snorted. "If you look like one and act like one, then you are one."

"Really? Then that would make you Jack's brother, wouldn't it, considering you look like him and are certainly acting like him?"

"Point taken. So not all spades are spades." Jeremy then guessed, "But I'll wager you're Bastard. Warmer waters as in the Caribbean? You might as well fess up to it."

"That I'm a bastard or that it's the name Jack picked for me from our previous voyage together? I put up with it from her . . . well, I put up with most things from her." But then in a darker tone Damon added, "I won't put up with it from you. You can call me Reeves or Captain Reeves, take your pick."

"Cap'n!" someone yelled from the top of the stairs. "You're needed topside before this argument comes to blows!"

Damon quickly closed and locked the door on the hostages. His nervous guard drew his pistol and headed up the stairs cautiously.

The other man, Paul Jensen, put a hand on Damon's arm. "You have an unusual crew, Captain. I've noticed they seem to only behave while you're on deck. They're a rowdy bunch, otherwise."

"When I hired you, Mr. Jensen, I warned there might be problems and asked if you were prepared to deal with them."

"And I am, sir. But are they your men or not? I've got your back, but I need to know who I'm guarding it from."

Damon smiled. "Thank you, and no, half of them are not mine. You've probably already guessed which half. We'll discuss this further, but in the meantime, I need to make sure none of the real sailors aboard get hurt."

Chapter Nineteen

W AS THERE A FIGHT?" Jeremy asked the first mate, who opened the door a while later.

"None of your business," Mortimer replied with his usual curtness. He dropped a small stack of books on the little eating table, then tossed a rolled-up hammock on the floor in the corner.

"Come now, Mr. Bower," Jeremy persisted. "A mutiny would most certainly be of concern."

"Mutiny?" Mortimer rolled his eyes. "Where the devil did you get that idea?"

"We heard the shouts. Nothing so grand then? A pity."

"You fish well, but when Damon wants you to know something, he'll be the one to tell you." Mortimer snorted and left.

Jeremy sighed.

Percival observed, "You are determined to goad him, aren't you?"

"He does prickle nicely, doesn't he?"

"Yes, but he also brings our food while it's still nice and hot.

Quite tasty, too, if you ain't noticed, dear boy. Might I suggest we keep it that way?"

"He doesn't strike me as a vindictive sort. Definitely disgruntled though. I wonder why."

"Ask."

"Asking gets nothing from him."

Percival moved over to examine the books. Jeremy read a few of the titles and wondered aloud, "What's a pirate doing with classical literature?"

"Pirated?" Percy suggested with a smile for such a brilliant thought.

Jeremy did chuckle over Percy's word for "stolen." "Possibly, yet he says he's not a pirate."

"We're to believe him?"

"I haven't decided yet. But something definitely doesn't add up here. What sane pirate talks to his captain like that belligerent one did earlier? The nasty little chap should've got knocked on his arse at the very least, and it even sounded like Captain Reeves wanted to do just that. I wonder why he didn't."

"Some men fastidiously avoid violence." Percival dusted off his sleeves.

Jeremy laughed, but groaned when it hurt and finally got out, "Yes, we know your druthers, old boy. But Reeves is capable of it. I saw it in his eyes briefly when I reached for him. He bloody well would have shot me if I didn't back off. At least he gave me fair warning."

"Oh, I say, I know that name, 'deed I do."

Jeremy raised a brow. "Reeves?"

"Yes."

"You waited this long to say so?"

"It only sounded familiar when he said it, but I've just

recalled why. There was a scandal a while back, well, longer than a while, over twenty-five years ago, actually, when I was a young buck going around with Nick and Derek. Lady Reeves's daughter, who was quite a beauty, went on holiday to the West Indies and briefly returned with a husband with whom she'd eloped. Her family didn't approve of the chap because he was only a planter, so she returned to Jamaica and was never heard from again. Her family assumed she died, but it was whispered they disowned her and that's the real reason she never came back again."

"You sure it was Jamaica and you're not remembering that name from me, because I lived there briefly with my father and his first mate, Connie?"

"I'm not confused, dear boy. You told Derek and me that story long ago."

"I'm afraid our captain is a bit too young to have been the planter Lady Reeves's daughter eloped with."

"No, no, I wasn't suggesting anything of the sort. I was just surprised to recognize the name. But you're right, Captain Reeves wouldn't be any relation a'tall to the East Sussex Reeveses, and besides, the planter wouldn't take his wife's name, now would he?"

Jeremy chuckled. "Highly doubtful, but then you can't discount pirates coming from upper-crust English families, either."

"Course not, point being your father—"

"Percy . . . ," Jeremy cut in warningly.

Percival delivered a soft snort. "I don't know why you still deny—well, I do know why, because you think I'll blabber it all over London, but—"

"Was it ever confirmed for you?"

"No," Percy grumbled.

"Then stop guessing over something that's such an old rumor. Why don't you help me figure out what's wrong with this crew instead."

"Wrong? Well, they're pirates, that's wrong enough, ain't it?"

"But I don't think they all are, and that's what's odd. That group who beat me down on Wapping Street were definitely the hardened sort, but listening at the door when the crew comes and goes from their quarters, it appears some of them aren't pirates a'tall, just typical sailors. And the first mate and captain are clearly not ordinary sailors themselves, might even be gentlemen."

"Oh! You mean from East Sussex?"

Jeremy rolled his eyes. "I concede that could be possible, since the Reeves family probably had other children, even grandchildren, cousins, nephews, et cetera, at least more'n one disowned or dead child."

"Don't know. Didn't know them personally."

"Percy, it's irrelevant where the captain and his mate come from. They could be royal bastards for all I care. My point is that it's clear the pirates don't like or trust their captain, so we should figure out how to use this fissure in the crew to free ourselves and Jack."

Chapter Twenty

Jacqueline was rudely awakened by two of the crew who were talking to each other quite loudly, as if they hadn't noticed she was still sleeping.

She gasped when she opened her eyes and saw that one of them was standing next to her cot staring down at her. A fearsome-looking pirate, he had a jagged scar running from cheek to ear on the left side of his face. Giving her a lopsided grin, he at least moved away from her now that she was awake. It didn't diminish her unease, which rose instead when she sat up, holding the blanket up to her neck, and realized Bastard wasn't in the cabin. She was alone with these two pirates. Had she slept all morning? She shouldn't have, not when she'd fallen asleep so quickly last night after her exhausting swim. If Mort had come back last night as Bastard had warned her, she hadn't heard it.

Indignation overwhelmed her when she saw the other pirate examining the clothes she'd hung on the chairs the night before. "Get away from my clothes. I assure you they won't fit you."

The scarred-cheek pirate laughed at his friend's red face. She didn't care. But she couldn't get out of bed with the pirates in the room. She noticed that the door was wide-open. A thoughtless mistake on their part? Or was there a guard out there again?

Her shoulders slumped when she saw a man's arm wave across the opening as whoever was out there stretched, likely bored with his duty. So she glanced about the room as she wondered why Bastard wasn't in it.

The drapes had been drawn open to let in the morning sun, and a tray of food was on the table. But nothing explained why two pirates were loitering in the room with her. If she was to have in-room guards now as well as one at the door, something must be amiss. With Bastard? If his wound was worse than he'd let on and he'd collapsed, they'd tell her, wouldn't they? Maybe not.

"What are you doing in here?" she asked.

"Changing the cap'n's bedding," the embarrassed one said belatedly, heading to the bed to do that.

"We are?" The other one looked confused.

"Get o'er here and help," his friend ordered.

She watched them for a moment yanking at the sheets before she raised her brow and asked the man in an amused tone, "So he has servants now?"

They both glanced at her at once, though only for a second before getting back to their supposed task, although Scar Face mumbled, "Not bleeding likely."

The other volunteered, "We help as needed, and just now it is. The captain doesn't need to be doing this in his condition—thanks to you."

"He probably won't appreciate your babying him just because of a little wound." Jack shrugged carelessly. "But make sure you tell him you changed his bedding. I don't want him to think I did it. Does he even know you're in here?"

At least one of them revealed a little nervousness at her guess, but it was nothing compared to the near panic he displayed when Bastard walked in. The captain was more than a little angry as he approached both men. One man made a wide circle around him and bolted out of the room. Scar Face backed away more slowly. He appeared more annoyed than afraid that he'd gotten caught.

"You know you aren't allowed in my cabin." A furious undertone was in Bastard's voice. "And how did you get in?"

"Followed the boy in with the food."

"If it happens again, you'll think Catherine's paramour had it lightly."

"No need for threats like that." The pirate displayed a little wariness now. "We just wanted to make sure you didn't damage the hellcat what stabbed you last night. Protecting our interests is all."

"Next time ask. Get out."

Bastard's anger didn't dissipate as the second pirate vacated the cabin. Jacqueline was fascinated by what she was witnessing. Not only was Bastard bare chested, his jaw was hardened, his shoulders tensed, and he was flexing the muscles in his arms as if he were itching to inflict mayhem on the pirates. She blushed a little, but only because his leaving his cabin like that, exposing the bloody bandage wrapped around his torso, let his whole crew see exactly what she'd done to him, if they hadn't already been told about it.

When his eyes moved to her, she saw the stormy expression in them. Sitting there with the blanket held up to her neck, she was hesitant to say anything because she wasn't at all familiar with this side of the man. But as he stared at her, his anger seemed to ease, and finally the tension left his body, too.

He crossed back to the door and closed it, telling her, "My men won't bother you again, but if anyone other than Mort or my cabin boy enters the cabin when I'm not here, you have my permission to raise hell."

"As in?"

"Scream really loud until I show up."

She raised a brow. "How many times do I get to cry wolf before it doesn't work anymore?"

"I'm serious."

"You don't think I'll do it just to see you come running?"

"I don't think you're stupid, no."

"But it would be interesting!"

He gave her a hard look, but it wasn't the least bit intimidating after what she'd just witnessed. He seemed more like the man she knew, which meant she could resume her usual goading.

She did wonder why a degree of disgust had been in his voice when he'd called those two pirates "my men," but she merely pointed out, "Your crewmen don't seem very happy to take orders from you. Why is that?"

"They're new" was all he said as he went to his desk, but he shook his head as he passed the dining table. "Your food is cold."

"My maid wasn't here to wake me," she quipped.

"I suppose I can fill that position for the duration."

Was he joking? She saw his grin as he sat down behind his desk. Carefully. Now all she could see above the desk were his handsome face and wide bare chest. Why the devil hadn't he put a shirt on? She hadn't shredded them yet, so he could have.

She would have gotten up to get one and throw it at him, but preferred not to expose her bare legs to him. But she simply couldn't stop staring at him. With muscles like that, no wonder he'd always found it so easy to restrain her.

She finally got her mind and eyes off his chest and arms and asked, "Should you even be out of bed yet?"

"The sawbones didn't say I shouldn't leave it." He shrugged.

"He should have, or is he not a real doctor?"

"Of course he's not a real doctor. His misnomer should have given you that clue. He's good at chopping off limbs, but I doubt much else. How bad do you think this wound is?"

"Obviously not bad enough," she hissed.

He was staring at her too intently, so she glanced at the table and wondered about making a run for it so she could get dressed. But he yelled toward the door, "Mr. Barker, have Jack—well, I suppose we'll need to call your brother Jackie for the duration—bring my guest another tray."

"I can eat cold food," Jacqueline said loudly enough for the guard to hear, though she still stared at her nemesis. "So don't do me any favors."

"I do you all sorts of favors. You're just usually too angry to notice."

She had no clue what he meant by that, but she gave up waiting for some privacy and shot off the cot to retrieve the clothing she'd spread around his chairs last night. She only blushed a little when she picked up her underclothes and realized they were what that pirate had been inspecting.

"You look adorable this morning, wearing my shirt."

She crossed back to the cot. "Did you buy this one for me?"

"No, I confess I like that color."

Pink used to be a fashionable color for men, but that had

been decades ago when bright satin jackets and knee-high britches were the choices of dandies, the more gaudy the better. Today men were much more staid in their dress. She was sure she'd laugh if she saw Bastard wearing the pink shirt. And since she'd rather he not think he amused her in any way, she decided not to give it back.

Laying her clothes on the cot, she reached for the rose brocade skirt, only to feel that it was still damp. She had decided on the sturdy traveling suit for the rendezvous for one reason, because even her day dresses were a little too fancy and she hadn't wanted the Mask, or as she'd hoped, Bastard, to think she was trying to impress him. Why couldn't that meeting have gone her way instead of his?

But she wasn't surprised that the heavier brocade hadn't fully dried yet, so she just put on her white petticoat. Made of fine batiste layered with only minimal puffing, each row bordered with a strip of white satin and dotted with tiny blue bows, it had been her hidden concession to elegance for the ensemble. Now it was no longer hidden.

She started to reach for her drawers next, but drew her hand back. She'd rather not give Bastard another performance for his amusement. She could wait until he left the room to put on the underclothes, so she unbuttoned the lower half of his long shirt and tied the lower edges around her waist. There, she was presentable and decent for the moment, even if her feet were bare.

"Nicely done."

If she liked the man, she would have given him a jesting curtsy for that remark. She ignored him instead and took her skirt back to the chair so it could continue to dry.

She took a deep breath. "I want to see my men today."

"I just saw them. You Malorys are all alike. Your brother tried to kill me."

"He's not my—" she started, but then smirked. "Is that why you're bleeding again?"

"No, I was armed, he wasn't, so it didn't come to a scuffle."

"I still want to see—"

"Then come here." He patted his lap. "Let's see how persuasive you can be." Her immediate glare had him add, "No? Then settle for knowing they're still breathing, and if you behave, you might get to visit them eventually."

Behave? Or just not try to kill him again? It was infuriating that he'd drop crumbs that he knew damn well she wouldn't pick up when he probably had no intention of ever letting her see Jeremy. Why would he? He was a bloody pirate!

Done with teasing her, he scolded, "You know you never would have made it to land last night. It was barely still in sight when you jumped. Do you realize the great distance you would have had to swim?"

"Another ship could have come along." She sat down in a chair facing him.

"That would have been an incredible long shot. You were just a speck in the water, Jack. Even if a ship sailed past you, chances are the people aboard wouldn't have noticed you even during the day, and certainly not at night. And dawn was a long way off."

"If you're expecting thanks for bringing me back, don't hold your breath."

His brows rose. "So you were willing to give up your life for your father?"

"Of course I would."

"But was that really your plan?"

She wished now she'd taken a seat that didn't face him. But she didn't have to answer. She didn't have to keep staring at those beautiful eyes, either, but she did.

She held her tongue waiting for him to press her, but he didn't. So she was surprised to hear herself say, "I'm a good swimmer. I had every intention of succeeding."

"Good to know that at least you aren't fatally resigned, so I suppose we can simply agree to disagree on the outcome. But tell me, why didn't you try to bargain with me first? You did before. Untold riches was your promise, wasn't it, if I betrayed the pirate for you?"

She snorted. "It didn't work last time, so why waste my breath?"

"But you haven't even tried seducing me to your side, another option that wouldn't require you to risk your life."

Seduce him? Why the devil would he say that? He knew how much she hated him. But then she'd never been nice to him, not once, had only wanted to kill or hurt him whenever she got close enough to do so. She had no idea how trying to be nice to him would play out other than to make him suspicious since he knew her druthers fairly well. Yet it was still a tempting thought—seducing him to her side, not by bedding him, but by just making him think she might. She might even be able to convince him to take her home. No, how could she when she wouldn't be able to resist punching him if she got that close. . . .

The cabin boy arrived with her second breakfast tray. He was a skinny lad about her height, with reddish-brown hair and freckles. He looked far too nervous, possibly because he knew, as everyone else did by now, that she'd stabbed his captain. She hoped she hadn't hurt the boy yesterday when she'd shoved him out of the way for her aborted leap for the railing. She gazed briefly at his britches, wishing she had a pair.

Bastard stood up to leave, telling the boy, "Keep an eye on Jack."

Jacqueline waited until the door closed behind him before she said, "Jack Barker, is it?"

"He wants you to call me Jackie."

"No, he wants everyone else to call you that to avoid confusion, but you and I will still call each other Jack. Are you from London?"

"Aye, but newly come from Reading in Berkshire with my brother Tom. He wanted to go to sea, has been hankering for it for years, he has, but he was reluctant to leave me behind, since he's all I got now, after our pa died. So he looked for a ship that would take us both on, and this one did. But I don't know much about being a cabin boy, well, not even a thing."

"Shall I tell you a secret, Jack? My mother was a cabin boy once."

His eyes got so wide, she laughed, but he asked, "Did her captain know she was a she?"

"He did, but she didn't know he did. It was amusing how that played out, to hear them tell it. But my point is that you don't need any prior experience for this job. You'll be told what needs to be done, so just follow orders as they're given and you'll do fine. And it's just"—she started to say Bastard, but she didn't want the boy to mimic her disparagement, which would get him in trouble, so she corrected herself—"the captain you need to be concerned with. Don't ignore small jobs others might give you if they see you idle, but don't let them interfere with something the captain wants done. He comes first for you, and you probably will want to keep busy. I know I would."

He started to fix the mess the pirates had made of Bastard's bed. "You'd want to be a cabin boy like your mum?"

"Goodness, no." She chuckled. "But I hate being idle, and there isn't much that I don't know how to do on a ship, thanks to my father and four uncles, all of whom captain their own ships. Come to think of it, you might consider asking some of the crew to teach you their jobs when you're not busy—that is, if you like sailing and aren't hankering to get back to land now that you've tried it."

"I like it. Didn't think I would, but I do."

"That's good, considering this ship is not about to turn back. Now, before you rush off to attend your captain, you might be able to help me with something."

He blanched. "I can't let you out of here. That was growled in my ear by the first mate."

"No, no, I wouldn't get another Jack in trouble, I promise you that. I was just hoping you might have an extra pair of britches I could borrow?"

Chapter Twenty-One

JACQUELINE WAS SITTING WITH her feet up on Bastard's desk. Her legs crossed, simply because she could since he wasn't there. And why the deuce wasn't he? Other than his brief visit that morning, he'd left her alone the entire day. When he ought to have spent the day in bed to let his wound heal. When she was beyond bored. When she might have flown at him with her nails if he had come in before she calmed down.

It hadn't been easy to force herself out of the frenzy she'd worked herself into after four hours of pacing and thinking of how badly she'd failed at getting herself, Jeremy, and Percy off a pirate ship heading for the Caribbean and how frantic with worry her mother must be by now. But it wouldn't be too much longer before she had company of one sort or another. Her growling belly convinced her of that.

When she finally heard the key turning, her heart skipped a beat. Which made her blink. What the devil? She was *not* excited that he was back. And it might not even be him. It could be Jackie with her dinner, so she stayed where she was.

But it was Bastard, and he only paused for a moment when he saw her in his chair. He was still shirtless, so she could see that his wound was still bleeding, though not as much blood was on the bandage as in the morning, so his dressing had been changed at least once today. And he was a bit sunburned.

"Why are you commanding your ship in your condition?" she demanded. "You have a first mate who could do it while you rest and recover."

"Did you miss me?"

He walked slowly toward the desk with that damned smile she hated. She still didn't vacate his chair, so he half sat on the edge of the desk, one foot on the floor, one leg dangling. And that was seeing far too much of him far too close. The man was too masculine, his chest too wide, his arms too thick with muscles, his eyes so light in contrast to his black hair and the stubble on his cheeks. She was having a little trouble breathing.

But he distracted her with "Mortimer might be my first mate and get things done nicely, but he doesn't like acting as captain or taking the wheel."

She scoffed, "You've likely got a half dozen men at least who know how to steer. Even I'm capable . . ."

"Of sailing us back to England?"

She growled to herself for telling him too much. "No, of course not."

"You don't lie very well, Jack. So your father even made a helmsman out of you? What else did he teach you?"

She clamped her mouth shut and bolted out of the chair to head back to the cot, tossing behind her, "The sun burned you. It was really stupid of you to go without a shirt for the entire day."

He didn't reply. Once she was seated in the middle of her narrow bed with her legs crossed, she guessed why. He was still looking at her legs, scrutinizing what she was now wearing.

He even put a hand to his forehead and sighed before he took his seat and, after another long moment of staring at her legs, said cautiously, "I don't need to ask where you got those britches, but do you really want to wear them?"

"Of course I do. It's how I always dress aboard a ship. If I had packed for this trip, you'd see that I have my own britches, tailor-made just for me for ocean travel. Wearing skirts that get tossed about in the wind is so ridiculous."

"You noticed wind in here, did you?"

He was grinning. She wasn't. Which might be why he quickly said, "But I believe we were discussing why I'm only half-dressed myself. So perhaps you don't know that it's nigh impossible to get blood out of white lawn, or any material, for that matter. I simply prefer not to stain my wardrobe just because you couldn't keep your dagger out of me."

Was he trying to make her feel bad about that? When she'd do it again if she could?

"But I did notice the sun, Jack, when Mort tossed a rain cloak at me. That was before noon or I'd be a lot redder than this."

She ought not to be talking to him at all and wouldn't be if she wasn't starved for conversation. His fault. Everything was his fault. How the deuce had she survived a week of this before? She couldn't remember pacing then, couldn't remember anything except her rage. And where the devil was it now? But she didn't want it now, did she? It might have kept her from noticing the boredom previously, but she had decided to try "nice" this time and then maybe, just maybe, seduce him into taking her home.

So she watched him for a moment before she asked, "How is your wound?"

"Would you like to examine it?"

Should she? No, definitely not. It was too soon to get that close to him.

But she pointed out, "The doctor will be coming to do that."

"What makes you think so?"

"Because he ought to check you for fever, infection, especially since you stupidly spent the day working instead of resting."

"If you keep that up, Jack, I'm going to start thinking you're worrying about me."

She snorted, then grit her teeth, which made him grin. The man was entirely too friendly for a kidnapping pirate. And much too easily amused. It was as if a joke were lingering in the room whose punch line she'd missed, and every time he looked at her, he was reminded of it. He couldn't really be so damned insouciant and cheerful when this situation was beyond serious, could he? That would make him—heartless.

"I've seen all of Dr. Death's incompetence that I care to. The crew might trust his tending, but I don't. Besides, he's likely drunk this time of day."

Her eyes flared wide. "Was he foxed when he stitched you last night?"

"You couldn't smell it?"

"And you let him sew your wound?!"

"Are you ready to play doctor, Jack?"

She stopped herself from laughing. This was the perfect opportunity to try to be nice to him when it was at his own suggestion and he wouldn't be suspicious about the change in her attitude. But what if she couldn't control herself when she got near enough to him to examine his wound? What if she socked him instead . . . ?

Chapter Twenty-Two

Y OU DON'T NEED TO agonize about it, Jack. I wasn't being entirely serious."

She could tell Bastard was still joking, so she sighed. "I wasn't aware that seriousness came in half measures. Remove the bandage and I'll have a look. For all you know, your foxed doctor made the wound worse, not better."

She didn't have to get close to him just to look. And it would be a good start, grudging help rather than offered help. So she went to the side of the desk. But he hadn't removed his bandage. He was staring at her legs again!

"You might want to untie my shirt if you're going to wear those."

"Why?" She glanced down at the britches. "They're a good fit."

"No, they're not. They're so tight around your hips and thighs that you might as well be naked."

"Oh."

The blush came instantly but left just as fast as soon as

she saw that he'd stopped looking at her. He was unwrapping his bandages and keeping his eyes on the task, so she quickly unknotted his shirt and pulled the now-wrinkled lower half of it down to her knees. But she definitely wasn't going to forget that his seeing her in tight britches bothered him. Seducing him might not be so difficult after all.

The square bit of padding the bandages had held in place was stuck to the wound. He pulled it off slowly without wincing before his eyes came back to hers. "Well?"

She tsked. "Look at it yourself. You can't tell anything about that wound with all that blood caked around it. It needs to be washed first."

"Go ahead."

She moved to his washstand and grabbed one of the little towels on the shelf under it. She soaked it in the water bowl and wrung it out, then came back and tossed it at him. "You go ahead. You know if I do it, it's going to hurt so bad you'll cry."

He burst out laughing. Once the dried blood was rubbed off, she could see the slit she'd caused was about an inch and a half. She winced a little even if he didn't.

She frowned and leaned closer, then exclaimed, "Good grief, the doctor only gave you one stitch and it's already unraveled. No wonder it's still bleeding."

He shrugged. "He probably got distracted when you called me a murderer."

She snorted at that reminder. "You didn't lock the door. I assume someone's standing guard out there?"

"Of course."

"Then send him for a needle and thread. You need proper stitching if you want that wound to heal anytime soon."

"Still determined to make me cry?"

"Good guess," she quipped with a tight grin.

But he did as she suggested, though he told the sailor to send someone else to fetch what was needed. Jackie arrived moments later with a needle and thread and a tray of food.

"Bring me a lit lantern or a candle," Jacqueline told the boy. "I need to pass the needle through a flame."

"So you received doctoring lessons, too?" Bastard said with some surprise.

"No, but I've seen a competent physician at work before, and I know a dirty needle is worse than no needle a'tall."

"But how are you with a needle?"

"I know how to sew, if that's what you mean. My cousin Judy wanted to learn embroidery and I wasn't going to just sit there and watch her do it, so I learned, too."

"I would have thought you'd have been out slaying dragons instead."

"She and I did everything together. I didn't like the sewing, but she was pleased that I tried it with her."

"And then she hunted dragons with you?"

She glanced up at him and noticed his grin. "Is that what you did as a child? Pretend to slay dragons?"

He laughed. "Actually, Mort and I pretended to slay pirates. But then we grew up in the Caribbean. I don't think there are any dragons there. Was that a real smile, Jack?"

It had been, for the briefest moment, but she wasn't going to kick herself about it. "I was just imagining a dragon romping through the islands. But Judy and I didn't need to play pretend. Our family is too big. There was always something exciting happening to occupy us instead."

"Did she reciprocate and try all of your activities as well?"

"Goodness, no. Some of the things I cajoled my father into

teaching me, she considered too unladylike for her. But she watched and cheered me on."

"Steering a ship isn't dangerous."

"Fetch me a rapier and I'll demonstrate."

He chuckled. "Lessons of that sort, really?"

"Much more fun than needlepoint."

To have such a normal conversation with him was a little disconcerting. A good start to her plan, but it still felt odd discussing their childhoods in such a whimsical way. But she didn't want to waste this opportunity to find out more about him, maybe even something personal that she could use against him.

So she said, "I would have guessed you grew up in England, not the Caribbean. You certainly sound English."

"Have I intrigued you again?"

"Again? Oh, that," she scoffed, thinking of the masquerade ball. "Any mystery is intriguing, and that's all you were—when you were wearing that ridiculous mask. Were you born in the islands?"

"Yes, of English parents. You'd be surprised how many Englishmen settle in the West Indies on the islands Britain has claimed."

"Which island?"

"If you're trying to distract me from my pain, you're doing a good job." He brushed his fingers softly over the hand she was leaning on his desk.

She jerked her hand away. She was out of her depth, trying to be nice to her worst enemy. She wished her fake relative, Andrew, were here to give her a few acting lessons. She was making a good start at being nice to Bastard, and she didn't want to ruin it by getting angry over his touching her.

"I'll wager your fancy cook has something for sunburns or

knows how to make a cream for it. You should ask, because that burn is going to feel worse tomorrow than it does today."

"You know about sunburns, too?"

"I fell asleep in a field one summer and woke up with burned feet and hands. Yes, it can be painful."

"Why were you without shoes?"

"I liked running about barefoot at that age—well, sneaking about. Shoes were too noisy for sneaking. But you ought to treat your sunburn."

He raised a brow. "Your concern is . . ."

When he didn't finish, she did, saying, "Suspect? I recall the cream stinging horribly for a while before it got around to soothing."

He laughed, but then he slapped his chest, leaving a white handprint on the pink skin. "This is nothing, Jack. I grew up under a much hotter sun."

She shrugged. "Suit yourself."

Jackie returned with a lit candle, which he set on the desk next to Jacqueline, reminding her, "Don't let your food get cold again, m'lady."

She gave the freckled boy a hard look. "What did we agree on?"

He blushed. "M'lady Jack."

"That wasn't it," she mumbled as the boy quickly left, then said to Bastard, "He really is nervous around you, isn't he? You should put him at ease."

"I haven't adopted him. He'll figure out in due course that I don't bite."

That was debatable, particularly since Bastard's expression implied the remark had been for her rather than the boy. But starting an argument wasn't on the agenda tonight, so she held her tongue and reached for the needle instead, but realized she ought to remove the broken stitch first before she put in neat ones.

"This will hurt," she said, but yanked the thread out before she finished the warning.

"You enjoyed that, didn't you?"

She managed not to grin, but glanced up at his face before she straightened. Damn, not again. Those sensual bright eyes of his, pinning her, stirring her insides, stealing her breath and voice. She closed her eyes, counted to ten, breathed again.

"Jack?"

"I was doing that imagining thing again," she lied, and moved away from him.

"So was I," he said in husky tones.

Chapter Twenty-Three

Y OU SURE YOU WANT her doing that?"

Jacqueline didn't glance at Mortimer, who'd entered the cabin silently and was now standing next to her. Her cheeks were still hot from that mesmerizing moment she'd just shared with her nemesis. It had been a mistake to get this close to him again, and she wasn't even done yet!

"She's a competent seamstress," Bastard calmly told his friend.

"She's a competent wound maker," Mortimer rejoined caustically.

Belligerence she could more easily handle, and being nice to Bastard's disagreeable first mate wasn't part of her plan. "If you've business here, state it, then get out. I need full concentration to apply this needle." She picked up the needle and passed it twice through the flame before pointing at Bastard. "And you get on the bed. I'm not getting a kink in my back for you."

He was grinning widely as he stood up and went to the bed.

But Mortimer crossed his arms and demanded, "Why are you willing to tend the wound you gave him?"

"I didn't volunteer, he asked me to. But are you under the impression that proper stitching isn't going to hurt?"

"So you just want to cause him more pain?"

"Of course, why else would I be doing this?" she quipped. "You can leave now."

"I'm not going anywhere. I'm sleeping in here again tonight."

That gave her pause. "Why?"

"You don't want a chaperone?"

She snorted.

Mortimer crossed over to the dining table to get a plate off the larger tray Jackie had brought before adding, "I was talked into giving up my cabin for the prisoners. Damon insisted I share his."

Damon? Bastard was giving up his name this time? Or had Mort just revealed something he shouldn't. But he didn't look as if he'd just blundered, and when she glanced at Bastard or, rather, Damon, he didn't look as if he cared. What the devil was different this time?

She'd asked for his name before, but he'd refused to give it. She'd been kept utterly isolated before, at least until Catherine had been allowed into the cabin to convince her to eat and, when she wouldn't, had let slip that Damon was her lover. There was no accounting for taste between criminals, she supposed, but really, the man would have done better with anyone other than that nasty witch. But this time, sailors, first mates, even cabin boys, had been let in to see her. Something was definitely different. Damon hadn't said what and probably wouldn't if asked. But she still tried.

"Damon is your real name?"

"I prefer Bastard."

"So do I," she snapped.

She should have known he wouldn't enlighten her, but realized it could simply be because she would be dying this time along with her father. So it didn't matter whom she could identify or what names she knew.

That thought made her grip the needle like a weapon, but only briefly. Be nice! Honey, not spit and fire. She took a deep breath and followed Damon to the bed, where he had lain down to accommodate her. Damon. The name had a nice ring to it, but she wasn't sure she'd call him that when she was too used to calling him Bastard. She supposed she could try, in the interest of her plan.

"This will hurt," she warned as she sat down on the edge of the bed. "The wound needs at least four stitches to keep it closed, but then you should be able to dress properly tomorrow without staining your shirts, with another bandage to guarantee it."

"Might as well make it five stitches then, just to be sure."

"Really?"

"Have at it, Jack, so we can eat. I apologize for delaying your dinner. It's been a long, tiring day."

The moment he'd entered the room, she'd forgotten how hungry she was. Now, she felt nervous. This wasn't white cloth pulled tight over an embroidery frame, but real skin, his skin.

She met his eyes. "Maybe you should get foxed first?"

He chuckled. "No, I'll be fine and so will you. Imagine you still hate me."

She pressed the needle through, but had to pause when her stomach churned. She wished she could close her eyes, but couldn't. *Just get it over with! You do hate him with every fiber of your body, but imagine he's white cloth.* . . .

She leapt away from the bed as soon as she tied off the last stitch and almost knocked down Mortimer, who'd come up silently behind her to watch. "That is a neat bit of stitching, girl."

"D'you have something that requires it?" she snarled. "I'd be happy to oblige."

Mortimer just laughed and took his plate back to the table to sit and finish eating while he watched her. Damon hadn't made a single sound during that stitching. If he'd winced at all, she hadn't looked at his face to see it.

"Wait until morning to rebandage it," she said without looking to see if Damon was getting out of bed.

He probably wouldn't. He might even have passed out, for all she knew. But the door wasn't locked yet. And she finally noticed the pile of bedding that had been dropped just inside it, so it appeared the first mate was really staying. But with Damon still in bed and Mortimer seated, she could probably get out of there and back into the water, but she wasn't going to. It was too late for that. The ship was far enough from England that she could never make it back.

She picked up one of the two remaining plates and sat down across from Mortimer, then ignored him. He was more likely there to protect Damon while he was in a weakened state, though the captain bloody well ought to seem weakened if he actually was.

And then Damon was standing next to her, picking up the third plate. He started to take it to his desk as he did last night at her insistence, so she said grudgingly, "You can eat here—on the other end of the table. I don't want to crane my neck if we're going to talk."

"Are we?" He sat down. "You actually want to?"

She shrugged. "Haven't we been?"

"I seem to recall the only thing you had to say to me before was how many different ways your father was going to kill me."

He shouldn't have mentioned that, or was he just testing the waters, so to speak, since she hadn't yelled at him once since he'd returned to the cabin. She was probably being too cordial. She'd be suspicious herself over such a complete about-face.

So she gave him a nasty glare before saying, "That was then, this is now."

"And what's different?"

"The bloody length of the trip, that's what!"

"Ah." He smiled. "Worried about boredom?"

"It crossed my mind," she mumbled.

Mortimer had finished his food by then and stood up to tell Damon, "I'd rather use a hammock tonight."

"It won't fit in front of the door."

"Is that really necessary? I can hold the key for you."

"You sleep like a log," Damon replied. "You're merely a fail-safe."

"You two bicker like old hens," Jacqueline put in with a tsk. "A full day has passed and I'm not stupid. Jumping ship is no longer an option."

"And we'd believe you why?" Mortimer asked as he spread his bedding in front of the door.

"D'you think I care if you do or not?" she retorted caustically.

"And now who's bickering?" Damon said.

Nothing else was said after that, so she regretted inviting Damon to sit at the table, especially when she felt his eyes on her whether she looked his way or not. And she was getting tired. Who knew boredom could be exhausting.

It wasn't quite dusk so no lanterns had yet been lit and might not be when she wasn't the only one who'd had an exhausting day. Finished eating, she stood up, but glanced at Damon when he mentioned, "You might be feeling a bit salty from your swim last night. I meant to offer you a bath earlier but got distracted. Would you like one now, Jack?"

Before she could reply, Mortimer said, "Bloody hell, Damon, I'm already bedded down. Can't that wait until tomorrow?"

Damon ignored his friend and was looking at her, awaiting her answer. This was something else he'd never offered her before, and yes, she would dearly love a bath, just not tonight with the two of them in the cabin.

"Do I get to hold the key while you two are on the other side of the door?"

"No."

"Then no."

"Smart girl," Mortimer mumbled.

She ignored the blond and headed to her cot, tossing back at Damon, "I do still hate you." She just wished it sounded more convincing.

After she'd hit her pillow a few times and curled on her side facing the bulkhead, she heard Mort say in a near whisper, "Does she think you're not sure?"

"There's always room for doubt."

Mortimer snorted. "You've got stitches to prove otherwise."

"But they're such nice stitches." Damon chuckled.

"I can bloody well hear you!" Jacqueline snarled back at them.

Chapter Twenty-Four

JACQUELINE WOKE WITH THE sound of hammering and shot out of bed with a growl, but then just stared when she saw what Damon was doing. Putting a latch on the door? On the inside of the door?

"Do you always oversleep?" He'd turned about to give her a curious look. He was wearing a white shirt again, opened halfway down his chest. No blood was on it. He'd even tucked it into his buff-colored pants and tucked those into his long Hessian boots. And his hair was still damp. He'd bathed or had seawater dumped on him, as some sailors did. Was he still getting dressed outside the cabin? She'd like to be awake one morning to find out.

She sat back on the edge of her cot. "I'm still on my London schedule, late-night parties, nothing needing my attention in the morning. And no maid to wake me any sooner."

He grinned. "But I just did that."

"So you did," she mumbled.

He finished what he'd been doing, then opened the door

wide before he left it and went to his desk. That must have been a signal for Jackie, because the boy immediately entered the room and set the food tray on the table. Jacqueline got no greeting from the nervous lad and he left rather quickly, so she went to the table and sat down facing Damon. Only a single plate of eggs and sausage was on the tray, along with a pot of tea and a basket of muffins.

"You've already eaten?"

"Unlike you, I'm an early riser."

It bothered her that he could stand by her bed and watch her sleep in a room filled with sunlight. Did he? No, why would he?

He added as an afterthought, "It's too bad you can't be trusted, Jack. You might otherwise have the freedom of the deck."

Her brows shot up. He'd never tempted her with that sort of freedom before. Why would he now? Bloody carrots again. He did like dangling them. But they both knew he'd never trust her on deck by herself, so saying something like that was cruel of him. Yet he wasn't, she realized, and was a little surprised how sure she was about it. He was many things, but he'd never been cruel to her. Did he mention it because he wished he could trust her? That was an interesting thought. Her strategy of being nice to him might be paying off.

Before she could ask him why he was treating her differently on this voyage, Jackie returned with a fresh bowl of water that he set on the desk in front of Damon. A little steam was coming out of it. Damon had already reached into his drawer for the shaving apparatus he kept under lock and key: razor, tin shaving cup, a short-bristled brush, and a can of soap chips that could be whipped into a lather.

Jackie got one of the little towels from the washstand and dipped it into the hot water, wrung it out, and wrapped it around the lower half of Damon's face, then started to whip up a lather in the cup. He'd apparently done this before, yet the lad looked so nervous Jacqueline ached for him.

She watched them while she finished her breakfast. When she was done, she pointed out, "Jack is frightened to death that he'll nick you."

"How else is the boy to learn without practice?"

"I can do that. I do know how."

"Come here."

She snorted. "Don't pretend you're agreeing to let me wield that razor."

"Indeed not, I have another task in mind for you. But you can give the boy pointers. A little teaching wouldn't be amiss." Damon wiped beads of blood from the nick Jackie just gave him.

She didn't leave her chair, merely told the boy, "Just keep the strokes steady. Any pauses have a chance to cut instead of scrape."

When Jackie was almost finished with the shaving, Damon asked her, "How do you, or more to the point, why would you know how to shave a man?"

"My brother taught me. He teased that I might want to shave a husband someday. I was young enough to be curious about the process."

"Your brother with a look-alike aboard?"

"Yes, Jeremy. My twin brothers aren't old enough to shave yet."

"You have twins in your family?"

"Gilbert and Adam, four years younger than I."

"Any other siblings?"

"Not that we're aware of."

He burst out laughing, then winced when he got nicked again for it. She was already scowling at him. "It's not funny. My uncle Tony had a daughter he didn't know about until she was already full grown. She's well entrenched in the family now, as well as any other bastards that we are aware of. We take care of our own."

"Commendable. Most families don't—at least don't take care of members of the illegitimate sort."

"Yes, swept under the carpet, so to speak. But we're not most families, Bastard."

"Apparently not. And you can use my name, now that you know it."

"I'm still debating whether to or not. The name Bastard suits you so well."

"Not really. My parents were married when I was born."

"To each other?"

That was a bit harsh and even earned her one of his rare frowns. She reminded herself to sheathe her claws. That she was usually painfully blunt wasn't going to help with her be-nice plan.

So she offered nonchalantly, "You know the name *bastard* has more'n one meaning."

"Yes, something foul you'd wipe off your boots," he replied curtly.

"Well, I wouldn't say—"

"Are you apologizing?" He raised a black brow while he waited for her answer. She hated conceding, even with friends, let alone with him! However, she could wave half of a white flag, even if it did cause a slight blush. "I'm dropping the sub-ject, Damon."

He nodded graciously—at least one of them could be!—and stood up and wiped his face. Jackie put everything in the wide bowl and left.

"What was the task you mentioned?"

"At your suggestion, I asked my cook about a cream for my sunburn. You were right, it does hurt a lot more today." He tapped the small jar on his desk before he removed his shirt. "And since it was your idea, I didn't think you'd mind apply-ing it."

She winced at how red he was in the bright light of day. But touch him? The thought flipped her insides a little. It *was* her idea. And it did fit in line with her be-nice-to-him plan. But it might also work with the seduction idea she was still toying with. . . .

She stood up and came around to the back of his chair, deliberately brushing against him as she leaned forward to pick up the jar. She had to clamp her mouth shut on her own gasp when her breast pressed against his shoulder. Maybe skip the seduction part! She hadn't thought that through yet, and it was a double-edged sword if she ended up being the one seduced!

She started to apply the cream to his shoulders, asking softly, "Are you sure you trust me to do this?"

"Mort's hands would do more damage than good. You've got soft hands, Jack."

He trusted her. He had to know with a burn under her fingers, she could make this painful. She didn't. She carefully spread the cream over his back and upper arms, aware that her breathing was getting erratic. She wasn't going to be able to finish, not when this was caressing of the most tender sort and having more effect on her than him! But she was wrong. His head leaned back, rested between her breasts. She could see that his eyes were closed, hear that his breathing was deeper. She was mesmerized for a moment; her hands stilled.

"Don't stop."

She stuck her fingers in the jar again and concentrated on something else. With him so relaxed, this was the perfect opportunity for her to get some answers.

"You've been treating me differently this time. Why?"

He stood up to put both of her creamy hands on his upper chest and held them there, his hands on the back of hers to guide them slowly across his skin. She was staring transfixed at what he was doing, so she didn't see his expression when he said, "Isn't it obvious? I'm attracted to you."

Nonplussed, she yanked her hands back. "You expect me to believe that when you've abducted me twice so you can lure my father to his death—where I'll no doubt die, too? And my poor mother—"

"Now you're jumping to conclusions and thinking the worst of me."

"Why shouldn't I?!"

He started to answer, then closed his mouth, put his shirt back on, and went to the door, telling the guard, "Bring it in."

A sailor carried in a wooden tub. It was barely bigger than the bottom half of a barrel, which it might have been, but it was still a tub.

"You think a bath will calm me down?" she fumed.

"It might if you let me bathe you."

She fried him with her eyes.

He sighed, feigned no doubt, before remarking, "I confess, this is one thing I didn't think ahead on, so no fancy tub for you. But this one will do, yes?"

"I think we had this discussion last night," she retorted.

"That was before I put a latch on the door for you. But be warned, if you think to keep it latched, the door will be removed and there will be no more baths."

She laughed for the first time in front of him. "As tempting as it might be to lock you out, I'm not starving myself this time around, and your door doesn't have a crack wide enough to slide plates through. You won't have to remove the door."

Four sailors came in with filled buckets. Actual sailors, not pirates this time, hair neatly cut, no flamboyance in their clothes, deferential nods in her direction, and not armed. She wondered why Damon had such a mix of men in his crew, but she was too eager to have her bath to ask about that now. When they were done, she walked over to test the water and found that it had been heated, then sucked the water off her finger and laughed again.

"It's salty." She turned to tell Damon. "How's that going to get the salt off me?"

"That extra bucket there has freshwater to rinse with. You've sailed before with your family. You should know freshwater needs to be conserved."

She did know that, she just found it amusing that he was offering ocean water to get rid of the residue of ocean water. But he must have shared the thought with her because he added, "It's worth laughing over, go ahead."

They thought alike too much! That was getting annoying. But he turned to leave and she realized he'd completely distracted her with the tub from getting any answers out of him.

She yelled at his back, "Which of my conclusions are wrong? You've got to tell me something! Are you working for Pierre Lacross?"

He glanced back, but only long enough to say, "Actually, I'm letting him work for me." And the door closed behind him.

Chapter Twenty-Five

CONRAD SHARP STOOD UP to refill their glasses before he remarked to James, "You're pensive tonight. Thinking about George?"

James chuckled at his first mate. "I'm always thinking about George. But traveling with you again, in this particular direction, stirs a lot of old memories."

Connie grinned. "Those were good times. Remember when you had that battle with Short-Dog McGee? A bloody giant he was, and shocked the hell out of us both when he barely even noticed your first punch. I don't think I ever laughed so hard when you were the one that got knocked across the room."

James gave his friend a quelling look. "So he had an iron gut. He didn't have an iron jaw. And I recall you went flying, too, before we figured that out."

"You have to admit it was funny when he dropped to the floor after you gave him a little tap on his chin. Of course with him over a foot taller than you, you had to jump up to deliver that blow!" Connie laughed.

"What I recall is, you dared me to take him on. Not one of your saner moments, old boy."

"But still fun."

"My own best recollection as Captain Hawke was when we bumped into Jeremy in that tavern, and the boy, working off his mum's description of me, asked if I was James Malory."

"I agree that was a great day. I'll never forget the expression on your face when Jeremy confronted you. Once you got over your surprise, you were a proud papa."

"I'm still proud of the boy, rather, the man. I was sorry to disappoint the youngun by not letting him come with us on this voyage. But I'll do anything to protect my children, Jeremy, Jack, Gilbert, Adam, even kill or die for them."

"It's not going to come to that, but in about three weeks when we get to St. Kitts, you'll no doubt be doing some killing."

James's expression darkened. "I anticipate with pleasure getting my hands on that bastard who stole Jack, and Lacross or whichever asinine pirate is pulling his strings."

"You don't regret retiring, Hawke, do you?" Connie asked to lighten the mood.

"No, the only regret I have from that time in my life was that I never kept my promise to Sarah Ross."

"The pretty neighbor you had in Jamaica?"

"Yes."

"But you got her away from that husband she wasn't happy with."

"Not far enough, but that's not what she asked of me."

James had rarely ever made promises back then and certainly not to women. He recalled vividly the day he did. Sarah had brought over a basket of treats that she'd baked for Jeremy. He knew from Jeremy that she often did that when James was away. But he was home that day and she asked if she could speak with him privately, so he walked with her in the garden behind his house. He'd bought the plantation that bordered hers to give Jeremy a home, not to actually become a planter. But he did anyway. The land was simply too fertile to ignore, and at Connie's request they planted crops on most of it, though James insisted on having gardens about the house.

When she didn't speak immediately, James remarked with a smile, "Your boy has been throwing rocks at my house again. I hope you don't think you need to apologize for him."

She gave him a wry smile. "I can't imagine why, but he's afraid of you for some reason. The rock throwing is to show you he's not."

"That's courage, to defy his fear."

"I suppose it is. I've tried to get him to come over here with me so he can see for himself that you're a nice man, but he refuses." At James's laugh, she asked, "What amuses you?"

"I don't think anyone has ever used that word to describe me, Mrs. Ross. But if this isn't what you wanted to talk about . . . ?"

"No, there's something else." She shook her head sadly. "I've decided that I must leave my husband. He and I were never suited and—and his gambling has grown worse, and now there is drinking—"

"Has he hurt you?" James cut in with a snarl.

"Goodness, I see now why you can strike fear into a child. No, it's nothing like that. I was just never happy here, and now it's so much worse. I don't want Damon to end up a pauper."

"Divorce him."

"I wish I could, but my family would never accept that stigma, and I do want to return to them. But my husband won't let me go if I try to take our son with me, and I won't leave without him, so I must leave in secrecy."

"Do you need money for passage?"

"No, but I hope you'll take us with you to England the next time you sail there."

He should have just told her the truth, that he didn't allow women aboard his ship unless they occupied his bed. Instead he'd lied and told her he had no immediate plans to return to England when in fact he was heading back to the homeland the next day to settle his score with Nicholas Eden.

"I was taken with her," James said to Conrad now. "She certainly was beautiful. And I was tempted, but she tugged at something else in me that made me want to help her instead of seducing her. She was so bloody melancholy, yet so gracious."

"But you did help her."

"Not really. I told her I'd get both her and her son to a ship that would take them to England. She came to the house the next day to get that help, but the boy bolted, and I saw bruises on her arms this time. I bloody well wasn't going to leave her there for more abuse. So I insisted she come with me and wait in Port Antonio, where we dropped her off. I promised that when I returned, I would help her get the boy away from his father. But Eden and then George proved too much of a distraction. I never did get back to Jamaica to help her."

"You tried your best. She was a woman of some means. No doubt she made other arrangements, might even have returned to England alone to get her parents' help in retrieving the boy."

"Her husband, Cyril, might have been something of a

wastrel, but from the few times I saw him in the fields with his son, I could see they obviously shared a closeness. So the lad wouldn't have come to harm before she could fetch him away from there." Then James rolled his eyes. "I haven't thought of her in ages. But I wish I'd kept my promise."

Chapter Twenty-Six

JACK OPENED HER EYES but didn't bother to get out of bed because she couldn't bear to spend yet another boring day practically by herself in the cabin. Although Damon had given her books four days ago, they weren't helping to distract her when she'd already read most of them.

Five trunks filled with clothes, soaps, and other amenities had been delivered that day she had her first bath. She'd been both delighted and furious that Damon had planned so well for her kidnapping that he'd even bought a wardrobe for her. Unless he'd stolen it. That was more likely. And she never did thank him. And he'd never explained further what he'd meant when he said Lacross was working for him even though she'd asked several times. Had he been lying? Bragging?

She hadn't seen a lot of Bastard, whom she'd got in the habit of calling Damon in the last four days, either, except to help change his bandage. She had started to enjoy that intimate contact with him, though she'd never let him know it. But the rough seas they'd encountered kept him at the wheel so much, a few nights he hadn't even gotten back to the cabin for his dinner, and when he did, he was too tired for conversation. She'd asked why he didn't have more men capable of manning the wheel, but he'd fallen asleep before she got an answer. Even Mortimer had abandoned her, moving out of the cabin three nights ago, so she couldn't question him, either.

Damon still wasn't letting her see Jeremy, but was allowing them to send notes to each other. She was grateful—and for this she thanked Damon. But she didn't trust him not to read the notes so she'd decided to make them cryptic, and to use phrases and references that only Jeremy would understand. She knew her brother had caught on when in her first note she'd asked him if he looked like Tony after a round at Knighton's or like Boyd. Unfortunately, he'd answered, *Like Boyd,* which meant he had at least one injury that was going to be slow to heal. Then Jeremy suggested she do what Reggie would do to get Nick to attend a ball with her. She'd laughed at that one, but didn't think her brother was really encouraging her to seduce the captain . . . well, at least not physically. But their cousin Reggie did use her feminine charms when she wanted to change her husband's mind about something, so Jacqueline got the idea. Damon had even suggested she try seduction. Did all men think alike?

Considering that Damon did confirm an association with Lacross, even though he'd been utterly vague about it, she let Jeremy know by writing, *Gabby and Drew once met our greatest enemy,* so he'd know Damon had confirmed it. Jeremy's reply to that was *Wish I had a knife so I could start sharpening it.*

Other than the notes, the only interesting things happening were the strong winds making the ship speed through the ocean, and the few times she'd heard sounds of arguing outside the cabin. Mortimer broke up one of those disagreements; Damon broke up another. It was a bit unnerving because it had sounded as if the pirates were trying to get inside the cabin. She'd quickly latched the door until it was quiet out there again.

But this morning, her seventh at sea, yet another argument started outside the cabin just as she was finishing her breakfast, and it sounded like a particularly nasty scuffle. Someone or something was thrown so hard against the wall that even her empty plate rattled on the table. Damon entered the cabin a few moments later, looking disheveled and angry.

"Let's go!" he ordered. She was too confused to move immediately, so he came over and took her hand. "I've decided to keep you at my side. It's the safest place for you."

Safe from what? But she was being pulled along with him out of the cabin, so she couldn't ask yet. She saw blood on the deck, not much, but it alarmed her. He didn't stop until he was at the unmanned wheel and turned it sharply to get them back on course.

He'd placed her in front of him, between him and the wheel. She could feel his chest against her back, though the physical contact didn't seem deliberate and was gone as soon as he was done turning the wheel. But he was still holding the wheel, which left his arms on both sides of her.

Jacqueline's grin showed up immediately. Freedom from that damned cabin—did she care why or that she had to share it with him? And she hadn't needed to make any concessions for it. Wind and sun on her face, the wheel in front of her, barefoot and in britches, this was such familiar territory for her that she didn't need to wonder why she was suddenly so happy.

She watched some of the crew working or loitering on deck. She'd seen nothing of this ship before, except to watch it sail away from St. Kitts. She didn't even know if it was the same ship.

Most of the crew were dressed like normal English sailors, were even barefoot like her. A few weren't; of the more flamboyantly dressed men, one wore an ancient green satin coat, tattered and frayed, and another, a dirty white silk shirt, with a saber hanging from each hip. They gave her such leering looks it caused a slight shiver down her back. Satin Coat even had four pistols stuck around his belt.

"You're allowed to ask why I haven't waited for you to seduce me," Damon said from behind her.

She choked back a laugh. "I don't care why I'm out here, just that I am."

"Really?"

She glanced back to note his frown. "Fine, if you're dying to tell me, go ahead."

"I'm not. We can discuss where you got those britches from instead."

She turned around to face him. He was looking down at the new floral-patterned britches. "I finished making these yesterday out of one of the dresses you supplied."

"Those were expensive dresses."

"Stop trying to evade. Why am I suddenly only safe at your side?"

"The pirates have been lusting after you ever since they saw you dripping wet after Mort and I fished you out of the ocean. They keep trying to get past my guards."

"But you warned them off."

"They're pirates, Jack, the dregs of the Caribbean. They

aren't known for being loyal under any circumstances, but certainly not to me. They're merely along for the ride."

"Explain," she demanded.

"Then let me be blunt. I can continue to fight them off and risk failing or give them a reason to back off for now."

"What reason?"

"They need to think you're sharing my bed."

Her eyes flared. That was a little too blunt. "That's not happening!"

He feigned a sigh. "I wish you wouldn't say that so adamantly, but I did say they only need to think it's so. The pirates know you stabbed me, and two of them saw you sleeping in your own cot rather than my bed. Perhaps if you made an overt gesture of affection toward me out here on the deck, the pirates will think you're my woman."

She gave him a suspicious look. "If this is some convoluted plan you dreamed up just to get me to smack my lips to yours, that's not happening, either."

He grinned. "If I thought that would work, I would have tried it long before now. So, no kiss?"

"Not one."

A much louder feigned sigh. "How disappointing."

Turning the conversation to a safer topic, she asked, "Why don't you train some of your normal crew to man the wheel?"

His answer was surprising. "That my only helmsman is Mr. Thomson, who takes over for me at night, is all that's keeping the pirates from mutiny. They can do most of the work on the ship as they did on the way to London, but they became suspicious when I hired a new crew there, so they don't even bother to help now. But none of them knows how to chart the course or man the wheel, so for now, they think they still need me."

"That's why you won't let me steer? You don't want them to know I can?"

He grinned. "I'm actually looking forward to the day you can prove it, but yes, if you can, I don't want them to know it."

"Mutiny? Really?"

"It's possible sooner or later. They're eager to get home, but they're more eager to get their hands on you. They could just keep Thomson alive to steer for them and tie the wheel down while the wind is steady from one direction or drop the sails when it's not. Poor Thomson won't get much sleep in either case."

"That's sooner. What's later?"

"Once we reach the Caribbean and they start recognizing islands, they'll figure out they can finish the trip without me."

"Then shouldn't we get rid of them before then?"

"Funny you should mention that. . . ."

He didn't elaborate, only laughed. She gritted her teeth. Sometimes he was forthcoming; other times, too damned tight-lipped. But she hated it when she amused him like this without knowing why.

"Seriously, Jack, the best way for you to stay safe is to pretend that you are sharing my bed."

She could indeed, and all sorts of things popped into her head about what he was suggesting. Touching him intimately, under duress, of course, but she still got a little excited over the carte blanche he was giving her.

"Are the pirates on the deck watching us now?" she whispered.

"A handful are."

With no hesitation at all, she moved a little closer to him and raised a hand to his shoulder, slowly moved it up his neck and into his hair. It was softer than she'd imagined. She ran strands of it through her fingers several times before she caressed him behind one ear.

Damon made a sound that told her he liked what she was doing. "If I were steering a carriage instead of a ship, I would have wrecked it by now. You're a wicked woman, Jack."

She threw back her head and laughed.

Chapter Twenty-Seven

JUDITH RAN INTO THE house on Berkeley Square, not waiting for Nathan to help her out of the coach. Henry was in the hall and immediately nodded toward the parlor because that was where Georgina was.

Amy and Katey were on the sofa with her. Amy stood when she saw Judith, saying, "Katey and I moved in with Aunt George to keep her company, since our husbands are both with Uncle James. Welcome back!"

Judith smiled slightly at her cousin and her half sister, but she moved to kneel on the floor in front of Georgina and took the hand that wasn't holding a brandy snifter. She noticed that all three women had snifters. Was this how they were getting through this nightmare?

"You're back from your wedding trip early," Georgina noted in a lackluster tone.

"Mother wasn't going to tell me any of this," Judith replied, guessing Georgina might be a little foxed. "But I suspect she's been as frantic as you are, so she gave in and sent word to me a few days ago. Nathan and I came straight here."

Nathan appeared in the doorway just then, but seeing the room filled only with women, he told Judith, "I'll collect your mother. She'll be annoyed that we're here and she's not."

Judith glanced back to say, "Thank you," and mouthed a kiss for him, then asked Georgina carefully, "How are you faring, Aunt George?"

"Stop looking at my glass," George scolded. "It keeps the tears away."

Judith sighed. Of course Georgina would be as upset as her mother was, if not more so. After all, it was her daughter who had been abducted—again. Judith had just never seen her aunt drinking brandy before.

"Have you heard anything a'tall?" Judith questioned. "Mother didn't tell me much in her note, only that Jack has been kidnapped again and my father sailed off to catch up with Uncle James to tell him."

"Tony should have been back by now," Georgina complained.

"You don't think he would have continued on with Uncle James after he found him?" Amy asked.

"I suppose he might have, but he still would have sent word back with that captain Jason hired for him. Instead they are leaving me in this horrid position of not knowing!"

Judith hesitated before saying, "I hate to mention it, but it's possible they haven't found the fleet yet. If Uncle James followed the sea currents to get to the Caribbean faster, it's unfortunately a very wide lane. Jack taught me that."

"Jack knows too much about sailing," Georgina said with

disapproval. "But are you suggesting Tony might not have even found James yet?"

"No, well, yes. I don't want to lie to you. It's such a wide shipping lane that he could have passed Uncle James's ship without spotting it, though I'm sure his captain is familiar with the lane and is doing diagonal searches."

"Which still could miss the fleet?"

Judith winced with a nod. "My father knows where Uncle James was heading, doesn't he? He can wait for him if he gets there first."

"So I'm to know nothing about what's happening for two to three bloody months?!" Georgina cried. "I'm going to the Caribbean."

"Now, George, you really don't want to do that," Katey said. "By the time you get there, they'll already be on the way home."

"But what's that got to do with Jack?" Judith asked.

"Your mother didn't tell you?" Amy said. "Jack was taken out to sea. Uncle Tony might even come across the ship that has her."

Judith frowned. "No, she didn't mention that part. How did you find out?"

Amy explained, "The night Jack went missing, Percy's mother showed up just before your father left for the ship Jason obtained for him. The old dame told us that her son, who mucks up everything except letting her know where he's going, told her he was heading for some excitement near the docks. But then his driver returned home without him and told Lady Alden about a terrible fight by the water on Wapping Street. He ran away from it just as it started, but he hid behind a tree and watched the mayhem play out to its conclusion, then came straight home to inform her."

"What was the conclusion?"

"The ruffians won. Percy, as well as Jack and Jeremy, were rowed out to a ship in the Thames that then sailed down the river."

Judith gasped. "It wasn't—?"

"It was," Georgina cut in furiously. "I got his note three days ago. But we already suspected who had them, and Tony sailed off to let James know that. The bastard even signed his note 'Bastard.' I suppose he figured we'd know him by the name Jack gave him. He wants James to meet him in St. Kitts, and if they can come to terms, he will release Jack."

Judith sat back on her heels with a curious frown. "That's a very different message than the one in his previous ransom note. No mention of an exchange this time?"

"No, just a meeting, which James won't even know about!" Georgina exclaimed. "Obviously the pirate didn't know that James sailed before he did. Ironically, they'll both end up on St. Kitts, though James probably won't stay there long enough to learn that's where Jack is—unless the pirate gets there first and is watching for him."

"That will be quite the surprise if Bastard approaches James expecting to have a parley with him," Katey said.

"Let's hope not," Amy put in. "Or Uncle James might kill him before he even knows the man has Jack."

Judith sighed. "I confess I'm somewhat relieved to know that it is Bastard who has her—and certainly that the demand is different this time."

Georgina stared at her incredulously. "Have you lost your wits, Judy?"

"No. While Jack reviled the man and professed to hate him, I also got the impression that she found him attractive. There was something she wasn't fessing up to."

Georgina looked horrified. "What the deuce are you suggesting?"

"I don't think she wanted to hate him. She might have said it in disgust, but she called him a polite pirate. And from everything she said, I don't think he wants to hurt her. I just think there's more to this than we know."

"Amy," Georgina said, a note of fury in her voice, "I'm going to need more brandy."

Chapter Twenty-Eight

Y OU LOOK ESPECIALLY BEAUTIFUL in candlelight."

Jacqueline didn't reply, didn't even glance up from her plate.

"I can see four, no, five, different shades of gold in your hair," Damon added.

Jack still said nothing.

"Giving me the silent treatment, are you?"

They were sitting at the table, had just finished eating dinner. Two weeks at sea and she still hadn't clapped eyes on Jeremy. Damon had even stopped allowing them to send notes to each other! Her being nice to Damon hadn't gotten her what she wanted most—a chance to see her brother, even though she'd asked several times. So she'd stopped being nice when Damon no longer needed her help with his wound, which had healed enough to no longer require elaborate bandaging. And he hadn't told her anything more about Lacross or what kind of mission he was running. But he still took her up to the wheel every day, which she had to admit—to herself—she enjoyed.

"That was quite impressive what you did today, saving

Jackie when the pirates tricked him into climbing all the way up to the topsail yard to fix a sail and he ended up hanging there by his hands. You kept him from panicking, Jack, and got him down safely."

"I told you I know how to climb a mast," she snapped.

"Just don't do it again."

She gave him a furious glare. "I want to see my friends!"

"Tell me about your family instead."

"No."

"Was that an adamant no, or do you just need coaxing?"

"Don't ask about them," she said stiffly. "You hurt one of us, you hurt us all. They're every one of them your enemy now, and I'm not going to tell you about your enemies."

"Then I'll tell you what I know. Your mother is an American. It was her family home in Connecticut where we first met. You have three brothers, but no sisters. Your father is so formidable that no single man can fight him and win, and five at once can't even bring him down."

She couldn't help smirking. "He trained with the best. His brother Anthony is the only one who can last a little while in a ring with him."

"Good to know."

"Why? You expect to meet my uncle Tony?" She chuckled. "Actually, I don't doubt you will. They're very close, you know. Uncle Tony often sails with my father, especially when a Malory needs rescuing. And after they get your note, it's very possible that the entire family will sail this time, and there are now too many Malorys to count. Consider yourself warned."

"That might depend on what I wrote this time."

"What did you write?"

"If you and I had a more agreeable relationship, I might tell you." The look he gave her left no doubt that he was talking about bed sharing, and bright color shot up her cheeks, which prompted him to add, "Still not ready to seduce me to your terms?"

"You'd slit your own throat?"

He laughed and stood up to walk to his desk. "I'll think about your request."

Her temper snapped with that answer, shooting her to her feet. "I want to see my friends! You said I could!"

He paused and leaned back against the side of his desk. He seemed a little surprised that she'd shouted those demands, but she didn't care. The silent treatment hadn't gotten her anywhere.

"I've changed my mind about that," he said thoughtfully. "You shouldn't see them while they're still injured."

Still? Still?! She flew at him in a fury and avoided his hand when he reached for her. She got in one solid blow because he hadn't even stood up straight to deal with her. But his confidence cost him. She got a whoosh out of him, a temporary loss of breath, before he flipped her about and put both of his arms around her to keep her from doing any more damage to him. And he was still leaning against the bloody desk!

It reminded her so much of their last voyage together. Every time she'd attacked him, she'd ended up like this, contained by his arms, helpless against his strength. But she was too furious to give up. Her brother had been hurt so much he wasn't close to healed yet. Damon had to pay for that!

Then she heard by her ear in the softest whisper, "Don't stop struggling, Jack. I like holding you."

She stopped.

"Truly? How disappointing."

But he didn't release her! She slammed her head back hard, might have hit his chin. She found his legs next with the soles of her feet and pushed to propel herself away from him, but even that didn't work! But it made him turn and set her on his desk. She got off one swing that missed before he moved in closer, between her legs, and wrapped his arms around her again, trapping hers beneath his.

"Better." He looked down at her. "I can do this all night, you know. Are you sure you want to?"

She answered by knocking her forehead against his upper chest.

"Splendid. Shall we make it even more interesting while we fight?"

He wasn't fighting, he was just holding her. And that meant he was going to kiss her. Warned, she was able to evade his mouth, but that didn't stop him from rubbing his cheek against hers, kissing her neck, licking her ear. She shivered, tried to slide her backside off the desk, but that just rubbed her against him. Oh, God, she wanted him, felt her body come alive with how much she did. It was beyond believable, but it was still happening. And he somehow knew it. But it changed nothing. She'd rather die than give in to those feelings for him.

He was holding her so close to him that the only way she could avoid his lips was to press her cheek to his chest. The compelling embrace was too intimate for her. She had a feeling he'd win if she looked at him. That was the trouble with his face, it was so handsome, it mesmerized her and made her forget, however briefly, she was at war with him. When that happened, it was too easy for him to kiss her, and far, far too easy for her to kiss him back.

She was still turning her head from side to side to avoid

getting kissed. Such a slow, gentle little war that wasn't at all satisfying other than that she was still winning it. She tried to get her arms out from under his until she realized her hands could touch the sides of his back. She dug her nails in so hard she probably poked holes in his shirt. Still he didn't release her, but he picked her up and tossed her on the bed. Before she could get out of the way, he was on top of her.

It happened, of course it would. He easily captured her mouth with the weight of his body holding her down. She still struggled, but the weak attempt ended the moment she felt one of his hands moving over her, softly on her neck, shoulder, down her arm. Such a simple caress, and yet she reacted as if it were torrid. Heat that had nothing to do with blushing permeated her whole body. She was enjoying herself! But before she succumbed completely, she needed to turn this around and take the lead so she could persuade him to let her see Jeremy. She should have done this long ago. Both Damon and Jeremy had suggested it!

She wrapped her arms around his neck and started kissing him passionately. She felt the intensity of his passion rise, too, as he deepened his kisses, teasing her with his tongue, exciting her beyond her wildest imagining. Persuasion had never felt so good, so she wasn't surprised when a moan of pleasure escaped her lips. He pulled back, his turquoise eyes lambent with desire, gazing down at her.

"Damon?" she said breathlessly.

He put his brow to hers and sighed. "It would be too easy to take advantage of you, which is why I won't. When you want me, really want me, I'm yours. But we know that hasn't happened yet. So for now, tell me what brought on the need to hurt me again? You're worried because your brother is still recovering from his injuries?"

That subject was guaranteed to dump cold water on both of them. It certainly worked for her. But he was only guessing that Jeremy was her brother, and she still didn't want to admit to Damon that he had two of her father's children to barter with. So she didn't answer immediately while she ran a few other possibilities through her mind. Jeremy's best friend? Or . . . ?

She finally said, "He was, still is actually, one of my suitors."

"A penniless suitor?"

"I exaggerated. He isn't entirely without means. Only Percy is."

"Too old for you, isn't he?"

"Gads no, did you see how handsome he is?"

"No, actually. The lighting wasn't good that night on the riverfront, and he was too bruised the last time I saw him, but what did you expect? He's a very big man. It took quite a lot to take him down. Now don't start again," Damon added when she stiffened. "I confess, I haven't seen him since last week, so the bruising is probably gone, but I doubt his ribs have fully mended yet."

"Show me."

"No."

"Then I don't believe you."

"But I'm to believe you? That you would bring a suitor to a rendezvous with another suitor?"

"To make the masked mystery man jealous, why not?"

"Because you're too blunt for a ploy like that, Jack."

"In matters of the heart, I can be brutally blunt, I agree. But I also wanted to see which one of them would be more jealous of the other."

"Process of elimination?"

"Exactly."

"But you told me you weren't really whittling down your list, or were you lying when you said you refused to marry this year?"

Did he have to remember everything she'd said? "It was time to figure out which suitors would wait around for me to try again next year, and which ones I should warn not to."

"I thought you warned them all not to pursue you?"

"And have no fun a'tall?" It occurred to her that he was using this conversation just to find out things about her that she wouldn't otherwise admit to. "Get off me."

He put his cheek to hers again and said softly, "We're still in the middle of a battle of sorts."

She snorted. "No, we aren't. I stopped shouting long ago."

"You still did me damage."

"How?" she demanded.

"Your nails."

She winced to herself, having forgotten about that. Served him right, though, for turning that conflict on the desk into an embrace where her hands could reach some part of him. But she wasn't hurting him now and stayed very, very still to get him to release her.

Nonetheless, she couldn't resist softly reminding him, "I hate you."

"I promise you won't always. Does that make a difference?"

"A promise you can't keep? No difference a'tall."

"But already you don't hate me as much. In the Caribbean, yes, your rage was beyond containing after you found that bloody ransom note. You would have killed me then in an instant. But what you feel now is only an echo of what you felt then. Why don't you admit it?"

"You ought to stop thinking you know me when you don't. Now let me up!"

He sighed again, deeply this time. When he inhaled, his chest pressed more tightly against hers, making her nipples peak, which shot heat up her cheeks this time. But he rolled to the side of the bed and got up. She rose more slowly, propping herself up on her elbows, and then was trapped in place, watching him remove his shirt and examine the damage her nails had done. Good God, she had to stop seeing him half-naked like this. Even aware of that, she couldn't manage to look away. But finding him so blatantly masculine, so incredibly attractive, brought her anger back. It wasn't fair!

And why the devil wasn't *he* angry? It certainly wasn't in his tone when he merely said, "I should cut your nails."

"I'd like to see you try."

He glanced back at her with a grin. "That might be fun. But be easy. You've—mostly—been behaving, Jack. Resist being stubborn for once and keep the bed for yourself. As you can tell, it's more comfortable." He put a hand up to forestall her getting back into high dudgeon. "I meant alone. I'll use the cot."

Well, that seduction did get her the bed at least. She laughed to herself before she turned over and got comfortable. But tomorrow, one way or another, she'd see her brother.

Chapter Twenty-Nine

Y OU MIGHT BE GETTING your feet wet on this ship, but if you really want a career on the sea, you'll want to sign on to a ship that's going to see more of the world."

Jacqueline had coaxed Jackie to sit with her on the quarterdeck while she ate the lunch he'd brought. She was giving Damon the cold shoulder again. She'd asked him first thing that morning to take her to her friends. This time she didn't get an answer of any sort.

She had noticed him watching her a lot more today than usual though. And while he asked her a number of questions of little import, he gave up rather quickly at trying to get a response.

"Do your family's ships sail to a lot of countries?" Jackie asked.

She smiled at the boy, but since they weren't quite alone and she didn't want Damon hearing her answer, she whispered, "Skylark Shipping is the name of their company, and yes, they have traders who sail to all parts of the world, even the mysterious Far East." Then she raised her voice to a normal level. "This ship, on the other hand, is doomed. There's no future on it for you other than a nautical education."

"How is it doomed?"

"Even if it doesn't get blown out of the water at the end of this voyage, your captain still doesn't have a long future ahead of him. I'd be surprised if he survives the year."

Jackie didn't appear frightened by her prediction that the ship was doomed. He just looked avidly curious. But he frowned at her prediction for his captain. "That isn't nice, m'lady."

Scolded by a child. She almost laughed. "D'you know why I'm here, Jack?"

"So you do still have a voice?" Damon said directly behind her.

She ignored the pirate, wouldn't even glance back at him. But Jackie couldn't get up fast enough, grabbed Jacqueline's plate, and nearly ran down the stairs. At least she'd finished eating first, but it was surprising how the boy could be afraid of the man, yet loyal to him at the same time.

"You shouldn't fill his ears with your woes," Damon continued. "It's not as if he can quit his job and hie off in indignation on your behalf."

He didn't move away. Had he tied off the wheel? She still wouldn't look back to find out. She waited to hear if he had anything else to say, but after a few silent minutes passed she began to feel a little uneasy. But she refused to ask him what he wanted.

"I don't mind your silence, Jack. It's an improvement over what usually comes out of your mouth."

She recognized testiness when she heard it. He did mind!

And his remark wasn't even true anymore. Since the day she'd gotten out of the cabin, she'd been cordial, mostly, except for last night, but definitely cordial in comparison to how she'd behaved before.

"So don't mistake my offer."

What offer? Ah, temptation to get her to talk. She wasn't falling for that. She got up and headed for the railing at the back of the ship, still without looking at him.

"Come with me," Damon said to her back. "You can talk to your friends—through a locked door. Don't ask for more than that."

She swung around wide-eyed. "Why now?"

"Because the wind is holding steady, so I have a few minutes to accommodate you."

She didn't care why, she was just so surprised and relieved that she would be able to find out how her brother was, from his own mouth. Damon's saying Jeremy was all right didn't make it true.

She followed on his heels, down to the main deck, then down the stairs to the next one. The galley would be down there and the crew quarters, which was where the pirates caroused when they weren't up on deck. She hadn't looked to see how many were up there, but she glanced back up the stairs hoping none would follow. The three-mast vessel was fairly large, so she was surprised there weren't more cabins for ship's officers, though Damon apparently had only one officer, his first mate. But only three doors were down here near the stairs, with another set of stairs that went down to the lowest level.

When he didn't leave her there, she turned to demand, "Some privacy, if you please."

He raised a raven brow. "Did I say that was part of the deal?"

Her brows snapped together. "You didn't say it wasn't. And if this was a deal, you should have said so and given me leeway to bargain!"

"Are you getting angry, Jack?"

She was. Damnit! "Five bloody minutes alone?"

He shook his head. "This is the most dangerous place on the ship for you to be, so you've got two minutes to get yourself reassured. Don't waste it."

"Jack?"

It was Percy asking on the other side of the door. Her raised voice must have drawn him to it. She'd been afraid she'd have to shout through the door to be heard, which would have been the case if the two were chained inside the room.

"Are you being treated well, Percy?"

"The food is rather tasty and they gave me a hammock to sleep in. It's a hellish contraption. I don't recommend it, Jack, 'deed not."

She heard laughter coming closer to the door, then Jeremy's voice next to it: "Percy had trouble figuring out how to stay in it long enough to sleep, but he's managing now. Are you okay, Jack?"

Hearing her brother's voice was such a relief she had to wipe back a few tears. "I'm fine—but not alone. The captain's here. You?"

"Not bad a'tall."

"He was black and blue—"

"Shut up, Percy," Jeremy said, then to her: "The bruising is gone. I promise you I've had worse after a tavern brawl, and you know how many of those I've jumped into."

"But something broke?"

Silence to that question, which had her holding her breath, then finally she asked the man who couldn't keep a secret to save his soul, "Percy?"

"I've kicked him away from the door," Jeremy said, then in exasperation: "Hell's bells, Jack, stop worrying about something so minor. I thought it might be worse, but I didn't have trouble breathing, and now it doesn't bother me to move anymore, so it was probably just a bruised rib that's mended itself." He added angrily, "And the captain lied. He said we'd get out on deck for exercise, but we haven't gotten out even once."

She winced. "That might be because I've been let out." She glared at Damon. "He doesn't want us to talk privately."

"And time's up." Damon took her arm. "You three will see each other soon enough."

She'd heard the growls from the upper deck just as he must have, so she understood why her visit was so short. And she clearly heard someone yell, "Get out o' the bleedin' way, blighter, or yer going tumbling down—"

The threat ended when Damon reached the top step and stood shoulder to shoulder with Mortimer, both with pistols drawn. The first mate had come to guard the top of the stairs to keep four of the pirates on Damon's crew from going down them. The thugs had apparently tried to catch her alone down there with Damon. One shout from them could have brought the rest of the pirates running. . . . She blanched when she realized what could have happened. Yet Damon had risked it just to reassure her that Jeremy was okay? Why the deuce didn't he just let Jeremy out to see her instead of taking her down there? But then she realized why. Because Jeremy, mended, was far more dangerous than four blustering thugs.

Damon had tucked her behind his back as soon as they got up there, so she didn't get a good look at the insistent pirates. But from earlier, she knew they were armed. The one wearing a green coat had four pistols tucked in his belt. Jackie had told her he called himself Bart Satin—no wonder he wouldn't get rid of that atrocious satin coat. She'd seen him too often on the deck, as flamboyant as his brethren, but more malevolent in the way he looked at her, as if the lust he felt wasn't the normal sort, but the deadly sort.

"Missing the rum keg already?" Damon said sarcastically, and waved his arm to the stairs behind him. "By all means, get off my deck."

A couple of them backed off with feigned laughs, but one pirate took the offer and walked past them to get to the stairs. Jacqueline squeezed around Damon's other side, putting herself between him and Mortimer, so the pirate couldn't try to grab her and drag her down the stairs with him.

Ironically, two weeks ago she would have cheered on the pirates if they'd tried to get rid of Damon. But that was before she'd been told they saw her as a prize for themselves. Before she knew Damon was protecting her. Before—fine, she could admit it—before she stopped wanting him dead.

She needed her own weapons, damnit. Living each day with the threat of mutiny hanging over them was starting to wear on her nerves. She'd accepted his story readily because she was so delighted to be out in the sun again. But she was beginning to hope it was all a lie, a staged ploy to make her behave. Damon was a pirate, the thugs were pirates, it was logical to assume they were his crew, but he'd said they weren't. Then why were they with him? And more to the point, why wouldn't he explain to her why they were part of his crew?

She leaned up on tiptoe to see over Damon's and Mort's shoulders why they weren't moving on yet. Ah, Four Pistols was still standing there. Murderous Lust. Bart Satin. Any of those names suited him, but Damon had another when he said, "Once more the instigator, eh?"

"Ye've no right keepin' her to yerself—Cap'n."

Bart said the word "captain" as if it were a slur. And he wasn't moving out of the way. Didn't he know he was standing there alone now?

"If one of your fingers so much as twitches toward your weapons, I will shoot mine," Damon warned. "Please put it to the test. One less of you is fine with me, but having you gone will be even better. Do you think anyone will care, Mort?"

"Bullies only think they're leading the pack," Mortimer replied. "No one will miss this one."

Bart had turned slightly toward the first mate as Mort was speaking, but it was enough for Damon to slam his pistol against Bart's head before the pirate saw it coming. He collapsed at their feet.

Mortimer said drily, "He would have backed down. A bully, yes, but a coward without the pack at his back."

"Don't begrudge me." Damon kicked the man down the stairs. "That was so long overdue, it should have been done before we even reached London. We both knew he was going to be nothing but trouble—and he wasn't backing down soon enough." Then Damon glanced at the other two pirates who were still slowly moving away from him and told them, "He's not dead, more's the pity, but next time he will be. Please relay that to him later."

They said nothing in return and their faces revealed nothing. They could be furious under those blank looks.

But then Mortimer groaned. "I suppose this calls for plan B?"

"For the time being," Damon replied.

Jacqueline merely raised a brow, waiting for an explanation, but when Mortimer said, "Bloody hell," and grabbed her arm, she dug in her heels. She was about to yell at Damon's back as he walked away, but Mortimer put his hand over her mouth so she couldn't!

Chapter Thirty

W E'RE BEING HAILED," CONRAD said, interrupting James's lunch.

James snorted. "Ignore them and have a seat. Your food is getting cold."

"You might want—"

"And don't steer any closer to them. I'm still hoarse from that shouted conversation I had with the barbarians yesterday. I'm not having another this soon."

"It's not your brothers-in-law hailing us."

James raised a brow. "Then who?"

"Come have a look." Conrad headed back out of the cabin.

James pushed his plate aside, grabbed his spyglass, and went out on the deck. He looked to starboard first, where the rest of his fleet were keeping up with him. The *Amphitrite*, Georgina's ship, was the only one within hailing distance. He'd made sure her captain kept abreast of him. It kept Warren and Boyd from trying to converse with him in shouts across the water, but they'd managed it yesterday anyway.

James joined Conrad at the rail on the port side and spotted the ship that had come into view behind them. "How do you know they're hailing?"

"They were flashing mirrors at us until they got our attention."

James trained his spyglass on the ship, which was still some distance away, but he could see there was no name, just an English flag flying from the topmast. No cannon, so it was probably a trader.

"Nothing droll to say?" Conrad asked.

James lowered the spyglass to the other ship's deck and after a moment burst out laughing. "I suppose we can drop the sea anchor and turn about to let him reach us. You could have just told me, Connie, instead of letting me think the Americans were pestering me again."

"I could have." Conrad grinned and sauntered off, whistling a jaunty tune.

JAMES WAITED IMPATIENTLY BESIDE the ladder that was lowered. A good twenty minutes later, the new ship was beside his, a rowboat had been lowered from it, and he was helping his brother aboard. "So you changed your mind after all, Tony?" James was smiling.

Anthony wasn't. "No. Jack's gone, Jeremy's gone, even that dunderhead Percy is gone."

A thunderous expression replaced James's smile. "You thought I had them? I don't. Jack was standing on the wharf with George when I sailed." Then in a growl: "Come with me."

James returned to his cabin and headed straight for the brandy decanter to pour two glasses. He handed Anthony one. "What happened?"

"You left," Anthony said accusingly. "Everything goes to hell when you leave."

"The devil it does."

"It does and only a day after you sailed, too."

"Tony, if you don't spit it out immediately—"

"They were taken out to sea, James, all three of them kidnapped. We suspect it's the same men who took Jack before—"

"What did the ransom note say?"

"I left before one was delivered. We felt the first priority was to let you know."

"Is your captain going back to London?"

"Yes, and—"

Anthony didn't finish because James was already stepping out of his cabin, bellowing, "Connie!"

It took only a few moments for the first mate to run up to the quarterdeck and guess, "You want me to toss him back over the side?"

"As if you could. Tell his captain to return to London immediately and let George know that I'll bring Jack, Jeremy, and Percy home. They're out here somewhere—"

"How the bloody hell did—?"

"I'll explain later. But I want all eyes watching for other ships, and find out if any have passed us this week. I may need to blast one out of the water."

James slammed the door shut before Conrad could delay him with more questions and, pinning his brother with a dark look, said, "Now that I've heard the end, start at the beginning. I need to know how this could happen again."

"I *was* going back to London with my ship," Anthony said testily, having heard James's orders.

"Now you're not, and this is not a good time to argue with me, Tony. If you haven't noticed, I need to kill something."

"Can't very well mistake that look—all right! It was evening, the second day after you sailed. George didn't know Jack wasn't in the house until she didn't show up for dinner. Jack's maid said she'd gone out with Jeremy and that she'd be home for dinner, but she wasn't."

"Leaving without letting George know where and why doesn't sound like my daughter. She'd at least leave a note so George wouldn't worry."

"Even if she thought she'd be home before George noticed her absence?"

"Did anyone look for a note from Jack?"

"The house was searched from top to bottom, first thing. I even looked for the notes from her mysterious suitor who'd been sending her single roses that week in case she'd gone off to meet him. Found the roses in her room, but no sign of his notes."

"There was a fellow at that masked ball they dragged me to who annoyed me because he refused to introduce himself to any of us before he took Jack out to dance. If— I'm going to kill that bastard! Did you search her jewelry box for his notes?"

"Of course."

"And the secret drawer at the bottom of it?"

"What secret drawer?"

James sighed. "Never mind. Jack wouldn't leave a note for George in that, anyway, since George doesn't even know about it."

"But you do?"

"I gave her the box. She started collecting tiny rocks when she was six, ugly little things, but since they sparkled, she thought they were special and hid them all over the house. But the servants started finding them and throwing them away, which led to Jack having quite a few tantrums—bloody hell, never mind all that."

Anthony still rolled his eyes. "You gave your daughter a hiding place for rocks?"

"It was a matter of diplomacy. The servants didn't like it when she screamed at them. It's too bad I never got around to mentioning it to George, since that drawer has a hidden latch in the back to release it. There could be something in that drawer that indicates what Jack was up to."

"Not just Jack. She had cohorts in Jeremy and Percy for whatever—"

James cut in, "What did Henry or Artie say about it? They usually won't let her out the door without finding out where she's going."

"Except when she leaves with family, apparently. Your retired-pirate-turned-butler Artie had the door that day and figured she was fine since she did leave with Jeremy, but George was still worried and sent for me and our brothers and also sent a man off to Jeremy's house. Danny showed up right after I got there to say Jeremy had left home with Percy, so we sent a man to Percy's house. It was late by then and George was crying the whole bloody time, so Jason left to pull some strings and get me a fast ship to come after you. It was a good thing he was still in London to be able to do that. We figured you'd want to know about this as soon as possible."

"When exactly did you sail, Tony?"

"Jason is an excellent string-puller. I was actually going to sail off that very night, well, at least that was the plan. But then Lady Alden arrived to say Percy had told her he was going to the docks for some exciting fun that night. The footman we sent to their house worried her when he told her Jack might be with Percy. She actually came to complain that Malorys were leading her boy astray again. George nearly kicked her back to the curb."

"So going to the docks was their idea? Bloody hell, they were looking for a ship to follow me, after I told them they couldn't and why—"

"No. I wish that's all it was, but it's not that a'tall. We know mostly what happened because Percy's driver came knocking at the door a bit later after being told his lady was at your house. Jeremy, Percy, and Jack didn't even go to the docks, just near them. They drove to the mostly deserted Wapping Street, which runs along the river. They went there to set a trap for someone, but that's all Percy told his driver. However, that 'someone' had set a better trap for them. The driver ran away as soon as the fighting started, and by the time he found a tree to hide behind and he could safely look back, the fight was over due to their opponents' far, far greater numbers, and Percy, Jack, and Jeremy were already being carried to two longboats that took them out to one of the ships anchored in the river. Dozens of the ruffians that had appeared out of nowhere to spring that trap stayed behind to load Percy and Jack's men in the coaches left there and drove off with them. And the ship sailed off. The driver stayed long enough to see that before he found his way home to tell his lady what happened."

"So you don't have the ransom note?"

"No, I waited two days for it to be delivered to your residence, but nothing arrived. Jason decided you needed to be warned about this before you got to the Caribbean so I sailed. He promised to get another ship and send it to St. Kitts with the note as soon as they receive it. So we can wait for it there— or find your children first. I thought I'd spot your fleet long before now, but we had to do a lot of zigzagging to make sure we didn't sail past you without seeing you a'tall."

"Which begs the question, did you pass any other ships heading this way?"

"No, and believe me, we were looking. I hoped I would find them first, play the hero, get them home before you even knew Jack was gone, though I'm not sure how I could have captured them with an unarmed merchantman."

"It's called ramming and it works fairly well."

"I suppose my captain would have suggested that if we'd found them first. I confess I do want to get my hands on Bastard, if it is Bastard this time. I know we've all assumed it is, but what d'you think?"

"It sounds like it, but that doesn't make it a certainty. Bloody hell, I wish you'd waited for the note so I wouldn't need to assume." James suddenly sighed. "But Jason was right to send you ahead. It's far better to know what's happened, so don't doubt that I'm glad you're here."

"There's no place I'd rather be at a time like this than standing by your side, Brother." Anthony's tone was darkly serious. "I want to catch those blackguards as much as you do. We will, never doubt it."

"I know, but it's going to be hell in the meantime."

Anthony nodded in agreement. "Then I'll do my best to distract you. I actually thought I'd already be here, you know. When you got me foxed the night before you sailed, I was sure you were going to shanghai me. Ros even thought so and had a bag packed for me."

"She did suggest it to me. She was worried that you would

be miserable with me gone as well as Judy off on her wedding trip."

"So why didn't you?"

"Because this trip was—will take more'n a couple months, while Judith will be back from her trip long before then. You would have been climbing the bloody walls if you weren't there to be assured she's still happy when she gets back."

"Oh, but now it's okay for me to climb walls? Actually—" Anthony bolted out of the cabin, but stopped in his tracks when he saw the ship he'd arrived on was no longer next to *The Maiden George*. It had tacked to the east to circle around for the return to London and was already far away.

"Suck it up, dear boy," James, beside him, said. "You just claimed to want a piece of Bastard. You won't get it unless you stay with me. And your daughter was in love. You know very well she's going to come home just as happy as she was when she left on her trip."

Anthony elbowed James. "I was joking, old man. Told you I'd be a distraction for you. Did it work?"

James snorted. "Yes."

"But once we have the younguns back, you can remind me that my baby returned home as happy as she was on her wedding day."

James didn't agree to that; he mentioned instead, "I still have that boxing ring in the hold that Nathan built me."

"An excellent—" After a glance at James, Anthony amended, "Actually, if you don't mind, I'll wait until you stop looking like you need to murder someone."

James sighed. "All right, but only because Ros expects me to bring you home."

Chapter Thirty-One

Y OU DIDN'T NEED TO manhandle me," Jacqueline growled as soon as Mortimer released her. "A simple explanation would have sufficed."

"That was a really risky thing for him to do, taking you down there with most of the pirates on that lower deck. And look where that's got us, me punished and you—whatever you are."

"How are you punished?"

"Getting stuck with you for the rest of the day, that's how."

She snorted. The man truly didn't like her. As if she cared. But she was back inside Damon's cabin, back behind a locked door, and that was intolerable, especially since the danger was already over. Or was it?

"What the devil is the plan you mentioned?"

He didn't answer. He'd gone over to Damon's desk to open the locked drawer and pulled four pistols from it. He sat down at the desk to check that they were loaded.

She waited for him to get around to answering when he was

done, but when he didn't, she demanded, "Take me to Damon so I can ask him."

"You bedevil him enough."

"I want to know—!"

"Good God, woman, shut up. You are the most stubborn, ill-tempered she-devil I've ever—"

"You're too kind," she cut in sweetly as she moved to a chair at the table and sat down facing him.

He was giving her a fierce look. "I'm only going to tell you this once. Behave, be very quiet, and you can probably go back on deck tomorrow—if we survive the day."

"What's that supposed to mean?" Again he was ignoring her, which made her yell, "I want to know why we're being punished!"

"Damnit, lower your voice! And stop asking questions. You aren't even being punished. You've got things to do in here now. I know, because I helped find some of those bloody books he wanted for you."

"How would you like it if you were buried in a black hole?"

"Eh? There's nothing dark about these quarters."

"I meant the hole you'll be in after I kill you," she said nastily.

"Save your threats for someone who cares. If you make me shut you up, no one's going to like that, least of all me, so for the last time, be quiet."

"For the last time, tell me why I need to be or get Damon in here to tell me!"

He got up to do as she asked. Finally! But he didn't cross the room to leave to get Damon. He took her by surprise instead, yanking her out of her chair and setting off all sorts of warning bells in her mind so her reaction was normal—for her. And the punch caught him nicely near his eye before she dodged out of the way of any retaliation. But his arms were just as long as Damon's. He got a handful of her hair and pulled her over to her cot and shoved her facedown on it.

"You couldn't make this easy, eh?" Mortimer growled as he put a knee in the center of her back. "How in hell he puts up with you is a bloody mystery. I wouldn't. I'd chain you to the damn bulkhead!"

"And that surprises me?" she hissed, then louder when he got her hands together and started wrapping a rope around them, "What are you doing?!"

"Following orders," he smirked.

"Liar! He wouldn't tell you to do this to me!"

She would have railed more at him, but he stuck a wadded cloth in her mouth. She started to push it out with her tongue, but he finished off the gag with another strip of cloth, tying it behind her head, catching enough of her hair in it to bring tears to her eyes.

When he was done, he leaned down near her head to say angrily, "No, he wouldn't, but I had orders to keep you quiet, even warned you to shut up, twice, but you just wouldn't listen, would you? Count yourself lucky I didn't return the black eye you just gave me."

He tucked the four pistols in his belt and left, locking the door behind him. She waited until she heard the door close before she turned over and maneuvered her feet over the side of the cot to stand up. At least Mortimer hadn't tied her ankles, too. Damned man could have just answered her questions instead of doing this!

She glared at the door next, wishing she could latch it to lock them all out of the cabin, but the latch was too high for her bound hands to reach. She ended up sitting uncomfortably in Damon's chair so he'd get the full brunt of her murderous gaze when he opened the door.

But it was a long time before that happened. When it did, all Damon did was tsk at the look she was giving him. Jackie followed him in with their dinner tray, but hurriedly left.

Damon locked the door again before he said, "Mort can be a clod sometimes, but I did get an earful about your retaliation, so I'm going to assume your blackening one eye is enough for today?"

Damon walked toward her as he asked that. Considering her scalp was still smarting, she disagreed, but she couldn't say so yet due to the gag and couldn't even shake her head no without it hurting even more. And then he swore when he was standing behind her and could see for himself how entangled her hair was.

"I apologize for my friend. He had limited options to keep you quiet. This was the harmless one, or so it was supposed to be. To be fair, I highly doubt Mortimer realized that he tangled your hair in this knot. It will take a few minutes to undo."

It took longer than that, he was being so careful in untying the knot without pulling out any more hair. The second the tied strip came loose, his fingers began to massage her scalp. It felt heavenly, so good, that she was quite tardy in spitting out the rest of the gag or recalling that she still didn't have the use of her hands. But he untied them a moment later.

"So has Mort been added to your kill-on-sight list?"

She could lean back in his chair now and did so as she rubbed her chafed wrists. "An-eye-for-an-eye style of revenge would mean plucking out every one of the hairs on his head."

Damon chuckled. "Not quite even, but—so, the black eye is sufficient?"

"I suppose."

He came around to partially lean on the side of his desk, facing her, before he asked, "Would it be sufficient payback to me?"

"Certainly not," she huffed. "Your tally of transgressions is far too long. And it's going to get you hung—or worse."

"There's worse?" He raised a dark brow. "And here I thought we'd moved beyond that."

"Whatever would make you think that?" she asked with feigned sweetness.

"You don't kiss me like you want me dead, Jack."

She didn't have an excuse for that. She felt herself blushing but said sharply, "Nothing about this was harmless. The harmless approach would have been to explain to me the necessity for quiet. What the hell was plan B?"

"A precaution. I made a move today that I'm not ready yet to back up. There was a possibility that it might have provoked the pirates to make their move now, before I'm ready for it. I wanted you safe in case they came up en masse for a fight. Your making noise would have incited them further because you're what they want. Your yelling and screaming would have given them an excuse to break in and 'rescue' you. You could have stayed quiet, you know."

"Why couldn't Mortimer just tell me that?!"

"He doesn't know how far we've progressed. He probably thought I wouldn't want you to know."

She was speechless, but only for a moment. "Whatever progress you think we've made has been reversed really far today. You could have told me what was going on. You could have told him that he could have told me! Instead I spent the day gagged and with my hands tied!"

"I apologize—"

"Not helping!"

"This is odd thanks for allowing you that visit today, which is directly responsible for what you're in a snit about now. Are you at least reassured that they're not dying?"

"They'd say they're fine even if they're bleeding to death."

"You know him that well?"

She frowned that he was fixated on one when she'd just mentioned both. "No, but I know they're chivalrous, and men like that will lie to keep a woman from worrying. So I'm only somewhat reassured. I'd still like to actually see them both."

"I don't want to watch you crying over a—suitor."

It was apparent in that moment that he knew he had her brother Jeremy. The pause was too significant. Bloody hell! But she refused to confirm it. He wasn't going to get to gloat to her if she could help it. So she left his chair if that's what he was waiting for and moved to the table to ignore him.

But she couldn't do that when she was still bristling over what had happened with the pirates after she'd spoken with Jeremy and Percy. "I don't believe they're all against you when you work for the same man and share the same goal. It's just Bart Satin who appears to be causing all the trouble for you."

"Your thinking that I'm loyal to that pirate is a misconception."

"Then take me back to London now, before you end up dying over this!"

"Would you care?"

It was a long moment—she actually had to think about it first!—before she said, "Of course not. But if you don't favor Lacross, then why are we here!?"

"For a different reason this time, so leave it go. You'll have answers soon enough."

He left the cabin, clearly telling her that she couldn't pull the information out of him until he was ready. But what was he waiting for?

Chapter Thirty-Two

S NUG BETWEEN THE WHEEL and Damon's broad chest again, Jacqueline was somewhat mollified over what had transpired yesterday. A freshwater bath that morning instead of the usual ocean water had helped, his way of saying he was sorry, she supposed. Still, just to be ornery, she'd left her hair unbound today so it would flit around his face in the wind. Yet all it got her was his body pressed firmly to her back and buttocks, and his chin resting on top of her head.

She laughed. "Okay, I get the point." She gathered her hair over one shoulder and tried to braid it, which wasn't easy in the wind. "An English gentleman would simply have asked me to stop behaving like a hoyden."

"I doubt a gentleman would be that blunt with you."

She grinned. "Probably not. Definitely not if he's courting me."

"You think I'm English?"

She blinked and turned around to face him now that he'd moved back to his usual position. She'd assumed he was

English, but she couldn't recall ever asking him to confirm it. "Aren't you?"

"Born of English parents, raised in the islands, but sent to England to finish my schooling. I suppose I am."

She chuckled. "It was beginning to sound as if you weren't sure. Did you like living in the islands? By the way, which island did you live on? Swimming in warm waters on hot days? Riding on beaches? Pretending to kill—your own kind?"

He laughed at the last question, her reference to his previous confession that, as children, he and Mortimer had pretended to slay pirates instead of dragons. But he only answered one of her questions. "I've never cared much for riding. My mother got me a pony when I was a child, but then she left and I outgrew it."

"That's an odd way to say she passed on. How old were you?"

"Seven. But I don't know if she's dead or alive. She ran off with our neighbor and we never saw her again."

Turning around, she saw the anger on his face. She so rarely saw him angry. Frustrated, yes, extremely so, but never this sort of cold, quiet anger.

"I've never hated anyone so much."

She wished he hadn't added that. She'd never known anyone who hated his or her own mother. It must be an abhorrent emotion to harbor, a contradiction of nature, and it stirred— she realized she felt sorry for him! She almost touched his cheek to comfort him before she caught herself and squashed the urge.

She immediately shook off that ridiculous moment of compassion and changed the subject. "What about your father? Is he still in the islands?"

"Yes."

It was said sadly, which was better than his anger, but still curious. Other than his annoying good humor, and that brief moment of coldness over his mother's desertion, he didn't usually show her any other feelings.

"Tell me about him?"

"We were close, and he was very supportive after my mother deserted us. He used to drink, perhaps a little too much, but that stopped completely after she was gone. He came up with all sorts of distractions to keep me from thinking about it, but I think they were meant to distract him as well. We loved her. I wonder sometimes if I would have grown up bitter and filled with rage if not for him."

"He sounds like a wonderful man."

"He is."

That didn't account for the sadness he'd revealed when his father was first mentioned. Damon could just miss him, she supposed, but if so, why didn't he just say that?

"Do you have family in England, too?"

"Yes."

That reply even produced a sigh! What the devil? "They've disowned you, haven't they, on both sides of the ocean?" she guessed. "And no wonder, considering the occupation you've taken up."

He rolled his eyes at her. "Wrong on both counts. And stealing beautiful women isn't an occupation, Jack."

She snorted. "Ah, yes, this must be what you call a minor offense. That is what you said at the ball, wasn't it? That you'd only ever broken the law one time and it was a minor offense because no one got hurt?"

"You're here merely as a means to an end, an important end."

All humor gone, she said furiously, "That's what you call killing my father?"

"I'm not the one who wants him dead." Damon's tone turned sharp. "How much do you really know about your father's past?"

She stiffened, wondering what he was implying. He couldn't know about her father's days on the high seas when he'd been a gentleman pirate. No one outside the family knew about that.

She prevaricated, reminding him, "I already told you he used to be one of London's most notorious rakes, which resulted in countless duels because of it."

"What about his ten-year absence from home? Was that because his family disowned him?"

"You've been listening to London gossip, haven't you?" she scoffed.

"There was quite a bit of it that night at the ball, all about him."

"You can't believe everything you get from the gossip mills."

"Except you just confirmed that some of it is true. And answer me this: Do you think I would harm your father when I want you as much as I do?"

Her cheeks lit up with warm color, her breathing stopped.

And it was in his eyes, his beautiful eyes, suddenly incredibly sensual. He couldn't do this to her again! Couldn't leave her wishing they weren't enemies! How dare he stir up her passions like this by saying something that—that provocative?

Chapter Thirty-Three

Damon watched her reaction carefully. He shouldn't have been so explicit, and yet, he'd definitely caught her off guard. Jack was an open book when it came to her emotions. She could change her tone, she could pretend things she didn't feel, but when it came to the rage she felt for him, she was never shy about sharing that. But they'd shared that brief moment of passion before she wrapped up her feelings in anger. But it was too soon. If she succumbed now before this played out, she'd have even more reason to hate him. But he hadn't yet figured out how he could get around his intention to escort her father to a prison cell.

She wasn't going to forgive him for that, any more than she would if he did what she thought he intended to do. It wouldn't matter that her father was guilty of piracy and had escaped justice until now. She would see it as a betrayal and it would be. But he hadn't anticipated wanting her this strongly, or wishing they could have met under different circumstances. And the more time he spent with her, the more he was conflicted. But he wasn't going to take advantage of her passionate feelings for him before she knew the whole truth. That would make him as bad as she thought him to be.

He was relieved when she walked away from him to stand at the railing behind him. It was far enough away to make any further conversation difficult, yet she couldn't get off the quarterdeck without walking past him. At least she didn't try to use his revelation about wanting her against him. Jack Malory seductive would be his undoing.

He could no longer wait to get Jack and her brother on his side. They were getting too close to the Caribbean, where he would have his parley with their father. Lacross's men had to be dealt with before then, before they got anywhere near James Malory. Jack's brother could certainly help with that, but not unless Damon explained a few key elements of his true mission to Jeremy and Jack. But not all. Damon wondered if the two siblings even knew that their father used to be a notorious pirate?

It had been a shock to spot Captain Hawke in London four years ago when Damon and Mortimer were celebrating the end of the university term. Barely changed, still big and menacing, but dressed like a gentleman now. The very man who'd taken his mother away from him and his father. And he'd seen it happen.

He had been seven years old at the time. The day had been hot and sultry despite the trade winds, and his mother had been behaving so nervously. She'd been dressed to go to town, even had a large bag with her, but all she'd told him was "We're going for a walk."

He loved walking with her, spending time with her. She always smelled wonderful and looked so pretty in her fancy dresses. She'd taught him to read, to ride, to swim. His father wanted to make a planter of him, but she never let Damon forget that he was a gentleman first, and gentlemen didn't tend the soil, they had workers to do that. He knew his father spent almost all his time in the fields alongside his workers because he simply loved to be outside and make things grow. Damon's mother never scolded him for joining his father because she understood that planting was fun for a boy his age. But he enjoyed walking with her the most, down their long drive, sometimes to town, or along the beach, but they'd never before walked through the sugarcane fields between their plantation and their neighbor's, at least not when the cane was tall—or when the neighbor was at home.

Damon's parents had told him that Captain Hawke was a planter, but Damon thought he looked like a real pirate.

Mortimer thought so, too. The man was big and muscular and never had a friendly countenance. Damon had never seen another man who looked as menacing as his neighbor did. But Mortimer wouldn't go with him to throw rocks at the pirate's house to prove they weren't afraid of him. Damon did that on his own. He just wanted the man to go away, back to sea, back to pirating elsewhere, and never come back. He got that wish, but the consequences had been devastating.

But that day, he didn't realize where his mother was hurrying to until he saw that giant neighbor of theirs waiting for them on his porch. Damon thought she was taking him there so the pirate could punish him for breaking his windows. His seven-year-old imagination went wild, envisioning the horrible tortures Captain Hawke had planned for him.

Damon balked. "No!"

"Damon, please, we need to hurry."

"You can't turn me over to him!"

"What? No, you mis—"

He'd already broken away from his mother and was running back home. She yelled after him, but he wouldn't stop even though he heard the tears in her voice when she called his name, which brought tears to his eyes, too, yet he couldn't go back to face that man.

Crying, she screamed a promise that she would come back for him. At least he thought she did, hoped she did, but he wouldn't turn around to find out for certain. Because of him.

His mother left with the man. And she never came back. His father was just as devastated by her desertion as Damon was, but he was furious, too, and swore he'd kill Hawke when he returned. Year after year, Damon waited for her to come back for him, but she never did. Neither did Hawke or his son, whom Damon had only ever seen a couple of times. Nor would they return, because the very next year, the captain's plantation was sold by an agent. Only years later did Damon suspect Hawke had seduced his mother into leaving her family. Why else would she abandon them? That's when he started to hate Captain Hawke.

But he should never have approached the man the night he saw him again in London four years ago, because he hadn't been sober or able to control his feelings of suspicion and hatred for the man. All he'd done was shout, "Where is my mother?" Actually, he'd done more, he'd also grabbed Hawke's lapels, which got him a single punch that knocked him on his arse and landed him in the hospital. When he woke up, a doctor was poking at him and telling him that he'd cracked his head in a fall.

He'd searched for Hawke again every chance he got when he was able to leave Oxford, but no one knew the name and Damon never saw him again. Until the day Damon and Mortimer were sailing home to the islands. Damon had been waiting for a hackney outside his hotel when he spotted Hawke and another man in a carriage. He'd had to run through the streets to keep up with them. They'd stopped at a sporting hall and gone inside. He'd followed them. The excited chatter and wagers flying around the hall revealed they were brothers, lords, and that the man he'd known only as Captain Hawke was actually James Malory, Viscount Ryding.

Damon had watched the fight for a few minutes. It had been brutal. He'd questioned the young gentlemen around him and learned that Malory lived with his wife and children in Berkeley Square. He'd married Damon's mother?! Damon had immediately gone to find the house and asked to see James's wife, but a rude butler had slammed the door shut in his face after saying, "Lady Georgina ain't receiving."

But Georgina wasn't his mother's name. Devastated once again to be unable to find out what had happened to his mother, and out of time with his ship soon sailing, he knew his questions would have to wait until he returned to England. But what he found when he got home to Jamaica changed all that.

"I thought you two were getting along, but it looks like she's giving you the cold shoulder." Mortimer joined him at the wheel, but nodded toward Jacqueline's back. "I got the black eye, she didn't, so I'm not apologizing to her."

"No, she's over that . . . well, she might not be if she sees you," Damon said quietly. "But we need to step things up before the winds turn warm."

"And her father catches up to us."

"He's going to be a week or two behind us, he's not catching up, we'll end up waiting for him in St. Kitts."

"I'll skip that first meeting, if it's all the same to you, now that we know he really was a pirate back then, not just what we assumed when we were younguns."

Damon grinned. "Lacross said that Hawke was worse than he ever was, which is hard to imagine, considering we know what he did to Andrew."

Mortimer scoffed. "I wouldn't believe a word out of that old pirate's mouth. He just wants to kill the man responsible for defeating him and tossing him in prison. And you, hating Hawke as you do, are more than willing to help Lacross get his wish."

"That was then—"

"You mean before you met his pretty daughter."

Damon gave his friend a quelling look. "Don't mix the issues."

"They're already mixed."

"No, they aren't. I do this for only one reason. My father. But I don't expect to have to fight Malory to get him into Warden Bennett's office. I can think of other ways to do that. Have you found out how many of the new men we can count on?"

"Only three. I think the others are scared of the pirates and won't do anything other than hide when the fighting starts. I don't think they'll join in on the other side, though."

"So that's five of us, and hopefully Jack's brother and possibly his friend. Still not good odds without a decent plan."

"So we did capture her brother? I'm surprised she gave that up."

"She didn't. It just became obvious the more she lied about it."

"Lied about what?" Jacqueline asked as she approached.

She was glaring at Mortimer, who snorted at her in response and left. Damon decided to get her attention on something else. "Perhaps a dress tonight for dinner? That's if you have any left that you haven't ripped up for britches?"

"I believe we've had this discussion about my preferences. And I've only ripped up one. Jackie packed thread to adjust his pants in case he outgrew them before reaching land again, but I already used up most of it."

Damon shrugged. "I merely thought you might want to look a little more ladylike for our guests this evening."

Chapter Thirty-Four

JACQUELINE DIDN'T ASK, DIDN'T need to. No one was aboard other than Jeremy and Percy that Damon would call "our guests." He'd tied off the wheel and escorted her to the cabin so she could have her bath and prepare herself—hours before dinner. Did he think she was like other debutantes who spent all day primping for an event? Did he even know any other debutantes? She'd laughed anyway, couldn't help it, she was so excited.

Damon arrived first near the dinner hour with a full bottle of brandy in hand, but paused to sweep his eyes over her and the deep rose gown she'd picked for the occasion. He might have ordered her clothes in the right sizes, but he hadn't specified debutante colors to the dressmaker.

"Magnificently feminine again." He grinned. "But I confess I was getting used to your shapely britches."

"The dress was your idea."

"Not for me, but for your friends." He put the bottle on his desk, then continued on to his clothes chest and donned a black jacket. With his white shirt and black trousers, and his black hair still wind-tossed about his shoulders, he looked rather dashing.

He moved back to his desk but merely leaned against it, his eyes moving slowly over her again. "And thank you for ignoring the evening gown. I'm not sure I could have survived that one."

She blushed slightly since she knew what he was referring to. The single evening gown in the trunk would have revealed far too much bosom, which she wasn't willing to share with him.

Percy came through the open door next. She was pleased to see him looking splendid, though definitely rumpled with no valet to attend to his attire, the same attire he'd been wearing in London. At least the wrinkles in his clothing indicated that he and her brother had been allowed to wash their clothes from time to time.

With a slight bow to Damon, Percy quipped, "My condolences, Captain Reeves."

"For?" Damon asked.

Percy gave Jack a quick hug before stating, "For the day her father gets his hands on you. Brutal with his fists, unparalleled with a pistol. I daresay you won't—"

"I get the idea," Damon cut in drily.

Jacqueline, frowning over what Percy had just called Damon, said, "You told him your last name but you wouldn't tell me? Or is that not your real name?"

"It is now."

She rolled her eyes at Damon's cryptic reply. Typical name-changing pirate, she guessed. But then Jeremy arrived, and even though he looked hale and hearty, she still started crying as she ran to put her arms around him, careful not to squeeze hard in case his ribs were still sore. He'd left his wrinkled jacket behind in his cabin. His hair was loose and so much longer that now he looked more the pirate than a London gentleman.

Jeremy whispered to her, "Is our presence the result of your trying the Reggie approach? Or because he came by last night and saw that my bruises have faded?"

"He was using your wounds as an excuse to keep me from actually seeing you."

"Ah, so that's why he said you won't cry now when you see me. Well, you weren't supposed to." Jeremy chuckled, wiping a tear from her cheek.

"It's such a relief to see you've recovered, Jer."

But behind them she heard Damon say, "That settles that, brother after all. I'm glad to see we can dispense with the lies."

She swung around. "So you were just humoring me by not calling me a liar?"

"I did want to applaud a few times because you delivered your lines so well, Jack. But be easy. Nothing has changed other than this is a night for truths. Shall we?" Damon waved a hand toward the table and walked over to it.

Jack turned back to Jeremy first and gave him a significant look, saying softly, "I had hoped we could take the ship from him and sail home, but that was before I saw how many men are on it."

"I'd rather continue on to save Father, but what truths is he talking about?"

"I don't know, but he's implied we're not here for the reason we think."

Jeremy chucked her chin with a grin. "Then let's hear him out and play it by ear."

She nodded and took her usual seat at the table. Jeremy and

Percy sat on the sides nearest her, which left Damon isolated at the other end. But he hadn't sat down yet. He went to the door to signal they were ready for the meal.

Jackie had the help of two sailors tonight in bringing everything in. A bottle of wine, glasses, four plates filled with food, and a tray of desserts. Four? Jack realized that Mortimer wasn't coming to help keep the peace. No doubt guards were standing outside the opened door to do that. Then Damon closed the door and took his seat. He was obviously confident that he could manage all three of them if it came to that, which was possible considering how damned strong and fast he was. Then again, he could simply be armed. A single pistol would stay their hands.

"Any relation to the East Sussex Reeveses?" Percy asked Damon as Jackie filled his glass.

"It's just a fake name, Percy," Jacqueline put in.

"No, it's my legal name," Damon said. "It was a stipulation of my great-grandfather's will that I take the family name to receive his estate. Yes, those Reeveses, Lord Percival."

"Know the property, 'deed I do," Percy mentioned. "Lovely location and quite large as I recall, though that was years ago. Went there as a child with my mum. Was there a title involved?"

"No, he was a second son. The titles are on my grandmother's side. She's the only relative I was able to locate while I was in England. Unfortunately, she's quite tetched with the loss of her memories, doesn't recognize her own servants, didn't even remember her own daughter, my mother. And she swears she doesn't have a grandson, so after my first visit with her I have been repeatedly turned away from the house that's now mine. Quite frustrating."

The wry smile had Percy say, "I had a great-aunt like that. She would fire servants just because she didn't recognize them."

"As does my grandmother."

"Then how did you find out about the inheritance?"

"There was one old servant who'd been there long enough to know my mother and refused to leave when she kept getting fired. She despised me without reason and wouldn't answer a single question I had about the family, but apparently, she sent word to the family's solicitor to complain about my first visit, and he tracked me down."

"Which begs the question," Jeremy said drily, "if what you just said is true, what are you doing here on a pirate ship, working for a pirate, and abducting a young lady and two noblemen?"

"I'm temporarily committed to another path."

Jacqueline waited for him to say more and was incredulous when he didn't. "I could have sworn you said this was a night for truths."

"The night is young."

She probably looked as angry as she was at his evasion because Jeremy nodded toward the bottle of brandy on the desk, saying to Damon, "How about a drinking contest after dinner, mate? First man to pass out loses."

"But you can't be beat at that game, old chap," Percy reminded Jeremy. "Everyone knows it."

"He didn't," Jeremy growled at their friend.

Percy looked so abashed that Jack refrained from kicking him. Percy let information roll off his tongue without the first thought to consequences and always had. This part of his endearing charm was usually amusing—at least for anyone not keeping the secrets he inadvertently revealed.

Damon laughed at the byplay. "Just out of curiosity, what prize were you after, Malory?"

"Full freedom aboard your ship."

"And the prize you were willing to offer me?"

Jeremy shot to his feet. "Not beating the living hell out of you."

Damon didn't stand up as well, but he did raise a brow. "So is that contest still on the table?"

"No, it's not," Jacqueline interjected sharply, and motioned to Jeremy to sit back down. "At least not tonight. Can we first hear why Damon invited you here?"

"Yes, you can," Damon said. "We're nearly to the Caribbean. I can no longer wait to form an alliance with the three of you."

Chapter Thirty-Five

JEREMY LAUGHED. "I'M SORRY, did you expect a response to that other than laughter?"

Jacqueline had been about to laugh, too, but she frowned instead, guessing that Damon had suggested an alliance because he was truly worried about the pirates on his crew.

"I'm not out to harm Jack or your father," Damon assured Jeremy.

"Liar, you want him dead!" Jeremy retorted.

"I never wanted him dead. I just have other objectives that involve him. Jack's presence was and is nothing more than a means to an end for me, a way of luring your father into helping me put Lacross back in prison."

Jacqueline's anger flared. "When you took me from Bridgeport, you had every intention of turning me over to Pierre Lacross! If you try to deny that, we're done talking."

"I had no intention of turning you over to them. That was part of Catherine and her father's plan, and I'd been assured you wouldn't be hurt, but I had doubts from the start. I just wanted to draw your father to Lacross's hideaway—"

"Which is located where?" Jeremy interjected.

Damon ignored his question. "At the time, I didn't really care who won that fight, I just expected there would be a fight, not a willing surrender that would have been a slaughter. Mort was to get you off the ship in St. Kitts while I took Catherine ashore so she wouldn't notice. But you escaped on your own before he could help you."

"If that's true, you wouldn't have sunk all those ships in Bridgeport!" Jacqueline said.

"And if I didn't, how do you think the situation would have progressed? I didn't want to end up dead or imprisoned after a fight at sea with your relatives. Besides, my intent was just to get your father's attention."

"Now I know you're lying," Jack said. "You had nearly a week to tell me that and didn't."

"You were too angry, and all your anger was directed at me. I didn't know you well enough then not to think you might scream that I was a traitor just to get even with me, and to hell with the consequences."

Jeremy asked her, "Would you have done that?"

"Possibly," she mumbled. "I wasn't exactly thinking clearly during that kidnapping."

Jeremy pointed out to Damon, "Why would it matter at that point if Catherine knew you weren't on their side—unless you still were?"

"Because until Lacross is either killed or captured, I still need the pirate to think I am helping him. When I took Jack away from Bridgeport, I expected your family to follow us straight to Lacross and finish him off. Instead Catherine blamed me for letting Jack go, I was thrown in their dungeon, and your father didn't show up as I'd hoped."

Jacqueline sighed. "And yet here we are once again your hostages, and you wonder why it's impossible to believe you?"

"I agree," Jeremy said angrily. "You're painting yourself pretty clean in all of this, mate, yet once again you're leading my father to his death."

"I never wanted him dead," Damon said just as angrily this time. "But I have other objectives that involve him."

"Which are?"

Jacqueline raised a brow when Damon refused to answer. Because he was angry now? What the devil did he expect?

"Did you really think this would be an easy conversation and that we wouldn't be skeptical of what you're telling us?" she asked Damon. "All things considered, you haven't even got to the heart of the matter yet and revealed what your objectives are regarding our father. Getting angry because we still have valid doubts is a bit pointless, don't you think? Why don't we eat this meal before it gets cold, then you can finish your explanation over dessert?"

Percy looked down at his empty plate. "Was I supposed to wait?" Then it started to slide off the table.

The wind had picked up, making the ship pitch. Jacqueline grinned at Percy's remark, though she held her own plate in place. Damon's visage was a little less dark. Jeremy scowled and reached for the wine bottle to refill his glass, apparently not giving an inch in his suspicions. Jack wasn't either after being a hostage to this man twice.

While they ate, she introduced a less provocative subject,

asking Damon, "Why didn't you invite your first mate to join us?"

"I did, but he declined. I believe he's embarrassed about the black eye you gave him."

Jeremy laughed. "Good for you, Jack."

"He deserved it" was all she said.

Dessert was being ignored. The wine bottle on the table was empty. Jeremy fetched the brandy from Damon's desk without asking permission, nor did he offer it to anyone else. He was a keg of unpleasant emotions and probably furious that he wasn't getting to trounce Damon yet. But Jacqueline's feelings were no better. She felt angry that she couldn't believe Damon and frustrated because she wanted to, which was self-serving because it had nothing to do with the situation and everything to do with her prurient feelings for the man. But that door would stay closed for her because the truth damned him as a pirate, or at the least a kidnapper and an accomplice to a pirate, and he hadn't even explained why yet!

But then Damon asked, "Why would I lie at this point?"

"When you get to the punch line we'll probably know," Jeremy shot back.

"I suppose you can consider this your punch line: I don't have full control of my ship. Well, I do, as long as I don't deviate from the pirates' plan. So far I haven't, because until we left London, our goals were the same—to get Jack aboard."

"Why capture her just to let her escape again?" Jeremy said derisively. "Or this time you're really going to hand her over to Lacross?"

"Neither. I took her again because I still need your father's help. She's my leverage to get it."

Outraged, Jacqueline pointed out, "You could have just knocked on the bloody door back in London and asked him for his help!"

"No, I couldn't. He would have no incentive to cross the ocean again just to help a stranger. You were safe, you were enjoying the Season, you were never actually harmed by Lacross. By all accounts, Jack, and especially since two months had passed since the abduction in Bridgeport, it appeared you and your family were done with the matter, so, indeed, I needed leverage to get your father involved again. But the note I had delivered to him a week after we sailed this time assured him you would be released to him if he met me in St. Kitts to talk. He should be a week or so behind us by—"

Jeremy's laughter cut Damon off. "Think again, mate. He sailed out of London two days before you did. He won't be getting any note, won't even know you have us."

Damon looked alarmed. "That's—unfortunate. The note wasn't threatening, but if he doesn't receive it—"

Jeremy was still laughing. "He's likely to kill you on sight?"

Damon gave Jeremy a dark look. "That's my problem, this one we share: The pirates want Jack. Once they saw what a beauty she is, they've been trying to get their hands on her. They know Lacross wouldn't begrudge them some enjoyment on the voyage home. I've been able to restrain them so far, but it won't be long before they decide they don't need me to finish their mission."

"I can vouch for that," Jacqueline put in.

Jeremy was already on his feet, furious again. "If everything you've said is true, you need to get rid of them before you approach my father for your parley, so why the hell are they still aboard? You need them to sail the ship?"

"I did on the way to England, but no longer. I hired a new crew in London."

"Then you have armed men on your side?"

"Only a few. The pirates have intimidated most of the new sailors."

"Hell's bells, man, you could have gotten rid of those black-guards the night you took us. You had a small army with you that could have helped you apprehend them. Why didn't you?"

"That's what I planned to do. But Catherine's parting gift to me was to warn her father's men not to trust me. So while the pirates aren't Oxford dons, they're not stupid, especially when it comes to their own survival. Five of them stayed on the ship that night and kept enough of the new crew I'd just hired with them so they could pull up anchor and sail off if they saw that little army heading their way."

"How many pirates are we talking about?"

"Fifteen."

"But you expected to only capture Jack, so what was your alternate plan for getting rid of them?"

"They rarely all come topside together, so as soon as we got to the Caribbean and the first island was in sight, I was going to start tossing them over the side. I can no longer wait for that. And make no mistake, I will be brutal about disposing of them if I have to be. But I'd rather imprison them and then turn them over to the authorities when we reach St. Kitts, not kill them."

"Commendable, but not when my sister's life hangs on your succeeding. Is this why you mentioned an alliance? You want my help in getting rid of them?"

"If you wouldn't mind," Damon said drily.

Jeremy laughed, but Jacqueline told Damon, "You could

have told me this to begin with to gain my cooperation. Why did you keep it from me?"

"I had hoped you'd stop fighting me—for other reasons."

Her cheeks lit up with color, but Jeremy turned deadly serious, warning Damon, "Don't even think about it. You might have had other reasons for getting involved in this, but you still did and she still suffered for it. And I'll give you the one reason why she'll never be yours. My father. So if you want my cooperation, she moves out of this cabin tonight and into mine."

"I can't, Jeremy, at least not yet." They all stared at Jacqueline, making her blush more deeply, but she still pointed out, "If the pirates think I don't have his protection anymore, they're going to come after me again, and they're all down on your deck, you know. Damon has forestalled them for the last week by keeping me by his side on deck, and—well, we also made them think I've been sharing his bed. I'm not!" she quickly added when her brother started to scowl again. "But it was working until he let me talk to you yesterday and there was another confrontation with a few of them afterward because they were hoping to trap us down there. But until you and Damon decide on the best approach to getting rid of them, nothing can look out of the ordinary, so I'm staying right here." Then she turned to Damon, her eyes flaring with the realization. "So we're allies?"

Chapter Thirty-Six

EALLY, YOU CAN STOP frowning, Jeremy," Jacqueline said with a tsk. "I'll be fine here. He's been a perfect gentleman this whole time, and now I know why. So are we his allies now or not?"

"He's defecting, so I suppose we are."

"I object to 'defecting,'" Damon said tersely. "I was never Lacross's man."

"We're not quibbling here, mate. You'll have our help, but without sharing the motives for your involvement, you can't very well expect me to believe everything you've said when your part could as likely be this: You went along with the pirate's plan for your own reasons—until my lovely sister became part of that plan. Now you're against it and so against him. You were willing to sacrifice our father, but now you're not, now you want his help instead. If you want to object to my view, hand over your reasons—or don't. I really don't care, since you had my cooperation the moment you said my sister is in imminent danger."

"And once she's safe?"

Jeremy stood up and moved closer to Damon, offering his hand. "The alliance will stand firm until my father says otherwise. But be warned," Jeremy added with a chuckle. "If you ever do get to talk to him, he'll demand a full accounting from you, not the vague explanation you've given us."

Damon nodded and shook hands on it before he finished off the last of his wine. Jacqueline was still coming to terms with being allies with him and what that meant for her. Now that Damon was on their side, he was no longer her enemy. He was no longer—off-limits. Her pulse beat faster with that thought. It was all she could do to keep her eyes off him, but she couldn't keep the smile from her lips.

"It's late." She stood up to give her brother another hug but had to grab the edge of the table to steady herself when the ship pitched again. Thunder cracked in the distance, suggesting rain was imminent. "You might want to get back to your cabin before the rain arrives. We can discuss plans for an ambush or a full deck-sweeping in the morning."

Jeremy signaled to Percy they were leaving, but put his arm around her shoulders to take her to the door with him, whispering, "Are you okay with an alliance?"

She chuckled. "Now you ask? Yes, absolutely."

She leaned her back on the door as soon as it closed and didn't get out of the way when Damon came over to lock it. "That went well, all things considered," he said.

He wouldn't meet her eyes. Did he have the same problem she had? She was gazing up at him and remembering what he tasted like until he added, "I'll be right back. I need to confer with Mr. Thomson about the approaching storm and make sure he's up to manning the wheel tonight."

Damon set her gently aside and walked out, leaving her utterly frustrated. She'd been about to wrap her arms tightly around his neck and kiss him the moment he locked the door! Bloody storm. And there was no telling how long he'd be.

With a low growl she moved to her trunk to undress for bed and grabbed one of his shirts to sleep in, but paused as she put it on, then suddenly removed it and removed her underclothes as well. She slipped the shirt back on and doused the lanterns as a precaution due to the pitching, then climbed into bed. She'd wait for him to return. Come hell or high water, he was going to be hers tonight. The decision was made. She'd desired him for too long. Even when he was her enemy, she'd been unable to stop those feelings. But now that they were allies, she didn't have to.

She hugged that thought to her, fully intending to stay awake. Yet the sound of his returning woke her. He'd been gone long enough for her to fall asleep? He'd brought a lantern in with him. He didn't notice that her eyes had opened, wasn't even looking toward the bed. He went to the washstand where the towels were stored to remove his wet clothes. He'd gotten soaked on deck. Nonetheless, she was surprised by what he was doing because she'd never seen him undress in the cabin before.

She slipped out of bed and quietly approached him from behind. His shirt was off. He was briskly rubbing the towel over his head when she grabbed it from his hands. "I'll do that."

He immediately turned and faced her, trying to take the towel back. He got his hand on it, but seemed arrested by the sight of her wearing his shirt and nothing else, his eyes moving down to her bare legs.

She tugged the towel back. "I insist."

She quickly began to rub the towel over his chest before he

tried to stop her again. When he didn't, she slowed down to enjoy what she was doing, moving the cloth over his muscular arms, his neck and shoulders. She didn't move around him to reach his back, she just stepped closer and swung the towel around him, catching it on his other side so she could slowly tug it back and forth across his back.

"Your boots," she said a little breathlessly.

He braced an arm against the wall and bent to remove them. She moved the towel to his head again as he did so, caressing him with her fingers through the cloth. Having carte blanche with his body was stimulating her senses, making her crave more. If she couldn't kiss him soon . . .

He straightened. "I can finish."

"So can I. Take off your wet trousers." When he didn't, she added, "Did you think you were the only one who could give orders? Take them off."

He still didn't comply, but he was staring at her in fascination—no, much more than that. Such desire was in his eyes that she could no longer control her own. She wrapped her arms around his neck and kissed him passionately. But she'd surprised him, maybe a little too much. He started to raise his hands to pull her arms down, which surprised her. She held on tighter.

"You don't need to seduce—"

"I'm Jack Malory, too bold for subtlety." She kissed him again, more hotly.

All the frustration of wanting him was in that kiss, now that she didn't have to deny herself anymore. That he was trying to resist compounded that frustration. This was no bloody time for him to be a chivalrous pirate! But then he groaned and lifted her, pressing her back to the wall. She curled her legs around his hips, thrilled that she'd just won this little battle.

Yet he still made one last attempt at gallantry, warning her, "Are you sure, because I'm two seconds from—"

"Shut up, pirate. I'm taking what I want."

He laughed. "I am so defeated. . . ."

Within seconds they were rolling around on his bed, both trying to rid themselves of the last pieces of their clothing. The buttons on her shirt went flying when he ripped it open. He stopped, looking startled, as his gaze roamed over her naked body before returning to her breasts. Cupping them in his hands, he said, "No chemise, no drawers. You are bold, Jack. And so beautiful." As his hands moved over her, she worked at the fastenings on his pants and ended up breaking them. At least now she could kiss every part of him within her reach. She couldn't keep her hands from wandering, either.

But he sighed deeply as he looked down at her. "We've done enough ripping. What's left has to be done slowly."

"You're not stopping—?"

"Not a chance. Believe me I'm more eager than you, Jack, but let me ease the way for you."

Gently he pushed her back down on the bed and began caressing her, which didn't ease anything and just made her want him now, right now! But she would give him a few minutes to show her what he was talking about because she felt a little too embarrassed to ask when she probably ought to know.

His mouth was so hot on her breasts that she was close to screaming. She did moan. A lot. Yet he was still behaving as if he had all the time in the world now, which was driving her crazy. But then he raised his head and gave her a sensual grin.

Finally! she thought. She started to wrap her legs around him again, but he slid down her body until his head was between her thighs and . . . oh . . . my . . . God!

The very moment his mouth touched her there, she felt out of control, her pulse exploding, spreading through her, lifting her hips and leaving her trembling, melted, and so utterly amazed. So that's what he'd meant? Good grief!

"Now you're wet for me."

She was? But she was now replete. Were they really not done? But the moment he climbed on top of her, bracing his arms on either side of her head and moving his hips against hers, she gave him the most brilliant smile. She wanted him again. No, they definitely weren't done.

Chapter Thirty-Seven

"DID WE SLEEP AT all?" Jacqueline wondered aloud the next morning.

Waking up wrapped alongside Damon, lying on her side pressed against his chest, had given her an instant, dreamy smile that hadn't yet gone away. He hadn't closed the drapes or turned off the lantern in the room last night. The lantern had burned out and the sun was streaming in. But the sunbeam on the wall was rather high. She had a feeling Mr. Thomson was doing a lot of yawning at the wheel, waiting for Damon to relieve him.

He had one arm across her back, keeping her close to him. His other hand was softly caressing the arm she had draped across his chest, moving from her shoulder to her fingers and back again. She could tell without looking up that he was grinning when he said, "Yes—I think."

She would have laughed about his not being sure, except she wasn't sure, either. But they must have slept a little, since she wasn't tired. She ought to be. It had been a night for education of the nicest sort. In fact, she felt quite energetic and exhilarated with him caressing her as he was doing. She decided she needed another kiss from this man and straddled his hips, grinning widely before she gave him one. He didn't hesitate to kiss her back, and before she knew it, he was on top of her, kissing her deeply, his hands stroking and exciting her in wonderfully sinful ways. Not until they lay beside each other breathless and satisfied, her not feeling a single regret—definitely her father's daughter—did she think about Jeremy and how furious he would be.

She sat up abruptly. "Is my brother going to be let out before you're on deck? The pirates might think he's escaped."

"No, Mort doesn't know about the alliance yet." With a sigh, likely due to the reminder of her brother, he got up to sit on the side of the bed. "But your brother might be wondering by now why he hasn't been let out." Damon leaned down to pick up something on the floor, then handed her a button with an abashed grin. "I'm sorry about your shirt. But I've seen you rip up clothes before, so I didn't think you'd mind."

She laughed. "It was yours."

"No, as soon as it's on your body, it becomes yours."

"Does that include you? I did notice you were a nice fit."

"Do you really need to ask?"

She grinned at him. "But don't expect me to be giving you any apologies in return. Nearly three weeks wasted when we could have been having that delightful time sooner if you—" Her eyes flared with sudden realization. "You weren't going to, were you? Ever?"

"Resisting you has been the hardest thing I've ever done, but I actually wanted your father's blessing—"

"Oh, good God. Now you're talking about never!" She

rolled her eyes at him. "It's a good thing I forced your hand then, isn't it? So we'll have some fun for the duration, then go our separate ways afterward, and you will never think again about doing the noble with my father. Really, he's not a normal parent by any means, and I don't want you dead anymore."

He leaned over and kissed her hard before he got up and walked to the chest at the foot of the bed. "It's adorable that you think you can control my actions, Jack, but you really can't."

She would have frowned at him, but she'd just gotten dazzled by the sight of his bare arse, such a manly shape, nicely rounded, tightly formed.

"Latch the door behind me, change into your usual, then meet me on the quarterdeck for breakfast."

She huffed as she got out of bed. They weren't done with that conversation, but they didn't need to have it today. She rinsed off at the water bowl, then dressed in her clean britches and tossed the pair she'd worn yesterday on the bed for Jackie to wash with the sheets. She stared at those sheets for only a moment, deciding she'd pull Jackie's ears if he mentioned the blood.

Stepping out of the room a while later, she was just in time to see Jeremy and Percy coming up the stairs from below. Two guards preceded them, and Mortimer and another guard came up behind them. Once they came up to the quarterdeck, the guards stationed themselves at the top of both sets of stairs leading up there. Well, of course it would need to appear that Jeremy and Percy were being let out under armed guard. She glanced across the main deck and saw no pirates on it yet, so she gave the two a bright smile when they reached her.

"Good morning!"

"We shall hope," Percy replied.

"Join the captain, Percy," Jeremy said as he put an arm around Jacqueline to detain her. "I need a word with my 'happy' sister." That should have given her a clue, but he added the moment Percy left them, "I know that look."

"What look?"

"Of a sexually fulfilled woman. I'm going to have to kill him now."

His expression told her he meant it, but she still snorted at him. "No, you aren't, since I'm the one who started it, and I'm not the least bit sorry that I did. It's not going to be the last time, either."

"The devil it won't be. The alliance didn't include you as the spoils."

She chuckled. "You need to rephrase that since he's the spoils, not I."

He narrowed his cobalt eyes, warning her, "You can't keep him like a pet, Jack. That's one mutt Father won't let in the house."

"Good grief, is that what concerns you? I don't want to keep him, I just want to enjoy him for a while. There's nothing permanent about a dalliance. So stop being a hypocrite, or do I need to remind you that I'm our father's daughter and he was the most notorious rake ever? You were a womanizer of the extraordinary sort yourself. If you think only men can—"

"You know bloody well it's different for a woman." His tone was quite angry. "I get called a bachelor, you get called—"

"Don't say it!"

"And yet there's a reason why there's no female equivalent for the masculine term *rake*. I rest my case."

She rolled her eyes. "Lucky for me it's not your decision, it's mine. So stop begrudging me this little bit of fun, Jeremy, and let it go."

His answer was to go over to the wheel and punch Damon in the gut. "You should have resisted, mate."

Damon grunted, bent over. "I tried—and failed, so I'll allow you one."

"I know she was the instigator, but there'll be more'n one if it happens again."

Jacqueline ran over to them. "You win, Jeremy. For the sake of peace, I'll stay out of his bed." She didn't blush, neither did her brother. But Percy did, which almost made her laugh. But Jeremy was giving her such a doubtful look that she was forced to add in a growl, "You have utterly ruined my mood, thank you very much. And don't think I'll forgive you for this interference. Now can we form a plan before Lacross's men come on deck and try to eavesdrop or, worse, put their own plan in motion?"

Chapter Thirty-Eight

So do we just grab them as they come on deck?" Jeremy asked.

"That would be ideal except ever since they started making attempts to get at Jack and I've had to fight them off, they've become wary of me and Mort. They never trusted me, but now they are fully alert, watching and waiting for me to try something. They might entrench themselves down there in the crew's quarters if any of their mates don't return, and we definitely don't want that to happen. They'll have cover, weapons, all our food, and they can hold my helmsman hostage. As long as they have him, they can sail the ship without me."

"So we have to get all of them up here. I see three of them now."

"Take a stroll with your guards," Damon suggested. "They'll stay close to you for the sake of appearances. The pirates need to think you're only up here for exercise. They should steer clear of you after you took down so many of them in London. Then again, they are an aggressive bunch of thugs and might want a little payback, so be careful."

"Or I can knock a few out just on principle. I'm due some payback as well."

Damon grinned. "Feel free to knock out as many—actually, don't. That could backfire on us. If it looks like you want to fight, they might shoot you before you reach them. Lord Percival, on the other hand, won't concern them."

Percy quickly squared his shoulders and tried to scowl. "Did I just get insulted?"

"D'you think you could knock one out if you took him by surprise?" Jeremy asked his friend.

Percy made a fist and stared down at it before he shook his head. "You know that ain't my cup of tea, dear boy."

"I can," Jack volunteered. "Never mind objecting, you know I can."

"You could," Damon allowed. "Except that would put you too close to them. All it will take is for one of them to get their hands on you, Jack, and the rest of us will lose. You stay right where you are."

"I'll be back in a minute." Jeremy headed down to the main deck with Percival and the guards.

"Is he going to start something?" Damon asked.

Jacqueline grinned. "Possibly, but more likely, just make them a little nervous. Are we going to do this today?"

He shook his head. "No, today we plan, and before we do anything, I need to lock Mr. Thomson safely in my cabin. We won't make much headway afterward if he gets injured or captured." Damon brushed back a lock of Jack's hair that had fallen over her face. "So . . . we're back to separate beds?"

She glanced around to make sure her brother was still walking on the main deck, then put her hand on Damon's buttocks and squeezed. "What do you think?"

"So you lied to him?"

"Course I did. He's being a hypocrite. He never denied himself any woman who cast her eyes his way before he married, and that was pretty much any woman who crossed his path. For him to deny me the same sort of pleasure is absurd."

"He was being protective and I'd expect no less."

"Are you going all noble again?"

He gently caressed her cheek. "As long as you want me, I'm yours."

She smiled brilliantly. "That was rather sweet—"

"What was?" Jeremy asked as he came up behind her.

She swung around to complain, "I thought you were getting some exercise."

"I was passing out nasty looks in preparation."

"For?" she asked.

"Our foolproof plan." Jeremy glanced at Damon. "Tell them to send up two of their men to fight me—hell, make it three. Say the crew is due some entertainment."

"That's not a bad idea, but challenging two should be enough."

"No, three. They have to think they can win, or the others won't come up to watch."

"You're assuming they will all show up, but what if they don't?" Jacqueline reminded Damon, "I thought you wanted to secure your helmsman first to keep him safe?"

"That won't be necessary if this impromptu fighting match that they can wager on lures all of them up here. But if it doesn't, we won't proceed beyond the fight and we can try again tomorrow. They might not be happy when your brother wins, but they shouldn't interfere. And at least we'll be able to count two or three of them sore or disabled for the next round."

"There are still fifteen of them," she told Jeremy. "How are we getting rid of the rest?"

"I'm going to be clumsy so a few of my swings will go wide and take out a few of the onlookers, and I'll keep it interesting so their eyes stay on me and won't be watching what the rest of you are doing."

"With the pirates gathered around your brother," Damon added, "we can take down the ones on the fringes before the others notice. It's a good plan."

It was, yet she couldn't help thinking about what would happen if they failed. They'd probably be killed and she'd be . . . She shuddered.

Noticing her expression, Jeremy chucked her chin. "You see any flaws in this plan?"

"No, but I'll need a weapon."

"You'll need to lock yourself in the cabin," Damon said adamantly.

"Not a chance! And before you disagree, they will expect me to be by your side as I've been all week. If I'm not, they will be suspicious and then nothing will go as you wish."

"She's right," Jeremy said. "Just try to stay out of the way, Jack. If even one of them gets their hands on you, it's all over."

"Exactly my point," Damon said. "You can stay on deck until the fight starts, but then you have to get behind a locked door. If you don't agree to that, Jack, then I'm not delivering Jeremy's challenge."

She glared at Damon for a moment before she mumbled, "Fine, I'll use the latch on the door. But you're going to miss my help."

Chapter Thirty-Nine

Aᴛᴛᴇʀ ᴄᴀʟʟɪɴɢ ᴍᴏʀᴛɪᴍᴇʀ ᴏᴠᴇʀ and relaying the full plan to him, the first mate went below to issue the challenge and wake up any sleeping pirates, promising a fight they wouldn't want to miss and taking wagers. Jeremy went down to the main deck, removed his wrinkled coat, and started stretching and jabbing at the air, typical preparations for a round of fisticuffs. Jacqueline stayed with Damon, trying to figure out a way to help without hindering. But she doubted she could knock out anyone with a single punch; disable, yes, but she didn't dare leave any of the pirates able to get back up before most of them had been captured. She wished she had some sort of weapon, but none was being offered to her.

Then Damon slipped her the little pistol he'd taken from her at the start of this voyage, saying, "Just in case." Knowing that he now trusted her with it gave her such a warm feeling she couldn't resist thanking him with an ardent kiss, even if it had to be brief. She knew the pistol was only for her own protection, not to be used in taking out any of the pirates, but she still felt more confident now that she had it and slipped it into the pocket of the britches Jackie had loaned her.

Jeremy's preparations were drawing the attention of the three pirates on deck. Jacqueline moved to the top of the stairs when one of them yelled at her brother, "Wot are you up to, toff?"

Jeremy motioned the pirate forward, his expression making it a dare. "I've offered some entertainment in the form of a challenge, and your captain thinks it will be amusing, so he's agreed."

"You're fighting him?"

"Eventually, but today I want any two of you who beat me down in London to dare try it again. Weren't you one?" The pirate's snort had Jeremy add, "No? Well, your mates have been invited and will join you shortly. Decide amongst yourselves who's brave enough to give this a go."

"Yer a bleedin' giant. Two to one ain't soundin' fair for our boys."

"Oh, come now . . ."

"Three maybe."

"Three it is."

Jeremy had probably agreed too quickly because one of the pirates snickered, "But four's a nice even number, I'm thinkin'."

Jack could see that Jeremy hadn't expected that, so his reply was deliberately insulting. "It's a cowardly number, but if that's what you think of your fellows, so be it."

That got him some nasty looks, but more pirates started appearing on deck, and the three who had haggled with Jeremy went over to confer with them. Jacqueline started counting heads, but it wasn't necessary. Mortimer came up the lower-deck stairs last and stood where Damon could see him, nodding and giving the signal that all the pirates were present. She saw Dr. Death, still wearing sinister black. She hadn't seen him since he'd treated Damon's wound. His deathly pale complexion was proof of his dislike of the sun. Next to him was Bart Satin, still carrying four pistols tucked in the waistband of his britches. She hoped that particular troublemaker would be one of Jeremy's contenders. And Scar Face and the other pirate who'd snuck into Damon's cabin to get a good look at her were laughing at the notion that Jeremy thought he could take down four of their brethren.

The rest of Lacross's men, all flamboyantly dressed and heavily armed, blended into one gang. She tensed when most of the pirates started toward Jeremy. The normal sailors got out of the way, many of them climbing the masts for a better view, though others gathered around with the pirates for a closer view of the fight that was about to get under way. She wished they would help her brother instead, but she supposed their not taking sides was better than helping the wrong side.

She gasped when she heard her brother say, "Five? Really? No brave lads among you a'tall?"

"No stupid lads."

She ran back to Damon. "You have to stop this. Now the challenge is up to five against one."

He gave her a grave look and a nod of agreement and pulled her forward to take the wheel. "Just until I get this under control," he said before she could ask, and he started down the stairs.

It was the first time he was trusting her with the wheel, but he'd picked a lousy time to do it because she didn't have a good view of the main deck from there. But no sooner had he started down the stairs than Mr. Thomson came up the other set that led to the quarterdeck. Looking tired but quite awake now, the helmsman was hurrying toward her, and the moment he reached her, she ran after Damon.

She'd only just bumped into his back when she heard Jeremy tell the prospective fighters, "Four, and you get to pick. Five and I pick. You decide, but keep in mind, there's at least one of you that I could flick over with a finger."

That got some laughter out of the pirates, and the shortest one among them had gone red in the face. But Jeremy's solution solved the numbers problem because the pirates chose the first option, and Damon turned around to whisper, "All eyes are on your brother. Now go lock yourself in the cabin."

Before the fight even began? She would have laughed at the suggestion if he didn't look so serious, so she merely reminded him, "That wasn't the deal."

He swore under his breath, something about stubbornness, but said, "You'll stay behind me, and the very moment I crack someone's head, you run to the cabin."

Mortimer pushed his way through to the center of the ring of pirates that was forming around Jeremy and ordered, "The contenders must hand over their weapons to me. This is going to be a—somewhat fair fight." But by the time five pistols and two daggers were dropped by his feet, he added, "Bloody hell, I need a sack," which drew even more laughter.

Still, he managed to stuff seven pistols around his waist and picked up the eight daggers from the four pirates who had stepped forward to participate. Finally, he raised his hand and said, "On your mark—"

One of them threw a punch at Jeremy before Mortimer could finish. The blond got out of the way and joined Percy behind the ring of onlookers, slipping him one of the pistols.

"Four is still a lousy number," Jacqueline whispered to Damon.

"Your brother must not think so, but you know him better than I. Can he do it?"

"Certainly—but he might not get in those missed swings we were counting on."

Three more swings toward Jeremy, all three misses. Jeremy was playing with them, apparently. Jack wished she had a better view, but at least she could still see her brother, taller than all the others, to know that he was enjoying himself!

But then Jeremy took his first swing at the pirate who was trying to slip behind him. A bystander went down instead and Jeremy complained, "Now see what you've done. That's what happens when you don't stay in front of me."

Jacqueline started to worry. Jeremy might have all their attention on him, but he should have taken down one of the four contenders first so he'd just have to face a manageable three, especially when the four could converge on him. She hoped he didn't think pirates would actually fight fairly. But she realized when another bystander went down that having the four contenders still standing was possibly keeping anyone else from interfering yet, if they planned to.

Two down, thirteen to go, and what was Damon waiting for? He wasn't. He hit the man in front of him with the butt of his pistol, helping him to the deck so his fall wouldn't make much noise. That was her cue to leave and she did, running back up to the quarterdeck and straight to the short set of steps leading down to Damon's cabin. Instead of going inside the cabin, she turned to the center railing in front of his cabin.

It was the perfect place to watch the fight because it provided an unobstructed view of the main deck and was only a few feet from Damon's cabin. She could still get behind his locked door if she had to, but she didn't think she'd have to since she also had a good view of both stairways leading up to the quarterdeck. If any of the pirates broke away from the fight on the main deck and headed toward her, she'd see it. She even put her hand in her pocket so she could quickly reach the little pistol if she needed it.

Damon and Mortimer were quietly but quickly disabling pirates on the edge of the crowd. Percy wasn't. He'd stuck his pistol in the back of one pirate and had given him a warning that was keeping him quiet. One was better than none for old Percy. The three armed sailors who'd been guarding Jeremy earlier had also taken out three pirates. When one of the pirates noticed what was happening, he shouted a warning, which set off the mayhem.

Jeremy got swarmed for a moment when his four contenders converged on him, but he was able to knock one out and push the other three back so they fell over their mate. Then he quickly went after the pirates who still had weapons. But for a moment during the brawl he came face-to-face with Damon and could have knocked him out as well. She saw her brother pause, seeming to consider it! She was about to yell something nasty at him when a pirate stuck a pistol in his back. Damon saw it and tackled that one away from Jeremy. Jack smirked, but her brother would still get an earful from her later about not honoring deals.

That's when an arm went about her neck, half choking her, and the tip of a dagger pricked the skin below her ear. Filthy black silk covered the elbow under her chin. She knew only one of the pirates wore that dark color. An icy chill ran down her spine, but then she got angry at herself. They'd been so close to winning and it was her fault that they wouldn't! She had to fix this.

"How'd you get up here?" she asked Dr. Death. "I would have seen—"

Foul breath crossed her cheek when he said, "Was already up here, pretty. Snuck up as soon as ye ran back to the cap'n to get him to leave his post, and I hid on the other side of his cabin. Fights are boring. If ye've seen one, ye've seen them all. But ye ain't boring, wench, and there's a nice bed only feet from here where we're gonna do a little bouncing."

"Take a look below. Your friends are done for."

"Then I guess they need to be helped up and given back their weapons, eh? And what do ye think will make the cap'n do that?"

He started to laugh, and of course he would, he was holding a knife near her throat—exactly what she'd been warned couldn't happen if Damon's side was to win. But she'd slowly been pulling the pistol out of her pocket so Dr. Death wouldn't notice, horribly aware that shooting someone behind her whom she couldn't see wasn't guaranteed to be successful. She had to turn her head enough to see some part of him she could hit because she didn't dare miss when she had only one shot. So she leaned into his elbow even though it cut off her breath for a moment and shot him where it would hurt him enough to let her go.

He didn't. He cackled like an old hen instead. "Oh, yer funny, girl. The reason I'm a sawbones is I had to cut off my own foot when I was a youngun. Ye just shot an empty boot."

The firing of the weapon drew a lot of attention her way, though, and just that momentary distraction provided enough of an advantage for Jeremy, Damon, and the others to beat down the last of the pirates who were still standing. But that wasn't helping her situation, which could give the upper hand back to the pirates, and she wasn't about to let that happen if she could help it.

"I think I set your boot on fire though."

"Nice try, girly."

"You can't smell it burning?"

That got him to lift his leg so he could at least see the empty boot, which loosened his hold on her a little, and that's when Damon dove at him. She grunted as she got knocked aside, but the pirate went down with Damon, and a furious punch knocked the pirate out. She almost laughed when she saw that Death's boot really was smoldering.

But Damon was already pulling her to her feet. "Did I hurt you?"

"No."

"Did *he* hurt you?"

"Just a scratch."

Of course Damon had to see for himself, but then he was hugging her fiercely. "Next time, can you do what I ask?"

"I could—maybe." She grinned. "But if there isn't a next time, then we don't need to find out if I will or won't."

"Not a good answer, Jack."

She laughed. "For me it was."

Chapter Forty

JACK AND DAMON WENT for a stroll around the deck after dinner to watch the sunset. Such brilliant orange and gold reflected so perfectly on the water of a becalmed sea was a magnificent sight. It was a pleasure to be on the ship now that the pirates were locked in the hold. The winners had had quite a celebration the day they'd won. Damon had even had the pirates' hoarded rum brought topside. But then the wind had died that night and no one had been happy about that—except Jacqueline. And six days later, she was still enjoying the calm because it gave her more time to spend with Damon. Now if her brother would stop being so annoying and find somewhere else to sleep . . .

She remarked, "I know all sailors hate a becalmed sea, and I thought that's why you've been so vexed, but—is it my brother instead?"

Damon gave her a wry look. "A little of both."

He directed her to the quarterdeck stairs since neither of them was in a hurry to return to his cabin, where Jeremy and Percy were playing chess. When the game was over, Percy would leave, but Jeremy wouldn't. He'd come into the cabin with a hammock after the pirates had all been tied in the hold and had warned Damon that was the only way he wouldn't beat him senseless for ruining his sister. Jack didn't get a chance to offer her opinion—well, she did later when she was alone with Jeremy, but nothing she said would change his mind about the sleeping arrangements.

She sat on the step below Damon, cocooned between his thighs, using him as a nice backrest as she gazed up at the sails, which were still flat and motionless. His hands circled her neck gently, his thumbs rubbing the skin below her ears. She was going to get frustrated again!

"We were so close to the islands." Damon sighed. "Now this."

She stretched her legs out in front of her and crossed her ankles, trying to ignore his caresses, which was nearly impossible, so she distracted them both with "So? There's really no reason to worry until we're out of fruit. But your supplies aren't running low so we're not at risk of getting scurvy, and your men have even been fishing, though I wish they wouldn't," she added in a mumble.

"Unless this calm stretches for leagues in all directions, your father will be disposing of Lacross without me and—"

"Wait, what?"

She turned about to face him, but remembered that the first night of the calm he'd asked them where James was sailing to. Jeremy, still not on friendly terms with him, had goaded, "Exactly where you thought he wouldn't go." But she hadn't realized that Damon had been left thinking that James was ahead of them simply because he'd left London two days before Damon had.

She didn't laugh at what had him so concerned, but she did confess, "You can't imagine how hard it was not to gloat over your failing on this second mission before you even got started because Father sailed before you did. But that was before we knew you wanted his help. I still don't understand why you didn't just present your story to my father when you were in London before your first mission."

"I considered it, but I wanted to do it on my terms, which is why I tried to capture him instead of you, not to deliver him to Lacross, but to get him to hear me out and agree to deal with Lacross with my help."

She sighed. "That is not the way to get on my father's good side."

"He has one?"

She snorted. "I meant an actual sit-down civilized talk."

"For reasons better left buried, I don't like your father. I was afraid that would get in the way of convincing him to listen to my explanation, and any number of things could have gone wrong because of it."

"Don't you think it's time you explained that?" When he didn't answer, she tsked. "What you don't know is that he sailed fully laden with cannons this time, so you probably took the lead less than a week out of London."

"Really?" He looked relieved until he added, "He still won't know where to find us."

She grinned. "But we know where to find him. We can wait for him on St. Kitts, where he's going to meet up with my uncle Drew, or on Anguilla."

"Anguilla? Why the devil would he go there?" An uncharacteristic sharpness was in Damon's tone.

Apparently, she hadn't reassured him enough yet. "Because we could only assume Pierre was behind this. He seemed the most likely culprit, but Father wanted to confirm absolutely that he wasn't still in prison. However, my uncle Drew Anderson has had ample time to find that out, so Father will want to confer with him first. So you needn't worry that you'll miss the big fight, if that was your concern. We'll get there first and we can tell Drew what's happened. And you might want to let him warn my father first, or my brother can, so he doesn't try to kill you on sight."

"Not your brother. He still wants a piece of me for ruining you."

She rolled her eyes and got comfortable again, leaning against his chest, using his two legs stretched out on either side of her as armrests. "I walked right into that ruination. You were just an innocent bystander."

"The men in your family won't take that view—unless we marry. As I'm stronger than you, you know very well I could have stopped you instead of letting you have your way with me."

She chuckled at his phrasing, delighted that they could joke about this. "It's silly of you to feel guilty—if you are feeling guilty—because I'm not the least bit ruined. So don't worry, you won't have to make the ultimate sacrifice. I never intended to be a virginal bride, or d'you really think I'd commit myself to a lifelong union without finding out first that I and my intended will be compatible in all ways?"

"That sounds like something a 'ruined' lady might say—after the fact."

She burst out laughing. "What a polite way of calling me

a liar. But I'm not your everyday lady, Damon, and I'm pretty sure you can agree with that."

"Indeed, a beautiful tempest, outrageously bold and opinionated, dangerously daring, willfully—"

"Okay! So I'm a hoyden. But I know love can make people do stupid things and ignore what's sensible. I don't intend to let that happen to me because love won't matter a'tall if a man isn't a good lover, isn't fun in and out of bed, ends up being a prude who wants to make love with his clothes on. The bedroom is a big part of marriage, and I refuse to get stuck with only half of the good part."

"And yet, an annulment can fix the unhappy-bed part if it came to that."

"Not in my family! We make sure first, then get the happy ever after."

"So—we aren't going to marry?"

She sat up and turned around, her brows snapped together. "This sort of teasing is no longer funny, so stop it. I still need the love part of the equation, which you and I don't have, so don't try to turn this ridiculous guilt you're feeling into something it's not."

"You want me."

She blinked at the reminder. "What has that got to do with anything? I'm attracted more'n I ought to be, which is why we had a delightful time in bed. It was fun and we could have had more fun if my brother didn't turn into a bloody guard dog. I'm the first to admit how frustrating that is because, yes, I do want you again before we run out of time. None of which negates what happened before this unexpected alliance, Damon. You hurt my family and I wanted you dead for it, for God's sake! That doesn't just go—"

He kissed her hard to shut her up. She stood up to kiss him back even harder, nearly knocking him back on the deck. Six days of abstinence when she wanted him this much . . .

He stood and picked her up. She loved being in his arms, pressed against his chest, having her arm around his neck. She couldn't resist kissing him again even though they were in full view of anyone walking out his cabin door. She wished he would take her somewhere private where she could do so much more, but they both knew Jeremy would find them all too quickly if they did because he never left them alone for long. But Damon quickly moved away from the lantern light to the shadowed side of his cabin, toward the back of the ship. For the moment, no one would see them there, but they had to be quiet with Jeremy on the other side of the wall.

When Damon put her on her feet, she stopped caring if anyone saw them because he started kissing her and soon whispered, "I know you're comfortable on a ship. I've seen you take the wheel, climb the mast. So you might enjoy this." He turned her around before he added, "Brace yourself, Jack."

She put her hands against the wall without asking why, but gasped when she felt him raise her shirt and pull down her britches and drawers. But she really sucked in her breath when she felt him kissing what he'd exposed, including her derriere. She peeked over her shoulder and saw him kneeling, his mouth moving over her tender flesh. He didn't stop kissing her and caressing her with one hand when he moved his other hand between her legs and slipped his finger inside her. Moving it slowly and then more quickly, he was driving her wild. She gasped as her body trembled, delicious sensations overwhelming her. This is what she'd wanted, needed, for too long! She slapped a hand over her mouth to stanch her cry of pleasure.

Damon patted her derriere and stood up to whisper in her ear, "I was right."

God, yes, he was. She turned around, reached for him, and got in one good kiss before they both heard the cabin door open and Jeremy calling her name. Damon quickly helped her straighten her clothes and led her back to where Jeremy could see them in the light from the lantern by the cabin door.

"We thought we heard a whale splash and tried to spot it," she told her brother.

He'd come to the top of the steps outside the cabin and gave her a doubtful look, then grumbled, "No touching, and stay out of the shadows," before he went back in the cabin.

Jacqueline growled under her breath. Her brother had become a mind reader, so uncannily on the mark with his timing. Every single time she and Damon had found an empty spot for some privacy this week, Jeremy would either show up or start shouting her name and looking for her until she showed up. He'd even climbed up to the crow's nest the night she and Damon had snuck out of the cabin, thinking Jeremy was asleep when he wasn't. Quite embarrassing, that, how quickly she'd had to fix her clothing before her brother peered over the side. But mostly, he just didn't leave them alone together. As chaperones went, he was the worst ever. But tonight they'd managed a few private moments. It just wasn't enough!

Damon was softly chuckling beside her. "I'm beginning to regret giving him his freedom."

"It was a wise decision and it worked out beautifully. Even though he is being aggravating now."

"Yes, he was the perfect foil to win the day with only bruises instead of bloodshed." Then Damon took her hand and brought it to his lips before he gave her his form of an apology for his mention of marriage earlier. "I'm still getting to know you, Jack. So some teasing you enjoy, and apparently, some you don't. Can we go back to enjoying the evening now that the stars are out?"

Mollified, she smiled and reached up to touch his face. "Thank you for what you did for me. I wish we could have more fun together."

The sky was pretty, black and star filled—and cloudless. Just one cloud would herald some wind returning, but the calm continued unabated.

"I could just take the beating your brother promised."

"Don't you dare. That won't get him to vacate the cabin."

He took her hand. "One more circuit of the deck before—?"

He didn't finish. The horribly loud sound of a cannon being fired drew them immediately to the back railing on the helm's side. But they hadn't been fired upon. It had just been a warning shot to get their attention. Jack saw a dozen longboats heading their way. They would already have seen them if they had really been looking for a whale behind the ship!

"It looks like our father is paying us a visit," Jeremy smirked, coming up behind them.

"You failed to mention he sailed with a bloody fleet," Damon said accusingly.

"Anderson ships and a few extra Father brought as well. He has no intention of letting Lacross escape justice this time. But what difference does it make that we didn't mention it when you intend to parley with him?"

"He's right, Damon," Jack said. "Father's coming with more help than you expected should please you."

"He's rowing over with an army, which means only one

thing. He intends to take my ship. There won't be any incentive for him to parley after that."

He was right—unless Damon held them at gunpoint again. But he wouldn't do that. She was sure he was going to put his trust in her and Jeremy to keep their father from killing him. Jack bit her lip. That wasn't the best plan of action considering Jeremy still had an ax to grind.

Chapter Forty-One

J AMES STOOD ON THE main deck of Damon's ship, not far from the ladder he'd climbed up. His men were searching the rest of the ship and had already told him prisoners who appeared to be pirates were in the hold. Jacqueline was clinging to his side, where she'd launched herself the moment he'd stepped aboard, she was so happy to see him!

She hugged him again before saying, "We stowed away."

"We did nothing of the sort," Jeremy corrected.

James leaned down and kissed the top of Jacqueline's head and clasped Jeremy's shoulder. "I'll have an accounting from you two later. Which of those two do I need to have a talk with?"

James was staring at Damon and Mortimer, the two taller, better-dressed men among the sailors forming a line for inspection across the length of the deck. Although her father cut a forbidding figure, wearing the ship garb he preferred—billowing white shirt open at the neck, tall Hessian boots over black pants—he didn't seem angry. Maybe he was a little annoyed because he'd come over for a fight but didn't get one since Damon had directed Mort to hoist a white flag and James and his men had climbed aboard without hindrance.

"That would be me." Damon stepped forward.

James slowly approached him, and no part of his expression warned that his fist was going to connect so brutally with Damon's gut, but it did. Once Damon was bent over from that, it was easy for James to follow with an uppercut to the chin.

It happened too fast. Jacqueline screamed, "Father, stop!"

Mortimer snarled, "Bloody hell," at the first blow and started to interfere, but five of James's crew were suddenly yanking him back in line, and James didn't even spare him a glance.

But Jacqueline pushed past her father and dropped to her knees by Damon's head and tossed back accusingly, "If you've broken his jaw, he won't be able to talk to you!"

"We just had a good talk," James replied. "When he wakes up, we'll have it again."

She growled in frustration at that answer, but her hand was gentle as she patted Damon's cheek to awaken him. James frowned as he watched her and demanded, "Is that, or is it not, the pirate you named Bastard?"

"It is," Jeremy answered for her. "But we formed an alliance with him."

"I gathered something of the sort, since I saw you and your sister on deck without restraints. Which is the only reason he's still breathing."

"I'm not saying he didn't deserve that, but I thought you'd hear him out first."

"To what point? There was an eyewitness to your abduction," James said. "Tony caught up with me to give me an account of it." Then James noticed Percy approaching. "Good to see you've weathered this adventure well, Alden."

"Oh, indeed, Lord M, though I've a much better appreciation for my valet now. Going to have to give the chap a raise when I get home."

"When you get there, do thank your mother and your driver for me. They let my family know what happened near the London Docks."

Jeremy pulled his father aside to give his own account of that, ending with "Yes, we were utterly foolish to think we could capture him. But he was willing to relinquish his upper hand just to protect Jack from Lacross's men. And if you have his ransom note, then you know—"

"I don't have it."

"Ah, well, that explains it." Jeremy nodded toward the still-unconscious captain. "He wrote the note this time, requesting a meeting with you in St. Kitts. He took Jack for leverage because he didn't think you'd cross the ocean again without incentive. Ironically, he wants your help to put Lacross back in prison."

"This isn't the way to ask for help."

"I agree."

"And I was already going to deal with Pierre."

"To be fair, he obviously didn't know that. He got stuck with the pirate's men this trip, so he had to pretend he was still following the same orders, when he wasn't—well, he says he wasn't. I'm not sure what to believe when he never gave any reasons for his own involvement in any of this—though I assume he won't be so reticent with you. But then the damned pirates aboard wanted Jack for themselves and were making attempts to get at her. The captain was fighting them off, but it was getting close to a mutiny, so he asked for my help in dealing with them."

"So it was just a temporary truce?"

"To last until you say otherwise."

James nodded. "Take your sister to *The Maiden George*. You're both done with this ship. And try to ignore Tony. He's been an utter pain in the arse this week since he joined me."

Jeremy grinned. "I was wondering why he didn't row over with you."

"And now you know why I didn't let him. I know he's just worried about Judy, but he's dealing with it by provoking me. Good God, I'm never going through that with Jack."

"I don't see how you can avoid—"

"By bloody well denying my blessing to all of her suitors, that's how."

Jeremy laughed. "Jack will probably have something to say about that, but at least you won't find out until next year what a colossal pain in the arse she can be." Then Jeremy went over to his sister. "Let's go, Jack."

She stood up, but reminded him, "I have trunks here that will need to be—"

James cut in, "You packed for your own abduction?"

She swung around to her father. "Of course not. Damon supplied me with clothes and other amenities. He prepared ahead. We didn't prepare enough. But we're allies now and—"

"Not anymore."

She gasped. "Jeremy gave his word!"

"That it would last until I arrived."

"No, that it would last until Damon gets to talk to you, and *then* you decide. And not the damned talking you already did with your fists."

James lifted her chin. "Is this gratitude because he protected you from the pirates on his ship—or more?"

She gave her brother a hard look before she said, "I hated him. I even tried to kill him. But that was before we found out he didn't really mean us harm. He was just trying to lure you into helping him dispose of Lacross. He didn't think simply asking you to help would work. Aren't you the least bit curious why?"

"He's twice abducted you, poppet. No, there's nothing he can say to absolve himself of that."

Despite the endearment, her father's tone was utterly unrelenting. Even Jacqueline knew not to argue when her father was like this. Yet she still said, "You've met him before."

James glanced down at the unconscious man. "If I have, it wasn't remarkable enough to remember."

"It was for him. 'For reasons better left buried, I don't like your father.' That statement of his clearly implies you've met before, but he wouldn't say how he knew you, or from where or when. Yet whatever occurred between you, it affected his decisions in this long chain of events. And as the pawn that was used as the lure, I still want to know why, whether you do or not." She marched to the railing, climbed over it, and yelled before she disappeared down the ladder, "Don't hurt his face!"

James tsked before he turned his full attention to Mortimer. "Your captain doesn't look familiar, but you, on the other hand . . ."

Chapter Forty-Two

Damon awoke behind a wall of iron bars. He pushed himself off the floor where he'd been dumped. The small cell had two benches, a chamber pot, and nothing else. There wasn't even enough room for him to stretch out. He definitely wasn't on his ship, but this one was actually moving. The wind that had pushed Malory's fleet into the calm before changing directions must have veered back and filled the sails. Or had several days passed since the cannon was fired at Damon's ship? He couldn't tell how long he'd been unconscious, though his jaw hurt like hell.

Trying the cell door to see if it was locked, he saw two guards blocking the entrance to the little corridor outside the cell. "What's going on? I demand to be released!" he shouted. "It's imperative that you fetch Lord Malory!" Neither guard answered his questions or fetched Malory for him, even though he bothered them about it for quite a while. Frankly, he was surprised the man wasn't there demanding answers of his own, but with the ship so quiet, he guessed it was the middle of the night.

Hours passed and the only sounds he heard were the creaking of the ship and an occasional cough from one of the guards. He wasn't tired, but he did bend his knees to lie back on one of the benches and must have fallen asleep. Metal clanking against an iron bar woke him, and he shot immediately to his feet when he saw who was making the racket with a dagger.

"Where's my first mate?" Damon demanded.

"That's your first question? Really?" But then James answered, "Mr. Bower is still on your ship. Very uncooperative fellow, wouldn't answer a single question. I got his name from one of your sailors. At least they were cooperative, though they had nothing pertinent to say."

"Did you hurt him?"

"No, I didn't see the point—when I have you. However, I left him in command of your ship with the request that he follow us. Quite a slippery fellow. He got away from me once before when he stowed away on my ship on my last voyage to Bridgeport. If he takes the opportunity to sail away now, I won't stop him."

"He won't. Now tell me the point of posting guards here when the door is locked? Surely you don't think I'm strong enough to bend bars?"

James's brow went up. "No, but all I hear is yet another question that doesn't address your own circumstances. Surely you aren't afraid to ask what I'm going to do with you?"

"Why ask what I already know? I've been assured by your children and their friend that this would be a meeting I wouldn't survive."

"And yet you forced the meeting anyway."

"To be honest, I expected to have leverage to discuss the matter with you, but I got on good terms with your children instead."

"Which sacrificed your leverage. A pity—for you. But one fair answer deserves another. The guards weren't for you, they were to keep my daughter away from you, of course. Like you, she seems to think your truce has made you friends of a sort, and because of it, she doesn't want you hurt yet. But since she isn't going to see you again, she won't know whether you get hurt. Come out of there." One of the guards leapt forward to open the door. "This reminds me too much of the time I put my nephew-by-marriage behind those bars."

"You lock up your own family?"

"He wasn't family yet. He'd been accused of stealing jewels, falsely as it turned out. You're accused of stealing my children, which has been proven beyond a doubt."

"There was a reason."

"Yes, and you might even get to mention it." And to the guards: "Bring him to my ring."

Having witnessed the two Malory brothers in a sporting ring in London, Damon would have guessed what James was referring to, except they were on a ship. But after a short walk, there it was, indeed on his ship, a large sporting ring in the center of the hold.

"The place where I restore my sanity." James waved his hand at the ring, actually smiling. "And where I drag my brother daily."

"You hate your brother that much?"

Lifting the ropes to get into the ring, James said tersely,

"Don't be absurd. And don't be hesitant." He motioned with his fingers for Damon to come forward. "I think you will prefer this to the other options I'm considering."

Damon stepped into the ring, but warned, "I won't fight you."

"Course you will. You have a bone to pick with me. This is the only chance you'll get to pick it."

Damon dodged the first swing by only inches and quickly pointed out, "I know you expect to win this fight and probably will, but what if you don't?"

"Don't look so suspicious, youngun. I'd actually be pleasantly surprised."

"But still kill me?"

James shrugged. "I see no cards on the table yet. You might want to play a few, Captain. You joined Lacross, why?"

Damon dove out of the way of the next swing, rolled, and came up nearly at James's back. He took his shot, a punch to the side, but the man was built like a brick wall, and his arm swung instantly backward in retaliation, knocking Damon into a corner. Bloody hell, he couldn't win if he couldn't hurt the man.

Damon leapt again to his feet, determined now to just stay out of Malory's reach. "It wasn't by choice. My father went heavily into debt to send me to England to finish my schooling. For one reason or another, he defaulted on his loans. When I returned home, it was to find nothing left, our home sold, his trading vessel sold. But that wasn't enough, so they imprisoned him as well. When I tracked him down, I tried to pay off his remaining debts to get him released, but the warden, Peter Bennett, refused to take my money—he wanted something else instead."

"Let me guess, your father's in the same prison Lacross was in?"

"Yes, on Anguilla."

"Bureaucrats don't usually snub their nose at blunt falling into their laps."

"Ambitious ones do. Bennett has his eye on the governor's seat at St. Kitts, which has jurisdiction over the nearby islands of Anguilla and Nevis, too. In order to get his name on the list of candidates to replace the current governor, he has to clean up his own record, as well as accomplish what the preceding governors of St. Kitts didn't do."

"Which was?"

"Settle a few outstanding warrants for men who were never captured or proven dead. He also has to remove the blemish on his own record—Pierre Lacross's escape. He wants Lacross returned to his prison—or proof that he's dead. He's very serious about this. He wouldn't even let me see my father while I was there and won't, until he has what he wants."

"He sent you to your death," James guessed.

"No, he gave me his own ship to use for the task. He wouldn't have done that if he didn't expect me to return it and Lacross to him. I have until the end of the year to accomplish the mission."

"How did you even find Lacross?"

Damon barely ducked the next blow. Malory was trying to corner him against the ropes, likely fed up with Damon's evasive tactics. If he was going to dance around the man, it had to be in the center of the ring!

"Before I left Anguilla, one of the men named in those outstanding warrants I mentioned walked right into my hands when I was hiring a crew. He either thought enough years had passed that he was no longer wanted, or he was too addled to realize he shouldn't be using his real name. Twice turned down within the week, he complained that even Lacross didn't want him, so I bought him a few drinks and he told me exactly where to find my target. But learning that Lacross was also hiring gave me an excuse to approach him and offer my services. I didn't expect to have to actually work for him, but I saw that he had too many men for me to attack his stronghold with my untrained crew. So I needed time to figure out a way to get him off that island without a fight or kill him if I couldn't and then escape."

"The best-laid plans . . ."

"Yes, in this case, they definitely went awry because of Catherine Meyer."

"The jewel thief," James said. "Is she really one of Lacross's bastards?"

"She claims she's his daughter and had only just found him herself. She spoke to her father at length that day but kept looking at me as she did. And then she approached me with his 'test of loyalty' for me and bragged that it was her idea. She said more than anything else, Pierre wanted to kill the man responsible for putting him in prison. But she also had her own agenda. She wanted to prove her worth to the old man, and because I arrived at the island with a ship and crew, she thought she could have me as her lover, help her father get his revenge, and make him rich to boot, all in one trip. But in the end, she only succeeded in making him rich—"

"With my family's jewels," James interjected darkly.

"Yes. Unfortunately, she insisted we leave immediately so I had no time to set up or enact a plan to capture her father that night."

"So to capture one, you must capture many? You don't think your plan went a little off track?"

"It wasn't my plan. You think I wanted the delay when it means my father must rot in prison even longer? Lacross didn't even think we could capture you, which is why he suggested one of your women instead. I didn't like it, and I never would have given Jack to him, but I expected you to attack once you had her back—but you didn't do that, you went home instead. And I got blamed for letting her go even though she escaped on her own before I could."

"Yet you tried again."

"I wouldn't have gotten out of his dungeon if I didn't at least pretend to go along with another attempt. But I got stuck with a full crew of Pierre's men this time."

"Not a good year for you, is it? Where is he?"

"I don't know."

"Wrong answer."

Damon couldn't breathe. Malory had just been toying with him, he realized, letting him only think he could dance around him all night. Doubled over, he gasped out before the next blow knocked him out again, "Wait!"

"I'd rather not" was said drily.

"There's a man . . . who will . . ."

"Bloody hell," Malory snarled. "Sit down and catch your breath."

Damon dropped to his knees first, then lay on his side on the tarpaulin-covered floor. Malory was pacing in front of him, obviously annoyed, though at whom wasn't clear. By the time Damon was able to sit, he decided the floor might be the best place to stay.

"When I first found the pirate, he was still building his

base. When I returned, it was mostly finished and there were a lot more men. When I was let out of his dungeon three weeks later, I saw that the ranks had grown, and his men were packing and tearing down structures because Lacross was moving again. There's a tavern keeper in St. Kitts who supplies them with rum. I'm supposed to get their new location from him when I return this time."

Damon tensed when the pacing stopped and James stood in front of him. "My daughter seems to think I should know you. From where?"

"Considering you knocked me out the last time we met four years ago, I'm surprised you don't remember."

"I'm never one to turn down a good fight," James said drily. "Refresh my memory about the one you seem to think we had?"

"You really don't remember?"

"Should I?"

"I suppose not. It was late at night, the street was dark and we spoke—I spoke, only briefly. I asked you where my mother was. You answered with your fist."

"That does ring a bell, actually, and you were quite belligerent in the asking, weren't you? Can you be more specific so we can clear up why you think I know where this woman is?"

Unable to contain the anger he'd harbored for years, he shot to his feet and spat out, "You seduced her into leaving her family!"

"I beg to differ," James replied blandly. "I've seduced hundreds of women, including unhappily married ones in my more rakehell years, but the one thing I've never done is try to lure a wife away from her husband. You appear to have mistaken me for someone else."

"Your memory might be faulty, but mine isn't. I know exactly who you are, Captain Hawke."

Malory's demeanor changed abruptly. Damon braced himself again. It was no wonder men feared this man when he could become so deadly menacing in the blink of an eye.

The neutral tone was gone when James said, "Aside from my family, barely a handful of people know that name. How do you?"

"You were my neighbor in Jamaica."

Again, Malory's demeanor changed. "Only the Ross family were close enough for me to call neighbors, from the plantation that butted up against mine. So you're the window breaker all grown up—and still daring?"

"And you're the man who stole my mother!"

"Give it up, lad. I did nothing of the sort. She was leaving Cyril of her own accord. Your mother told me of his drinking and gambling—and that she'd never been happy there. But there was a desperation, too, to leave immediately. She didn't say what the urgency was and I didn't know her well enough to pry. But in any case, she was aware that I had a ship anchored nearby and she asked me for passage to England."

"Is that where you took her?"

"No, I had other business to attend—"

"Yet you still took her away!"

"Yes, I did, but not far a'tall, just around to the other side of the island, where she could find a passenger vessel in Port Antonio to take her and you to England. It was far enough away from your home that your father wouldn't look for her there. And I promised I'd help her retrieve you when I returned, but unfortunately, I never made it back that way."

Damon found it hard to let go of the anger he had harbored

for this man for so long, thinking what he did. In fact, Damon couldn't. He was supposed to just believe an ex-pirate?

"You don't look convinced, Captain. I don't actually care other than to say, no one calls me a liar without seriously regretting it. So before it comes to that, perhaps I can be a little more clear. I have no shame in admitting that I am the black sheep of my family for good reason. I was wild and reckless and had been since I came of age, so I wasn't particular in those days about the women I bedded, including wives who weren't happy in their marriages. However, I drew the line at stirring up trouble in my own backyard, as it were. And your mother tugged at something in me that wasn't prurient, might even have been compassion, though I was quite sure I was no longer capable of that feeling back then. She was gracious, beautiful, but so very melancholy. And yet she was still kind to my son, bringing him hot meals and treats when he was there alone with just the servants. Now you've twice asked me where she is and I've told you where I last saw her, but I haven't a clue where she ended up. She was crying that day when you bolted instead of going with her. If she left the island, it would have been to get help to fetch you out of there, which I assume didn't happen?"

"No, my father and I never saw her again."

"Did you look for her in England? That was where Sarah wanted to go."

"Of course I did, with no luck."

"Then you might want to check the harbor records in Port Antonio where I left her. That's if they even keep them this long—it was nineteen years ago, wasn't it?" At Damon's nod, James added, "Perhaps she never made it to England. For all

I know, she might still be in Port Antonio, or perhaps she went to America."

"That suggests I'll be alive to check those records."

"I regret that I wasn't able to keep my promise to your mother. A boon for you will remove that regret."

Chapter Forty-Three

If you don't stop laughing, Tony—"

"Yes, yes, you'll toss me over the side." Anthony tried to whistle instead, but it wouldn't get past his curled lips.

Jacqueline was avidly listening to her father and uncle's conversation as she finished off a breakfast pastry and tapped her foot impatiently under the dining table. She was torn between wanting to check on Damon's condition after his second "talk" with her father, and not wanting to miss a single word her father said about him. She had arrived at her father's cabin directly behind Tony, so she didn't think she'd missed anything pertinent, even though Jeremy had already been there.

At least now they knew why Damon had gotten involved with Lacross and that he wasn't a criminal. But why the deuce couldn't he have told her and Jeremy? Perhaps because he didn't want them to know that he hated their father, believing what he did? If he'd told them any of that, Jeremy wouldn't have agreed to an alliance. He would have helped to get rid of the pirates for her sake, but he wouldn't have agreed to a truce with Damon afterward.

Anthony was still smiling when he added, "But you have to admit, old boy, that your helping a damsel in distress just isn't—you. You bloody well wouldn't do it."

"She cried."

"Yes, so you said. Don't like that watery display m'self, but I didn't think you shared my aversion."

"She wanted to leave her husband. By all accounts Cyril Ross was a good father, but he was still something of a wastrel and far too fond of gambling. I believe Sarah had her own money, which gave him leave to gamble even more. Even if she wasn't unhappy with him, it was a situation bound for ruination. So she was right to leave Cyril when she still had money to do so, before he got tossed in prison and she and the boy ended up penniless on the streets."

"It's hard to imagine that kidnapper as a boy," Anthony remarked.

"Well, even as a boy he had quite an aversion to me," James said in disgust. "Used to bloody well throw rocks at my house as if that might chase me away."

Anthony started laughing again. Jacqueline couldn't help grinning, picturing the child throwing stones at a pirate's house. How brave he'd been!

Jeremy said, "I remember him as a boy, but I remember his mother more. I was utterly infatuated with her, she was such a beauty, but a very sad woman."

"You were infatuated with anything in skirts back then," James said with a grin.

"True," Jeremy allowed, then told Anthony, "But Damon

was no more'n six or seven at the time. Of course, Father and I were rarely in residence. Father bought that place to give me some stability after he found me, but we were still more often at sea. And the Rosses were already living there when we moved in. I found Damon on the beach one day and tried to talk to him, but he backed away from me and asked, 'Are you a pirate, too?'—then ran off before I could answer. Obviously he thought Father was a pirate and objected to one living so close to his family."

James snorted. "Sarah Ross tried to take the boy with her the day they were supposed to leave with me, but the boy ran off and she started crying, refusing to leave without him. But she was afraid that he was running straight to his father. Apparently, she was desperate enough to try to escape while Cyril was somewhere on their property."

Jacqueline felt a pang of sadness for the child getting left behind. She remembered Damon's anger when he'd told her about his mother. She'd assumed he hated her for leaving him, but it had been James he'd hated for taking his mother away.

"Why didn't you just hide her in your house and deny him entrance?" Anthony asked.

"Did you miss the part about my sailing that day? Jeremy was already on the ship. And I solved her dilemma by insisting she come with me to Port Antonio on the other side of the island, and promising that when I returned, I'd help her fetch the boy. But that was the year I returned to England to even the score with Nicholas Eden by capturing his wife."

Anthony grinned. "I would have given anything to see your face when you found out the wife you kidnapped was our dearest niece Regina."

"Not one of my finer moments," James said sourly.

"But ultimately, it got you back in the fold . . . well, after you let our brothers beat on you some, just retribution, et cetera."

"You were in that fight, as I recall, and didn't pull any punches."

"Of course I didn't, at least until I realized you weren't even trying to defend yourself. Good job on that, old man, to appease the elders that way."

"They were too angry to notice."

"Well, all under the bridge, as they say. But Jeremy was the clincher. The elders' finding out you had a son nearly full grown—if they could have gotten him into the family without you, you might not have been forgiven so easily."

"I don't need that reminder," James replied. "But speaking of that eventful year, I had intended to fulfill my promise to Sarah Ross when I went back to Jamaica to sell my plantation."

"Did you?"

"I never actually got there. As you know, I had a delightfully beautiful cabin boy on that return to the Caribbean."

Jacqueline smiled at the mention of her parents' unusual courtship. They still teased each other about it to this day.

Anthony rolled his eyes. "I suppose that's one way to describe George."

"But as you know, she spotted one of her brother's ships when we docked and snuck off on me. So I merely found an agent to sell the plantation for me so I could chase after my future bride instead."

"Did you actually know you wanted to marry her at that point?"

"Not quite. I was too bloody annoyed by her defection to wonder why it bothered me quite as much as it did. And then

George and I returned to England after her brothers dragged me to the altar."

"So you left your amazing attempt at heroics vis-à-vis Mrs. Ross half undone?"

James gave his brother a dark look. "It's one of my few regrets. But I've assumed all these years that when she gave up waiting for me, she paid someone else to fetch the boy for her so they could sail to England together, or she went home to get her family to help. Neither of which apparently happened."

"If she left to protect the boy's future, it seems odd that she never went back for him," Anthony remarked.

"I agree, and unfortunately, it likely means she died before she could. I know she loved her son. I can think of no other reason she wouldn't have returned for him. So for his mother's sake, I'm going to help him get his father back."

Thrilled to hear those words, Jacqueline got up and headed to the door until her father queried, "And where do you think you're going, Jack?"

She turned about. "I want to see how much damage Damon sustained during your talk."

"A few paltry bruises."

"I still want to see—"

"Jeremy, go with your sister."

She stiffened. "You won't let me talk to him alone?"

"That, poppet, isn't going to happen—ever."

Jacqueline flounced out of the room. Unfortunately, Jeremy stayed right on her heels. But after what her father had just said, she accused her brother, "You told him about Damon and me, didn't you?"

"*I* didn't."

"Did Percy?"

"Percy was on deck a lot after the pirates were captured. He might have seen you and Damon with your arms around each other at the wheel. But he's not good at guessing, Jack. If he let anything slip to Father, I'm sure it was just that you and Damon got quite chummy. Course, Father is good at guessing."

She groaned. "Is Damon still locked up?"

"Why wouldn't he be? Father's help doesn't mean make the man comfy."

"I merely thought—damnit, Jeremy, we're his allies! And he had good reasons for doing what he did. He shouldn't have to remain in that tiny little cell any longer!"

Jeremy shrugged. "I'll mention it to Father later. You shouldn't, or Damon won't get released until we reach St. Kitts."

On the lower deck, she stopped at her cabin first without telling Jeremy why. She grabbed a jar of ointment to use on Damon's new bruises, which her father no doubt gave him. Jeremy just rolled his eyes at her when he saw it.

When they reached the cell, Damon immediately came to the bars. Jeremy at least turned his back on them, but he still didn't leave her side. Jack barely noticed, her eyes looking worriedly for injuries on Damon, but he had moved normally, quickly, and she saw only a slight bruise forming on his chin. Still, she opened the jar and reached through the bars to apply the ointment to his wound.

"You can't seem to stop taking care of me, Jack." Damon grinned.

"You can't seem to stop getting in the way of a Malory."

He caressed her cheek through the bars and said softly, "I'm sorry for abducting you—twice. I intend to make it up to you one day."

"Better not try it, mate," Jeremy warned without turning around.

"I was sorry to hear about your father—and what you thought about mine."

Damon sighed. "I don't know why my mother left, and I may never know. But I could have prevented what happened to my father if he'd just let me know he was in trouble. His letters never gave a clue, even came from Jamaica, as if he still lived there. I can only assume he asked one of his old friends to send his letters and intercept mine, so I wouldn't know what had befallen him. I'd even told him about receiving an inheritance while in England, but he still didn't ask for my help."

"Pride?" she guessed.

"Enough to keep him rotting in prison until I got home," Damon replied in disgust. "I don't understand that sort of pride."

She couldn't begin to imagine the shock he'd had, coming home to that. "Why would he even send you to England if he couldn't really afford it?"

"But he could. The crops were very lucrative, weather permitting, and he'd even purchased a ship to double his profits. I liked that ship. I learned to sail on it. But England was what my mother wanted for me. She often said to Father and me when I was a child that it was expected of a Reeves to have an extensive education. Despite her leaving us, he still loved her and wanted to honor that wish. What I didn't know was that he liked to gamble."

"Ah, that fondness causes more ruination than it does riches."

Jeremy turned about. "Time's up, Jack. You got your assurance that he doesn't need a sickbed."

As Jeremy pulled her away, she sighed, and glanced back for another look at Damon. It had better not be the last time she saw him, and she was encouraged when Damon called out, "This isn't the end, Jack." She just wasn't sure what he meant by that.

Chapter Forty-Four

James was true to his word. For the few remaining days that Damon was on *The Maiden George* with them, Jacqueline wasn't left alone for a moment. Damon had been let out of his cell and given a cabin, but she might as well have been in the cell herself since even a guard stood night duty outside her door. During the day, one of her relatives or another guard was constantly at her side. If she tried to whisper something to Damon, she got dragged away.

It was intolerable! And what was the bloody point? But she was afraid she knew. She'd showed a little too much concern for Damon aboard his ship, and her father had decided their "friendship" was over. He might be willing to help Damon because of that ancient history they shared, but that didn't mean he had forgiven Damon for his part in all this. She should just be happy for the resolution that had occurred and let it go at that since he had survived meeting her father, but—she wasn't done with him, hadn't enjoyed him nearly enough thanks to her brother's interference.

When they neared St. Kitts, James directed the fleet up the coast to anchor at the home of Nathan Brooks, Drew's father-in-law, which was on the beach but far from the main harbor. This precaution was in case any of Lacross's men were in town, watching for them. Brooks wasn't at home, but his servants welcomed his son-in-law and friends.

Only the family and Damon had rowed ashore to the beach house. Jacqueline wasn't invited to join the war council that night, but of course Jeremy was! Well, at least he wouldn't be eavesdropping with her outside a window this time, though here she was on a terrace with the French doors wide-open, a warm breeze blowing up from the beach—which ended up being a hindrance. Warren, Drew, Boyd, and Anthony were discussing strategy, but she wasn't catching every word from where she stood leaning back against the wall next to the open doors because the strong breeze was blowing them right back into the large open room.

Damon said something so quietly that she caught only the word "tavern," but in response, she definitely heard her father growl, "Why didn't you tell me this sooner? Jack!"

She wasn't going to try to hide that she'd been eavesdropping. She immediately walked through the doors and saw how furious her father was.

Damon was telling him, "It can't be helped. His instructions were explicit. I have to give the tavern keeper the password and have Jack by my side when I do it to prove I captured her. The man won't give me Pierre's new location without both."

"I refuse to put my daughter in danger," James said adamantly.

"We could threaten the tavern keeper until he gives up the location," Warren suggested.

"Unless he doesn't know it," Drew put in. "Pierre is a wily old bastard. One of his men might be waiting there for Damon, the tavern keeper only serving as a go-between to receive the password before nodding to the pirate. If there are a lot of people there, we'll be flat out of luck figuring out who the second man is."

"Then we hire a local woman to pretend to be Jack," Jeremy said.

Drew snorted. "Good luck finding a blonde her age on this island."

"We can't risk that," Damon put in. "The tavern keeper might question Jack to make sure it's really her."

Jacqueline understood now what Damon had meant when he'd told her, "This isn't the end." And they weren't even asking her opinion.

"This is a simple matter," she said. "I just need to stand there looking angry and coerced to prove Damon completed his mission. Once he gets the location, we leave. What could go wrong?"

"The tavern could be full of bloody pirates, that's what," James said.

Drew chuckled. "A handful, maybe. Lacross won't leave too many of his men sitting idle for months waiting for Damon to show up, if he even stationed any there. But we can go in before Damon and Jack enter to check the place out, pretend to be customers, and be on hand to protect Jack. But not you, James. You would be recognized."

"We will need to go in with just Reeves's ship," Boyd mentioned as if the plan were already agreed upon. "All of our ships arriving at once would be a red flag—in case there are more pirates there. And we should probably go in the morning. The tavern might be too crowded tonight."

"Nathan has a small stable here," Drew added. "Some of us can ride to the tavern and be there before Damon and Jack arrive."

"And I'll go with Damon and Jack as escort," Jeremy said. "I can look the part of a pirate if need be. The tavern keeper won't know the difference."

"I will as well," Anthony said, then smirked. "Father and son pirates." James rolled his eyes at that because the two still looked so much alike, but Tony added, "You denied me the last fight, which ended up not being one. You're not keeping me from any more, old boy."

"Then it's settled?" Damon asked.

James nodded. "I'll sail with you and stay out of sight. But I'll be close by if I'm needed. And you will protect my daughter with your life. I hope we understand each other?"

"Perfectly," Damon said.

No one in the room doubted that James had just issued a polite death threat.

Chapter Forty-Five

A PRETTY MOON WAS shining on the water and the breeze was warm on Jacqueline's cheeks as she stood on the balcony of Gabby's old room, which she'd been given for their brief stay. The yard had a green lawn and a few palm trees, but the lawn didn't extend far before the beach started. The house was small, local in design with its open, airy rooms, although most of the furniture was English. Warren and Boyd had rowed back out to their ships to sleep in their cabins. James and Anthony were sharing Nathan's room for the night. She wondered if Jeremy and Damon were sharing a room, or if Damon had one to himself.

She was considering asking one of the servants when she saw Damon below the balcony, walking across the lawn. He wasn't looking for her window and appeared to be in a pensive mood. "Psst!" She tried a few times to catch his attention. When he looked up, she signaled him to wait. She yanked on her britches, pulled on her boots without stockings, tied her nightgown around her waist, and climbed over the balcony railing to hang from the bottom of it before she even thought to look if there was anything to give purchase for her feet. But then she felt his arms go around her legs and she let go, twisted about, and slowly slid down his body to the ground.

She started to laugh but his mouth cut her off, and that kiss was incredibly voracious, setting off all sorts of delicious sensations inside her. It felt like years since she'd touched him, tasted him, when it had been only a few days, but it hadn't been enough then and it certainly wasn't enough now when she needed so much more. So she didn't object when he took her hand and they started running away from the house along the grass bordering the sand.

He didn't slow down until the ships anchored by the house were far from view. No watch was likely to have been posted on any of them this far up the coast. It was still nice to feel a little isolated. The beach was empty, illuminated by a bright moon, and the air was balmy on their cheeks. They strolled, hand in hand, on the sand for a while. Jack felt so happy and kept stealing glimpses of Damon's handsome face.

"I didn't think I was going to see you alone before the battle," he said. "We'll be sailing directly to it as soon as we get the location tomorrow."

"I doubt it will take long. There are enough armed ships in my father's fleet that you can probably sink whatever island Lacross is on."

He chuckled. "Not quite sink, but your father decided against bombarding the base because he wants to deal with the pirate personally. The cannons will only be used to blast an opening if there are any high walls."

"That gives them warning. They could scatter."

"But not escape. It's a new base, might even still be under

construction—unless Lacross found another ancient fort to fortify."

"My father is letting you go along for the battle?"

"Why wouldn't he?"

"I'm more worried about why he would, when he might think you'll die in the fight. Don't do that."

He laughed and pulled her into his arms, hugging her tightly and whirling her around. "You can be very silly, Jack, about some of the orders you issue."

Jack looked up at the moonlit sky and smiled dreamily, but then she heard him add, "There are many tales about mermaids in the Caribbean, beautiful women who entrance men, put them under a spell, and make them do their bidding. They're dangerous, but no man can resist them. Are you one of them, Jack?" He put her down and ran his fingers through her long blond hair before kissing her.

She grinned against his lips and said whimsically, "Maybe."

Damon sat down on the sand and drew her onto his lap. Lights twinkled in the distance by the harbor. She cuddled against his chest. His kisses were soft, his mouth moving from hers to her cheeks, down to her neck. Gently, he was stirring her desires, making her wish she could share such moments with him every day. Without spotting her brother or sailors every time she turned around, she could touch him as she wanted, however she wanted. But on this beautiful night in this beautiful place she was oddly content to be in his arms as he held her close.

A caress on the side of her neck made her shiver, causing him to ask, "Are you nervous about your part tomorrow?"

"Not a'tall. It's likely to be quite boring, then I'll get stashed back here while you men get to go have all the fun."

"That sounds like a complaint. You can't really want to go along for the fight?"

"Why can't I—want to, that is? I thought you said you knew me quite well."

He rolled his eyes at her grin, and she ran her fingers lightly along his neck. If she hadn't been basking in this closeness they were sharing, they wouldn't be talking now, but since he hadn't stopped kissing her the whole while, she hadn't tried to silence him yet. But she gasped when one of his hands brushed too close to her breasts, and when he did it again more slowly, definitely caressing her there now, she thought she would probably regret making love on a beach when she woke up tomorrow with sand in her bed. . . . She laughed at the thought. No, she wouldn't.

"What's amusing?"

She repositioned herself to face him, putting her legs on either side of his hips. "I'll tell you—when you return safely tomorrow." She leaned forward and kissed him.

But then they heard, "Really, Jack, climbing out windows at your age?"

She leapt immediately to her feet. "Damnit, Jeremy—"

"No complaints, dear girl, after I've been standing over yonder when I ought to be in bed just so you could have some time to talk. Anything else doesn't get to happen . . . ever . . . again. So come along." He held out his hand to her, but she ignored it and flounced past him instead, so she didn't hear, "And you, Captain, won't be warned again—stay away from my sister."

She managed not to slam the door to her room when she got back to it. But her frustration didn't last long. That interlude, having Damon all to herself again, had been too nice.

In the morning, she had a quick breakfast before they all

rowed out to Damon's ship. She'd come ashore in her rose brocade traveling dress and she wore it now, although she'd left off the matching spencer jacket because the weather was so hot here in late August. Warren, Drew, and Boyd had departed earlier to ride to town and be inside the tavern when they got there. James was still chafing at the necessity of remaining out of sight until Pierre's new location was obtained.

It didn't take long to reach the harbor, where they got the last available berth, so they didn't have to row ashore. Jeremy and Anthony had raided Nathan's wardrobe and blended in perfectly. Jeremy had a bandanna tied about his head, and Tony was wearing an old tricorn hat with a pink feather. Neither man wore a jacket, and both had pistols stuck in their belts. They walked Jacqueline ashore, one on either side of her, following Damon and Mortimer, who led the way to the rendezvous site.

The tavern was near the docks and was crowded even at that early hour, which wasn't surprising with so many ships presently docked. The patrons appeared to be an even mix of traditional sailors and men of a rougher caliber, not necessarily pirates, but not friendly sorts, either.

"Anyone you recognize—not counting ours?" Jeremy asked Damon in a low voice as they entered.

"No."

The Anderson brothers were seated at a table near the entrance where they could keep an eye on the whole room and anyone who walked through the door. But every eye in the room fixed on Jacqueline. Laughter was cut short and silence descended for several long moments. It was what Jack had expected. Ladies didn't usually frequent such places. If the room weren't so crowded, she might have pretended to struggle a little or at least pulled her arms away from her uncle and brother, who were clasping them. But the last thing they wanted was for anyone there to try to help her.

They moved forward to the long bar, where the man behind it was watching them closely.

Damon leaned forward and gave him the password. "As you can see, I have Pierre's prize."

The man nodded. "Wait." He entered a back room to the side of the bar, leaving the door open.

"Be easy," Damon whispered behind him.

"Smells like a trap," Jeremy whispered back, but after glancing behind himself and not seeing anyone getting up from the tables, amended, "Or not."

The tavern keeper returned and handed a note across the bar to Damon, who glanced at it before putting it in his pocket. He started to thank the man—until Catherine Meyer walked out of that same back room and came around the bar to stand in front of him.

She was grinning, nearly laughing. "Success at last!" she crowed, then turned her gloating expression on Jacqueline. "My father will be so pleased to finally meet you, Jack. And who are these fellows?" She was giving Jeremy a long, appreciative look.

"Your father's men make lousy sailors," Damon said. "I hired a few more in London."

Catherine's eyes came back to him. "Where are his men? I didn't notice any of them on the deck of your ship as you sailed in."

"You were watching for us?"

"Of course. And his men?" She didn't exactly look suspicious—yet.

"Last night they celebrated being so close to landing,"

Damon said. "They're likely still sleeping it off. I saw no reason to wake them just to come ashore since we aren't staying here. And why are you here?"

"I finished my task successfully, too." She laughed. "Those New York bankers' wives are so rich! And since it was nearing the time of your return, I decided to wait for you here. I've only been here a few days. Good of you to not keep me waiting too long."

"Again, why?"

"Because I'd rather deliver her to my father, if you don't mind."

Damon stiffened. "I do mind."

"Too bad." Catherine smirked and signaled to her men.

Nearly half the room stood up!

Jacqueline was immediately shoved behind her escort, which left her standing next to Catherine, who was quickly opening her purse no doubt to get a weapon to detain Jack. Jacqueline socked Catherine's nose first, which Jack found so utterly satisfying! Catherine slid to the floor, screaming and trying to stanch the blood from her nose.

Jacqueline reached down and pulled the purse off Catherine's arm to get whatever weapon was in it. She also saw a lot of jewelry in the bag, mostly rings and bracelets, yet another fortune for her damned father.

"Stay down unless you want a boot to your face, too," Jack told the pirate's daughter, pointing the little pistol from the purse at her as well.

A lot of fighting was going on in the rest of the room. But the Anderson brothers had made a big dent in the numbers, having taken a lot of Catherine's men by surprise from behind. Anthony and Jeremy were making quick work of those who'd charged them. Damon wasn't abandoning his bulwark station directly in front of Jack, merely beating down anyone who got close to him. Mortimer had charged into the middle of the fray. Unfortunately, some of the normal sailors couldn't resist a fight, either, and didn't care whom it was against. Some helped, some didn't. Still, the fight was over rather quickly, considering most of Catherine's crew was in that room. And Jacqueline had the evidence in her hands that would assure Catherine Meyer would get her just deserts. Now, if apprehending her father could be this easy. . . .

Chapter Forty-Six

S TANDING ON THE DECK of *The Maiden George*, Damon said, "He's been building a small army, but whether it's a useful army remains to be seen. If Lacross just wanted numbers in anticipation of dealing with your allies after he killed you, then he might not have been particular in who he sent his captains to hire, and they may not all be willing to fight for him."

Damon had been asked for any more information about the pirates that he could warn them about, before they debarked. Spotting the anchored ships with no harbor was the only indication they had that they'd found the actual camp. But this island was a jungle thick with foliage, and at a glance, nothing of a camp was sighted.

Two ships from Malory's fleet had turned about to go ashore farther back, Warren Anderson leading those crews, so the base, if it was in there, would be mostly surrounded to prevent escape. James was giving his in-law time to get into position.

"How many ships are usually anchored at his base?" James asked next.

"I've only ever seen one or two, though Lacross's captains might have taken others out so they could hire more men."

James lowered his spyglass. "Three are here presently. They will be burned. And no old fort this time, but too much jungle. Whatever he's built in there is mostly hidden. All I just spotted through the trees is a portion of a wooden wall." James directed one of his men over the side, then explained to Damon, "He's going to find out if they have any high walls that need to be knocked down. It was annoying having to get past them the last time I dealt with Pierre."

"What if he's not—at home?"

"I will be extremely disappointed. Is Red with him this time around?"

"Who?"

"Never mind. If you'd seen her, you'd know I'm referring to Pierre's old flame. A pirate herself, she may have retired after he went to prison. Gabby told me Pierre's obsession with her infuriated Red, so Red probably wasn't lured in again." At Damon's raised brow, James added, "Not pertinent to this fight, Captain. At least Catherine Meyer has already been apprehended, and no other ships left St. Kitts while we were there that might have warned Lacross that we are coming."

There had been time in the harbor on St. Kitts to unload the pirates on Damon's ship before it returned to James's fleet. "I warned the governor to prepare his jail for a lot more prisoners," James continued. "He wasn't pleased to hear that after we'd already turned over the fifteen you had in your hold and the lot from the tavern. But he ordered a pen built to contain them all until trial. My in-laws will see to delivering the rest to him, while you and I escort Pierre to his home on Anguilla."

"Will he be able to walk?"

James raised a brow. "Do you care?"

"No," Damon said, remembering what had been done to Andrew—and what would have been done to Jack. The man deserved punishment.

"Then I expect he will need to be carried."

A blast was heard and a bright flash came from the trees as a single cannon was fired. James laughed as the cannonball fell far short of any ship and rolled harmlessly down the beach and into the water.

"Pathetic," James said. "But that's our cue that they know we're here. Shall we?"

The longboats had already been lowered and were mostly filled. Malory's brother was in one. Jeremy wasn't. He'd been left behind at Nathan Brooks's house to guard his sister and had complained loudly about it as he and Jack were rowed ashore there. The Andersons were rowed to their own ships, and Damon had been invited—it wasn't really a request—back to *The Maiden George* to sail with James. Damon might have smirked over Jeremy's complaints, considering how aggravating Jeremy had been in his diligence to keep his sister chaste—after the fact. But Damon understood why James wouldn't risk his firstborn son to a stray bullet, especially when their numbers were great enough that one more man wouldn't turn the tide either way. Watching Jack being rowed away from him, Damon had sworn to himself it wouldn't be the last time he saw her.

The longboats had barely reached the beach when a wave of men burst out of the trees. They were yelling, brandishing pistols, sabers; one even held an ancient pike—dozens of men were charging in their direction.

"One shot each to stem the tide!" James commanded.

Damon was wading ashore when he fired, but other shots came from twelve longboats, not all at once, but close enough that the front line fell as well as the second line, and the men still running forward started tripping over bodies. It had been a pointless charge, and Damon was afraid that Lacross had ordered it to buy himself time to escape. It wasn't that small an island. It could take days to find him, maybe even weeks, if he managed to slip into the jungle. So Damon grabbed a saber from one of the downed men and fought his way through the remaining pirates to get to the buildings behind the trees.

"Wait up, Captain. You don't get this pleasure."

Damon turned to see that James was close behind him and not wielding any sort of weapon . . . well, other than his fists, which he was using liberally. But barely any pirates were left standing, so Damon cautioned, "This might not be all of Pierre's men."

"I do hope not."

They entered the clearing beyond the trees cautiously. But there were only one long building with the door standing open and several smaller ones, which some of James's men were heading toward to search now.

Damon glanced around the clearing. "He hasn't gotten much built since he moved here."

"Pirates don't make good carpenters," James replied, and sent his brother and a handful of men to check the back of the larger building.

Damon poked his head through the doorway for a glance

inside before they entered. An upper floor hadn't yet been built, and the ground floor was open space that hadn't yet been divided into rooms, so there were no other doors behind which men might be waiting to ambush them. They walked to the kitchen area in the back, which hadn't yet been enclosed. Lacross was sitting alone at the end of a long table that was filled with half-empty plates. He appeared oddly unconcerned by their arrival. Damon wondered if the pirate had really sent all of his men down to the beach to make one single effort without providing for any contingencies.

Pierre said calmly, "I see you're not in chains, Hawke." And then with an accusing glare at Damon: "Why is that?"

"You should have kept your vendetta between men," Damon replied. "Involving women was an inexcusable mistake on your part. We already apprehended your daughter. Catherine succeeded in stealing more baubles for you, which will be used as evidence to convict her."

Pierre merely shrugged. "It's a shame about the jewels. I was looking forward to the money they would bring. Building a proper base is costly."

Damon was disgusted by the man's utter disregard for the daughter who'd tried so hard to please him that she was going to prison for it.

Anthony came in from the rear of the building and stopped behind the pirate to stick a pistol in his back. "Drop your weapons."

"I'm not armed," Pierre insisted, though he didn't raise his hands to prove it. "There was no point."

"You have one second to drop—"

Metal hit the floorboards under the table with two distinct thuds. Anthony yanked Pierre to his feet and pushed him away from the table. Damon quickly removed two more pistols from the pirate's belt. No wonder he'd sat there so damn calmly.

James shook his head as he came forward. "Dying just so you can take me with you, Pierre? Was that your final escape plan?"

"I'm not going back to prison!"

Two of the Anderson brothers had come in, and Drew suggested, "Kill him and get it over with."

"What the devil, Drew?" Boyd said. "I thought you agreed with your father-in-law that Lacross won't pay enough for his crimes with a quick death."

"Who said anything about quick?" Drew shot back.

Boyd snorted. "The man wants death rather than prison again. We didn't come here to give him what he wants."

"Point made, Yank," James said, right before he delivered his first punch. "But he needs a few things broken to remember me by."

That ended up being a jaw, some ribs, one arm, and a collarbone before Pierre lost consciousness. Damon winced a few times, not for the pirate, but because he'd escaped a similar beating and still wasn't sure why. Malory's children's brief alliance with him must have carried more weight than he'd thought.

When they went outside, the third Anderson brother approached James. "There are nearly thirty more of Lacross's people who tried to hide in the jungle—servants, doxies, and the men who weren't willing to die for Lacross. They surrendered without a fight."

Damon looked behind Warren and didn't see anyone else. "Where are they?"

Warren turned around. "Give it a moment. There were a damned lot of bushes to navigate through."

But the captured bunch started appearing through the trees, sailors pushing them forward, and Damon's eyes suddenly flared. "Father?"

Chapter Forty-Seven

IT WAS NEARING DUSK by the time the three ships docked on the island of Anguilla. One was going to give Damon and his men passage to Jamaica after they were done here, since he would no longer have the use of the warden's ship. He was surprised Malory had arranged that after his earlier parting remark: "All for nothing, eh?" Damon had tried to get Malory to go about his business, assuring him that Damon could see to Lacross's delivery to the prison, but Malory had just ignored him. But he had to try again. If James ended up arrested for old charges against Captain Hawke, Jack would never forgive him.

"Still no bloody coaches to be had on this island," James complained when the wagon arrived to take them to the prison.

As Pierre, who had been slipping in and out of consciousness, was being laid in the back of the wagon, Damon tried again to dissuade Malory from going to the prison. "You needn't inconvenience yourself. I'm capable of delivering him—"

"Enough, Captain. I intend to see to this personally."

"There's a reason you shouldn't," Damon finally said. "I told you I had warrants for other pirates I was supposed to bring in. Hawke was one of them."

"I appreciate the warning, but I'd already gathered as much." James climbed up onto the driver's perch. "I intend to get that warrant off the books. Now come aboard and tell me what your father had to say for himself."

Damon was too relieved not to oblige. "He found out in prison that he and Lacross had one thing in common, getting revenge against you, so Pierre offered to take him with him when he found a way to escape. I've already told him he was wrong about you—we both were—that you didn't seduce my mother into leaving. But now he has no idea why she left, so that is a mystery that may never be solved."

James gave him a doubting look, but since Damon wasn't satisfied by the brief talk he'd had with Cyril, he wasn't going to argue about it with Malory.

"My father is not a pirate, nor even a fighter. But he's capable of captaining a ship and was given the one Pierre stole when they escaped to hire men for Lacross's crew, which is why I never saw him with the pirates before today. He admitted they ran out of money, so Catherine was given use of that ship to get more. If not for that, I still might not have known he wasn't in prison any longer."

"Bennett is going to answer for that today and admit that he lied to you when we bring him Lacross. That gives you leverage to demand that Cyril's name be stricken from the prison records."

A while later, entering Peter Bennett's office without waiting to be announced—James did that, simply opened the door and walked in—they caught the warden by surprise, and he apparently didn't like surprises. He stood up, his expression furious.

Damon forestalled whatever outrage Bennett was about to spew by saying, "Allow me, Warden Bennett, to introduce James Malory, Viscount Ryding."

Bennett's expression changed instantly. "A lord? On Anguilla? You do me great honor, m'lord! What brings you—?"

"You are ultimately responsible for setting a series of nasty events in motion, Mr. Bennett. I'm here to put an end to them."

"I don't under—"

James interrupted again. "You will remove Cyril Ross from your inmate ledger."

"About that . . . ," the warden began uncomfortably.

Wanting to leave the dreary prison as quickly as possible, Damon said, "Yes, I already know you don't have him. You will still clear his charges in full since I've fulfilled your demands for his release. Pierre Lacross is outside and will need to be carried in, and your ship is returned in good condition."

"And the infamous Captain Hawke?"

"Hawke died nearly twenty years ago in England, where his death was recorded," James said.

"But we should have received word if that is so. Are you sure?"

"The proof is that I killed him, or will you discount my word?"

"Certainly not, m'lord. And I will see to it personally that this news spreads throughout the Caribbean."

Of course Bennett would, since he wanted the accolades

for it, Damon thought in disgust. But the man had opened the ledger on his desk and made notations to it. Damon peered at it to see what was written and was satisfied.

Damon turned to leave, but James wasn't quite done. He glowered at the warden and said in one of his less pleasant tones, "You, sir, have too many other things on your mind to properly attend to this prison. You will transfer Pierre Lacross to a more secure containment from which he will never escape again, or you will resign the position so someone who actually wants it can be installed. If Lacross ever leaves this prison again, other than to go to his grave, it will be your head I will come after. I trust we understand each other?" At Bennett's profuse agreement, James added, "Then I bid you good day."

"He doesn't deserve the governorship," Damon grumbled on their way back to the harbor.

"A simple matter to assure his name is never put on the appointment list," James replied. "That's not a favor I'm doing for you, Captain, but what I already intended to do. My obligation to you has ended."

Damon stiffened. That could mean any number of things, including that Malory might now give him the beating he felt Damon was owed. Before that happened, or didn't, at least before they parted, he had one more boon to ask of James Malory. Damon was just having a damned hard time forming the words that were so important to him. And they'd reached the harbor! The wagon had stopped between Malory's two ships. He was already getting down from it.

"Lord Malory, wait. I will regret it to the end of my days if I, that is, I wish leave to—I want to marry your daughter!"

"Are you utterly insane?" was all James said before he walked away and boarded *The Maiden George*.

Damon sighed and headed to the other ship. Yes, he was insane to think Malory would have answered any other way. And Jack would likely tell him the same thing. She might want him and was bold enough not to deny that, but she'd thought he was joking when he'd mentioned marriage to her and had even gotten annoyed at him.

Mortimer was waiting for him on the other ship, and the captain immediately gave the order to cast off. If Damon were in command, he might have tried to race Malory to St. Kitts before Jack was taken out of his reach. But he wasn't, and while he would risk James's fury for her, it would be pointless because she didn't want to marry him.

"You haven't said yet whether you intend to stay in Jamaica," Mortimer said.

"I haven't decided, though I doubt I will now that I have that bloody big estate in England to deal with. I'd rather Father return there with me. And I'm still hoping my grandmother will have a good day and be lucid long enough to answer my questions about my mother. For that to happen, I will need to live there, not just visit."

"You really think you can still find your mother after all these years? You know now that she wanted you with her, and yet she never came back for you. I hate to say it—"

"Don't. I—I have to know in either case. This wondering about what became of her is hell. But you're welcome to join me, you know. You'll always have a home with me if you want it."

Mortimer chuckled. "I took that for granted. But you know my family had money. I probably should decide if I want to do something with that education we labored over, or maybe find myself a pretty wife."

"Good luck with that. The pretty ones seem to come with too many bloody in-laws."

Mortimer snorted. "Only your pretty one does. I still don't know how you put up with that tempest."

Damon tapped his chest. "Let's hope someday you find out for yourself. Is my father in his cabin?"

"Yes, and he's anxious to speak with you. I think he's worried about what happens next—for him. You gave him no assurances yet?"

"No, I haven't. The surprise at finding him with Lacross hadn't worn off yet. I anguished over the delay in getting him out of prison, and all the while he'd found his own way out. I'll speak to him now."

Damon found his father pacing the floor in the cabin they would share. Cyril looked hale and fit, though his brown hair had turned gray at the temples. If he had suffered deprivation in prison, he had recovered from it these last months.

But his father looked wary now, which made Damon ask, "Did you think you would be taken back to prison?"

"You sailed here, where the prison is located."

"To clear your name. You are completely free now, Father, so be easy about that. We sail to Jamaica now. Your plantation was sold, but I will find you another before I return to England."

"You're not staying—so you learned the truth?" Cyril said cryptically.

Damon frowned. "What truth?"

Cyril wrung his hands. Damon didn't think Cyril was going to answer, he was silent so long, but then he said, "That—that I gambled too much. And drank too much after you left. The two combined guaranteed I could never win. I understand that now and will never fall into that dual trap again."

Damon was still frowning. He did vaguely recall that his father had been drinking before he went off to school, and even before his mother left, but most men drank to some degree, and it had never seemed to affect Cyril's ability to run the plantation. But there had also been the occasional argument Damon overheard between his parents about money, so maybe Malory had been right about Cyril's having gambled even back then. And if he fell into that ruinous cycle again?

"Perhaps you should return to England with me," Damon suggested. "The Reeves estate is mine now. You're welcome to live there with me for the rest of your life. You will never have to work again."

Cyril smiled wryly. "Idle hands are the devil's hands, Son, and I am a farmer at heart. Be it my land or another's, there is great satisfaction in an honest day's toil. In the islands I'm respected as a planter, in England—no, I'm never going back there."

"Give it some thought before you decide."

"Do not for a moment think I am ungrateful, Damon. Look at you, Son, what a fine man you've become. So well educated, you speak like a fine gentleman now. I can't tell you what it means to me that you would risk your life, your reputation, and do so much to get me out of prison. I'm so proud of you."

Seeing tears forming in Cyril's eyes, Damon hugged him tightly. "You've been a wonderful father."

"But after all these years, I much prefer these islands, and I have friends in Jamaica, even a mistress I may marry now that I'm no longer wallowing in anger and self-pity."

"My mother isn't dead."

"She is to me," Cyril said a little too sharply. "I loved you from the day you were born, and loved her, too, for giving you to me. I'll always love you, Damon, never doubt that. But I understand you have new obligations now and we must live an ocean apart. I won't make the same mistakes to lose this second chance you're giving me. I swear it."

Father and son embraced, and both had tears in their eyes now.

Chapter Forty-Eight

JACQUELINE RAISED HER HEAD slightly from her pillow and opened one eye to see who had just burst into her bedroom without knocking, but she should have known. Only her cousin Judith would make such an entrance.

"Are you actually sick this time?" Judith demanded.

"No."

"A sprained ankle perhaps?"

Jacqueline put her head back down and dropped a listless hand over her eyes. "Ennui, if you must know. The last trip to the Caribbean was too exciting, which apparently has nasty aftereffects. Now, nothing interests me."

"Is that all? You're merely suffering from boredom?"

"What else?"

Judith plopped down on the bed and pulled Jacqueline up to sit in the middle of it with her. "Oh, I don't know—maybe you lied when you said you didn't fall in love with your pirate?"

"I did nothing of the sort. But I might be experiencing moments of—I don't even know what to call it. Misery, I suppose."

Jacqueline couldn't bring herself to talk about this yet, that she was worried that Damon didn't love her, that he'd only used her to get her father's help. He'd gotten that, and now she might never see him again!

"And tears?"

"Don't be silly, Judy, you know I don't cry."

"And yet boredom does not cause misery—"

"It does for me!"

"—while love certainly can cause misery for a number of reasons. When you're separated from your heart's desire, is one. When two people have unresolved feelings for each other, is another. When you think he doesn't feel the same way you feel about him, that's a hundred times worse than the other two reasons. When you think he's betrayed you, that's a thousand—"

"Judy! We were talking about me, not you, and why haven't you forgotten the miserable parts of your romance with Nathan? You're married now and over-the-top happy."

"Which is why I can think of that time of doubts now and laugh."

"I don't have doubts, nor am I miserable like that. I'm just so bored!"

"Well, lying in bed all day for no reason, of course you are. But your mother has a fix for that. She's going to host a ball."

"The devil she is! My mother never has parties of any sort unless they're for the extended family. She'd never, ever arrange a ball."

"Yes, she would." Judith smiled. "She is in your father's study making the invitation list right now."

"Why would she?"

"As I said, to get you out of bed."

Jacqueline snorted. "The Season is over."

"Yes, but that only means the debutantes have gone home—or are having engagement parties. London doesn't come to a halt just because the Season is over. The *ton* will still have their entertainments."

"But not my mother. Besides, Father wouldn't allow it."

"You really think he would butt heads with George about it? She is so thrilled to have you home, safe and sound, and wants to see you happy."

"Well, maybe not. She did cry for nearly a week after we returned, and he's still making amends as if it were all his fault."

"Joyful tears, but that's not the kind she shed while you were away."

"He knows. But my mother should have been reassured by Damon's note—I read it, and as he told Jeremy and me, it wasn't at all threatening."

"When do mere words reassure a mother? She was still worried sick about you the entire time you were gone, while you were off fighting pirates and having a grand old time. My mother even offered to buy them a ship so they could hie off to search for you themselves, but saner minds prevailed, since that would have been like looking for the proverbial needle."

"It wasn't all grand," Jack reminded her cousin.

"The last week or so was, to hear you tell it—well, until he went one way and you went another. For God's sake, Jack, the very moment he was no longer your enemy, you told me you were tossing him in bed. Admit it—or admit that you're in love."

"Nonsense—but, about that ball . . . If Mother makes it a masked ball, I might attend. Damon's had time to return to England if he is going to return. He could sneak into a masque like he did before."

"So you do want to see him again?"

"Certainly. I wasn't nearly done with him. He was magnificent—when I didn't have anger clouding my eyes. I miss him. I so wish you could have met him, you'd love him."

Judith raised a brow. "I will, but you don't?"

"Just a figure of speech."

Judith squeezed Jacqueline's hand. "Why are you denying these feelings?"

"Because it's too soon," Jack mumbled, still unwilling to admit what she was really feeling, even to herself, though she did allow, "But next year I might love him."

"I wouldn't have expected to hear such nonsense from you at this point, Jack Malory," Judith scolded with a tsk. "You've said you miss him, said you're not done with him—and don't think I don't know what you meant. But you can't keep doing *that* and not get with child, and then your father really will kill him."

"You don't understand—"

"I understand perfectly since I was part of that pact we made not to marry until next year. But everyone, including me, warned you how unrealistic it was. And answer me this: D'you really think you'll find someone else who makes you feel the way he does? Why the devil would you still want to wait when you've already found your perfect man?"

"Father isn't going to let me have him," Jacqueline whispered.

"Oh." Judith sighed. "There is that."

Chapter Forty-Nine

D AMON ARRIVED IN EAST Sussex to an empty house, no butler at the door, no one in the halls. What the devil had happened here? But then a young maid ran from the back of the house, ignoring him, and went out the front door, which he'd left open.

Incredulous, he followed her outside and called, "Wait! Where is everyone?"

The girl paused long enough to turn and say, "At the family cemetery, sir. Our lady is being buried today. If you've come for the funeral to pay your respects, you may still be in time. I overslept!"

She ran on and disappeared around the side of the large mansion. Damon didn't move, felt poleaxed. Now he'd never be able to catch his grandmother at a lucid moment so she could answer his questions. That hope was gone forever. He wished he'd gotten here sooner. But it had taken a week in Jamaica to get his father settled in a new plantation, then Damon had spent another week in London trying to see Jack. But every time he knocked on the door to her house in Berkeley Square, one of two butlers—they really did have two—slammed the door shut. Only the first time, after he'd given his name, was he told, "Cap'n's orders, you ain't welcome." They wouldn't even take the flowers he'd brought her, so he'd had someone else deliver them, but they wouldn't accept those, either!

He'd still kept an eye on her house, hoping to catch her when she left it, but she never did. He was going to have to try something more drastic when he returned to London, even if it meant confronting her father. There would be no pleasantness this time with that man—well, there never had been, but Malory's boon was over and he'd made it absolutely clear that Damon couldn't have his daughter.

But Damon was prepared to brave anything for her—if she would have him. He just needed a chance to speak to her without her father in attendance, to tell her he hadn't been teasing when he'd asked her to marry him. He should have admitted it that day on his ship, but she'd seemed so annoyed at the idea. Would she still be? Was there really no hope of his ever making her his wife?

He knew where the cemetery was, on both sides of the small chapel beyond the tall hedges at the side of the house. The chapel spire could be seen above the hedges, which is how he'd found out it was there. He'd investigated it just once, fearing he'd find his mother's grave in there, but he didn't.

He hurried to the chapel, but when he passed through the fancy entrance cut into the tall hedges, he was surprised by the number of vehicles on the other side. So many people were there, standing outside the small chapel and coming out of it— servants, tenants, local gentry, even that solicitor, Mr. Harrison, who'd tracked him down and was the only person there whom he'd ever spoken to at length.

The coffin was already being carried out of the chapel. He'd missed the service, but at least he could see Agatha Reeves buried. She might have called him by a half dozen wrong names, thinking he was other men she knew, but she'd still been his grandmother, and he wished he could have known her when she'd still had all of her faculties.

A grave had already been dug in the side yard next to the chapel, branches of an oak tree shading it and flowers planted all around it. If not for the gravestones, a visitor might have thought this private family cemetery was a pretty garden. Only Reeveses were buried here. He noticed one grave that was nearly a century old as he slowly followed the procession.

While the coffin was being lowered into the open grave, he moved to stand next to Mr. Harrison, a middle-aged man with brown muttonchops and friendly green eyes. He had offices in the nearby town of Hastings.

Damon nodded a greeting and asked quietly, "How did she die? Peacefully?"

"I'm sorry to say it was likely a painful death."

"You're not sure?"

"Well, there's no telling at what point she died on her fall down those stairs. I was told that a footman was helping her down them, but Lady Reeves thought he was her husband and then recalled her husband was dead. She screamed dreadfully as she tried to get away from the imagined ghost, and then—she tumbled backward." Harrison sighed. "Nasty business, when your mind plays tricks on you like that. But I'm glad you're here. I wasn't sure if you were even in the country. I heard you sent word to Lady Reeves that you were returning to the West Indies. It meant nothing to her, but Mrs. Wright let me know. Such a busybody that woman, but utterly devoted to her mistress."

"I returned a week ago. I had no idea my grandmother died"—Damon waved his hand at the coffin—"until just now."

"My condolences, sir. But we will need to speak at the house later. Your grandmother made her will years ago, before her affliction, when she was of sound mind. She excluded the members of her family from whom she was estranged, namely her uncle by marriage and her daughter."

"Agatha was estranged from my mother? Good God, man, you didn't think that was something I should know?" No wonder the housekeeper had been so nasty to him!

Mr. Harrison shrugged. "I was the family solicitor, but I didn't know them well and certainly wasn't privy to their secrets. It could have been no more than a mother-daughter tiff that never got resolved. But those were Lady Reeves's instructions when she made the will. She didn't specify you in the will, but she didn't exclude you either, so as her closest living relative, her worldly goods are now yours. It's a long list, mostly properties, even a small castle in Scotland. Oh, and a house in London."

"Empty?"

"No. It had been her mother's house. Lady Reeves didn't stay there often and probably hadn't been there in years, but a few servants were retained in case she did want to use it."

He'd rather have Agatha back than another inheritance. "She was Scottish?"

"Her ancestors were, and not to speak ill of the dead, but

I always wondered if that was where she got her inflexible disposition."

"You said she had an uncle?"

"Well, yes, though I doubt he is still alive. He was her husband's uncle."

"Why didn't you mention that before when I asked you if I had any other relatives?"

"Because Lady Reeves warned me never to mention his name on threat of dismissal. He was estranged, after all, from both her and her father-in-law."

"Why?"

"I asked once and got fired for it. It took months of profuse apologies from me to be reinstated, and I never questioned the lady again. But Giles Reeves would be your great-great-uncle on the paternal side of this family, the older brother of your great-grandfather, whose estate you now own. As I said, I highly doubt he still lives."

The chaplain had begun saying prayers over the open grave. Damon noticed Mrs. Wright, Agatha's disagreeable housekeeper, standing on the other side of the grave, crying. Damon moved to stand next to her, facing the chapel.

Agatha had been sixty at least, but Mrs. Wright was younger by some ten years. No gray was in her brown hair yet, but her austere demeanor made her look as old as his grandmother. She'd been his grandmother's housekeeper for several decades. She might even have worked here when his mother still lived here, but that was just one of the many questions she'd refused to answer for him, so he wasn't sure.

She was the only one left who might be able to tell him if his mother had ever come back here after she'd left Jamaica and where she was now. He'd ridden to Port Antonio as Malory had suggested and had learned the harbor did keep records, but unless his mother had given a false name, there was no record of her booking passage on any ships leaving from there the year she'd left home or any year after that. He'd visited the inns near the port in case she'd stayed at one, but they didn't keep records that dated that far back. He'd even checked Port Antonio's cemetery. It had been a wasted trip.

He wasn't sure what to say to Mrs. Wright when it had been so apparent on his earlier visits that she disliked him. Perhaps he could begin by reassuring her that she could keep her job if her disposition would improve.

"Come for even more gains?" was whispered spitefully.

"What the devil does that mean?"

"For someone who didn't know this family at all, you have gained from it rather substantially."

He turned to face her and said just as quietly, "I would rather have gotten to know my grandmother, to have had at least one damn conversation with her where she didn't think she was talking to someone else of her acquaintance. Do you honestly think I'm glad about her death?"

"Why wouldn't you be? She would have hated you as much as she did your mother—if she even knew you existed, but she didn't."

"Why would she hate me?"

The woman clamped her mouth shut. He'd seen her do that before. It meant she wasn't going to say another bloody word. She was beyond infuriating!

He tried to curb his anger, but his voice was still sharp when he told her, "I'm not going to fire you, despite your disagreeable nature, but I do insist you tell me what you have against me, and whatever it is, it needs to end now."

"I would as soon leave your employ."

"Just to avoid telling me the truth?"

"Neither you nor your mother were ever to be welcomed here," Mrs. Wright hissed at him. "She came and wasn't let in the door."

He sucked in his breath and demanded, "My mother came here? When?!"

"Many years ago, but as I said, she was turned away at the door."

"As I would have been? Because grandmother couldn't remember her own daughter?"

"Oh, no, that was before Lady Reeves started to forget the people she knew. My lady was not a forgiving woman."

"What did my mother do to cause such strong antipathy that it would be extended to me?"

"Why don't you ask her?"

"Bloody hell, I told you before I don't know where she is and you wouldn't tell me!"

Mrs. Wright looked behind him. "I suppose she read of my lady's passing in the newspapers."

Damon immediately swung around. Another carriage had just arrived, and a well-dressed middle-aged gentleman was stepping down from it. He was tall, black haired, and had an air of importance about him. The woman with him pulled the black veil down from her hat to cover her face before she took the hand he offered to assist her to the ground. But Damon saw her face in the moment before she covered it. She was still beautiful despite the years. He'd cherished that face his whole life.

He felt such a welling of emotion, he wasn't sure he could move, but it shattered when he heard Mrs. Wright nastily say, "If she thinks she can get in the house now, she can't. I know my lady's wishes—"

"Shut up, Mrs. Wright. You're fired."

He approached the couple and stepped in front of them, blocking their way. But standing this close to his mother, words failed him. He thought he'd never see her again! And she was crying quietly. Did she still love the woman who wouldn't even speak to her and had struck her from her will? She must. The bad feelings had apparently all been on Agatha's side.

But his mother's escort drew his own conclusions about Damon's standing in their way and said sharply, "If you think you can stop her from attending the funeral—"

Damon threw up a hand to halt the diatribe. He didn't even look at the man, couldn't take his eyes off Sarah, his mother. But he realized she must have brought a solicitor with her, thinking she would be prevented from seeing her own mother buried. An understandable assumption when she hadn't been let in the bloody house when she'd come here before.

He wanted to draw her close, give her a thousand missed hugs, but breathless, all he could do was say, "Mother."

She said nothing, and through the veil he thought he saw an expression of curiosity on her face. Oh, God, she didn't recognize him. Of course she wouldn't! She hadn't seen him since he was a child.

The solicitor hesitantly asked, "Damon Ross?"

His mother collapsed in a faint.

Damon leapt forward to catch her, but so did her escort. It was an awkward moment, but at least they kept her from falling to the ground.

Alarmed, Damon told the man, "Step aside," as he picked his mother up in his arms.

"Put her back in the carriage," the man suggested. His proprietary manner was beginning to annoy Damon.

"Is something wrong with her that I should know?"

"No—just shock, I would imagine. She was told you were dead."

Chapter Fifty

W HO TOLD HER I was dead?"

Damon said the words instinctively since he had no intention of waiting for an answer he'd rather hear from his mother. He quickly carried her to the house. It was a long walk, but she was a willowy wisp of a woman and he barely felt her weight. The door was still open. He took her straight to the parlor and gently laid her on the gold brocade sofa. She still hadn't awakened, and there wasn't a damn servant in the house to fetch him some smelling salts.

"We haven't been properly introduced. I'm Brian Chandler of Essex."

Damon glanced at the man who'd followed him and was standing beside him. Damon was a little more than annoyed at him now, and his tone reflected it. "Go away and close the door on your way out. This is a family matter."

"I'm not leaving, and you don't need to wait for your answer. Cyril told her you died after he threw divorce papers at her."

Damon stiffened. "You're lying! My father wouldn't divorce her. He loved her."

"I wouldn't have thought he did considering the callous way he informed her, and yet that might explain the grief and rage he displayed the day we visited him. Fury might have impelled him to divorce her, but in his heart he knew he shouldn't have. But he did, the papers were legal, and he blamed her for your death, for not being there to nurse you back to health when you had pneumonia. Your mother was devastated by the accusation and the horror of losing you. But obviously, since you are alive, Cyril just said those things to hurt her."

Furious, Damon grabbed the man's lapels. "Who the hell are you?!"

"You're upset. Perhaps it would be better if your mother tells you."

"By God, if you don't say—"

"Don't hurt him, Damon," Sarah beseeched as she sat up. "He's your father."

Damon, as if he'd been burned, let go of the man and swung around to face the woman he hadn't seen in nineteen years. "You're lying!"

She was taken aback. "No, I'm not. Why would I?"

He didn't know, but it couldn't be true! This was too much all at once! Finding his mother. And a father he didn't know? He gave the man a furious look and got a half smile in return. Bloody hell?!

"I'll leave you two alone," Brian offered. "But not for long."

"Damon, come sit with me." Sarah patted the sofa. "I am still shocked, but this joy is beyond containing. You're here, alive, and good God, look at you! You're even more handsome than your—"

"Don't say 'father,' because I'll need to ask which one you are referring to."

"Don't be bitter, please."

"How can I not be when everything I know to be true isn't?" Then in anguish: "Why did you leave me?!"

She shot to her feet and threw her arms around him. "I never would have left that island without you if Cyril hadn't convinced me you were dead. He even said you were buried on the property. I was too destroyed to ask to see the grave. He must have realized that having divorced me, I could have taken you from him legally. The courts usually favor the father, unless the mother comes from nobility and the father doesn't. Even if I didn't have a marquis with me, he knew my family could sway the courts. He'd already lost me. He was obviously desperate not to lose you as well. He did love you, Damon, as if you were his own."

"When did you come back for me? When did he tell you I died?"

She squeezed Damon harder. "Four months after I left. I will tell you all of it, just let me hold you for a few minutes and convince myself that you're real, that I'm not dreaming. I come here to bury my mother and find you, my son, alive— and I almost didn't come." She leaned back with wide eyes. "Good God, I wouldn't have found you if Mother didn't die. What a sharp, sad twist of fate."

"Why did you come to the funeral when Grandmother obviously never forgave you—for having me?" he guessed.

"My mother wasn't always so harsh. She was loving and kind when my father was alive, though even then she was excessively proper. I think she would have rather gone to hell than have scandal touch her name. Her father was an earl, so she was a lady in her own right, while my father wasn't a lord because his father was a second son. But we did have a living earl on my father's side of the family, my great-uncle Giles, and besides, the Reeves family was much richer than hers, so the marriage was quite acceptable to both sides. And they were in love. They probably would have eloped if they'd been denied. Mother loved him so fiercely. Father died when I was still a child. She was never the same after that."

"I found her too late to know her."

"What do you mean?"

"You didn't know her memory was failing?" Damon tapped his head. "She was living in a world of her own up here."

"No, I didn't know. But perhaps it was a blessing for her, relief from the ill will she harbored. I'm surprised Uncle Giles never told me. He and I were close and kept in touch. Maybe he didn't know about Mother's condition either."

"How did you come to marry Cyril instead of my real father?"

"He was a bought husband, a tenant farmer on our estate, who was paid handsomely by my mother to marry me— enough to buy his own farm in the islands. Mother was furious that I'd fallen from grace, and that I'd done so with a married man who couldn't make it right. But Brian and I were deeply in love. You can't fight love, darling."

"You can when you must."

"But I didn't have the will to. And I've never regretted the results. You. And Cyril was a good father to you. He was even a good husband to me for a few years. He loved us both, even knowing that you weren't his. But his realization that he couldn't really make me happy began to fester, which caused him to drink—and that led to his gambling. The profits he made from his crops just went to pay off his gambling debts. And he kept demanding more money from me."

"Agatha gave you money before kicking you out of her life?"

"No, she was going to send me off penniless, but my grandfather, even as angry as he was at me, gave me money before I left. But what I'd done caused a rift between him and his brother, Giles, because Giles introduced me to Brian, his neighbor in Essex. My mother and grandfather both blamed Giles for not chaperoning me properly."

"Then why would your grandfather leave me this property?"

"It's been in the Reeves family for centuries, but it's not the entitled estate. Giles has that—and I know he will be delighted to reinstate you as *his* heir when he learns the astounding news that you are alive. Soon after you were born, I wrote to Uncle Giles, told him of you, and he informed his brother, my grandfather. Sadly, my grandfather died without reconciling with his brother. But a male heir is still a male heir, illegitimate or not, and I was married before you were born, which took the edge off that."

"I know where Hawke took you, but I still don't understand why you left me that day, why you didn't return for months. Did you leave so you could be with Brian?"

"Damon! Of course not. I'd had no contact with him since I left England because I thought he was still married. I didn't know he'd been widowed. I left because Cyril thought I had an endless supply of money when I didn't. It was just a matter of time before he found it and squandered it. I felt I had no choice but to take us away before that happened. I was afraid for your future. I wanted you to attend university."

"You could have hidden your money where he couldn't

find it. You could have told me we were leaving the island, instead—"

"You were so young! I was afraid you'd tell Cyril."

He realized he was blaming her now. First Hawke, now her, when it was ultimately his own fault that he hadn't gone with her that day. "I'm sorry. I just feel robbed of all the years I could have been with you, too."

"Yet I did come back for you that year. I waited a month for Captain Hawke to return to help me retrieve you. When he didn't, I hired three men to escort me back to collect you, but they robbed me of all but a little of my money, and I had to get a job in Port Antonio to earn passage. That's when I wrote to Giles to tell him how dire my situation had become. I thought he would just send me money. He sent Brian instead."

"I can't believe Cyril would tell you that ridiculous tale of my death. Did he know you were back and sent me away so I wouldn't be there?"

Sarah frowned. "Possibly. He had many friends in that town, and it took Brian hours to find a carriage to drive us to the plantation. But we weren't coming to steal you away. As Brian, your real father, is the Marquis of Marlowe and he was with me, there was no doubt that Cyril would have had to give you to us. I know you loved him, might even have fought to stay with him, but, Damon, he is not your real father. You belonged with me, should have been with me all these years. You might forgive Cyril for that dastardly lie, but I can't. I didn't get to see you grow up!"

She started crying again. Damon was torn between wanting to comfort her and still being angry over what she had revealed. He was a bastard. And, oh, God, how ironic that Jack had named him that. His chances with her had just dropped a hundredfold.

All he could say was "A marquis? I bloody well won't call him lord."

"Dearest, he didn't know about you until he came to rescue me. I had begged my uncle not to tell Brian. He was still married then. Finding you today is as much of a shock to him as it is to me."

"I can't believe Cyril would tell you what he did. I'm not saying he didn't, just that I can't believe he would." Damon paused, thinking about his conversation with Cyril on the way to Jamaica. "Actually, I think he was going to confess it recently, when he asked if I'd learned the truth, but he must have changed his mind and spoke of his gambling instead."

"I don't blame Cyril for divorcing me. I do blame him for lying and costing me all these years without you. I feel that loss as poignantly as you do, Damon. When I think that you could have grown up with your real father—"

"You and he . . . ?"

"We're married now and have been since we returned to England that year."

Damon nodded and finally sat down on the sofa with her. "I think Cyril stopped gambling after you left, applied himself to work, even made enough to buy a ship to double his profits. Life was good for a while, and all we lacked was you. But after he sent me to school in England, he was alone and started gambling again. When he couldn't pay his debts, he was imprisoned. I only found out this year and gave him a new start in Jamaica."

"You're too kind."

"He's the only father I've ever known and I love him. He'll always be my father."

"And now you have another. But tell me about you. Are you married? Do you hope to be?"

After he gave his mother a modified account of his adventures over the last year and stunned her with the revelation that Captain Hawke was really James Malory, Viscount Ryding, she said, "A Malory girl? That family is well known, and a bit notorious. Now I understand why. Are you sure that's who you want?"

"More than anything."

"Well, your father's credentials should pave the way for you."

"No," Damon said curtly.

She raised her brows. "You sound like you resent Brian. Please say you don't, when he was blameless in all this."

"He's not blameless for seducing an innocent girl while he was married," Damon said a bit harshly.

"Ah, well, that was actually my fault, not his." She blushed. "He tried to resist me, but I wouldn't be denied."

Oh, good God, that sounded far too much like his own situation and was exactly how Jack had behaved toward him. He laughed and hugged her close. "You're absolutely right, Mother, he's utterly blameless."

The door opened and Brian Chandler poked his head around it. "That sounds like my cue to return."

"You were eavesdropping?" Sarah accused with a chuckle.

"Of course."

Damon stared at the man, really looked at him this time. He'd never wondered why he didn't resemble Cyril. Brian was as tall as Damon was and built much the same. Brian, too, had black hair, and some of their facial features might even be the same. If they stood side by side, people might see the resemblance immediately and guess they were related. And so they were. The annoyance, the resentment Damon had felt earlier, it all slid away.

He stood up and held out his hand. "Perhaps we should meet again, Father?"

Chapter Fifty-One

BACK IN LONDON THREE weeks now, Jacqueline was leaving her home for the first time tonight. But they weren't going far. While Georgina had planned this ball and had attended to every minute detail, they didn't have a ballroom at their house in Berkeley Square, but Brandon Malory certainly did at his grand mansion in Grosvenor Square, yet another inheritance from the previous Duke of Wrighton.

Jack was hopeful now that Judy had confessed that while the ball might have been Georgina's idea, making it a masque had been hers. It would give Damon an opportunity to sneak in, like the last time—if he was in London, if he heard of it. One too many ifs, but Jack could still hope.

"Your mother gave me a pile of invitations to take to Regina, who would know who else to invite, since your mother was mostly just inviting family. But I kept half of them and have invited some of your previous beaus."

Judy had told her this earlier in the week and Jack had complained, "I wish you hadn't done that."

But Judy had pointed out, "How else were we to hide him in the mix?"

"So you invited Damon?"

Judith had grinned. "After everything you said the other day confirmed what I already knew you were feeling, of course I did. You'd already told me he owns the old Reeves estate in East Sussex, so I sent it there."

"How could you know what I'm feeling? I don't even know!"

"Yes, you do."

Yes, she did, and while he might not even be in England to have received his invitation, she was hopeful that he would be, which led to this bubbling excitement she could barely contain. Which is why she wasn't listening to what her parents were saying as they sat across from her in the coach, until she heard, "She says she's not in love, but I think the arrow struck her true."

"Good God, George, don't you dare mention Cupid to me," James complained.

Jacqueline raised her brow. "Trying to get my attention, are you?"

"It worked." Georgina smiled. "But I wasn't serious. We know you refuse to fall in love this year."

"About that—"

James interrupted, "It's rude to correct your mother, so don't."

Jack squinted her eyes and scrunched her mouth at her father, but wasn't about to argue with that tone of his. She'd never imagined she would have to elope one day, but obviously that was the only way she was going to get herself married to

Damon. If he asked. If he showed up to ask. He bloody well better show up.

Brandon, along with his parents, was waiting by the door to greet them, but the street was already crowded with vehicles, and the music was playing, so the ball had already begun. Judith had followed directly behind them with her husband and parents, so Jack waited for Judy and hooked her arm to her cousin's before entering. Georgina did the same thing, entering with Roslynn. Which left the three men. But Nathan, seeing James's expression, left him with his brother.

Standing alone with James, Anthony guessed, "You're expecting something unpleasant. What?"

"Reeves is going to be here."

"He wouldn't dare."

"There's never been any doubt about his temerity. And while George assured me she invited no pirates, your minx sent off some invitations, too, and Judy is privy to all of Jack's secrets, so she might have invited him. But you're going to help me spot him before he gets anywhere near Jack."

"If I must," Anthony said drily, but after entering the ballroom with James and seeing how many couples were already on the dance floor, including Jacqueline, he added, "Did George really invite this many? Or has every gate-crasher in London come out for this?"

"The latter. How often does a Malory host an extravaganza? The *ton* will be rabid with curiosity to find out why we did."

"Point taken. But in this crush, we're not likely to—" Anthony began, but amended, "Well, that didn't take long a'tall. Take a gander at the terrace. Reeves might have an invitation, but he wouldn't want his name announced in a room full of Malorys.

He appears to be sneaking in the back way to avoid that, but just this moment he put on his mask. Shall I toss him out?"

"Bite your tongue, that pleasure is mine."

"Well, now's your chance to catch him off guard, while he's got his eyes clapped on Jack."

A few moments later, James told Damon, "You were warned."

The punch had already been delivered. Doubled over—bloody déjà vu—Damon gasped, "God, not again. Must you always lead with your fists, Malory?"

"You were warned."

Damon didn't straighten yet, but he risked a black eye and porcelain being smashed into his cheek to peer up at James to gauge just how angry he was—and wished he hadn't. "What is the bloody point of a masque if you guess who's who? I could say you have mistaken me—"

"You're not that stupid."

"I love her."

"So you are that stupid," James said. "The anguish you've twice caused my family won't ever be forgiven. And you really were warned."

James gripped a handful of Damon's hair on the top of his head in preparation for the next blow, which would likely knock him out. The half mask fell off. The thought did cross Damon's mind that he could fight back, but that brought an image of Jack crying over her parent being hurt, so that was out of the question.

He did have one second to get out, "What if Jack loves me? Would you really deny her happiness?"

"With you, yes. This country is overflowing with eligible

men, and I'll find her one m'self in a decade or two—" The pause was unexpected before he added, "Does she?"

"I don't know," Damon was forced to admit.

"Good." James drew his fist back.

"But I'm going to find out." Damon tore himself away.

He left a damn lot of hair behind in Malory's fist, but quickly weaved his way onto the dance floor. He'd spotted Jack immediately, her domino short this time, barely covering her eyes—as if she wanted him to recognize her. He whisked her away from the fellow she was dancing with, hopefully not another Malory who might object.

Her eyes widened slightly, but then she laughed. "No mask? I'm disappointed we aren't going to play that guessing game again."

His smile was brilliant. "No, you aren't."

"No, I'm not. I've missed you!"

"I thought I might be coming to my execution here. I couldn't think of any other reason your mother would send me the invitation."

"And yet you came anyway?"

"Yes."

"She didn't send it, Judy did."

"No, I actually got two invitations; one was from your mother."

Jack's brows went up. "Really? Then maybe you were right about an execution. Shall we find out? Quickly, before my father joins her!"

"Dragging me to my death wasn't what I had in mind for tonight," he said as Jack pulled him to the two women standing with Anthony Malory.

"Don't be silly," Jack said. "Mother wouldn't carry her pistols to a ball."

When they walked up to the trio, Anthony immediately started to reach for Damon, but Georgina actually put out an arm to stay him, which gave Jack time to say, "Mother, I would like you to meet Damon—"

Georgina cut in, "No, I don't think so," and gave Damon a resounding slap.

There was actually some applause in the room. Well, a lot of Malorys were present, and they were well aware of Jacqueline's second trip to the Caribbean.

But Jacqueline stared at her mother and asked, "Just once, yes?"

"For tonight."

"Is it my turn now, George?" Anthony asked.

"No, it's my turn," Jacqueline told her uncle, and pulled Damon away again.

Back in the center of the dance floor, where they would be temporarily shielded by other couples, she didn't even pretend to want to dance. She did put her arms around Damon and leaned up to kiss his red cheek, whispering, "Better her than him."

"Funny you should mention that," he said cryptically. "I do understand, you know. You're their only daughter. I twice caused them anguish, which I heartily regret."

"I suppose it will take time to smooth those edges."

"I would expect so."

"But they will relent when they see how happy you make me."

He drew in his breath. "Do I?"

"Well, that depends on why you're here."

"I'm here to ask you again to marry me. I wasn't teasing

before." He had started to lead them in the dance, but stopped as he waited breathlessly for her answer.

"I wasn't ready to hear it then, but now I am. Shall we sneak out now?"

He began to laugh. "Shouldn't I ask your—"

"Good God, no. You can't ask him or we'll never get out of here."

"I was going to say your mother. One parent's approval would be nice."

Jack rolled her eyes at him. "She just slapped you. She's not ready to approve, either."

"But I'm heir to two titles now. Will that make a difference to your father?"

She laughed. "No, but—two? How did that happen?"

He told her briefly about finding his mother, and the lie that had been told to her to keep them apart. "I can't even be angry at Cyril for lying to her—well, I can, I am, it cost me so much. And yet if it hadn't played out as it did, I never would have met you."

"I beg to differ. You and I were destined. We would have met somehow."

He smiled. "You think so?"

"It's what every woman in my family would say."

"But not you?"

"Don't be silly. Who am I to dispute a consensus that big?"

"You did, as I recall. You would have made your destiny wait a full year."

"Not anymore."

His turquoise eyes perused hers, and he looked a little too serious when he said, "Are you sure? Because I haven't actually heard you say yes."

She grinned. "Yes." She kissed his cheek. "Yes." She licked his ear. "Definitely yes." And slid her lips across his face to say against his mouth, "D'you need more convincing that I'll marry you?"

He crushed her to him for a moment before he said, "The first yes did it, but by all means, continue."

She shook her head. "If we're going to slip out, we probably need to do it now, before my uncle tells my father that you're here."

"He already knows. Frankly, I'm surprised he hasn't ordered the doors locked and the crowd to part."

"He wouldn't want to feed the gossip mills. He doesn't care about creating scandal about himself, but wouldn't want even a whiff of it to spread to me, so he won't make a scene. It's mostly my extended family here tonight, but there are still other members of the *ton* in the room." A quick glance around her and she had to amend, "Actually, a lot more than were invited. But that would be why he hasn't ripped you out of my arms yet. He probably does know exactly where we are and is just waiting until the music ends."

"Wonderful." Damon groaned.

"We can elope to Scotland and inform them afterward."

"Impulsive as ever."

"No, but now that I've decided I'm not waiting for next year after all, I don't want to wait another day. Although it's going to take more'n a day to get to Scotland."

"But less than a day to get to Essex, where my father already has a special license for us."

Her brows went up. "That sort of title?"

"Yes—and an extra name. If you marry me, you will be Jack Reeves Chandler. I've just met my real father."

She started laughing and wouldn't stop.

"It's not that funny, Jack."

"Oh, but it is."

Then Judith bumped into them deliberately and exclaimed with wide eyes that swept over Damon, "So *this* is him? And you haven't eloped yet?"

Jacqueline grinned. "We were about to. Damon, this is my cohort in all things secret, my dearest, dearest cousin and best friend, Judith Malory Tremayne. Judy, meet Damon Reeves. He's got a third name, but if you don't know it, then my parents won't be able to pry it out of you and figure out where we went, so it can wait. Give us an hour's head start before you let them know I've hied off to get married. Tell them I'll send word tomorrow where the after-wedding party will be held."

"They're going to worry."

"No, they'll be too angry to worry, and they'll hear from me before that changes."

"Are you sure you don't want a big wedding like mine?"

Jack grinned. "The family and I enjoyed yours just months ago, and besides, you know my father was never, ever going to give his blessing, no matter what, not for Damon, not for any man. I was giving him an extra year to get used to the idea, but it just wasn't happening. So, fait accompli instead, which is more exciting and fun!"

They didn't run out of the room, which would have drawn people's attention, but they did move rather quickly to the entrance and then started running along the curb to Damon's coach. Jacqueline was laughing, so happy she couldn't help it. And Damon's driver had been warned, so the moment they were in the coach, it started moving, and they started kissing. She couldn't help that either! It had been far too long since she'd seen him, tasted him, felt him in her arms.

"Wait—" he tried.

"No!"

He chuckled. "Just for a moment."

He was getting something out of his pocket, and he brought her hand to his lips to kiss it before he slipped a ring on her finger. The beautiful large emerald was surrounded by so many diamonds, Jack laughed.

"It's the perfect wedding ring to receive from a pirate," she teased. "Are you sure it's not ill-gotten booty?"

He smiled tenderly. "My father gave it to me, a Chandler family heirloom. They are expecting us. They were as hopeful as I that you would say yes. They've missed so much of my life, they are thrilled to be part of our elopement. We have their blessing, at least."

"You know we might have to marry again someday for my parents."

"If they ever accept me, certainly."

"My mother approves. She did invite you to the ball, after all."

He rolled his eyes. "Just so she could slap me."

Jack grinned. "You had to expect that, and it may even happen a few more times. But she wants me to be happy, and she could see that I am with you."

"Are you?"

She kissed him soundly to answer him, but it wasn't long before she wanted more. "Can the driver go any faster?" she asked breathlessly.

"I think this is as fast as we can go at night without running off the road. Besides, considering what we're doing, I don't want to face a clergyman and my parents just now."

She laughed and reached under her gown to pull off her

drawers before climbing up on his lap to make love to him. The bouncing of the coach was exceptionally nice once she felt him inside her!

In the throes of passion, she cried out, "Faster!"

"I told you the driver—"

"Not the driver. I meant you!"

"Now that I can happily accommodate."

Chapter Fifty-Two

"THEY ARE ARRIVING," DAMON warned.

It was morning. Jacqueline had been awake for only a few minutes but had heard the carriages and voices below their window, too. She probably shouldn't have sent off that missive to her parents last night, right before the wedding.

Damon's parents had welcomed her warmly and led them into the parlor, where they'd awakened the clergyman who had been standing by all evening. The room had been filled with every flower on the estate! Although the man was a bit sleepy, he'd performed the ceremony with dispatch, but in a moment of confusion he'd asked, "Who gives away this woman?"

But Jacqueline had laughed. "I do!"

After she and Damon had taken their vows to be man and wife, they'd raced upstairs to their bedchamber. Not that they hadn't already made love twice in his coach on the way to Essex. But missing him as much as she did while they were apart had made her insatiable, and she hadn't gotten her fill of him yet.

"I'm not leaving this bed," Jacqueline said now.

She climbed on top of Damon to straddle his hips and was only a little surprised that he was already hard enough for her to mount. She grinned down at him and wiggled her hips.

"Do I need to teach you that you should let me lure you into—"

"Do I need to divorce you already?" she countered.

He went very still. She punched his shoulder. "You're the one who needs teaching about what's a tease and what isn't. You're never getting rid of me—Bastard." She giggled as she said it.

He rolled his eyes. "You really do find that funny, don't you?"

"Don't you? Especially since your real father has already legitimized you as his firstborn and heir. By the by, I like him and your mother. At least one of us can say that about the other's parents."

"I'm sure I'll like yours—someday."

She chuckled. "Probably not." Then she gasped as he twitched inside her.

A lambent light entered her eyes just before she leaned down to put her lips to his. She hoped, she really did, that this need to devour him would settle down eventually . . . well, at least settle down to moderation. Once a day, maybe twice. Had she really thought when she was on the ship with him in a sea becalmed but with her passions running wild that one more week of him would have sufficed? Such a silly notion.

The kiss got hot. Gooseflesh spread across her bare back where his hands moved. They were both naked, never having put on any nightclothes last night, even when he got up to pour them wine, or when she got up to stoke the fire in the wee hours when it got a little chilly in the room. They had made love for most of the night. Maybe it wasn't morning and was afternoon instead?

He finally gripped her hips for a harder thrust, but he gasped and tried to flip her over. She fought to stay mounted. He let her win. She rewarded him by grinding her hips to his, but she got the reward, that beautiful explosion of sensual delight.

And the gasp "Oh . . . my . . . God!"

He laughed as she threw back her head to enjoy the full luxury of that climax, but then he did the gasping as he followed with his own. She ended up staring at him and marveling once more that he was hers. She hadn't been glad of the day she'd met him, but if she'd known then what she knew now, she would have been. So many variables could have revealed the truth sooner if he hadn't been desperate to help the father who raised him, if he hadn't hated James for taking his mother away, if he hadn't had to get a pirate back in prison one way or another . . . if . . . if . . .

She shared one with him now. "Half of my rage when we first met was because I wanted you even then, but knew I couldn't have you."

"Do I need to say again how sorry—?"

She put a finger to his lips and smiled. "No, but you can promise never to keep any secrets from me again." She gave him a wicked grin. "Imagine how much sooner we could have been doing this if you'd been honest from the start."

"Or you might have killed me."

"I had my chance and merely gave you a paltry wound. What does that tell you?"

"How lucky I am?" He cupped her cheeks and gazed deeply into her eyes. "I love you, Jack. I think I have from the start."

Emotions bubbled up inside her and made her eyes a little glassy. She couldn't have found a more perfect husband if she'd conjured one up. He'd given her adventure and excitement, passion and now love. He'd stirred every one of her emotions, bad and good.

With only the good ones remaining, she could tease, "I figured you must, since you've braved my family to have me. But it's nice to hear."

He raised a brow, saying pointedly, "Yes, it is."

She chuckled. "Of course, I love you—now."

"Now?"

"Did you think it was instantaneous?" She laughed. "No, no, only the lust was. Love took longer, although it probably happened sooner than my stubbornness allowed me to admit. But it's well seated now, this glorious feeling. And we wouldn't be married if I didn't now love you wholeheartedly."

The sudden pounding on the door had Damon leaping out of bed because he hadn't locked the door.

Jacqueline yelled, "We'll be downstairs shortly!"

Damon glanced back at her to whisper, "You know that was probably him."

"Probably." She grinned. "Pour us a bath to share in that lovely bathing room you have. My father can wait a bit longer."

"I'll share it," he said on his way to the little attached room. "As long as we just bathe. I really don't want to keep him waiting."

"I make no promises."

JACQUELINE DID ACTUALLY MAKE one while she was drying off after their bath. With a blush, she said, "I promise our love-making won't always go so quickly."

"I'm not about to hold you to that, love, at least for a few more weeks. Even then, I may have to make that same promise to you, I want you so much. But eventually we will take our time."

They did finally get downstairs. Jack was wearing her pale green ball gown again and hoping her mother had thought to bring her some clothes. The marquis's mansion was nearly as big as Haverston. Following the sounds of conversation, they headed straight for the large parlor, where tea and crumpets had been served. It appeared that more of her family than she'd expected had come here for this reckoning.

Grinning like a fool because she was so bloody happy, she took Damon around and proudly introduced him. The women gave congratulations and hugs, the men were more hesitant or droll in their remarks.

Jeremy chucked her chin, his expression as bland as their father's usually was. "I don't need to ask if eloping was your idea, when we know you don't have a jot of patience, Sister. But you couldn't just settle for sex and let us kill him?"

She pretended to give it a moment of thought. "A lifetime of sinful sex or I give you some legitimate nieces and nephews? D'you want to ask that question again? And you're the worst chaperone ever, Jer!"

He finally grinned. "Actually, by definition, I was the best. But it's written all over you, how happy he makes you, so"— Jeremy glanced at Damon—"welcome to the family, mate. Just don't tell my father I said that."

"Understood," Damon said as they shook hands.

"And you might want to steer clear of him," Jeremy warned. "At least today, or for a week, actually—"

"I get the idea," Damon cut in.

"No, I'm not sure you do. He's really not happy with you, and that equates to a lot of pain for you." Then Jeremy looked at Jacqueline. "This won't be like his war with Nick and Warren and settle down to mere verbal barbs. You're his baby girl."

She smiled. "Yes, I'm exactly that—and more like him than you know. If I'm not worried, you shouldn't be."

Anthony joined them and put an arm around Jacqueline's shoulders, his tone quite droll as he remarked, "You might want to turn off that bloody glow, puss. It's throwing salt in the wound."

"I haven't found a switch for that, Uncle Tony."

He stared at Damon. "Well, my condolences, younggun. You should have run while you had the chance."

"I did run, in the only direction possible. I'll always run straight to Jack. She holds my heart."

"Gad, let's not wax maudlin," Tony complained, then to Jack: "Your mother isn't known for patience."

Jacqueline laughed and grabbed Damon's hand again to head to her mother. Georgina, standing with Danny and Kelsey, ignored Damon but put her arms around Jack. "You've denied me the joy of planning your wedding."

"If I had done it the way everyone else does, Mother, would it ever have happened? Father walking me down the aisle and giving me away? Really?"

"I could have talked him around," Georgina insisted.

"With someone else, maybe, but with Damon?"

Georgina tsked and nodded toward James, who was talking quietly with Sarah Chandler. "Possibly. He knows Damon's mother and has regrets concerning her."

Jack chuckled. "He already relieved himself of those regrets by not trouncing Damon in the Caribbean. He won't give him any more boons."

"I heard, and I was partly to blame for his not returning to help Lady Chandler. Which is why I won't slap her son again."

"If you really want to have that big wedding, he'll marry me again just for you."

"Will you come home in the meantime?"

"No."

George snorted. "Then there's no point." But then she hugged Jacqueline fiercely, whispering, "Give me time. I'll get used to this."

"I love him, Mama."

"Good God, children grow up too fast."

Jack grinned. "Was that your blessing?"

"Yes, I believe it was. Now go make peace with your father, but do *not* take your husband with you. You can leave Damon safely with us."

Jacqueline didn't hesitate. She marched straight to James and put her arms around him. "Don't be mad."

"I'm not mad."

She peered up at him. "Don't be furious, either."

He didn't deny that one.

"Fine. But no more bruises on my husband's body or I'm going to have a very, very long wedding trip."

"You're having one?"

"He has his own estate in East Sussex. I was going to opt for a week or two alone with him there before we allow visitors—as long as there are no more bruises."

"You'll invite me. I'll make no promises."

She laughed. "One of us needs to give ground on this, Father."

"No, you already had your way. You married him. He hasn't realized yet what a prize he stole from us."

"My alone time with him has just doubled to a month."

"Jack," James said warningly.

"I should be pregnant by then," she said with a brilliant smile. "I'm certainly going to try to be!"

"Where do they keep the bloody brandy here?" he growled.